D0957433

"I can help you, Drucilla," said Kevin. "We can help each other. One gamble —a big one—and you can have more than you ever dreamed of. Money, security, social position, a wealthy husband, if you want one."

"How?"

"The Tremayne fortune. Beth was her grandmother's only remaining heir. And you are going to be Beth Cameron."

"You must be mad," she said.

"No," he said. "You are going to Newport. You are going to convince the grandmother, the lawyers, and all of Newport society, that you are Mrs. Tremayne's long-lost granddaughter."

The
PASSIONATE PRETENDERS

by

Diana Haviland

A FAWCETT GOLD MEDAL BOOK

Fawcett Publications, Inc., Greenwich, Conn.

THE PASSIONATE PRETENDERS

Copyright © 1977 by Diana Haviland

All rights reserved, including the right to reproduce this book or portions thereof in any form.

ISBN 0-449-13810-0

All the characters in this book are fictitious, and any resemblance to actual persons living or dead is purely coincidental.

Printed in the United States of America

10   9   8   7   6   5   4   3   2

The
PASSIONATE PRETENDERS

One

───────

DRUCILLA mounted the steps of the boardinghouse, then hesitated in front of the door. She wanted to put off the moment of her return, but the high-piled rain-clouds overhead threatened a downpour at any moment. Besides, she was hungry. She realized that she had had nothing but a cup of coffee all that day, and now it was almost evening.

She opened her purse, although she knew without looking what she would find. A dollar and some change. All that was left after she had paid Beth's funeral expenses. And she owed the landlady three weeks' back rent. Still hesitating, she looked up and down the shabby street, as if hoping to find some haven other than Mrs. Baxley's theatrical boardinghouse. Only a few blocks from New York's notorious Five Points district, Mrs. Baxley's had nevertheless managed to retain an air of seedy gentility. Inside the hallway, however, Drucilla was enveloped in the mingled odors of fried fish, cabbage, Macassar oil and patchouli perfume.

In that spring of 1872, Macassar oil was popular with gentlemen, and even the antimacassars that covered the backs of all the chairs in the boardinghouse sitting room did not prevent the plush from getting oily stains; and patchouli perfume was a favorite with the actresses who lived at Mrs. Baxley's boardinghouse.

Drucilla wrinkled her nose in distaste. Even as a child at the County Farm in Ohio, she had been oddly fastidious and had been made to suffer for it—often. And now, she reminded herself, she was still in no position to be critical of her surroundings. If she didn't find work soon, she wouldn't be able to afford even Mrs. Baxley's place.

She pushed the thought away, unwilling to give in to the despair that threatened to overwhelm her. Right now she would have her dinner, and then she would go upstairs to bed. With a hot meal and a night's sleep, she would be ready to start making rounds again tomorrow.

The other boarders were already seated around the long dining room table when she came in but, as she started forward to take a chair, Mrs. Baxley intercepted her.

"Just a moment if you please, Miss Reed," the landlady said firmly. "You're not sitting down at my table until you've paid me the back rent you owe me. I haven't wanted to bother you before, but now . . ."

"I'm going to an audition tomorrow," Drucilla said. "As soon as I get a part, I'll pay you."

"You've been telling me that same story for weeks."

Mrs. Baxley didn't bother to lower her voice, and several boarders stopped eating to listen. A man who had arrived at the boardinghouse only last night gave Drucilla a penetrating stare from under his straight, heavy brows. His expression was one of cool interest, without a trace of sympathy. She looked away, only to be confronted again by Mrs. Baxley, who was obviously unwilling to move out of the entrance to the dining room. The landlady stood in Drucilla's path, as if carved in stone. She was a large woman, and her black bombazine dress with its full skirt and leg-o'-mutton sleeves, made her look even more formidable than usual. She set her heavy jaw at a pugnacious angle, as if challenging Drucilla to try to pass.

But Drucilla's legs were weak, and she was beginning to feel lightheaded from hunger. As often happened to her at such times, her voice began to fail. It emerged as something between a croak and a whisper.

"I spent the last of my money on the dress for Beth. . . ."

"Plain foolish, if you ask me, but that's not my problem. I have this house to run and bills to pay, and you theater people don't seem to understand . . ." She broke off and looked at Drucilla sharply. "What's wrong with you?"

"I'm tired and . . . the funeral . . ."

"Not going to faint, are you?"

Drucilla shook her head, her voice having deserted her completely. She swayed slightly and caught at the dusty rose-colored drapes that framed the archway between the hall and the dining room.

She turned away from Mrs. Baxley and stumbled down the hall and upstairs to her room, half-afraid the landlady would follow her. But, looking over her shoulder, she saw that Mrs. Baxley had gone into the dining room.

Drucilla reached her bedroom at the end of the hall, and closed the door behind her, then sank down across the lumpy iron bed. If she could sleep, even for an hour, she would find new strength with which to face Mrs. Baxley and hold her off for a few days longer. But when she closed her eyes, she saw Beth Cameron as she had looked when Drucilla had found her, white and still, the bottle of laudanum on the worn rug beside her. Beth had left no note but Drucilla had known what despair, what terror, had led the other girl to take her own life.

She opened her eyes and sat up, fear sweeping aside her exhaustion. She wasn't like Beth. She was strong. She would survive.

She forced herself to get up, to smooth her dress and tidy her hair. In the wavy mirror over the battered dresser, she saw her face, white and drained, under the heavy masses of red-gold hair; the violet eyes with their thick lashes, the high cheekbones and small, pointed chin. She pinched her cheeks to give them color, and thought longingly of a new dress, one that would accent her graceful, slender figure, that would deepen the color of her eyes and set off her fair complexion. How could she hope to get even a small part in one of the New York theaters, when she looked so shabby? She had to get work, and quickly.

"I could put a new lace collar on this dress," she thought. "I'll take it off the green one—that's too old to wear at all—and I'll have to mend my stockings."

She should have bought those detached stocking feet she had seen in a shop on Broadway the other day; they were meant to be sewn on to the legs of stockings that had become worn in the soles. But she had been confident she would not need any such makeshifts, not here in New York City.

She sighed, remembering her foolish daydreams: she would have a dozen pairs of new stockings—all silk —and elegant kid shoes with pointed toes; ruffled petti-coats with real lace trimming and blue satin ribbons.

She lifted her skirt and glared at the frayed hem of her petticoat. Everything she wore was clean and ironed but threadbare from too many washings in too many boardinghouses like Mrs. Baxley's. Her daydreams of success in New York's splendid theaters had become a little threadbare, too.

The theaters were here, and even finer than she had been told: Booth's, the Grand Opera House, Wallack's, the Fifth Avenue Theater. Marble walls, frescoed ceilings, plush seats and splendid gaslit chandeliers. But the man-agers of these theaters wanted actresses with experience, and Drucilla's two years of touring with a small, down-at-the-heels stock company did not qualify her for a part in a first-rate New York City production.

One good-natured manager had admitted she might have some talent but said that she would need formal training. How she could afford such training when she didn't have enough money to pay her boardinghouse bill was her problem.

Last month, a gray-haired, red-faced character actor in his fifties had offered to help her with her career. Over dinner he had made it plain that the price of his help would be "a close and warm relationship." She thanked him for the dinner, but said she would rely on her own abilities to further her career.

That had been two months ago, early in January, a few days after Beth Cameron had come to live at the boardinghouse. Beth, too, had been unwilling to become a successful actress except on her own merits—at first. But, unlike Drucilla, Beth had lacked the inner strength to stick to her resolve. Drucilla tried not to remember what had happened to Beth: a job in one of the wretched "concert saloons" down on Chatham Street; then, when the establishment had been raided, two weeks on Blackwell's Island. Drucilla was the only one at Mrs. Baxley's in whom Beth had confided. Her term in jail, brief though it was, had broken her completely. Two nights after she had returned to the boardinghouse, Drucilla found her lying dead, the empty laudanum bottle beside her.

Beth, who had had the same ambitions as Drucilla. . . .

"I'm not like Beth," she told herself again, as she leaned toward the mirror and arranged her hair in a chignon. Since she was banned from Mrs. Baxley's dining room, she would have to find a meal at an inexpensive restaurant. A glance at the window told her that the rain, which had been threatening all that day, had started falling. The wind drove the drops against the pane like a shower of gravel. No matter. She reached for her cloak and put it over her shoulders. Then she heard the knock at the door.

Mrs. Baxley faced her, ready for battle. "I want to talk to you . . ."

"I was on my way out to dinner."

"Not yet, Miss Reed." She pushed Drucilla aside, came into the room and stationed herself in front of the open door. "You wouldn't be planning to slip away and leave me with an unpaid bill, would you?"

"Certainly not. I want to get something to eat, that's all. Since you refuse to let me dine here . . ."

"Of course, I refuse. If I let every out-of-work actress eat at my table, I'd soon be in the poorhouse."

"I'm going to get work, I've told you. It's only a question of time. I'm not a beginner. I've toured through Ohio and Kentucky and . . ."

"That's not the same as working on the stage here in New York. We've had the finest performers in the world here. Charlotte Cushman. Rachel. Lola Montez. You think a manager would hire an insignificant little nobody like you? Oh, you're pretty enough, or you would be if you had a little more meat on your bones. But your voice . . . When you're scared, like you were downstairs, you can't get a word out."

"I wasn't scared. I was tired . . . and hungry . . . that's all."

Drucilla straightened her slender body and looked the landlady squarely in the eye. "Besides," she added, "I happen to know that Sarah Siddons often lost her voice before a performance. But she . . ."

"Sarah Siddons? Are you comparing yourself to . . ."

"Why not? She had to start at the bottom, too . . ."

"Now listen to me, my girl," Mrs. Baxley said. Her tone, all at once, was almost friendly. "There's other kinds of work you can get, if you'll forget your silly notions and face facts. A pretty girl like you don't have to go hungry."

"What kind of work are you talking about?"

"I have a friend . . . has a place down on Chatham Street. He's always on the lookout for fresh, pretty little things who can sing and dance a bit."

"Chatham Street. There are no theaters down there, only concert saloons."

Concert saloons like the one Beth had worked in, just before she died. It had music and dancing but only to hide the true purpose of the place, Beth had told her later. And Beth had told her more. How the concert saloon was raided by the police, after one of the patrons, a young man from a good family, had been stabbed and robbed and left in an alley. Such incidents were commonplace on Chatham Street; but the young man's family had been important enough to apply pressure in the right places, the saloon had been closed, and the girls rounded up and shipped off to the prison on Blackwell's Island.

Even now, remembering Beth's description of what had been done to her in that grim, stone fortresslike prison, Drucilla shuddered.

"Well," Mrs. Baxley was saying, "shall I give you the name of my friend's place?"

"No. I'd never work in a place like that—never."

"Don't put on airs with me. If you want to go on living here, you'll have to pay up, and you can't do that with fancy talk." Her voice was soft, wheedling. "You wouldn't have to work down there forever. You could earn enough to pay up your back rent, and buy some pretty new clothes, too. What chance have you got, dragging around to auditions in a shabby rig like that?"

Mrs. Baxley was right, of course. An actress had to look successful and confident, and how could she if her dress was faded and out of style and her shoes cracked and run over at the heels? No matter. Drucilla wasn't ready for Chatham Street, not yet. Not after the stories Beth had told her.

"I can give you the address of the place, and I'm sure my friend will be able to put you on right away."

"No doubt. And you probably get a commission for every girl you steer down there."

"That's none of your affair. Do you want the job or don't you?"

"No, I don't."

Mrs. Baxley abandoned her friendly approach. "Please yourself. But in that case, you're not spending another night here."

"Very well. I'll pack my trunk right now and . . ."

"Don't bother. I'll be keeping your trunk for security. When you've paid up, you can have it, not before."

It was dark out now, and the rain was still pelting against the window. Drucilla thought of the wet, dirty streets, of having to sleep on a bench or in an alley.

Mrs. Baxley, as if reading her thoughts, swung the door open all the way. Her voice rang out, down the

13

length of the hall. "You can sleep in the gutter for all I care."

Drucilla wanted to beg, but she couldn't. She swept past the landlady in silence, fastening her cloak around her.

"Remember," Mrs. Baxley called after her, "your trunk stays here until you've paid your bill."

Drucilla quickened her steps and stumbled against the tall man with the straight, heavy brows who had stared at her with cool interest, but without sympathy, when she had tried to enter the dining room a little while ago. Now, in the light from the flaring gasjet overhead, she saw that his eyes were gray and alert, his face deeply tanned. His hard, thin-lipped mouth curved in an ironic smile as he stepped aside to let her pass.

Drucilla went hot with shame, knowing that he must have heard Mrs. Baxley's last words. She lifted her skirt and walked downstairs, her head held high. As always, when she was afraid or humiliated, she sought refuge in daydreams. Now she was a star in a play, making her entrance, descending a long stairway; in a moment the audience would burst into applause. . . .

Then she was outside the boardinghouse, and the rain was whipping against her face, soaking her thin cloak, molding her blue serge dress against her body. The wind was raw; it chilled her, it tore at her cloak and her hair. At the foot of the steps, she grasped the iron railing for support.

She did not hear the footsteps behind her, did not realize she wasn't alone, until she felt a hand under her elbow, supporting her. She turned and saw the man who had overheard her quarrel with Mrs. Baxley a few moments before. She looked away. "Please leave me alone," she said. The light from the gas lamps along the shabby street wavered and swam before her eyes.

He handed her a handkerchief. "Go ahead," he said, "you've earned a good cry after that scene with our landlady."

She pushed his hand away. "I have no intention of crying," she said. Those years at the County Farm back in Ohio had taught her the futility of tears and given her a stiff-necked pride.

"All right," he said. "But you're done in, I can see that. And you're getting soaked, besides."

"I can't go back in there . . ."

"You don't have to. I'll find a hansom and take you to dinner. You will have dinner with me." It was a statement, not a question.

"I don't even know you. . . ."

"My name's Kevin Farrell. Now, wait here." He released her arm, and she clung to the iron railing as she watched him striding through the rain toward the curb. A few minutes later, he was helping her into a cab.

"The Fifth Avenue Hotel," he told the driver. Then, as the hansom turned the corner and started off up Broadway, he leaned back against the seat, brushing the rain from his black cheviot suit.

"No, please, Mr. Farrell. I'm not dressed for the Fifth Avenue Hotel."

"If you walk into the dining room there with the same dignity you showed when you went down those stairs at the boardinghouse, no one will care what you're wearing." His gray eyes flicked over her. "You're shivering," he said, taking her hands in his. "You mustn't get a chill." He rubbed her hands until the icy numbness began to disappear. She felt that he was communicating his own energy to her through the simple gesture. "Better?" he asked.

"Yes, thank you. You're very kind. . . ."

"When you get to know me, perhaps you'll change your mind," he said, but he was smiling. "No sense your getting pneumonia and going to an early grave, like your friend." He paused, his eyes direct, probing. "It was pneumonia, wasn't it?"

She was too exhausted to lie. "Beth Cameron died of an overdose of laudanum. She may have taken it by accident, as Mrs. Baxley told the police, but . . ."

"But you don't think so."

"What does it matter—now?"

"Perhaps it does matter, more than you think. You paid for Beth Cameron's funeral, didn't you? Had she

15

no relatives to take care of the expenses?"

"I don't know . . . she told me stories, sometimes. But I was never sure. After she got out of jail . . . her mind wandered a great deal. The things they did to her there. . . . Please, can't we talk about something else?"

"Of course," he said. "At least for the moment. Have you been here in New York long, Miss Reed?"

"Only three months. I . . . suppose you heard everything Mrs. Baxley said to me . . . you must know all about me."

"I know you've had a run of bad luck, but who can tell? It may be about to change."

"I don't understand."

"You don't have to—yet. Right now, what you need is a hot meal and some wine to warm you. Have you ever dined at the Fifth Avenue Hotel?"

"What do you think?" she said bitterly.

"You'll enjoy it. It lacks the tradition of the Astor House, perhaps, but the city is moving north, and the Fifth Avenue is now considered far more fashionable."

When they entered the marble lobby of the hotel, Drucilla saw that Kevin Farrell was right. She took his arm and stared, in wonder and fascination, at the elegantly dressed women and their escorts who strolled past.

This was the kind of setting she had imagined when she came to New York: the marble stairways, the frescoed ceilings, the velvet drapes.

She was painfully conscious of the clothes of women around her, of the contrast between their expensive and elaborate gowns and her worn blue serge, with its frayed white soutache braid, under the serviceable but dowdy black broadcloth cloak. The women who strolled through the lobby of the Fifth Avenue Hotel that April evening wore gowns of brocade, satin-de-Lyon, or striped silk, trimmed with Chantilly lace, velvet ribbons, or passementerie. Their shoulders were bare. Jewels sparkled in their elegant coiffures, swung from their ears, and encircled their throats.

"Come along," Farrell said. "The dining room's right ahead."

Drucilla's fingers tightened on his arm. She felt the hard muscles under the cheviot of his jacket and, just as when he had taken her hands in his back in the cab, so now again she drew strength from touching him.

She looked up at him as they entered the huge, crowded dining room with its myriad gas lamps and, for the moment, forgot her self-consciousness. She saw that he was a big man, his shoulders were wide; he had a large-boned frame, but he moved with animal grace. He looked completely at ease in these, to her, intimidating surroundings. Why, she wondered, had he been living at Mrs. Baxley's run-down boardinghouse? Of course, she reminded herself, he had been there only one night.

He helped her with her cloak, and they followed the headwaiter to a table near one of the tall windows.

"Shall I order for you, Miss Reed?"

She nodded. A glance at the menu had shown her a bewildering array of elaborate and unfamiliar dishes.

"Oyster bisque to start with, I think. Then the venison in port wine sauce. . . ."

The hot, creamy bisque was delicious. Drucilla forgot her surroundings, forgot her embarrassment at being unsuitably dressed. Only when she was almost finished did she become aware that Kevin Farrell was watching her, his gray eyes alert under the heavy black brows.

"Tell me, Miss Reed, what are your plans now?"

"I don't know . . ."

"You could still go down to the concert saloon Mrs. Baxley told you about and get work there."

"I'd rather starve."

He laughed. It was not a pleasant sound. "I doubt that," he said. "I know you've gone hungry, but starvation—that's something else. It has a way of changing one's mind about a lot of things."

He took a sip of wine, and studied her over the glass. "I'm curious about you. You might have done what Mrs. Baxley suggested, you know. Taken work at the concert saloon long enough to get some money, and then gone back to making rounds to the theaters."

"That's what Beth thought."

"Oh, yes," he said. "Beth Cameron. Tell me about her."

"She went to work in a concert saloon. There was some trouble—one of the customers was stabbed. The place was raided, and Beth and the rest of the girls who had been working there were sent to Blackwell's Island."

Drucilla shivered. "Beth was thrown in with thieves, with common prostitutes. . . ." The words came slowly at first but then, her tongue loosened by her weariness and by the wine, Drucilla found herself telling Kevin Farrell about Beth's last weeks. He listened, nodding from time to time, or putting in a word or two to show that he understood. It was a relief to share the painful memories, even with this hard-eyed stranger.

"They do terrible things to the girls out on Blackwell's Island. You can't imagine . . ."

"I think I can," Farrell said quietly. "I should imagine most prisons are pretty much alike—"

"Perhaps. But Beth wasn't like the other girls there . . . she couldn't . . ." Drucilla looked away, embarrassed.

"And so," he finished for her, "she came back from Blackwell's Island, back to the boardinghouse and then, a few weeks later, she took an overdose of laudanum." Farrell shrugged, then looked at Drucilla sharply. "Had she no family to turn to?"

"Her father's family was wealthy. She told me about them many times. She showed me some pictures of her parents, and a few pawn tickets for some jewelry. A necklace her father had given to her mother, and her mother's engagement ring and . . ."

"She hadn't the money to redeem the jewelry?"

"No, but—she gave me the tickets in case. . . . It doesn't matter now."

"Perhaps not. But tell me, what more did she say about her father's family? Did she tell you their name?"

"Beth used her mother's stage name—Cameron. Her mother was an actress and her father . . . Beth said he was a weakling, under his mother's thumb. And his mother, Beth's grandmother, disapproved of having an actress in the family."

"I suppose she made no secret of her disapproval," Farrell said.

"The old lady made life miserable for Beth's mother."

"Go on," Farrell demanded.

Drucilla told him the stories she had heard from Beth during the evenings they had spent together at Mrs. Baxley's boardinghouse. She told him that Isobel, Beth's mother, had left her husband, fled the family mansion in Newport, and returned to her native San Francisco. There she gave birth to her daughter, then went back to the stage. She toured the West, performing in mining towns.

"It was a hard life. Isobel lost her looks, then started drinking. When Beth was sixteen, her mother died. Beth toured for awhile, in Nevada and Colorado. Small parts with second-rate troupes. She came East because she wanted to get work in a real theater."

"You two had a lot in common," Farrell said.

"Oh, yes, we even looked somewhat alike. Her hair was red like mine, but darker. Her skin was very fair. Even after she got out of prison, thin and ill as she was, there was something about her, a special kind of beauty. . . . But she'd always had a cough and after that time in prison, it was worse, much worse. She couldn't sleep without taking laudanum."

Abruptly, Drucilla picked up the huge menu and used it to shield her face. She felt Farrell's hand close over her own. "Don't," he said.

"I'm perfectly all right. I'm not going to cry and make a spectacle of myself. I never cry."

"All right then," he said. "Put down the menu, and try some of this venison. It's better than Mrs. Baxley's cold mutton and cabbage, I promise you."

It wasn't until the end of the meal that Farrell brought up the subject of Beth Cameron again. "Didn't Beth ever try to get in touch with her grandmother, to ask for help?"

Drucilla shook her head. "Never. She blamed her grandmother for all the bad things that had happened to her mother. She wouldn't even use the family name."

Farrell put down his wineglass. "What was the family name?"

"I'm not even sure I remember. What difference does . . ."

"Think, Drucilla."

"Oh . . . yes . . . Tremayne, that was it."

Kevin Farrell drew his breath in sharply. He leaned back in his chair, his lips set in a thin, hard line, his eyes looking past Drucilla as if she had ceased to exist.

The orchestra at the other side of the hotel dining room began to play a waltz. Drucilla sipped her wine. The gas lamps on the walls blurred before her eyes and she knew that she was getting a little tipsy.

"I . . . didn't mean to bore you, Mr. Farrell," she said, when the silence between them had grown unbearable. "You did ask me about Beth."

"Be quiet," he said harshly. "Drink your wine."

She looked at him in bewilderment. What had she done, or said, to cause this shift of mood?

She pushed back her chair and started to rise.

"Where the devil do you think you're going?"

"I . . ." She realized, with sudden, painful clarity, that she had no place to go.

As if reading her thoughts, he asked, "What are your plans for the future, Miss Reed?"

"My plans can't possibly be of any concern to you. In fact, I don't understand why you've taken me out to dinner at a place like this. . . ."

He smiled. "Why does any man take a pretty girl out to dinner?" He refilled her glass. "Of course, the word 'pretty' doesn't do you justice. You're beautiful, desirable. . . ."

She looked down at her worn serge dress.

"Yes, even in a dress like that one," he said. "Although with the right clothes . . . a silk gown—purple, I think. Your eyes are the color of violets."

Drucilla kept her eyes fixed on her lap and thought about the wet, fog-shrouded streets outside the hotel. Where would she spend the rest of the night? She had enough money in her purse to buy a bed in one of those horrible lodginghouses in Five Points. Those places were far worse than Mrs. Baxley's boardinghouse. They offered only pallets laid down on the floors, without sheets or coverings. From six to ten persons shared a room without regard to sex. The prices, she had been told, varied from ten to twenty-five cents.

"You look frightened, Miss Reed," Farrell said. "Don't be. You've had a bad time of it, but I think your luck is about to change for the better."

Two

DRUCILLA set her jaw and forced herself to look at Kevin Farrell. She would have to make a decision, and she didn't have much time. She remembered the aging character actor who had promised to help her with her career in return for a "close, warm relationship."

"So you think my luck is going to change for the better," she said. "And I suppose you're the one to change it."

"That's possible."

Drucilla shook her head slightly, trying to dispel the effects of the wine. During her years with the touring company, she had had offers from men in the audiences in many of the towns where she performed. Offers of money, of finery. What had stopped her from accepting?

Not the conventional religious teachings, the threats of hell-fire and damnation she had listened to during her years at the County Farm. And certainly not the example set by the other women in the touring company. She wasn't cold by nature, either. But she had always believed that she would have to care for a man before she could give herself to him.

"You'll get over that notion, my dear," one of the older actresses had told her. "Men are all the same in the dark, you know. Besides, after the first time, you might get to like it."

Now, looking at Kevin Farrell across the table, she thought:

He's young. He can't be more than thirty. And good-looking, too. But there's something in his face, a kind of hardness. And his eyes can be as cold and remote . . . But when he held my hands, back there in the cab . . . Then panic swept through her as she told herself: *I don't know anything about him, really. He's a stranger, a complete stranger, how can I possibly—*

"I'll pay your back rent at the boardinghouse, Miss Reed," he was saying. He smiled at her. "I'll even buy you a purple silk dress. Tomorrow."

And tonight she would have to share his bed.

Her words came unbidden, unplanned. "Mr. Farrell, I'm most grateful for your generous offer, but I cannot accept . . ."

To her chagrin, he threw back his head and laughed.

"Good Lord, you're not playing a part with that touring company. This isn't one of those melodramas about the wicked landlord and the sewing machine girl."

She looked down at the table.

"I have no designs on your . . . virtue . . . if that's what you're thinking."

"You're not dispensing charity out of the goodness of your heart," she said flatly. "You're not that sort of man."

"You're quite right. Nevertheless, my offer stands. You'll get a chance to repay me, perhaps, but not in the way you obviously had in mind." When he smiled at her, his face lost its hard, wary expression. There was something teasing, almost boyish, in his gray eyes. "Sorry to disappoint you, my dear."

Her cheeks flamed and she stood up so quickly that she knocked over her empty wineglass.

"Sit down," he said.

"I'm leaving."

"In a moment, we'll both leave."

"And just where do you think we'll be going?"

"Back to the boardinghouse. I'll settle your account with Mrs. Baxley."

"Oh, but I . . ."

"Be still. You must learn to take one thing at a time. Tonight, at least, you'll have a fairly decent place to sleep."

On the ride back to the boardinghouse, Kevin Farrell lapsed into silence. Drucilla was grateful, for she needed time to compose herself, to sort out her confused thoughts. But it wasn't easy for her to think clearly. She was tired, and the ample dinner and the wine had lulled her into a daze.

She made herself sit up and look out the cab window. The rain had stopped. Lower Broadway and the streets that branched off it, were shrouded in heavy fog. The gaslights blurred and wavered before her eyes.

In spite of the bad weather and the lateness of the hour, the streets and narrow alleys were far from deserted. During her few months here in New York, Drucilla had become accustomed to seeing the steady procession of prostitutes along Broadway day and night, loitering at shop windows and in front of hotels and theaters. Even now, although it was close to midnight, these women continued their promenade, moving slowly under the murky flare of the gaslights through the foggy April night.

Some were handsomely dressed: they wore fine cashmere shawls over the low-cut bodices of their silk and taffeta gowns. But others were shabby, and the flounces they trailed over the wet pavement were torn and soiled; their rouged faces were haggard, their eyes desperate. Most of them were in their early twenties, but Drucilla had seen some who must have been no more than thirteen.

She turned from the window, and looked at Kevin Farrell. Had he been telling her the truth when he had said she would get a chance to repay him, but not in the usual way? What else could he possibly want of her? She would do almost anything, rather than go to work in a concert saloon on Chatham Street. . . .

At the boardinghouse, Kevin Farrell paid Mrs. Baxley the money for Drucilla's back rent; the landlady shrugged, took the bills, and watched with knowing eyes as he escorted Drucilla upstairs to her room. But he did not try to follow her inside; instead, he said good-night and went on to his own room on the floor above.

Reassured, Drucilla sank down on the edge of the narrow bed and undressed quickly. Then she pulled her nightgown over her head, lay down, and covered herself with the thin blanket. She was too exhausted to mind the lumpy mattress tonight. From down below in the street, she heard the clatter of horses' hooves on the wet cobblestones and a woman's shrill laughter. She closed her eyes, buried her face in the pillow and, in a few minutes, she was asleep.

The first light of dawn pierced the torn places in the windowshade. Drucilla awoke, her body rigid, her nightgown drenched with perspiration. She had been dreaming. Confused memories of her nightmare crowded into her mind.

Beth's face behind a barred window of the grim prison on Blackwell's Island. Beth, lying across her bed, white and still, the laudanum bottle beside her. Drucilla knew it was no use trying to go back to sleep.

She got up, put on her wrapper, and lit a spirit lamp. She filled a saucepan with water from the pitcher beside the bed, then took a tea cannister from the shelf and put a few precious spoonfuls in her teapot.

She was interrupted by a knock at her door. No one at Mrs. Baxley's boardinghouse should have been stirring so early; theater people usually slept late.

She opened the door. The gaslight in the hallway was dim, and Kevin Farrell's face was shadowed.

"I heard you moving about," he said. "Let me come in."

She hesitated, but only for a moment, then stepped aside. What else could she have expected, for all his assurances of last night? He had only waited until everyone in the house was asleep before coming to her room.

Now he glanced over at the spirit lamp. "I see you're about to have tea. May I join you?"

"As you wish, Mr. Farrell."

"Call me Kevin. Under the circumstances, I think it's more suitable, don't you agree?"

"Under the circumstances, there is no need for you to make conversation at all. You paid my rent, and now you—"

"Good Lord, you do have a suspicious turn of mind. And you're bad-tempered first thing in the morning, aren't you?"

He put his hand under her chin and tilted her face upward, studying her features. She started and tried to pull away. "Or are you afraid?"

She jerked away. "I'm cold, that's all. This room's like an icebox."

"True enough. Get back into bed." When she hesitated, he lifted her off her feet, carried her to the bed, and put her down on it. "That's better," he said. She watched him warily, her body tense. But he sat down on the chair beside the bed, and leaned back. "Now, suppose we have a little talk, while we wait for the water to boil for tea. . . ."

"Damn you," she said, "why don't you stop pretending? You didn't come down here at six in the morning to drink tea or . . ."

"I know this is an unconventional hour for a social call, but our meeting last night wasn't exactly conventional, either. I told you then that you'd have a chance to repay me for taking care of your rent, and I also told you I had no designs on your virtue. Obviously, you didn't believe me. I didn't mean to terrify you."

"I'm not afraid of you or of any man," she said, hoping her voice would not betray her.

He shrugged. "You're a fool, Drucilla. You might have had an easier time of it if you'd learned to use a woman's weapons."

"I don't know what you mean."

"Obviously." He leaned forward, his eyes glinting with

26

amusement. "Tears can be most effective, when a girl's as young and beautiful as you are. And if you admit you're afraid, you appeal to a man's protective instinct." He laughed and added:

"Forgive the lecture. I'm sure your mother must have tried to teach you to use feminine wiles. . . ."

"I never knew my mother. She died when I was born. My father brought me up."

Kevin nodded. "That would explain something about you."

"My father did the best he could for me," Drucilla interrupted. "He was a schoolmaster, and he taught me the same as if I'd been a boy—he thought girls and boys should have equal education. He even talked about sending me to normal school. But—he died when I was ten."

"You're quite alone in the world, then? No close relatives?"

"No relatives at all, that I know of." Thinking she saw a look of pity in his face, she added: "I've always managed to take care of myself."

"You weren't doing a very good job of it last night, when I found you out there in the rain."

She knew she should resent his patronizing tone, but she found that she was grateful for his presence at the moment. Talking to him, she was able to push her nightmares to the back of her mind.

"The water should be boiling now," she said, leaning forward in bed.

"Don't get up," he ordered. "Brewing tea is one of my many accomplishments."

A few minutes later, she was agreeing. "You do make a good cup of tea."

"I make an even better one with freshly drawn water. At any rate, remember that when making tea, you should always bring the pot to the kettle, never the other way around."

She was reminded of an Englishman who had been a part of the touring company back in Ohio, and who had been endlessly critical of the way tea was prepared in America. "You aren't English, are you?" she asked.

His face fell into harsh lines. "Christ, no," he said. "I'm Irish. We lived in England for awhile, though."

"We?"

"My mother and I. All that was left of our family. We left Ireland during the famine."

Drucilla had heard terrible stories of the potato famine that had ravaged Ireland during the fifties, of whole families wiped out by starvation. Those who managed to raise the passage money to emigrate to America found that they had to face conditions nearly as bad in the New World. They had been scorned by those whose ancestors had been among the earlier waves of immigration: the English, the Scottish, the Dutch.

Some found work in the homes of the wealthy, as housemaids, grooms, or coachmen. They had enough food, but they did the hardest work for the lowest wages. Here in New York, many Irish immigrants had settled in the Five Points district, back of City Hall near the East River. Here, there was scarcely a house to be found without a saloon or "bucket shop" on the first floor; many of the tenements also served as brothels.

In the cellars of the Five Points' tenements, whole families of Irish immigrants crowded together in unspeakable filth, and plagues were frequent.

Drucilla wondered why Kevin Farrell had left England to come to New York and how he had managed to prosper here. Before she could ask him more about himself, he said: "You're feeling better now, aren't you? There's a bit of color in your cheeks."

She sipped her tea. "I'm quite all right." Then, responding to something sympathetic in his tone, she added: "I had some terrible nightmares, just before I woke up. I—"

"Tell me." He smiled. "They say, if you tell your nightmares, you'll never have them again."

"I was dreaming about Beth . . . about that horrible prison she was in, just before she . . ." She shuddered. "Please, I can't talk about it."

"All right," he said, pressing her hand. "But tell me this . . . you do have those pawn tickets here in your room. The ones Beth left you?"

Drucilla nodded.

"Fine. Today we'll go down to the pawnshop and re-claim her jewelry."

Drucilla pulled her hand away and threw him a suspicious look. Had he gone to all this trouble, just to get his hands on Beth's jewelry? It didn't seem likely, for he was obviously prosperous, well-dressed, and had enough money to take her out for a sumptuous dinner last night, and pay her back rent.

Nevertheless, she told him: "Beth's jewelry isn't worth much. Her mother had to leave all the really valuable jewelry behind when she ran away. All Beth had left to pawn was a garnet ring, a gold chain with a locket and . . ."

Kevin interrupted impatiently: "I don't give a damn if those trinkets are made of paste and tin. We're going to get them." Then, seeing Drucilla draw back, obviously startled by the harshness of his tone, he added: "She would have wanted you to have her jewelry. Be dressed in half an hour. I'll have a cab waiting outside."

He rose, turned, and left the room. Drucilla remained seated in bed, holding her empty tea cup. She stared after him, then slowly got up, and began to dress.

After Kevin and Drucilla had left the pawnshop on Division Street, with Drucilla carrying the parcel of trinkets in her purse, they stopped for a hearty breakfast in a large, cheerful-looking restaurant on Lower Broadway. She was surprised to find that, in spite of having eaten a lavish dinner the night before, she was able to do justice to a generous serving of ham and eggs, with hot biscuits and coffee.

Later, when they had returned to Drucilla's room at the boardinghouse, Kevin said: "You hold on to the jewelry, but be sure you keep it in a safe place."

Drucilla went to her trunk, unlocked it and, pushing aside her neatly folded underthings, she took out a small, square box covered with threadbare, pale blue velvet.

"This belonged to Beth," she explained. She opened the box to put the jewelry inside.

"Anything else in there?" Kevin asked.

"Only a few old photographs."

"Let me see them."

She handed him the photographs. She was not particularly surprised by his tone of command and his brusque manner. She had grown accustomed to taking orders during her dismal years at the County Farm in Ohio, and she had learned to obey at once, without complaint or question. The matron had had a heavy hand, and had administered swift punishment for the slightest infractions of the rules, or for any show of reluctance in carrying out her commands. But Drucilla reminded herself that she was no longer a helpless child, and Kevin was not her master; she felt a flare of resentment, even as she complied with his demand.

Kevin was apparently unaware of her feelings at the moment. He was studying the photographs as if he wanted to engrave every detail into his memory forever.

"Who's this?" he asked, holding out one of the pictures for Drucilla's inspection. She looked at the likeness of a slender young woman with delicate, even features, whose long, abundant, light-colored hair fell in curls over her shoulders. She wore a white lace dress with a full skirt, in the style of twenty years ago; she held a wide-brimmed straw hat, wreathed with daisies.

"That was Isobel—Beth's mother. The picture was taken a little while before she married Beth's father."

Kevin nodded and held out another photograph. "And this? The happy young couple, I assume?"

"Yes. Beth told me it had been taken right after her parents eloped. He was good-looking, wasn't he?"

Kevin shrugged. "Maybe. Pity he wasn't man enough to stand up for his wife against his mother." He broke off, and drew out a third picture.

"That's Beth, at six months, with her mother. It was taken in San Francisco, Beth told me. That was after her mother had run away from her father."

Kevin put the photographs back into the box.

"And that's all Beth left you—these pictures and the jewelry?"

"Yes, that's all. But I really can't understand why

. . . Do you always take such a deep interest in someone you never even met?"

Drucilla stopped short as a new idea crossed her mind.

"Or did you know Beth?" All at once, her imagination, nourished on the romantic dramas she had acted
in, began to work feverishly.

Maybe Kevin had known Beth out West. That must
be it. He had seen her on the stage there and fallen in
love with her; he had followed her to New York, only to
arrive too late.

Drucilla looked at Kevin and sighed. "Tell me, did
you . . . were you and Beth . . ."

"Be quiet, will you? I have to think."

He strode to the window and, turning his back on her,
he stared down into the street. Hurt by his harsh tone,
Drucilla lapsed into silence. She busied herself putting
the photographs neatly in order, along with the jewelry.
Then she locked the case and returned it to her trunk,
covering it with the pile of underthings.

Still Kevin did not move. He remained lost in his own
thoughts. His hands were thrust deep into his pockets,
and, although she could not see his face, the set of his
broad, heavily-muscled shoulders conveyed an air of
barely controlled tension.

Then, all at once, he turned to her and smiled. "Come
on," he said. "We're going out again."

"But where . . ."

"I promised to buy you a purple dress, didn't I? We'll
drive to the Ladies' Mile, and you shall have the most
elegant purple dress in New York City."

Three

———

KEVIN Farrell was as good as his word, and Drucilla forgot her misgivings about him, as she went from one to the other of the fashionable shops that lined Broadway from the St. Nicholas Hotel to Thirty-fourth Street. She had never dared enter them before although she had looked with longing at their show windows. Now for the first time in her life, she would be able to choose a dress without counting the cost—a dress that would set off her red hair and white skin, and complement her eyes.

She found the dress in the elegant new Lord & Taylor department store at Broadway and Twentieth Street, a magnificent building with an iron frame construction, which allowed ample space for window displays; it also had a steam elevator to carry customers to each of its five floors. Fashionable New York City was moving uptown, and the finest shops were moving, too.

After much pleasurable indecision, Drucilla finally settled on a walking dress of lilac silk and ombre-shaded satin, in tones from palest mauve to the deep purplish-blue of a midnight sky. The reflection of the satin over-skirt changed her violet eyes to deep purple. The silk bodice fitted closely and tapered over her small waist; it emphasized her high, rounded breasts, while the over-skirt, with its elaborate and intricate draperies, concealed what she believed to be the one defect in her figure—her almost boyishly slender hips.

Kevin Farrell had insisted that she buy not only the purple dress, but one or two others as well, and whatever else she might need to add to her wardrobe. The purple dress was ready-made, but the saleswoman promised to have the alterations completed by the following day. Two other dresses—a pale blue peau de soie, and a China silk in a soft cream color with tiny lavender and green flowers embroidered on it—would take a little longer to complete.

The following day, as Drucilla stood in the dressing room at Lord and Taylor's store, turning and swaying gracefully before the mirror, she was still trying to find answers to the questions that had tormented her since her meeting with Kevin Farrell. Why was he buying her these clothes, if not for the obvious reasons? And why was he so interested in Beth Cameron, a girl he had never met, and why—

"Is something wrong with the dress, Miss?" the sales-woman was asking. "We'll be happy to make any further alterations you desire."

"Oh, no. It's a wonderful dress." Drucilla smoothed a flounce on the satin overskirt with a loving hand. "It makes me feel— Oh, I've never had such a beautiful dress."

The saleswoman concealed a smile. So many of her customers fussed endlessly, no matter how becoming a dress might be. A few criticized and found flaws to prove that they were accustomed to only the best.

The clerk, who had been with Lord & Taylor for many years and had worked in the older store at Grand and Chrystie Streets, was not impressed by these critical customers. Although they were now the wives and daughters of New York's growing nouveau riche society, she knew that their origins were often as humble as her own. But this beautiful young girl with the glowing red hair and violet eyes, who stood before the mirror lost in admiration for her new dress, was something of a puzzle.

Her old dress of blue serge, which the saleswoman had wrapped up for her, was frayed and worn; furthermore, the girl had made it plain that she was not used to shopping in fine department stores. And yet, there was a quality about her, an air of good breeding. Her voice was soft and well modulated; her diction as perfect as that of any daughter of the Jays or Livingstons, two of the first families of New York. The saleswoman shrugged slightly. Her customers' private lives were not really her concern, but she knew more about them than they perhaps imagined.

"You should always wear that color, Miss. It might have been created for you." She made a few small adjustments in the overskirt, then added: "Perhaps you would like to see something in millinery. We have a new hat—it just came in yesterday from Paris. Do let me show you."

Drucilla hesitated, then, remembering Kevin's instructions, she said: "I'd love to see it."

It was indeed the perfect hat to complete the costume: a flirtatious little chip that perched saucily over one eye, and was trimmed with the same ombre satin as the dress. It was topped with three ostrich plumes, shaded from pale mauve to deep violet. Drucilla bought it, and then, throwing caution to the winds, also bought scented mauve gloves and a tiny purple velvet purse.

Kevin, who was waiting for her on the street floor, paid the bill without raising an eyebrow, then said, "All this elegance is much too beautiful to keep hidden. I'll take you out driving and you can show off your finery."

In the weeks that followed, Drucilla discovered another side of New York City, one she had only heard about until now. Instead of trudging from one manager's office to another, she now explored an exciting city that was growing in population and in amusements, some elegant, others raffish, all pleasurable.

Kevin had hired a fine, shiny victoria and a team of sleek bays, which he drove with considerable skill. She learned during those weeks that Kevin could be the perfect companion when he chose to be. He knew the city well and took obvious pleasure in showing it to her.

The weather turned warm early that May, and it seemed to Drucilla that all of New York was congregated in Central Park. Elegantly dressed ladies took afternoon walks with their escorts on the Mall, a stately esplanade. On Wednesdays and Saturdays, Kevin took her to hear the promenade concerts that were given in the ornate music pavilion beside the Mall. They sat together at the Casino on a terrace above the esplanade and enjoyed a light repast while listening to the music.

One afternoon, he led her down the steps near the Mall, and took her boating. She was charmed by the swans that floated on the lake. It was plain to her that many of the couples in the other boats were far more interested in their own courtships than in feeding the swans. She found herself looking at Kevin and wondering why he had not yet showed any awareness of her as a desirable woman.

True, he had held her arm when helping her into the boat, but that was only common courtesy. What was wrong with him, she wondered. And with her? That first night, at dinner, she had been thoroughly relieved when he had told her he had no wish to sleep with her. Now, after spending so much time with him, her feelings were changing. She remembered how he had lifted her in his arms to carry her back to bed, that morning he had come to her room at the boardinghouse. Suppose he had not let her go, but had made love to her then? She looked at him and saw the ripple of hard muscles under his jacket as he rowed the boat out to the center of the lake. She felt a shiver of excitement.

Nevertheless, she was grateful when he diverted her thoughts, asking her: "Do you ride, Drucilla?"

"No. That is, not very well."

"All the same, I'm going to take you riding tomorrow morning. I'll teach you some of the fine points. And then we'll have breakfast at Mount St. Vincent at One Hundred and Sixth Street. It's considered a bit raffish, but you're no more conventional than I am."

No, there was no figuring him out. He would take her

to a restaurant where gentlemen of rakish tastes entertained their equally free female companions; but he did
not so much as try to kiss her. He also took her to a part
of Coney Island where, as he calmly told her, no well-
brought-up young lady should go, certainly not without
a chaperon. She was annoyed by his frankness, but at
the same time, she was delighted when he took her to
dinner at the Wooden Elephant, a huge restaurant built
in the form of an elephant with enormous glass eyes
which, when lit for the night, shone like beacons.

One afternoon in the middle of May, he took her
driving in the victoria in Central Park, and regaled her
with anecdotes about New York's leading citizens, respectable and otherwise. It was the fashionable hour of
four o'clock, and all the city had turned out to enjoy the
fine weather. He pointed out the broughams of the old
New York families: the Jays, the Stuyvesants and the
Livingstons. These vehicles were as uncompromisingly
respectable as their owners and were driven by dignified old coachmen who had served the families for many
years.

But Kevin also called Drucilla's attention to the car-
riages of such celebrities as Josephine Wood, the madam
of New York's most fashionable brothel, and Madame
Restell, the city's most successful abortionist. "Madame
Restell has a mansion at Fifty-second Street and Fifth
Avenue—much to the chagrin of her neighbors."

"But can't she be run out of town, a woman like that?"
Drucilla asked.

"You don't know New York, my dear. It would seem
that Madame Restell knows too many intimate secrets
about too many important families. No one dares affront
her."

He went on to tell Drucilla about John Allen, who
was driving by in an elegant four-in-hand. "He owns a
dance hall and brothel on Water Street. Several of his
brothers are preachers. I've heard that John Allen himself was once a student at the Union Theological Semi-
nary. But I suppose he finds his present trade more
profitable."

"That's—horrible!"

"Oh, I don't know. Allen runs a lively establishment. His girls wear low-cut, short red dresses and red-topped boots with bells around their ankles. The effect is quite fetching."

Drucilla gasped and looked away, sure that Kevin had gotten his knowledge about John Allen's establishment firsthand.

"Sorry," he said. "I didn't mean to shock you. Look, over there—that's right. That's called a demi-d'Aumont. It's a new kind of vehicle, and the woman inside is Mrs. August Belmont."

Drucilla scarcely listened. Instead, she wondered about Kevin Farrell. What kind of man was he? What was his business and why his interest in her? He had told her she was beautiful, but New York was full of beautiful young women, splendidly dressed. Yet, for the past three weeks he had spent nearly every day, every evening with her. He had paid her casual compliments, had pressed her hand and, a few times, had put his arm around her waist. But he had not attempted to kiss her.

She was sure he was not shy with women, nor inexperienced, and his virile looks, his powerful physique, drew admiring glances from women; wherever they went these last weeks, Drucilla was aware that other women found her escort attractive.

Now, sitting there beside him in the victoria, she wondered what it would be like if he were to make love to her. She was still a little afraid of him, of his brooding silences and swift changes of mood. But fear was mingled with longing as she thought of his mouth on hers, his hands on her breasts. . . . Deep inside her, something quivered, then tightened. . . .

Lost in thought, she was not immediately aware that Kevin had turned the victoria and was driving the team out of the park, onto Harlem Lane.

"Where are we going?" she asked.

"There's a little inn on the river road near the High Bridge," he said. "I thought you might like to have dinner there."

"Is it very far?" She looked at the lengthening shadows

that fell across the open fields on either side of the road. "It's getting late."

He shrugged. "If you're afraid to have me drive you back after dark, we can stay at the inn overnight."

"Certainly not . . . I . . ."

"In separate rooms," he added. He shook his head. "I can't make you out, Drucilla. One minute, you're prim and proper, and the next . . . Tell me, what kind of girl are you, really?"

"I've told you about myself," she said.

"You've told me your father was a schoolmaster in Ohio, that you were shipped off to the County Farm when he died, and you toured with a stock company. But there's still a lot I don't know. Why did you decide to become an actress?"

"It would be hard to explain. Acting is all mixed up in my mind with so many other things. Freedom . . . and excitement . . . and . . . fine clothes. . . . And being someone else, not myself. . . ."

She waited for him to jeer at her, but instead, he said softly, "Go on."

"I guess it started at the County Farm outside Cincinnati. Sometimes I'd play-act for the other children, but mostly for myself. I used to do a lot of play-acting when the matron locked me up in the shed."

"The shed?"

Even now, remembering, she felt sick in the pit of her stomach, but she forced herself to go on. "The shed was an awful place. We were locked in there as a punishment. It was next to a cesspool, freezing cold in winter and always damp. The windows were boarded up, and there was no candle. I used to imagine all kinds of terrible things were waiting for me in the dark. Then I started remembering stories from the books Papa used to read to me, and I'd pretend I was someone else: Marie Antoinette, in prison, waiting to go to the guillotine. Or Joan of Arc, right before she was burned at the stake. . . ." She broke off, embarrassed. "I guess you think I'm crazy. But it helped."

"How long were you at the County Farm?"

"Until I was fourteen. Then they found me a job as a

chambermaid in a Cincinnati hotel. It wasn't quite as bad as the Farm, but I hated it all the same. I'd only been at the hotel a few months when a troupe of actors stopped there, and the manager gave me a ticket to a performance. It was wonderful, the lights and the costumes and—I knew I had to be part of it. I couldn't go back to scrubbing floors and making beds at the hotel. So, when the troupe moved on to Kentucky, I went along."

"Just like that?"

"Well, you see the manager's wife had a new baby and two other small children, and I offered to take care of them, to help with the sewing—anything—if I could get a chance to act."

"I see. Sounds as if the manager got a good bargain."

"He did, but I got what I wanted, too. It wasn't easy, sleeping in barns and sheds, or dirty little inns along the river, and some of those backwoods audiences were pretty rough. But the actors were kind to me, and after awhile they let me take small parts in the shows."

She fell silent, aware of his eyes on her. She had seen that look before and, as always, it made her uneasy. "Now you know all about me," she finished.

"Not quite," Kevin said. "I've known a few actresses in my time, and they were—forgive me—they didn't refuse to take a man's money in exchange for their favors, as you did the night we met."

"That's not fair," she began, but her anger quickly subsided, for she knew that there was some truth in what he had said. "The other actresses in the troupe told me I was being foolish not to let a man . . . but I couldn't help it. I always thought I'd have to love a man before I could . . ."

"And now?"

"I suppose I still feel that way."

"You said 'love.' You didn't mention marriage."

"Marriage?"

"You've heard of it, no doubt?"

"I guess I never thought about it," she said, ignoring his sarcasm. "I don't know if I'd want to get married, ever. But love—that's different."

"And have you ever been in love, Drucilla?"

She looked at Kevin, at the hard line of his jaw, his thin-lipped mouth, his gray eyes under the heavy black brows. A slow, languorous tide of feeling moved within her; fear and desire mingled. She forced herself to draw away from him, to sit up very straight on the seat beside him. "I'm a virgin, if that's what you're asking." The words came out, unplanned, unbidden, and a moment later, her face flamed with embarrassment.

Kevin threw back his head and laughed. Drucilla writhed inwardly. No respectable girl should ever use such plain language in speaking to a man.

She turned away and looked out at the shining ribbon of the Hudson, far below, and at the shoreline opposite. The May afternoon was giving place to evening. The sky above the New Jersey hills was turning rose and gold, and the low-lying clouds were edged with crimson. The air was heavy with the scent of sweet new grass and the first delicate leaves of the oaks and birches that lined the roadside. The breeze from the river loosened a strand of her hair and blew it against her cheek, but she made no move to tuck it back under her hat.

"Don't be embarrassed, Drucilla," Kevin said, almost gently. "You spoke your mind. I like that. I don't want you to pretend with me, ever. You don't have to. We're too much alike."

"We are?"

"I think so. We both got a bad deal from the world when we were too young to fight back. Now, we want something better. You seem to think you can get what you want—money, security, happiness—through a career on the stage. Although perhaps, after what happened to Beth Cameron . . ."

"I won't end like Beth."

"How can you be sure?"

"Because I won't give in—I won't take the easy way, like she did. I'll fight for what I want, and I'll get it."

"I believe you mean that."

Kevin turned the carriage off the road and into a wooded path that led between the trees to the edge of the river. The huge, heavy trunks of the oaks screened them from the road.

"I can help you, Drucilla," he said. "We can help each other."

"I don't understand."

"One gamble—a big one—and you can have more than you ever dreamed of. Money, security, social position—a wealthy husband, if you want one."

There was a tension in him, a controlled energy; his eyes were on hers, hard, demanding. The look frightened her, and she gave a nervous little laugh.

"Don't laugh at me. Not now, or ever. And don't say anything. Just listen. You can have what you want. All it takes is nerve—and luck."

"What makes you think I'm lucky?"

His hands closed on her shoulders. "You are lucky. You were Beth Cameron's friend, her only confidante. Now, you're going to *become* .Beth Cameron."

She looked at Kevin, trying to understand his words. "You must be mad," she said at last. "Even if I were willing to take part in such a . . . a deception, what could I hope to gain?"

"A fortune. The Tremayne fortune. Beth was her grandmother's only remaining heir. Old Mrs. Tremayne hasn't much longer to live. She's in her seventies, and I think all that's kept her going so long is the hope of finding her granddaughter. Beth was to have inherited everything, if I had found her in time."

"If you had found her? You've been searching for her then. That's why you asked me all those questions about her. Who are you? What was your connection with Beth?"

He was silent for a few moments. He looked out across the waters of the Hudson, which by now had turned a glowing rose color.

"All right," he said at last. "It's time you knew. I was hired by Mrs. Tremayne's lawyers to find Beth."

"You're a—detective?"

"That's right. I used to work for the Pinkerton Agency; you must have heard of them. Now I work for myself.

The profits are higher—or they will be, if you help me." The line of his jaw hardened. "If I'd arrived in New York a few days earlier . . ."

"If only you had. Poor Beth. If you had found her . . ."

"I have, I tell you. You're going to take her place."

"I couldn't possibly . . ."

"You're going to convince her grandmother, and the lawyers, and all of Newport society, that you are Beth Cameron."

She pulled away from him. "No. It's impossible. Think what you're asking."

"I have thought. Ever since that first night we met, I've thought of nothing else. You can do it, Drucilla. I've worked out every detail, considered every risk. Now listen. You're coming to Newport with me. I'll take you first to the lawyers, then to the Tremayne mansion. Once you've seen it, you'll realize how much you have to gain. The Tremaynes are wealthy, their fortune goes back nearly a century. And when the old lady dies, everything will go to you."

"You told me that night—at the Fifth Avenue Hotel —that I'd be able to pay you back. Is this what you meant? You'll want a share of the fortune."

"Of course. I won't be greedy, I assure you. You'll have more than enough for yourself. And even before you come into your inheritance, Mrs. Tremayne will give me a liberal fee for finding her granddaughter. So you see . . ."

"I see that I want no part of this horrible scheme." She shivered. "You said we were alike, but you were wrong. Whatever happened to you back in Ireland during the famine, and afterward—it left you twisted, corrupt."

"Stop it. You're talking like a fool."

"I don't care what you think of me. Just drive me back to the city—now."

"Not yet."

"Then I'll drive myself." She tried to take the reins, but he jerked them out of her hands.

"I'm offering you a fortune, and you're too frightened to see it."

She stood up in the victoria. "I'll walk back if I have to." She tried to climb down, but he took hold of her and pushed her back into the seat. The horses reared in panic, and Kevin had to use all his strength to subdue them. Then he turned back to her. "Sit still, damn it, or you'll have us both over the cliff and into the river down there."

"I don't care . . . I want to go back . . . I want . . ."

He took one hand from the reins and before she knew what was about to happen, he struck her across the cheek with his open palm. The force of the blow brought tears to her eyes. Her voice shook as she said: "It means so much to you—that money."

"You're damn right, it does. And it should to you, too. You said you'd starve before you'd go to work in that saloon, like Beth did. Remember? Fine words. But I have starved. Not for a day or a week but for years. I saw my father and my brothers and sisters die of starvation. It's a slow and terrible way to die. Have you ever seen anyone die that way, Drucilla?"

"No," she said. "Not even at the County Farm."

Even there, nobody had starved. The food was coarse and cheap—oatmeal, stews made from the toughest cuts of meat, thin, watery soups. But nobody starved.

"I saw the people in my village, children and grown men and women. I saw their skins grow rough and dry, their bodies become misshapen. They had sores on their bodies and between their fingers. I saw them lying in the road with a greenish froth on their lips, from eating grass, because there was nothing else for them to eat."

"But you said you left Ireland with your mother. Weren't conditions better for you in England?"

"We begged our way to Dublin, then my mother got the fare to take us to Liverpool. She never told me how. When I was a little older, it wasn't hard for me to guess—but I never dared ask. In Liverpool it was just as bad, maybe worse. By the end of 1847 there were more than three hundred thousand Irish refugees in Liverpool, jammed into miserable cellars that had been condemned years before. The English didn't want us there, and we didn't want to be there but, without passage money to America, we had no choice. We'd been there only a few weeks when my mother took sick. It was typhus. I tried to get money. I begged in the streets, then I stole. And got caught, and put in prison for a month."

"But you couldn't have been more than . . ."

"I was eight, to be exact. At any rate, by the time I was released, my mother was dead. No one could even tell me where she was buried."

"Oh, Kevin, I . . ."

"It was better she died. Those women who survived had to sell themselves in the streets for food, or for passage money to America."

His eyes were bleak. "You asked me why money was so important to me. Because without money, honor, common decency can't exist."

Was he right? Was it possible that if he had not come along to help her, when she had been put out of the boardinghouse, she would have grown desperate enough to sell herself?

He was speaking quietly, without emotion. "For the next few years I lived like an animal. I stole food, but I became more skillful at thievery. After the first few months, I didn't get caught anymore."

Unable to speak, Drucilla put a hand on his arm. Her anger had disappeared, and she felt only pity. "I didn't know. I'm sorry . . ."

"I didn't tell you all that so you'd feel sorry. I wanted to make you see what the world can be like for people like us." He moved closer, so that she felt his warm breath on her cheek. "Now you see why we have to do this thing, together. And you will do it, won't you?"

His arms went around her, pressing her against him so hard that she found it difficult to breathe.

"You will," he repeated. "Say it."

"Yes. I will." Her arms held him now. Her body moved against his with a will of its own. A hot dizziness swept her, different from any feeling she had ever known. Under the thin China silk of her bodice, her breasts were crushed against the hardness of his chest. Then he was looming above her, so that she lay back in his arms. His lips found hers, and his tongue explored the moist warmth of her mouth.

The early twilight now shadowed the oak grove; the river had turned from crimson to indigo, with the setting of the sun.

"We'd better drive on to the inn," he said.

"Not yet, Kevin. Please, not yet."

"Drucilla, if we stay here—surely you must know . . ."

"I know." Her eyes were purple in the dusk.

He drew a long, uneven breath. His fingers moved to the buttons of her bodice and a moment later, his mouth touched the soft swell of her breasts, which were barely covered by the delicate lawn of her lace-trimmed chemise. She stroked his dark hair, her hands trembling with her need for him.

She was tormented by her hunger, but she was afraid, too, uncertain of what lay ahead. She allowed him to lift her out of the carriage, and then he was carrying her deeper into the grove, close to the cliff's edge, where the new grass was thick and soft, still warm with the heat of the day. He lay down beside her, and the sweet-scented darkness of the May evening enveloped them.

He drew her close. She felt the warmth of his flesh, searing her through the thin material of her chemise, the single garment she still wore, and the hardness of him that made her realize he was ready to take her now, this moment. But she was not ready. She needed time. She put her hands against his chest to hold him off.

"What's wrong?"

Unable to speak, she made a small sobbing sound.

"You're not afraid, are you?" He raised himself on one arm and looked into her face. "Yes," he said slowly, "I think you are." He began to stroke her hair then, to take out the pins so that it fell around her face. Then he kissed her, a long, lingering kiss. His lips moved along her throat. Under the thin lawn of her chemise, his hands stroked her thighs. Then she felt him draw the chemise from her body. "That's better," he said softly. "Now . . ."

His tongue touched her breasts, and her nipples hardened. This time the sound she made was one of pure pleasure. His hands moved to her legs, his touch gentle, slow. She felt her body relax, her thighs parted, and his hand moved upward. Her hips arched to meet his touch.

When he took his hand away, she nearly cried out in frustration, but a moment later he was positioned above her and her long, slim legs were locked around him, her hands drawing him down. . . .

A moment later, her feverish urgency gave way to shocking pain. She pressed her mouth against his shoulder to stifle her cry. Then, as he began to move inside her, slowly at first, then faster, thrusting into the center of her being, the pain faded, giving way to a new sensation. Guided by instinct she began to move, matching her rhythm to his, seeking and finding the final explosive moment, the ultimate release.

The night breeze from the river stirred the trees, and she saw, between the branches, the stars that flickered dimly in the spring night. She turned her head to look at Kevin who lay beside her, his eyes closed.

She raised herself up on one arm and reached out to touch him. Her long hair brushed his face, and he opened his eyes.

"Are you all right, love?" he asked.

She laughed softly. Never had she felt such peace, such fulfillment; she lay still, savoring the warmth that had moved from the deepest part of her to every nerve of her body.

It wasn't until later, when they were driving back to the city through the warm, scented darkness of the night, that she remembered, as if from a fevered dream, Kevin's fantastic plan to take her to Newport and pass her off as Beth. He had spoken of a fortune and of her chance to make a socially acceptable marriage to a wealthy man. But surely now, after what had happened between them, he would change his mind.

She looked at his shadowed face; in the moonlight, it looked cold and remote. His eyes were somber, brooding. In spite of herself, she felt a stirring of doubt. Perhaps the moments they had shared back there by the river had not meant as much to him. He had had other women before her. More beautiful women, perhaps, certainly more experienced women.

Perhaps he had made love to her not only because he had desired her, but also to bind her to him, to make her a willing pawn for his dangerous scheme.

Four

THE TRAIN rumbled across the green Connecticut countryside, and the compartment on that June afternoon was warm and oppressive. Drucilla moved uneasily on the plush seat. Although her blue silk traveling suit was correct for summer, she now wished she had worn something lighter. The neck of the fashionable Watteau casaque came up to her chin, and the sleeves covered her arms right down to the wrists.

While she might have been more comfortable in a simpler costume, she had to admit that the blue silk was becoming, with its elaborate ruffles edging both the casaque and the underskirt. Her hat, too, was most fetching, a small, forward-tilted confection adorned with mauve and pale blue blossoms.

At this particular moment, however, she was not concerned with her appearance. Her palms were moist and she felt a growing tightness in the pit of her stomach.

"Go on," Kevin Farrell urged. "Repeat that last part of the story again and let's make sure you have it down pat."

She drew a long breath. "My mother and I were in Virginia City with a touring company, when she became ill. She was appearing in a production of *The Specter Bridegroom* at the time, but one night she was unable to go on. The doctor said she had consumption. Another member of the company replaced her."

Drucilla hesitated, then seeing Kevin's lips press together in a hard line, she went on quickly. "Later, mother recovered a little, and when the troupe moved on to Yellow Canyon, she was able to resume her role, but . . ."

"No, damn it. You've got to concentrate harder. Your mother went back on the stage when the troupe was in Sacramento. It was some months later, in Yellow Canyon, that she collapsed completely and you had to go on in her place. Can't you remember anything?"

"I'm sorry," Drucilla said. "I'm trying. But now that we're getting closer to Newport I'm beginning to feel afraid."

"I don't care how you feel. Feelings are a luxury you can't afford right now."

"I know that. But I don't see why it is so important that I memorize the name of every town in the West where Beth's mother appeared on the stage."

He seized her by the shoulders, his face dark with anger.

"Not Beth's mother. Your mother. Isobel Tremayne was your mother. You are Drucilla Tremayne."

"Nice of you to let me keep my own first name," she snapped.

"I have my reasons for that."

"I know—you explained. I'm not stupid, Kevin."

"Prove it, then. Repeat that part of your story about your mother, and your first appearance on the stage. And this time, get it right."

"Not now, Kevin. Later, when I . . ."

"Repeat it."

How hard and implacable he was, holding her that way; his gray eyes were pitiless.

"My mother and I were in Virginia City when she fell ill . . ."

This time she went on to the end of the recitation without a mistake. Only when she had finished did Kevin release her. Tiny beads of perspiration moistened her upper lip, and she dabbed at them with a handkerchief.

"Maybe we both need a break," he said. He looked at his watch. "Nearly two. Suppose we go into the dining car."

She shook her head. "You go, Kevin. I couldn't swallow a bite of food."

"Nonsense. You hardly touched your breakfast. You must be famished."

He stood up. "The food on these trains is excellent. I could relish a beefsteak, I think. Or perhaps some venison."

How could he think of food at a time like this? How could he appear to be so calm and self-possessed, when tonight they would be arriving at Newport, and tomorrow they would have to face Mrs. Tremayne's lawyers? If she had not known otherwise, she would have thought Kevin was bound for Newport on a pleasure trip.

"Come along," he said, holding out his hand to her. "You may order something light, broiled trout perhaps, and blancmange for dessert."

The mention of food, together with the stuffy warmth of the compartment and the jolting and swaying of the train, were making her a little nauseated.

Ever since that evening back in May, when Kevin had revealed his plan for her for the first time, she had been hoping desperately that he would change his mind. She had dreaded the idea of passing herself off as Beth, no matter how much money was at stake. But she knew that if she refused to do his bidding, he would leave her.

After he had made love to her in that shadowed grove overlooking the river, she had known, beyond doubt or question, that there could be no other man for her. Rather than risking his displeasure, she had agreed to do what he wanted—to memorize the story he had prepared for her, to go with him to Newport and face Mrs. Tremayne's lawyers. Then old Mrs. Tremayne herself— if the daring scheme ever got that far.

But visions of arrest and imprisonment loomed before

her, growing more terrifying now that they were on their way to Newport.

"Come along, Drucilla," 'he was saying impatiently.

"I can't. I . . . Please don't be angry."

He looked down at her. "You really are frightened, aren't you? But there's no reason to be. Once we get to Newport, everything will go exactly as I've planned."

"Kevin, don't make me go through with this." She was close to hysteria, and only by the strongest effort of will was she keeping her self-control. "I . . . don't think I can."

"Go on."

"It's so dangerous. You could go to jail for years, and so could I."

"But we won't. Not if you keep your head." Then, more gently, he added, "It's natural for you to be nervous, I suppose. But you must think of it as stage fright, nothing more."

"This isn't a play. You want me to convince an old lady that I am her granddaughter. It's wrong . . . it's a sin . . ."

She turned her face away and fixed her eyes on the flat landscape outside the train window, the elms and maples with their first delicate green leaves, the farm houses and the ponds, blue and sparkling in the afternoon sunlight.

"Even if Mrs. Tremayne does believe us, and later, she finds out the truth, it could kill her."

"Stop it, Drucilla. Right now." His voice cracked like a whip.

He stood over her, and said harshly, "Your moral scruples do you credit. But haven't you forgotten that Charlotte Tremayne drove Beth's mother away, simply because she had been an actress before her marriage? Didn't you tell me that Beth hated the old lady so much that she refused to ask her for help, even when she was at the end of her rope, in that miserable boardinghouse?"

"But Beth never knew her grandmother. She only knew what her mother had told her. Maybe old Mrs. Tremayne was sorry afterward. Why else would she have told her lawyers to start the search for her grand-daughter?"

"I don't know, and I don't care. But look at it this way. You'll be doing Charlotte Tremayne a favor. You'll be giving her back her granddaughter. And offering her a chance to salve her conscience in her old age. From what Mr. Pollock, her lawyer, has told me, the old lady's not been happy these last years. She lives alone in that big house of hers. She has no close relatives, few friends. Now, when you arrive, she'll have something to live for. Think what it will mean to her to have a lovely young granddaughter to present to Newport society."

It all sounded so plausible, the way Kevin put it, and yet something deep in Drucilla's mind rebelled. But she saw that it would be useless to try to explain her feelings to Kevin. Hadn't he told her feelings were a luxury she could not afford?

"Even if I can carry this off, if I can convince Mrs. Tremayne I'm her granddaughter, how long do you expect me to keep up the pretense?"

"Not too long, my dear. I agree that it would be a strain to go on with this charade indefinitely." He sat down beside her again, put his arm around her, and, as always, she drew warmth and confidence from his touch. "You are arriving in Newport right before the beginning of the season. Do you understand what that means?"

"You've told me that wealthy people come there from all over the country, and there are balls and picnics and swimming parties. But I don't understand how that will help me to get away from Mrs. Tremayne before I . . ."

"The reason for all that feverish activity is the need to marry off young girls to suitable men. Eligible young girls, of course."

"Oh, but I . . ."

"You will be most eligible, for you will not only have the Tremayne fortune to back you, but the name as well. The Tremaynes are old Newport society. Their money goes back a century. Compared with them, the Vanderbilts, the Astors, the Goulds are upstarts. Yes, Drucilla, you will surely find a suitable husband."

She stiffened and drew away. Once before, he had

52

spoken of her finding a husband in Newport, but then that same evening he had made love to her, and surely that had changed everything. How could he possibly expect her to marry another man, loving him as she did?

"When you marry," he went on calmly, "you can leave Newport, and begin a new life. You will visit your grandmother from time to time, of course, but there will be no need to live under the same roof with her."

"I couldn't . . ."

"Of course you can. And you will. With your many charms, you'll have no trouble convincing the lucky bridegroom that you are all you claim to be."

Did he know how much he was hurting her? He must know, surely, for she had made no secret of her feelings about him. She had given herself to him, had held nothing back, only because she loved him. But he had never once said that he loved her.

"That night by the river," she said softly. "It meant nothing to you, nothing at all."

He took her hands in his. "Drucilla, please. You must forget about that night. For your sake, as well as mine. We both have so much at stake."

"Yes, of course," she said dully. "The Tremayne fortune."

She wanted to plead with him, to declare her love and convince him that she wanted no other man, ever. But he did not love her, perhaps he could not love anyone. Her pride gave her the strength to hold herself erect, to move away from him.

She stood up slowly.

"Where are you going?" he asked.

"To the dining car with you."

"I thought you said you weren't hungry."

"I've changed my mind."

As he took her arm, he said: "I knew you'd be sensible. There's no future for us—together. In Newport, with a little cleverness, you can arrange a future for yourself that any girl would envy."

He opened the door of the compartment and led her out into the narrow passageway. "You're quite right, of course," she agreed.

But even as she spoke, she knew that she was lying. And she felt a confidence, a determination. She would not be defeated. Kevin might not love her now, but he would one day. She would make him love her.

It was late evening when Kevin and Drucilla left the train and took the ferry to Newport. Even now, in June, the sea air held a chill, and Thames Street, a narrow thoroughfare close to the harbor, was blanketed in pearly fog.

She breathed deeply, filling her lungs with the salty air. "It is very quiet down here, and the buildings look so old. I was expecting something quite different."

"This is the oldest part of the city," Kevin said, helping her into a hired closed carriage. "It dates back before the Revolution." He got in beside her and, after directing the driver to take them to the Aquidneck House, he closed the door. The horses started off at a brisk trot. "Wait a few weeks," he went on. "The social season has not begun yet. When it does, you'll see a change. Not down around here, but in the fashionable part of the city. Bellevue Avenue and Ocean Drive."

In spite of the long train trip and her fears about what might happen tomorrow, Drucilla could not help catching his enthusiasm.

"You will see Mrs. August Belmont, driving down the avenue in her demi-d'Aumont. You remember, I pointed her out to you in Central Park."

"Oh, yes. I'd never seen such a carriage before. Four horses and two postillions, outfitted as jockeys."

"That's right. She is one of the social arbiters here. Then there are such famous hostesses as Mrs. Nicholas Beach, Mrs. Paran Stevens, Mrs. Sidney Brooks. Social lionesses, every one. They'll be arriving with trunks of dresses from Worth in Paris, and jewels from Tiffany. And guest lists a yard long."

"But Kevin, how can I possibly hope to be accepted? I don't belong here. My father was a schoolmaster. I scrubbed floors and emptied chamber pots in a Cincinnati hotel. . . ."

"Be quiet. You're as good as any one of them. And

as much of a lady. Good Lord, Drucilla, you must not be awed by these people. Don't you realize that half of society today built fortunes on war profiteering? They're a hell of a lot worse than either of us."

"I don't believe you. Those ladies we saw driving in Central Park, they looked like . . . like creatures from another world."

"Listen, my love, those fine ladies are the wives and daughters of men who made millions by supplying the Union Army." He laughed, his mouth twisting. "And with such supplies."

"I don't understand."

"Some of the leading financiers made money by selling to the government ships that were unseaworthy. Rifles, outmoded and defective, bought from European armories. Shoddy uniforms, boots with cardboard soles, rotten food."

"But that's . . . horrible."

"Oh, they're quite elegant now. Their wives and daughters queen it over Newport society, and cut to ribbons any unfortunate newcomer they choose to find unacceptable."

"But you think they will find me acceptable?"

"Naturally. You are Mrs. Tremayne's granddaughter. Believe me, they'll flock to Peregrine Court to meet you."

"Peregrine Court?"

"The Tremayne mansion. The original house burned down, a few years before the Civil War, and Mrs. Tremayne built a new one, on a lavish scale. She had gone abroad with her husband some years before, and those old English manor houses intrigued her. Peregrine Court is a fine Tudor-style mansion of gray stone. The lawns run right down to the Cliff Walk."

"But what does the name mean?"

Kevin laughed. "Mrs. Tremayne was impressed by the pursuits of the old English nobility, falconry among them. She had a pair of stone peregrine falcons carved on the pillars of the front gate. The motif is repeated throughout the house. I'm told it's quite imposing."

"You've never been inside the house, then?"

"Not yet. I have not even met Mrs. Tremayne. Mr.

Pollock hired me. I always met with him in his office. I shall go there to see him tomorrow, to tell him I've found the heiress to the Tremayne fortune."

He pressed her hand reassuringly.

"Oh, Kevin, I . . ."

"Here we are. This is the Aquidneck House. It's old-fashioned but quite comfortable. Besides, you won't be staying here long."

The lobby was not nearly so imposing as that of the Fifth Avenue Hotel, where Kevin had taken her on the night of their first meeting; the walls held the dampness and chill of the sea air, and Drucilla found herself shivering slightly as she stood beside Kevin at the front desk.

He had reserved a room for himself on the same floor as Drucilla's. "But it will be at the other end of the hall," he had explained to her. When she had to sign the register, she wrote her own first name, then hesitated a fraction of a second; feeling the hard pressure of Kevin's hand on her arm, she added the name Tremayne for the first time.

She could not help noticing the quick, sharp flicker of interest in the desk clerk's eyes, as he looked at the signature. Then she and Kevin went upstairs to their rooms.

Although her bed, with its soft mattress and fine, thick woolen blankets, was far superior to the one at Mrs. Baxley's boardinghouse back in New York, she found that sleep eluded her. She heard the sound of a foghorn, punctuating the quiet of the June night, over and over again.

She closed her eyes and tried to visualize the house called Peregrine Court, the gray stone Tudor mansion overlooking the sea. She tried, too, to picture the aristocratic old lady who lived there, Beth's grandmother. No —her grandmother now.

Think of it as a play, she told herself. Say your lines as Kevin taught you to do and trust him . . . trust him. . . .

But how was it possible to trust a man as ruthless as Kevin Farrell? How was it possible to love such a man?

Only that afternoon, he had told her she must marry someone else, someone suitable.

But he cared for her. He might not be willing to admit it even to himself, but she knew it was true. In the darkness her lips curved into a smile. Some day she would make him admit his love. Right now, she would help him to get what he wanted, but afterward she would make him see what she already knew, that they belonged together.

Her smile faded. Suppose something went wrong. Suppose that lawyer, Mr. Pollock, discovered the truth about her. Lawyers were clever, trained to ferret out deceptions, and surely, a woman as wealthy as Charlotte Tremayne would have only the best lawyers.

All right, then, what if the deception were brought to light? She and Kevin would be arrested, separated. She would be sent to jail, as Beth had been, but not for a few weeks. For months. Perhaps for years.

She pushed her blankets away, put on her robe and slippers, and moving silently, she left the room. The long, gaslit hallway was filled with shadows, and she could still hear the foghorn calling.

Kevin answered her knock and stood looking down at her.

"What are you doing here? Someone could have seen you . . ."

He drew her into his room and shut the door. "This isn't Mrs. Baxley's boardinghouse. You should be more discreet, love."

"I'm sorry . . . it's only that I. . . ."

He smiled, and Drucilla saw a teasing, almost boyish look in his eyes. "Dare I flatter myself that it was your uncontrollable passion for me that brought you here?"

"Don't talk nonsense," she said sharply. "Can't you see I'm frightened? And if you had any sense you'd be frightened, too."

"What makes you think I'm not?"

Was he still teasing? She thought there was an undertone of seriousness, but she could not be sure. After all, he had been in jail once, as a child.

He put an arm around her and held her against him.

"I have no intention of getting caught," he said. "We're not going to end up in jail, my sweet. You are going to be the belle of the Newport season."

"And you? You won't go away and leave me? I know I won't be able to carry any of this off if you leave me."

"Then I'll have to stay for awhile, won't I? But we'll have to be careful about seeing each other."

"You do want to go on seeing me . . . you want . . ."

His arms went around her. "What man wouldn't want you? I've seen a few more beautiful women in my time, but you—there is something about you that makes a man forget every other woman he's ever had. That makes him want to . . ." He fell silent and she could see the hot light in his eyes, feel his uneven breathing. In another moment . . .

But to her surprise, he released her. "Go back to your room, Drucilla. You must be calm and rested tomorrow. You may sleep in the morning, if you like. I'll go to see Mr. Benjamin Pollock." He was quite businesslike now. "Only after I've had my talk with him will you have to meet him. You will show him the jewelry and the photographs. He'll ask you a great many questions, but as long as our stories match, he should be satisfied."

"And then?"

"Then, my love, you will go to Peregrine Court and be introduced to your grandmother."

Mr. Benjamin Pollock was a tall, thin, gray-haired man in his late forties. He had a soft voice and impeccable manners, and Drucilla saw a keen intelligence in the lawyer's pale blue eyes. She was grateful that Kevin had laid the groundwork for her meeting with Mr. Pollock.

She wore a simple, high-necked dress of pale gray muslin, trimmed with white lace. She knew she looked demure, almost schoolgirlish, but she made no secret of the fact that she had appeared on the stage.

"Stick to the truth, wherever you can," Kevin had said. "In that way, you will speak with greater conviction, and there will be fewer opportunities for Mr. Pollock to trip you up. But," he added, "no matter how carefully we have rehearsed your story, there is no way we can anticipate every possible question. You may have to improvise."

Now, seated beside the wide, golden oak desk, with Kevin a few feet away, Drucilla confronted Mr. Pollock.

"I appeared on the stage for two years after my mother was no longer able to work," she was saying. "Mostly in the West, Nevada, California. . . ."

Mr. Pollock sighed and shook his head. "That will displease Mrs. Tremayne, I'm afraid."

"No doubt it will," Drucilla said. "My mother told me all about my grandmother's prejudice against having an actress in the family. But I cannot change what I have been—even if I wanted to."

"Did you choose your career? Or was it forced upon you by circumstances?" the lawyer asked. His alert eyes never left her face.

"That cannot be answered simply," she said. "I liked my work at times, but even if I had not, I was trained for nothing else."

"You have had no formal education, then?"

"Traveling from place to place as we did, it was impossible for me to go to school."

"And yet . . ." The pale eyes narrowed slightly. "Your speech and your manners are those of a young lady who has had some education."

Drucilla glanced at Kevin, who sat in a leather chair against the wall; with his long legs crossed, his arms resting on the arms of the chair, he looked completely at ease. His face was impassive, giving her no clue as to what she must say.

"One of the actors in our troupe had been a school-master," she said. "He tutored me whenever he could." Then she added, with what she hoped was exactly the right amount of spirit, "Actors are not vagabonds nor are they illiterates, Mr. Pollock—no matter what you or my grandmother may think."

"You have inherited your grandmother's stiff-necked pride, at any rate," he said. "I assure you, I did not mean to offend. But I trust you can understand Mrs. Tremayne's feelings about having an actress in the family. Today, with the changes brought about by the war, our standards are, perhaps, more liberal, but to a lady of your grandmother's generation and background . . ."

"There is no need to explain," Drucilla said graciously. "My grandmother is an old lady now, and I have not come here to revive the feud that divided my family years ago."

"Why did you come?" Mr. Pollock spoke in a quiet, almost offhand way, but Drucilla was not deceived. She drew a deep breath, but before she could answer, Kevin said:

"She came at my request, as you know. You hired me to find Charlotte Tremayne's granddaughter, and I have done so. I explained to Miss Tremayne that her grandmother has no close living relatives, that perhaps she now regrets having driven her daughter-in-law away . . . that she wishes to make amends."

The lawyer turned back to Drucilla. "Now, suppose you tell me your reasons for accompanying Mr. Farrell to Newport. Are you motivated solely by the desire to bring peace of mind to a lonely old lady?"

Drucilla could not ignore the hint of irony in the lawyer's soft voice. "I had another reason," she said.

"Indeed?"

"I have no other living relatives. I am quite alone in the world. I have spent these last years, since my mother's death, among strangers. I have lived in boardinghouses. I . . . want to belong somewhere, to establish a tie with at least one person who might mean something to me. Can you understand that, Mr. Pollock?"

"I think so. It cannot have been easy for a young girl like yourself, cast on her own resources."

"I have my profession," Drucilla said. "I am a good actress . . . I could have been a better one, with the right training."

Mr. Pollock picked up the photographs that were spread on the desk, the same photographs Drucilla had shown to Kevin back in New York. "I suppose you inherited your mother's talent," he said. "And her beauty, as well, if I may say so. You do not look like her, however. She was more fragile . . . more ethereal."

"She was never very strong," Drucilla said.

"I know. Mr. Farrell has told me something of her unfortunate history after she left Newport. How she was taken ill in Carson City . . ."

"Virginia City," Drucilla corrected him. Then she smiled sweetly. "I suppose all those western names are a bit confusing to an easterner like yourself."

"I have visited the West. Only a few years ago, as a matter of fact. I went to California on business. You made your debut in Sacramento, didn't you?"

"No, Mr. Pollock. I made my first appearance on the stage in Yellow Canyon in Nevada."

"I don't believe I've ever heard of the place. Is it a large city?"

"It's not a city at all. Only a mining town. You must understand that in the West, many touring companies perform in places you would not call theaters. A town hall, a barn, a tent."

"Yes, quite so. A difficult life for a young lady like yourself."

"Yes, it was." Drucilla spoke with conviction, recalling her own experiences in Ohio and Kentucky. She had never played in a mining town, but she was sure that she had known equal hardships: nights spent in dirty, crowded trains, sleeping in her clothes; performances in leaky, mosquito-ridden tents before half-drunken backwoods audiences; greasy, badly cooked boardinghouse fare, and never enough of it. "I came to New York hoping I could improve my circumstances."

"And did you find success in New York?"

"No . . . I was unable to get a part . . . I'm sure Mr. Farrell told you . . ."

"How were you able to live, then?"

"I had some savings."

"You could not have had much."

What was he leading up to, this soft-spoken man with his shrewd eyes? He was no fool, and if she tried to represent herself as having been too virtuous, too pure, she would not, she was sure, convince him that she was telling the truth.

She would have to take a risk, and without being able to consult Kevin beforehand.

"I . . . I . . ." She looked at Mr. Pollock appealingly, from under her long, heavy lashes. "I do not wish to tell you this, unless . . ."

"Go on, please."

"You must promise not to tell my grandmother."

"Miss Tremayne, I assure you that Mr. Farrell has already told me everything about you."

"But he does not know everything—no one does."

Kevin's head went up, like that of an animal scenting danger.

"I see. Do you want to speak in front of him now?"

"I believe he is a man of the world, as you are, Mr. Pollock. But my grandmother is an old lady, living by the standards of another generation, as you have pointed out . . ."

"Very well. We will keep your confidences, will we not, Mr. Farrell?"

Kevin nodded, his eyes wary.

"I worked in a concert saloon, as an entertainer. I had no money, and I could not find work on the stage. I did it only for a few weeks, and then Mr. Farrell found me . . ."

"A concert saloon," Mr. Pollock said, and it was obvious to Drucilla that he knew the reputation of such places.

"I give you my word, I did nothing to be ashamed of. Not then. Not ever."

"Suppose Mr. Farrell had not appeared when he did. Do you think you could have gone on living a virtuous life—in such surroundings?"

"Does anyone know what he might do if he were desperate? Do you, Mr. Pollock?"

Now it was Mr. Pollock who was thrown off balance. "Quite so," he said. "I did not mean to distress you. But I must consider Mrs. Tremayne. It is necessary for me to have all the facts about you, before I present you to her."

"I understand," Drucilla said. Remembering Kevin's advice about how to arouse a man's chivalrous impulses through a show of feminine weakness, she reached into her gray silk reticule and drew out a tiny lace handkerchief. Turning her face away, she dabbed at her eyes.

"Please, Miss Tremayne, do compose yourself," Mr. Pollock said. "If you behaved unwisely, when you were alone in New York, that is understandable. I'm sure— no real harm was done."

"But you won't tell my grandmother. If you want to consider her interests, you can surely see . . ."

"Of course. Charlotte Tremayne has had more than her share of trouble during her lifetime. She lost three sons in infancy. Your father was the only one of her children to survive, and when he was still quite young, she lost her husband. If she protected your father more than was wise, perhaps it is understandable. He was her whole world, and after he died, she became something of a recluse. Not entirely. But she gave up her home in New York and remained here in Newport throughout the year. She has taken no part in the social activities for years now."

"I know so little about the Tremaynes—my mother did not like to speak of . . . How did my father die, Mr. Pollock?"

The lawyer's face assumed a distant, cautious expression.

"Mrs. Tremayne may tell you about that. If she wishes to. I will go to see her at once. I will tell her that her granddaughter has been found." He stood up behind the wide oak desk. "I realize this has been an ordeal for you, Miss Tremayne. Mr. Farrell will escort you back to the hotel, and I will let you know when your grandmother is ready to see you."

He allowed himself a smile. "I do not think you will have long to wait."

Drucilla leaned back against the seat of the surrey Kevin had hired. She allowed herself to relax, to breathe the fresh salty air and enjoy the sunlight on her face.

"You would have made a fine actress, even on the New York stage," Kevin was saying. "Your account of your brief stint at the concert saloon was touching."

There was mockery in his gray eyes, but she could tell that he was pleased with her. "I thought it would make me sound more believable."

"It was clever," he conceded. But then he added, "Almost too clever. We're not out of the woods yet."

"Mr. Pollock said he wouldn't tell Charlotte Tremayne that part about the concert saloon." She put an anxious hand on Kevin's arm. "He'll keep his word, won't he?"

"I think so. Remember, finding you is a credit to Mr. Pollock as well as to me. We both stand to profit by our success. Mr. Pollock doesn't want to rock the boat, any more than I do."

"She must be a very unhappy old lady," Drucilla said. "And a lonely one."

Kevin shrugged. "I suppose so. But if her son left her, he had good reason. She destroyed his marriage, remember that."

"Kevin how did he die? Mr. Pollock was unwilling to tell me."

"He didn't tell me, either. I only know Horace Tremayne left Newport shortly after his wife ran away. He died in California. I don't know the circumstances of his death." He dismissed the matter. "I've no doubt your grandmother will tell you the whole family history in time." He shifted the reins to one hand, and put the other on her arm. "You did well today, Drucilla. I was proud of you."

If only he would go on to say he loved her. She needed that reassurance now. Only his promise of a future together would give her the courage she needed to go on with this deception.

She slipped her arm through his and moved closer to him, resting her cheek against his shoulder.

"Careful, love," he said. "Remember, for all its high-toned ways, Newport's a small town. We wouldn't want to start any gossip about the Tremayne heiress."

Five

LATE in the afternoon of the following day, in response to a message from Mr. Pollock, Kevin Farrell drove Drucilla to Peregrine Court. He reined in the horses before the tall iron gates, and while they waited for the gatekeeper to admit them to the grounds, Drucilla caught a glimpse of two pillars, one on either side of the gates. Each pillar was topped by a carved stone figure of a falcon, wings spread, as if preparing to descend upon its prey. In the fading sunlight, the stone birds had a faintly sinister look, Drucilla thought.

Kevin must have sensed her mood, for he reached over and pressed her hand. "Mr. Pollock didn't waste any time setting up this meeting. Your grandmother is obviously eager to see you." Even when they were alone, he made a point of referring to Charlotte Tremayne as Drucilla's grandmother. His words were reassuring, and his touch even more so; from their first night together, she had drawn comfort from his presence. She pushed her fear of the coming interview to the back of her mind. As long as Kevin was beside her, she would manage. She relaxed and looked about her as the surrey rolled up the winding road that led to the house.

The shadows were gathering, and the gray stone house loomed up before her, against a background of clouds edged in rose and warm gold. It was surrounded by fine old oak trees, and although it had been built in the English Tudor style, it did not look out of place, here on the coast of Rhode Island. The trees, the wide, beautifully kept green lawns that sloped down to the Cliff Walk, and the sea below, surging against the jagged rocks, provided the ideal setting for such a house. Peregrine Court looked as if it might have been standing here for centuries. There was a solidity about the fine stone facade, topped with towers at either end. The sun gleamed on the oriel windows that were set at intervals along the first floor.

Drucilla was deeply impressed, but she felt out of place here, an interloper. What was she doing, in preparing to enter this house, to claim kinship with the family that had built it?

She smoothed the folds of her dress, which was of violet silk, simple and becoming. She knew she looked respectable, even dignified, in spite of her eighteen years. She had braided her shining red hair, and had arranged the braids in a neat coil at the nape of her neck.

Kevin helped her down from the surrey, and she tried hard to think of the house as a stage set, to remind herself that she was playing a role and must play it to perfection; but when she stood beside him, in front of the massive oak door, she had to use every bit of will power she possessed to keep from getting back into the surrey and begging Kevin to take her away from here.

But Kevin pulled the doorbell and the door opened at once. "I am Kevin Farrell, and this is Miss Drucilla Tremayne," he told the maid. The woman, tall and thin, in her forties, stepped aside to admit them. She wore a starched white apron over a neat black dress, and a small, frilled white cap perched atop her head.

Inside the entryway, she said: "Mrs. Tremayne will see you now." But, when Kevin started to follow, she added politely,

"Just Miss Tremayne, if you please, sir. Mrs. Tremayne has asked that you wait." She gestured toward a small parlor, and added, "Please take a seat, sir."

Drucilla felt her heart sink, as Kevin turned to leave her. She threw him a desperate look, and he smiled at her, his gray eyes warm and encouraging. She lingered for a moment, until he had taken a seat in a tall-backed, velvet-covered chair that looked very old but beautifully made.

"This way, Miss," the maid said, and Drucilla followed her down the long, high-ceilinged hallway. She caught a swift impression of dark walls, hung with heavy, intricately worked tapestries. A massive, pierced-panel staircase led to the upper floors of the three-story house. On each newel post, she saw a peregrine falcon, carved of dark wood.

She thought that the heavy, Tudor-style furniture, the high-backed chairs, the inlaid tables and chests, must have been brought from England. She had never seen anything like them before, except in pictures in some of her father's books.

Now the maid was opening two sliding doors, and standing aside. She said, "Miss Drucilla Tremayne, madam."

Drucilla took a deep breath and moved forward, into the library. It was an imposing room, and, like everything else she had seen here so far, it filled her with awe. At any other time she would have taken pleasure in examining the furnishings more closely: the huge, carved oak desk, the bookcases filled with calf-bound books with titles in gold, the square, velvet-cushioned sofas. But now she could only look at the woman who had risen to greet her. Charlotte Tremayne. Beth's grandmother. *Her* grandmother, now.

The rays of the setting sun, streaming through the oriel windows, revealed a woman who had once been beautiful, and who still retained traces of her beauty in the finely chiseled nose, the delicate lips, the firm, somewhat arrogant jawline. Her white hair was parted in the center, and swept up in an intricate coiffure of loops and coils which added to the dignity of her appearance.

There was dignity, too, in her carriage. She wore a

brown silk dress, decorated with intricate beading, a high collar and close-fitting sleeves.

"So you are my son's child," she said. Her voice shook slightly, and it came to Drucilla that she was not the only one who was uneasy about this meeting; it must be an ordeal for Mrs. Tremayne, as well, and the older woman did not have Drucilla's strength and resilience. To her surprise, Drucilla felt some of her fear ebbing away, to be replaced by an unfamiliar impulse: sympathy and a wish to protect Mrs. Tremayne from undue strain.

Whatever Charlotte Tremayne had been, whatever she had done to her son and her daughter-in-law, she had suffered afterward. Drucilla was sure of it. Her face was deeply lined and pale. Only the hazel eyes held vitality —and a kind of tremulous hope.

"Edith will bring tea for us shortly," Mrs. Tremayne said. "Please sit down, no, there, by the window. I want to look at you."

Drucilla took the chair indicated.

"Horace's child," the old lady said shortly. A spasm of grief crossed her face.

"But perhaps," she continued, seating herself opposite Drucilla, "you think of yourself as Isobel's child only. That would be understandable. She brought you up alone."

Drucilla nodded, not sure an answer was expected.

"I suppose your mother spoke of me sometimes. And not very kindly?" Charlotte Tremayne said. She gave Drucilla a challenging look, sharp and direct.

"I have told Mr. Pollock that I want to forget the past, the bitterness and the conflict."

"But surely," Charlotte Tremayne went on, "living with Isobel, you must have heard many unpleasant things about me."

"Yes, I did."

"She told you I was a cruel, possessive old woman who resented her for no other reason than that she had been an actress before she married Horace."

Drucilla decided it would be of no use to fence with Mrs. Tremayne; she might be old and frail, but there was an inner force here that could not be denied.

"Yes, she said such things."

"She blamed me for breaking up the marriage, for driving her away from this house."

"She did."

Mrs. Tremayne gave Drucilla a level look. "Your mother was quite right. Everything she must have told you about me was the truth."

Drucilla stared at Mrs. Tremayne. She had expected the woman to deny her guilt, to disclaim all responsibility for the breakup of her son's marriage.

Mrs. Tremayne smiled sadly. "You are very young, my dear. It will be difficult for you to understand what I must tell you. But you have a right to know."

Drucilla looked away, and thought, "But I have no right, none at all."

"My husband, Robert, wanted sons to carry on his business enterprises," Mrs. Tremayne continued. "I gave him three sons in the first three years of our marriage." She closed her eyes briefly, and her thin lips pressed together. Then she said evenly, "The first was stillborn. The other two died, each before he was a year old."

Drucilla heard the old grief, the despair reaching out across the years.

"Five years later, when I had almost given up hope, Horace was born. Your father, my dear. He was premature, very small and sickly—but alive. And I was determined to keep him alive. I had nurses for him, of course, but it was I who made him survive; I who fed him and bathed him and cared for him when he was ill. And he was ill, much of the time, during those first years." Mrs. Tremayne raised her head. "But he survived." Her hazel eyes, still bright under the drooping, wrinkled lids, glowed with triumph. Drucilla felt a grudging admiration for the old lady who had surely been a fighter in her time.

"When Horace was six, Robert went down to New Orleans on business. While he was down there, the city was ravaged by an epidemic. Yellow fever. Robert was stricken. He died within a few weeks."

Drucilla shuddered, thinking that the Tremaynes, for all their wealth and pride, had known much sorrow and loss. The proud old lady seated opposite her had not been invulnerable.

"I had only Horace left, and perhaps I protected him too much, pampered him more than was right—or wise. But I was so afraid of losing him, you see. He was educated here at home, by the finest tutors, but when it came time for him to go to college, I had to let him leave, of course. He met Isobel in New York, saw her on the stage in a music hall, and was taken with her. She was not very talented, but she was fresh and pretty —and young. She had a certain charm, I suppose."

Mrs. Tremayne's voice turned icy. "She was wrong for my son."

"How could you have been so sure? Perhaps if you had helped her, supported her . . ."

"She was wrong for Horace, I tell you," the old lady repeated stubbornly.

"Because she was an actress?" Drucilla's pride in her profession gave an edge to her voice.

"I've no doubt that's what she told you. And believed herself. But it was more than that. I might have overlooked her . . . origins—although it would not have been easy. You must remember that the Tremayne name is an old and respected one. There was a Tremayne who served in the squadron of Oliver Hazard Perry, during the battle on Lake Erie. We have had statesmen in our family, and scholars. And long before that, back in England, the name was known and honored. There were Tremaynes who fought to defend Charles Stuart and died with him; others who accompanied his son into exile and came back after he had been restored to the throne." She looked at Drucilla closely. "I suppose none of this means anything to you. You probably don't even understand what I am talking about."

"Indeed I do," Drucilla said. "I have always been fond of reading history books and my . . ." She caught herself just in time; she had been about to say that her father had given her an excellent grounding in the subject.

"Surely, traveling around as you did, you had no time for any sort of education. Mr. Pollock said something about your having been tutored by one of the actors in the troupe with which you traveled, but I scarcely thought . . ." She broke off and looked faintly incredulous.

"My mother provided me with books," Drucilla said.

"Surprising. When she lived here, she never opened a single one of these books." Mrs. Tremayne indicated the rows of leather-bound volumes on the shelves. "She looked at the fashion journals from Paris, but that was all."

Drucilla felt her muscles tense, and she wished with all her heart that Kevin was beside her, to give her confidence.

But Mrs. Tremayne only shrugged and said, "Your mother, my dear, was a pretty, frivolous little fool." She leaned forward. "I do not think you are like your mother. Nor like my son, either."

Was it going to happen now? Was Mrs. Tremayne going to expose her for the impostor she was?

"You are like me, however," the old lady said calmly. "That often happens, you know. A set of characteristics skips one generation, only to appear in the next. I've observed that in many families."

Drucilla's relief was overwhelming; she allowed herself to relax.

"If your mother had been a strong woman, she would have stood up to me. She would have helped my son to become the man he ought to have been."

"Is that fair?" Drucilla asked. "If, as you have said, you overprotected and pampered him all the years he was growing up, how could you have expected that his wife would make a man of him?"

Drucilla expected an angry, defensive retort, but instead, Mrs. Tremayne said, "I won't deny that. I must share a measure of blame for all that happened to your father. For what Horace became. But do not misunderstand me. Your father was a fine man, in his way."

"Was he? I would have thought that after my mother ran away, he might at least have tried to find her. Surely, it was his duty, as her husband. But instead he went on living here, in luxury, while my mother . . ."

71

The accusation was drawn from her by the memory of Beth, ill and broken from all she had suffered. Beth, who had been driven to take work in a concert saloon; who had returned from the horrors of Blackwell's Island to die by her own hand.

"If your son had tried to find his wife, to make a home for her . . . it would have been so different."

Mrs. Tremayne's lips parted. Drucilla thought she was about to speak, but instead, a puzzled frown appeared between her brows.

"I'm sorry," Drucilla said. "Perhaps I should not have come here at all."

"Where else do you have to go? Your home is here, with me. We must both forget the past. You are young and very lovely. We must think of your future. You . . . will stay?"

Drucilla knew that it was not easy for a proud woman like Mrs. Tremayne to ask for any favor. And she was asking—pleading, now. It was in her voice, in her eyes.

"I'll stay," Drucilla said.

Mrs. Tremayne resumed her self-possessed manner. "A sensible decision. I hope you are as sensible as you appear to be. Now, we must make plans. You will be presented to society here in Newport in a few weeks, as soon as the season begins. We'll have a ball, I think. There hasn't been a ball in this house for so long. When my husband was alive, the ballroom was always filled with guests, and sometimes, when the weather was fine, we would set up a dance pavilion on the lawns, back of the house. Ah, but in those days, society here was quite different. We entertained the Livingstons, the Jays, the Brevoorts. And plantation owners, up from Charleston. You know, Newport was a mecca for Charleston planters and their families, before the war. The climate down there is impossible in summer . . ."

Drucilla smiled politely. Here was an old lady, lost in memories of the past, painting a picture of a vanished way of life.

"We still get some fine southern families here during the season. But we get the others, wealthy, of course, but no real background. Astors, Vanderbilts, Goulds."

Drucilla stared at Mrs. Tremayne, thinking that she must be secure, indeed, in background as well as fortune, to dismiss these millionaires' names in such cavalier fashion.

"Money does not necessarily confer breeding," Mrs. Tremayne added.

"I did not suppose so," Drucilla said, "but still . . ."

"In New York City, people may be accepted because of wealth alone. Newport is different." Mrs. Tremayne laughed—for the first time since Drucilla had met her. There was a touch of malice in the sound.

"I don't suppose you know, for instance, that J. Pierpont Morgan made his first big fortune by buying up obsolete carbines that had been condemned by army inspectors."

"Why, no . . . I . . ."

"He bought them for a ridiculously small price, and sold them to the Western Army Headquarters for nearly four times as much."

"But if the weapons were obsolete, surely . . ."

"The army had to discard the whole shipment of Morgan's carbines when soldiers firing them had their thumbs blown off. And that, my dear, is only one case out of many. There are speculators, profiteers, lording it over society today."

"Why . . . that's what Kevin said."

"Kevin? Oh, yes. Mr. Farrell. A shrewd young man. And handsome as sin. I watched from the window as he was helping you out of the surrey. You came to know him well?"

"No—not really, but we did converse on the train coming up here." Drucilla kept her eyes on her hands, which were folded primly in the lap of her silk dress. Surely, there was nothing in her voice to betray her. But Mrs. Tremayne was a sharp old lady. Those hazel eyes missed little.

"Yes," she said, "a handsome young man." Then she shrugged. "No family, no background, of course. Shanty Irish, from what Mr. Pollock said."

"Hardly that. He had to leave Ireland during the famine, but . . ."

"Ah, yes. Many did. But most became servants, stable-hands—or beggars. Mr. Farrell, it would appear, bettered himself to a degree."

Mrs. Tremayne stood up. "I'll ring for Edith now. She will bring our tea. Or perhaps you would rather go to your room and rest for awhile. In that case I will join you there, after I've finished with Mr. Farrell, and we can have our tea upstairs."

"I think I'd prefer that," Drucilla said.

"Very well. Mr. Pollock will, of course, pay Mr. Farrell the reward for finding you, but I want to offer him my personal thanks."

She rang for Edith and when the woman appeared, she said,

"Miss Drucilla and I will take tea in her room shortly. Show her upstairs, and tell Mr. Farrell to come in here."

A few moments later Drucilla, standing at the foot of the broad staircase, saw Edith directing Kevin to the library. He raised his head and looked up at her for a moment, and she gave him a little smile, to tell him that things had gone well.

He nodded to show he understood, but it was not enough. She longed to go to him, to feel his arms around her, to be alone with him, and tell him everything that had happened. Whatever might come of this meeting with Charlotte Tremayne, of her acceptance as the missing granddaughter, she wanted to share it with him, for he had made it possible.

He had taken her, shabby and half-starved, out of the rain-drenched street in front of Mrs. Baxley's boarding-house and had brought her to this place of comfort and safety and luxury such as she had never imagined.

But now, as she stood, one hand resting on the newel post with its carved falcon, watching him turn down the hallway, it was as if an immeasurable gulf spread between them—as if this moment, for which they had schemed and planned, was tearing them apart.

"This way, Miss Drucilla, if you please," Edith was saying.

Drucilla followed her up the stairs. "I won't lose him,"

she told herself. "I won't let him go. Somehow, I'll find a way for us to be together."

The next two weeks flew by in a flurry of plans for Drucilla's introduction to society. At her insistence, Mrs. Tremayne had agreed that the ball could be put off; that she could be introduced to a smaller group at a formal dinner. But even so, there were endless plans, a caterer to be brought from New York, a new gown to be designed and made by Madame Janine, who was staying at the Aquidneck House.

"You will, of course, wear the Tremayne diamonds," her "grandmother" said. "Your mother wore them, when she was a bride, here, but she left them behind, when she . . . went away."

Drucilla thought that had been unfortunate, for the Tremayne diamonds would have kept Isobel and Beth in comfort for some time. However, she only nodded and said, "Thank you, grandmother. I am sure they are very beautiful."

The fittings with Madame Janine occupied a great deal of time, for the talented Frenchwoman, who had opened a shop in New York, but was spending the summer in Newport, obviously hoped that the wardrobe she was creating for Drucilla Tremayne would bring her many new customers from among Newport's wealthy summer visitors.

The gown for the dinner was to be a delicate shade of aquamarine, the bodice shaped with deceptive simplicity, and cut quite low, to provide the proper setting for the diamond necklace Drucilla would wear. The wide skirt would be caught in elaborate folds with tiny, turquoise bows.

In addition, Madame Janine would provide for Drucilla a riding habit of pearl gray broadcloth, dresses for yachting parties, for afternoon teas, and dancing receptions.

"And something simpler but chic—for a picnic," she said, showing Drucilla a length of blue and white sprigged muslin.

"A picnic?" Drucilla thought that such a simple form

of amusement would be of little interest to the wealthy Newport summer visitors.

"Oh, but they are splendid affairs," the dressmaker said, her dark eyes glowing with enthusiasm. "There are flowers and cases of champagne, and the finest delicacies, supplied by Mr. Ward McAllister. He is said to be the social arbiter here in Newport."

Drucilla recognized the name, for Mrs. Tremayne had remarked that Ward McAllister would be one of the guests at the dinner party, along with Mr. and Mrs. August Belmont, and a number of plantation owners from South Carolina, who still continued to come to Newport to escape the humid heat and the threat of fever back home.

The evening of the dinner was warm and clear. The chandeliers in the great dining hall had been polished until their prisms glittered with icy fire. Standing on the threshold, Drucilla heard the soft, tentative notes of the string quartet that had been imported from New York and installed in the musicians' gallery overlooking the hall.

She knew she should go up to her room where Clarice, Mrs. Tremayne's own personal maid, would help her dress for the dinner party, but she remained where she was in the grip of a mounting tension that had begun early that morning.

She had managed to put on a convincing performance for Mrs. Tremayne these last two weeks, but she wondered if she would be able to be equally convincing with the guests tonight. Unlike the woman who was supposed to be her grandmother, these guests would have no emotional need to believe that she was the Tremayne heiress. Her "grandmother" had counseled her to say nothing about the years before her arrival at Peregrine Court, except that she had been living with her mother.

But suppose Mr. McAllister asked a probing question. He was famous for his interest in the backgrounds and origins of every member of society; indeed, that very year, he had drawn up a list of a committee he called the "Patriarchs," which would, in turn, decide who should be accepted and who excluded from the social events in New York City during the coming season. Was it possible that she would be able to convince such a man that she was all she claimed to be?

She shivered and felt an impulse to flee to her room and plead illness, but she knew that sooner or later she must bear the scrutiny of people like Ward McAllister, Mrs. Belmont, and the rest. She felt as if the walls of the house were closing in on her, trapping her. She picked up her skirts and hurried out onto the wide terrace behind the house, and down the marble steps. The broad lawn sloped gently in the direction of Cliff Walk, and the ocean below.

The grounds of Peregrine Court had been a revelation to her from the first day she had seen them, and she still found them breathtaking. Mrs. Tremayne had explained that the landscaping had been designed to look like the Tudor gardens of England. From the terrace, Drucilla took a path leading to the topiary garden, where towering hedges had been trained and clipped into the shapes of fantastic birds and animals. Benches had been placed at intervals between these hedges, but Drucilla was much too restless to sit.

It was getting dark now, and the hedges looked black, instead of green; she found the effect disquieting. A white marble summerhouse, like a miniature pagan temple, loomed ahead, and she caught her breath sharply when she saw a man step around the side of the building.

Then she recognized Kevin Farrell.

"Drucilla, this is an unexpected pleasure." He walked toward her with his familiar, easy stride, looking calm and self-assured. She felt her own fears ebbing away. She could not help noticing how handsome he was, in his dark gray coat and ivory-colored trousers.

"Does Mrs. Tremayne know you're here?" she asked.

"Certainly, she does. Didn't she tell you? I have been hired for the evening." Then, seeing her bewildered look, he added, "I'm to keep an eye on the Tremayne diamonds and the jewels of the other ladies. It's customary at affairs of this kind."

"I see," she said, and she felt a sharp pang of disappointment. "I thought perhaps . . ." Her pride would not allow her to finish.

"I wanted to see you, of course," he said. "There hasn't been much chance since the day I brought you here."

"You've—missed me, then?"

"You are a little fool." But warmth stirred deep in his eyes and he spoke softly, so that the words were a caress.

He reached out and drew her into the shadow of the summerhouse, and his touch sent a swift current moving through her.

"Kevin," she whispered. She closed her eyes and he drew her to him. Her head tilted back and her lips parted.

But he did not kiss her, as she had expected he would do.

"We mustn't take foolish risks," he said.

She pulled away, her eyes open now, and blazing. "You're right," she said, her voice trembling. "I'll return to the house now."

His hand closed on her arm. She saw his slow, teasing smile. "Drucilla, you surprise me. Have you lost your modesty altogether? If I can wait a few more hours, surely you can."

"Wait for what?"

The mockery was gone from his face, and his eyes were filled with his hunger for her. "After this damn dinner party, when the last of the guests have gone and Mrs. Tremayne is asleep, you will meet me here."

The hard edge in his voice, the assurance that she would come to him when he wanted her, filled her with anger. "I'll think about it," she said.

His arms went around her, and his lips found hers in a savage, bruising kiss. A moment later he released her; she turned and fled back to the house between the dark rows of towering hedges.

Drucilla was still somewhat shaken when, a few hours later, she stood beside Mrs. Tremayne to receive their guests. But something of the old lady's quiet dignity, her unshakable poise, communicated itself. Drucilla held her head high and felt the weight of the Tremayne diamonds against her skin. She turned to smile at the Belmonts and was aware of the pear-shaped diamond earrings swinging on either side of her face.

She glanced at Mrs. Tremayne, who gave her a faint but encouraging smile. The old lady, in her dark blue silk, her white hair piled high on her head, was obviously glowing with pride and satisfaction. She greeted her guests with the air of a dowager queen.

By the time a servant announced that dinner was served, Drucilla had begun to feel more confident. All her life, even when she had been back at the County Farm, or working at a chambermaid in Cincinnati, she had felt that she had been meant for something better. And tonight she was preparing to step into the shining world she had only dreamed of until now.

The Tremayne diamonds were no longer icy weights; warmed by the soft, creamy skin of her bosom, they were a part of her.

When Ward McAllister offered her his arm, she took it without hesitation, and moved gracefully into the dining hall at his side.

"This is your first summer at Newport, I believe," he said.

"That's right."

"And before that?"

"I lived with my mother. We traveled a good deal."

"Europe?" he asked.

"California," she told him.

"Mr. McAllister spent some time in California during the Gold Rush, my dear," Mrs. Tremayne interposed.

"Indeed?" Drucilla said, her eyes glinting wickedly. "You do not look like my idea of a prospector, sir."

He cleared his throat, "I went to California to join my father and brother in their law practice," he said. His Napoleon III mustache nearly quivered with outrage as the ladies in their vicinity laughed at Drucilla's seemingly innocent mistake.

She had known Ward McAllister's background perfectly well, for Mrs. Tremayne had told her about him. "An odd sort of man . . . more interested in giving parties and arranging entertainments for others than in undertaking the work of a real man—railroads, shipping, the stock market. But he comes of an excellent family. He is a descendant of Richard Ward, who was the Royal Governor of Rhode Island, and Samuel Ward, the Revolutionary Governor."

Nevertheless, Drucilla had taken pleasure in pretending to believe that he had been one of those dirty, crude, and hairy prospectors of whom she had heard.

"There must have been a great deal of work for a lawyer in California during the Gold Rush," she said. "All those disputed claims."

"We did well enough," he said. "But I didn't fancy the life among those frontier barbarians. No, indeed. I was relieved to return to my native city, Savannah."

"I have always felt Savannah to be the only civilized city in Georgia," said a square-jawed matron with iron-gray hair, whose firm mouth belied her soft, gentle drawl.

McAllister smiled. "Coming from a South Carolina lady like yourself, Mrs. Seaton, that is indeed a compliment."

Mrs. Belmont leaned across the candlelit table and said, "I had thought your family would be with you tonight, Theodora."

"Radford was forced to remain in Charleston on business for a little longer than he had expected. He will be here by next week, in time for your ball, Caroline. And the girls will be with him, of course."

She smiled sweetly at Drucilla. "If he had known what a charming granddaughter Mrs. Tremayne had, he would have come, whether or not his business was finished," she said.

Drucilla acknowledged the compliment with an inclination of her head, but she thought, uneasily, that the matchmaking had begun already, even as Kevin had predicted it would. No matter. There would never be any man for her except Kevin, however many well-bred gentlemen tried to join their family fortunes with that of the Tremaynes.

"You will be coming to Mrs. Belmont's ball at By-the-Sea, won't you?" Mrs. Seaton pursued.

"Yes . . . that is . . ."

"We will be there," Mrs. Tremayne said firmly, clinching the matter. "We are looking forward to visiting your new villa, Caroline. I only hope it won't mark the beginning of a mass migration to Newport. There are certain people who would be more at home in Long Beach or Saratoga."

Although Drucilla had grown fond of Mrs. Tremayne during the past few weeks, she could not deny that the old lady was a snob, and probably always would be. If she ever found out the truth about Drucilla's background, she would be absolutely outraged.

And yet, Drucilla thought, how senseless it was, judging a person by such narrow standards. She was not ashamed of her parentage. She had never known her mother, but her father had been a good man and a gentle one, with a store of learning equal to that of anyone present here tonight. And he had instilled his love of learning in her. She was proud to be his daughter.

Mrs. Seaton's gentle but insistent drawl cut across her thoughts. "I trust that you will save a dance for my son although, now that you have been introduced to Newport, I'm sure you will be absolutely beseiged by admirers."

Radford Seaton must be a very shy young man, Drucilla thought, or perhaps an unattractive one. Otherwise, why would his mother have to plead his cause so blatantly?

Still, it was obvious that Mrs. Tremayne approved of Mrs. Seaton, otherwise she would not have been invited to this select dinner party tonight. So Drucilla smiled and said, "You flatter me, Mrs. Seaton. I should be pleased to meet your son, of course. And I will remember to save him a dance."

The last of the guests left after midnight. Mrs. Tremayne and Drucilla climbed the wide staircase together.

In the hallway above, she stopped and put a thin, blue-veined hand on Drucilla's arm.

"You were a credit to the Tremayne family tonight," the old lady said. Then she added, "I had not thought to know any happiness in this house again. But you have changed all that."

Drucilla felt the sting of tears. For the first time since she had come to Peregrine Court, she did not plan or pretend. Impulsively, she put an arm around the old lady and kissed her wrinkled cheek.

Then she said, "Good-night, grandmother. Sleep well," and went on to her room, at the far end of the hall.

Clarice put the diamonds away and began to unfasten Drucilla's gown.

"It's enough for you to see to my grandmother," Drucilla said quickly. "She must be very tired and waiting for you now."

"But who will assist you?" Clarice sounded scandalized.

Drucilla repressed a smile as she thought of all the years she had dressed and undressed herself, done her own hair, mended her clothing, in drafty dressing rooms and tents. But she only said, "I will find a lady's maid of my own, as soon as possible."

"Perhaps I might be able to recommend a suitable person," Clarice offered.

But Drucilla had no intention of allowing someone else to choose a personal maid for her. She would have to choose for herself, and carefully, for it would be difficult, she sensed, to keep secrets from another woman who would be in such close contact with her.

After Clarice had left her, Drucilla lay back on the bed, and stared at the canopy overhead. The minutes dragged by. She would have to wait until the house was silent, until the hands of the small painted china clock told her it would be safe to leave.

It was close to three in the morning when she got up, changed to her simplest dress, the pale gray muslin she had worn on the day Kevin had brought her to see Mr. Pollock. She put a dark shawl over her hair and about her shoulders. Then she hurried out to meet Kevin in the summerhouse.

She still felt an edge of anger, because of his arrogance, his assumption that she would run to meet him whenever and wherever he chose. But stronger than anger, more consuming than pride, was her need to be with him.

She slipped out of the house by the back way, and ran lightly across the lawn, the sea breeze blowing her skirt out around her.

Six

MOONLIGHT edged the dark outlines of the hedges with silver, and turned the small stone summerhouse frosty white. The breeze from the ocean was stronger here, and Drucilla had to clutch her shawl about her.

She pushed open the door and Kevin's arms reached out for her. In the light that filtered through the small-paned glass windows, he was a dark, half-seen shape.

"The party's been over for hours," he said. "What took you so long getting here? Did something go wrong? Did the old lady question you? She doesn't suspect anything, does she?"

"No. She said . . ." Drucilla felt her throat tighten at the memory. "She said I was a credit to her. That she had not thought to be happy in that house again, but now . . ."

"That's fine," Kevin said. "I told you that you could do it."

He embraced her and she felt the length of his body against hers and knew the hunger that was in him. But she held back and said, "I . . . wasn't sure whether I would come to meet you at all, tonight."

"Don't be coy," he said sharply. "You're not impressing those dinner guests now. You're with me." He took off her shawl and pressed his face against her hair. "You don't have to be Miss Tremayne right now. Only Drucilla."

Only Drucilla. She understood his meaning. Only the bedraggled creature he had found in the rain outside Mrs. Baxley's boardinghouse, the girl who had not known where she would sleep that night or where her next meal was coming from.

"I am Miss Tremayne now," she reminded him.

"Not here with me." He tried to embrace her again, to draw her down on a wide cushioned bench that stood against the wall. "I was watching you tonight, you know. From the back of the musicians' gallery. You looked so beautiful, I had all I could do to keep from carrying you out of there and . . ."

He bent over her, his hands rough and urgent, his breath warm against her cheek. Still, she could not yield. Instead she began to speak quickly, her words a barrier between them.

"The dinner was most successful. I know I made a favorable impression on Mrs. Belmont, and Mrs. Seaton —she's visiting here from South Carolina—and although I was afraid of Mr. McAllister at first, because he was asking me so many questions . . ."

"Tell me about it later," he said. "We have better things to do now."

He tried to kiss her, but she turned her face away.

"Damn it, don't play games with me. I want you, now, and you want me."

Yes, he wanted her, she had no doubt of that; but she needed more from him than desire. She needed tenderness, reassurance. "Kevin, listen to me, please. We have to . . . reach an understanding. I've done all you asked. You have your money from Mrs. Tremayne, the reward for locating . . . her granddaughter. Now I have to know, what is going to happen to me?"

He released her. "That should be obvious. You are going to be the belle of Newport this season, courted by all the eligible young men. And I . . ."

"What will you do?"

"I'll stay here for the summer. I will have many more assignments of the kind I had tonight. Mrs. Belmont has already hired me for the ball she'll be giving next week."

"But when summer is over, what then?"

She tried to see his expression in the moonlight that filtered in from above, but his face was a pale blur.

"By then, you will have enough confidence to carry on without me. Indeed, you may have become engaged. You will certainly have every opportunity. And I will move on."

She felt a tightness in her throat. "Where will you go?"

"Who knows? The West, perhaps. California or Nevada. Or perhaps the Caribbean. Since the end of the war, this country has been expanding in so many directions that a man who has some money and is willing to take risks can make a fortune. But why waste time talking about the future? We're together now."

When she did not respond, he demanded roughly, "What's wrong? That first time, back in New York, you were willing enough. Perhaps I taught you too well— perhaps you've come to believe you are the Tremayne heiress."

"You know better than that," she said.

"Then why are you . . ."

"Because I've fallen in love with you. And I want more than we had that first time."

"I see." His voice was cold. "You're asking for a declaration of eternal love. Or perhaps a proposal of marriage?"

"I'd be a good wife to you, Kevin. I'd go anywhere with you. And I'd make a home for you. I'd . . ."

"Stop it. I can't marry you. It wouldn't work."

"Then don't marry me, only take me with you. I need you so."

"A tempting offer," he said. "But . . . no, my dear. You're very young and filled with romantic notions, but you'll grow up in time. For a woman, security, a home, a husband, those are the important things, but for a man like me . . . I would make you miserable."

"I'm willing to take the risk," she said.

"I'm not," he said. He turned and started toward the door.

"Wait," she cried, hurrying after him. "Where are you going?"

"Back to the hotel, of course."

"No. Not yet. Please, not yet . . ."

She put a restraining hand on his arm. He stood quite still, remote, withdrawn, looking down at her, his eyes coldly silver in the moonlight.

Then she heard the sharp intake of his breath, and a moment later she was in his arms. He bent her backward, his body pressed to hers. She heard a low, roaring sound in her ears, blending with the surge of the waves against the rocks below Cliff Walk. "You do love me. You do, Kevin . . . say it."

But he remained silent. She wanted to free herself, to run back to the safety of the house, but she could not. She was furious with herself for giving in, but even as her mind fought to resist, her traitorous body clung to him, melted into his body, and her hands pressed the hard muscles of his back.

He lifted her off her feet and carried her into the shadows at the far end of the summerhouse, to the cushioned bench, and set her down upon it. His face loomed above hers, his touch blotting out reason.

Her lips parted to receive his kiss.

The ball at August Belmont's villa, By-the-Sea, was a spectacular affair. As long as Drucilla remained in Charlotte Tremayne's company, she was poised and calm. She knew that her dress was most becoming, one of Madame Janine's prettiest creations. The underskirt was of white grosgrain, the tunic bodice of pale blue peau de soie, trimmed with white lace and satin piping. Around her neck she wore a single strand of pearls, a gift from Mrs. Tremayne.

When she stepped into the ballroom at her "grandmother's" side, she was overawed by the sight of so many beautifully dressed women, all graceful and self-assured, as they circled the floor with their partners to the lively rhythm of a polka. The ballroom had been transformed into a bower of white roses, gardenias, and lilies, with trailing green vines for contrast.

Mrs. Tremayne led the way to a velvet and mahogany loveseat. After introducing Drucilla to the two young ladies seated there, she took her leave; Drucilla watched, with a sinking heart, as the old lady crossed to the other side of the room, where she sat with a group of matrons in dark silks.

There was no room for Drucilla on the loveseat, so she took her place on a small gilt chair beside it, and tried to find something to say to Catherine Tyler, a plump little blonde with pale lashes and rather prominent front teeth, which gave her a disconcerting resemblance to a rabbit; and Georgina March, whose light brown hair had been piled high in a coiffure that must have taken at least an afternoon to arrange.

It became obvious to Drucilla, after the first few minutes, that both girls had known each other for years, back in New York City, and that they had attended the same academy and dancing classes. Their conversation was about people and events completely unfamiliar to Drucilla.

"Shall you be going to Mr. McAllister's *fête champêtre* on Saturday?" Catherine asked. Her question was directed to Georgina.

"Yes, indeed. He is the only man in Newport who knows how to conduct such an outing with style," Georgina replied. Then, to Drucilla, "Don't you agree, Miss Tremayne?"

"I really don't . . . this is my first season in Newport." *As you know perfectly well,* she added silently.

"Oh, yes, of course," Georgina said.

She turned away and a moment later was deep in discussion with Catherine about a picnic that had been held the summer before, without the assistance of Mr. McAllister, and which had been a complete disaster. Drucilla smiled and tried to get a word in here and there, but both girls were ignoring her.

Kevin had told her about the social snobbery here in Newport, and now she was beginning to understand what he had meant. She realized that the dinner at Peregrine Court had given her a false sense of security; under Mrs. Tremayne's roof, with that indomitable lady by her side, she had been safe from the sort of treatment she was receiving now.

The two girls changed the subject of their discussion from the picnic to last year's theatrical season in New York.

"I was quite disappointed by the performance of Miss Maria Copeland in *The Fatal Dowry*," said Catherine Tyler. "What is your opinion, Miss Tremayne?"

"I did not see *The Fatal Dowry*."

"Oh, really?" The pale lashes blinked rapidly. "What was your favorite play of last season, then?"

"I did not attend the theater at all," Drucilla said.

"You surprise me," Catherine said sweetly. "I should have thought you would be interested in the theater because of your mother's profession . . ." Her hand flew to her mouth, but Drucilla knew she was not the least embarrassed. "Forgive me, my dear. Perhaps I should not have mentioned your mother."

Drucilla opened her lips to reply, but before she could get a word out, Georgina launched into a discussion of a costume party that had been held at Newport last summer.

Once more, Drucilla was shut out. She remained seated for a moment longer, then excused herself and fled from the ballroom, through the open French doors and out onto the terrace.

But the orchestra had begun to play another polka, and the two girls inside were forced to raise their voices, so that Drucilla heard every word.

"What did you mean about her mother? Do tell me, Cathy."

"You mean you really don't know? Her mother was an actress—a cheap little performer without talent. She managed to trap Mrs. Tremayne's only son, Horace, into an impossible marriage. Of course, she did not fit in here, and then . . ."

"Go on . . ."

"She ran away and lived a most abandoned life afterward. Performing in mining towns. No one knows all the details, but the rumors are simply not to be repeated."

"Poor Drucilla. No wonder she was so ill at ease. Still, she is Mrs. Tremayne's granddaughter and is received by Caroline Belmont."

"It's all very mysterious, I grant you. But we'll know all about her before the end of the season. I'll ask Mr. McAllister. He can always track down a person's background, however hidden . . ."

Drucilla had to lean against one of the pillars of the terrace for support; the mingled odors of roses, gardenias, and lilies had become overpowering. She found it difficult to take a deep breath, and the lanterns, strung along the wall, blurred before her eyes.

She had known unkindness before—from the matron at the County Farm, from Mrs. Baxley. But these people here in Mrs. Belmont's ballroom should have been different. Safe, secure behind the bastions of wealth and status, why should they feel the need to tear a newcomer's reputation to shreds?

A moment later, however, she forgot about her hurt at the snobbery of the Misses Tyler and March and thought, "Good heavens, suppose they do start prying. Suppose Mr. McAllister does. What might *he* discover?"

She felt a cold lump of fear in the pit of her stomach. Her fingers went to her throat and closed upon the strand of pearls, twisting them. She began to shake with pent-up terror.

"Don't do that," said a drawling masculine voice. "If you break your necklace, I will have to remain here and help you search for every pearl."

She whirled around and looked up at the young man who had spoken. He was tall and slender but well built, with light brown hair and an aquiline nose.

"Forgive me," he said. "I did not mean to startle you." Then, smiling, he added, "Permit me to introduce myself. I'm Radford Seaton."

"Oh, yes—I've met your mother . . ." She struggled to regain control, but the memory of the conversation she had overheard from inside the ballroom was still disturbing. Had Radford Seaton heard it, too? But, of course, he must have, since he had been standing so close to her.

"If you will excuse me, Mr. Seaton . . ." She began.

"Please, don't go," he said. "I was unable to attend the dinner at your grandmother's home, but if you will overlook that and give me the pleasure of this dance, I'll try to make up for my tardy arrival in Newport."

"I don't know all of these dances," she said.

"But you do waltz, surely?"

There was an unmistakable air of quiet good breeding about this young man that put Drucilla somewhat more at ease. She did not want to go back into the ballroom, to expose herself to the gossip that might be spreading even now, to curious, hostile stares. But she could not remain out here all evening, and it would surely be easier to return in the company of Radford Seaton.

"Miss Tremayne, may I tell you something? Every young woman who is as lovely as you are is fair game for those less favored. Oh, yes, believe me. They can be cruel, but only because they are jealous."

"You're very kind, sir."

"No. Only truthful. Listen, Miss Tremayne. The waltz is starting."

Her mind flew back to an afternoon at Mrs. Baxley's boardinghouse, when Kevin had taught her to waltz. The lesson had been delightful, but brief, for there had been little time and so many things to be learned before she was to come to Newport.

But now, in Radford Seaton's arms, she had no difficulty getting into the rhythm of the waltz, even though she could not forget how different it had been, dancing with Kevin. She had only to half-close her eyes to remember the touch of his hand, his tall, splendid body, wide and muscular through the chest and shoulders. If only she could be dancing with Kevin now . . .

Damn Kevin. But no. Why turn her anger on him for what was her own weakness? He had not forced her to submit to him that night last week in the summerhouse. He had had no need to use force.

"Miss Tremayne?"

She blinked and turned her face up, focusing her

eyes on Radford Seaton. Thank heaven, he could not read her thoughts.

"I beg your pardon," he said, a half smile touching his mouth, his blue eyes alight with amusement. "I did not mean to bore you. I suppose the business of running a plantation is of no great interest to a young lady."

She realized he had been saying something about his home near Charleston in South Carolina, but she had been lost in her own thoughts and had caught only a word here and there.

"Oh, no . . . I mean, yes. I am very much interested."

He laughed softly. "You're not still brooding about those malicious little cats, are you?"

"No, indeed. I was enjoying the waltz so much that it was hard to think of anything else. You are a fine dancer, Mr. Seaton."

"You're very kind," he said. Then, "Are you planning to go to Ward McAllister's picnic?"

"Picnic?"

"He calls it a *fête champêtre*. Thinks French is more elegant. To give him credit, though, he manages such outings in fine style. Music . . . flowers . . . a carpenter to put down a floor for dancing. He plans everything down to the last napkin. He even has the farmhands dress like French peasants—and sometimes he rents a flock of sheep and a few teams of oxen for atmosphere."

"Now you're teasing, I'm sure."

"I give you my word, Miss Tremayne." He laughed, and she joined in the laughter. For the first time since she had overheard the conversation between Miss Tyler and Miss March, she was beginning to relax.

"It sounds like the picnics given by Marie Antoinette. I've read that she and her courtiers used to dress up like milkmaids and shepherds."

He raised his eyebrows slightly. "Few young ladies as beautiful as you remember what they learned in school."

"I did not go to school," she said, remembering her carefully memorized lies. "My mother kept me supplied with books, however. She had respect for learning—even though she was an actress."

"Miss Tremayne—Drucilla—please stop thinking about what you overheard."

"It isn't easy. I . . ."

"Then remember only that you are a Tremayne. And if you hold your head up and ignore the silly snubs you will surely encounter, you will soon be accepted as a Tremayne."

When the waltz ended and they were seated in an alcove under a trellis covered with roses, he continued. "The Tremaynes and the Seatons have been friends for generations. My family has been coming here to Newport every summer since the middle of the last century. Of course, during the war, it was impossible, but . . ."

He broke off, his blue eyes somber.

"It was my mother who began the rebuilding of Seaton Barony. It was difficult without slave labor, but she managed. She is a most capable woman."

Remembering the firm jawline, the cold blue eyes, Drucilla said, "I'm sure she is."

"My father was killed at the beginning of the war," Radford went on. "And I was fourteen—no help to her at all."

"At least you did not have to fight."

"That's not quite true," he said. "I got into the fighting just before the war was over."

"But you were still only a boy."

"That did not matter. The Confederacy was fighting for its life. And a boy grows up quickly in combat. But, forgive me—I had not meant to dwell on such matters. Indeed, I . . ."

He was interrupted when Mrs. Seaton, majestic in a gown of heavy, steel-blue satin, swept up to them.

"Ah, Radford, I see you have already met Miss Tremayne." She turned to Drucilla. "How pretty you look tonight, my dear."

Drucilla murmured an acknowledgment, and Mrs. Seaton went on, "Radford and I will be at Mr. Mc-Allister's farm for the picnic, and I do hope . . ."

"I was about to ask Miss Tremayne to accompany us, mother," Radford said. He was perfectly polite, but

Drucilla thought she recognized an undertone of tension in his voice. And who could blame him? Why on earth should Mrs. Seaton feel that a young man like her son was not able to ask a girl to a picnic without her prodding?

Fortunately, at that moment, the orchestra launched into the first notes of a lively polka, and Radford, taking courteous leave of his mother, led Drucilla back onto the floor.

"You will go to the picnic with me, won't you?" he asked and, breathless with dancing, she nodded.

For the rest of that summer, as one blue and golden day followed another, Drucilla embarked on a round of social activities; Ward McAllister's picnic was followed by an endless series of lawn fêtes, balls, yachting parties, and musicales. Radford Seaton became her regular escort, and while his mother was sometimes present, she kept to the company of the other dowagers who sat to one side, passing judgment on the young girls, their dress, their conduct, their eligibility.

Although Drucilla did not pretend to herself that she was in love with Radford Seaton, she did enjoy his company, his easy, polished manners, his skill as a dancer. She could not help noticing that other young girls found him attractive, too. But though they preened and flirted, Radford did not appear to be interested in anyone but Drucilla.

Other young men showed interest, too, and for the first time she began to realize that her beauty could be a potent weapon. The young girls might snub her but their brothers, and sometimes their fiancés, were definitely attracted to her.

She was also to learn that Radford, although he had never spoken of love, was deeply jealous of any other man who might look at her. Once, when she accepted an invitation to a musicale from a young New York stockbroker, a clever and personable young man, Radford spent the evening glowering at her from across the room, so that she was unable to enjoy the performance.

Later, before retiring, she went to speak with Charlotte Tremayne in the old lady's room. She mentioned Radford's behavior, and Mrs. Tremayne said, "He's very fond of you, Drucilla. Surely, you know that. Why, he hasn't paid the slightest attention to anyone else, since the night of the Belmonts' ball."

"But he hasn't said a word to me about . . ."

"He will ask me first, of course," Mrs. Tremayne said. "That's customary, you know. I am your only relative. It would not be proper for him to ask you to become engaged, without first requesting my permission." Then, putting her hand on Drucilla's arm, she asked, "How do you feel about him?"

"He's very charming. And kind."

"And that's all?"

Drucilla looked away. There was no way she could tell Mrs. Tremayne that she was not in love with Radford Seaton because there could be no man for her but Kevin Farrell.

"My dear, is it that you don't want to speak to me about these matters? I realize that you cannot feel close to me, as you should, because of your memories of your mother."

"It isn't that—truly, it isn't. There is nothing to discuss, that's all. I like Radford, but I'm not in love with him."

"Love?" The hazel eyes flashed under the wrinkled lids. "Love is for servants and little immigrant girls. For a young lady in your position, love must come after marriage. Radford Seaton is a young man worthy of your consideration."

Drucilla longed to cry out, "You don't know. I'm already in love." But instead she only said, "It would please you, wouldn't it, if I became engaged to Radford?"

"The Seatons are an old and most respected family," Mrs. Tremayne said. Obviously, as far as she was concerned, this was a most significant point. "Seaton Barony was one of the great plantations of South Carolina."

"A curious name," Drucilla said.

"The land was given to the Seatons in the form of a royal charter from King Charles II, after he was restored to his throne. New titles were created for the colonial landholders: they were called barons, cassiques and landgraves. And so—Seaton Barony."

Drucilla concealed a smile. She was constantly impressed, and a little amused, by Charlotte Tremayne's ancestor worship.

". . . lost all their slaves, of course," Mrs. Tremayne was saying. "But Theodora Seaton is a most remarkable woman. She would not admit defeat, and while she had to sell some of her land, she used the money to put the rest back under cultivation, with paid field hands. She made a number of shrewd investments, too, I believe."

She looked at Drucilla meaningfully. "She will expect Radford, as the only son, to continue to rebuild the family fortune. And she will expect him to marry a girl from a family as good as her own." Her eyes sparkled. "She might even overlook the fact that the girl was a Yankee."

"Grandmother, are you saying you would want me to marry him? Because if you are, you must know . . ."

"Drucilla, please don't talk romantic nonsense. The kind of love you are thinking about is found only in storybooks. But you probably don't even know what love between a man and a woman means—now do you?"

Mrs. Tremayne's last words brought a wave of guilt mingled with pleasure, for Drucilla was remembering her meeting with Kevin in the summerhouse. His arms around her, the fierce hunger he had kindled in her. And the exquisite sense of fulfillment afterward, when she had lain in his arms, her face pressed to his chest. She remembered it all and, with her memories, her need for him returned.

Mrs. Tremayne touched her hot cheek with cool, gentle fingers. "There, child, I did not mean to embarrass you. Your modesty is quite proper, of course."

She stood up and rang for her maid. "There is no question of forcing you into marriage, my dear. But it would please me if you would at least consider Radford Seaton as a possible choice."

The following day, the weather turned hazy with a threat of rain. Gray mist swirled along the Cliff Walk, and Drucilla, driving a light surrey, felt the air damp on her face.

The groom who had brought the surrey around to the house at her orders had offered to drive, but she did not want anyone along on this particular occasion.

Thank goodness, Charlotte Tremayne spent the hours between lunch and tea in her room resting. Drucilla suspected that, at her "grandmother's" age, this was a necessity during the arduous social season.

For Drucilla, the luxury of Peregrine Court had suddenly become oppressive. Since her talk with Mrs. Tremayne the night before, she felt that she was being pushed into a situation she could not handle. She had to see Kevin, to make him understand what was happening.

She knew that it was risky, going to his hotel this way, but she had worked it all out in her mind, when she had lain awake the night before.

Now, driving the surrey along the Cliff Walk, she felt her spirits rise. It was a pleasant drive, in spite of the cloudy weather; the Walk ran along a broken wall of rock, high above the ocean. On one side, Drucilla could see the masses of fallen rock far below, scattered along the shore, with the waves foaming up over them. On the other side were the carefully tended green lawns belonging to the great estates.

She drove past the Forty Steps, once a natural stairway of stone, leading to the ocean's edge, now reinforced with wood. On the landing at the head of the steps, townspeople and servants from the estates held their own dances on warm summer evenings, to the music of fiddles and guitars.

Overhead gulls wheeled and made their poignant cries, graceful gray and white shapes against the darker gray of the clouds. Drucilla touched the sleek mare lightly with the whip; she wanted to reach the Aquidneck House before the impending shower broke.

Inside the comfortable old hotel, she asked the desk clerk if Madame Janine was in. When the man said that she was, Drucilla proceeded to her suite. Although impatient to be with Kevin, she knew she could not visit him openly. She had devised her call on Madame Janine as a cover-up, in case she should be seen by someone who knew her.

She had brought along the latest copy of *Madame Demorest's Mirror of Fashions,* and had marked a sketch of a walking dress on one of its pages. Since her arrival in Newport and her acceptance by Charlotte Tremayne, Drucilla had never ceased to marvel over this new way of life: To see a dress, order and have it delivered within a week, sooner, if she demanded it; to have others care for her clothes, arrange her hair, cater to her every need; to sit down to an afternoon tea with enough food to have served her for the whole day when she lived in Mrs. Baxley's boardinghouse.

Sometimes she wondered whatever became of the food that was always left over. But she never dared to ask Charlotte Tremayne. The old lady took this style of life for granted, and Drucilla tried, without success, to adopt the same careless attitude.

She had to admit to herself that it could be pleasant, at times, not to have to worry about the cost of the gaslighting that kept Peregrine Court illuminated each evening, the fresh flowers in every room of the house, or the sensuous pleasure of soft, delicate fabrics against her skin.

She knocked at the door of Madame Janine's suite, and the dressmaker admitted her to the parlor that also served as a workroom. Scraps of silk and brocade were piled on tables, along with stacks of French and American fashion magazines and paper patterns. An open box held a collection of tinted French kid gloves in pearl gray, primrose, and soft beige.

Madame Janine greeted Drucilla, saying, "But my dear Miss Tremayne, I'm delighted to see you. Had I known you were in need of my services, I would have been pleased to come out to Peregrine Court." She drew forward a small gilt chair. "Please, do sit down. Would you care for some tea?"

Drucilla shook her head and showed the dressmaker the copy of the *Mirror of Fashions.* "I saw this sketch —yes, here it is. I would like to have it made . . ."

"Ah, yes. Charming, indeed," the dressmaker said. Then, for nearly an hour, she and Drucilla consulted together on the proposed costume. What type of lace should be used to trim the bodice? And the fabric for the dress, should it be of the fashionable new striped silk? Or perhaps satin-de-Lyon? Amber buttons or jet?

Drucilla found herself growing taut with impatience, but she knew that this ruse was necessary, and she forced herself to listen to the dressmaker's remarks, to put in a suggestion here and there. All the time, she wanted only to be with Kevin, and he was so close, in his room upstairs.

At last, she was able to take her leave, with Madame Janine assuring her that the walking dress would be ready for a first fitting within a few days.

Then she proceeded quickly to the floor above and down the hallway, dim in the hazy afternoon light. "Suppose he isn't here?" she thought as she knocked on his door.

Then she heard footsteps, and the door opened.

"Drucilla, what are you doing here?"

"It's all right," she assured him. "We're quite safe."

He stood aside as she entered the room. She saw that he was wearing only his trousers and that his dark hair clung damply to his forehead. He smelled of soap and bay rum.

"Is something wrong?" His gray eyes were alert and wary.

"Must something be wrong for me to pay a call on you?"

"Don't act coquettish with me, love. Save that for Radford Seaton."

He had seen her with Radford, of course, at Mrs. Belmont's ball and probably at other affairs as well. And he was jealous.

"Very well," she said, smiling up at him. "I only wanted to talk with you. I've missed you, Kevin."

"I shouldn't think you'd have time to miss me, with your busy round of activities. You're the belle of the season, as I said you'd be. And the elegant Mr. Seaton should keep you from getting lonely."

"He's a most charming young man."

"That's fine," he said. "And is that what you came here to tell me? In the middle of the afternoon, when you might be seen by anyone? I'm sure there are at least a dozen disappointed mothers who would be happy to rip your reputation to shreds because you snared the eligible Mr. Seaton."

She laughed. "I took care of that. My dressmaker, Madame Janine, has a suite on the floor right below yours. I went to see her first, and spent plenty of time with her."

"I see." He relaxed slightly, but made no move to take her in his arms, as she had hoped he would do.

"If you're sorry I've come, I'll leave."

"You know better than that." He drew her against him and kissed her lightly. She reached up and stroked his hair.

"All the same," he said, "it might be wise for you to go, my dear."

"How can I?" she asked, pointing to the window, where the first light drops of rain had begun to trace silver lines down along the glass. "No gentleman would send a lady out into a rainstorm."

He smiled down at her. "But I never claimed to be a gentleman."

She moved closer to him and put her hands on his naked shoulders. "You want me to stay, don't you?" she whispered.

His mouth found hers in a long, searching kiss. He left her only long enough to draw the heavy drapes and, a few moments after, they were together on the wide, soft bed, and his hands were stripping away her dress, her petticoats. She reached out for him, drawing his face down against the curve of her breast.

Later, she lay close to him and listened to the rain, pounding heavily against the window. She breathed in the salty air from the sea. She felt safe, relaxed.

She thought Kevin had fallen asleep, but then she saw that he was looking at her with half-closed eyes. He ran his hand gently along the smooth, creamy skin of her shoulder, then pushing back the sheet, traced the line from her waist to her knee.

"Kevin, we can't . . . I have to leave now. It's getting late."

"And perhaps Radford Seaton is calling on you this evening? Is he?" He took his hand away and moved to the other side of the bed.

"Kevin, I don't want to talk about Radford—not now."

He got out of bed, his eyes hard and cold as granite, and stood looking down at her.

"Has he asked you to marry him, Drucilla?"

"What if he has? Mrs. Tremayne approves of him and besides, you . . ."

"Go on." He reached for his clothes and started to dress, but his eyes did not leave her face.

"You don't want to marry me—you said so . . ."

He drew a deep breath, and she felt a swift surge of hope. He did care. He did.

"Are you in love with him?" he asked her very quietly.

"You told me I could not afford the luxury of feelings," she retorted.

There was anger in his eyes, but there was something else, something she did not understand. She reached out to him, but he moved away and went to the window. "That's quite true, of course. A marriage between you and Seaton would be most sensible."

She felt her heart sink and was conscious, all at once, of the damp chill in the room. When he saw that she was trembling, he handed her his own robe. "Put this on," he said.

She got up and put on the woolen garment which was, of course, far too large. He fastened the cord around her waist, then took her hands in his. She remembered that first night, when he had taken her hands that same way during the drive to the Fifth Avenue Hotel; remembered the warmth and comfort she had drawn from his touch.

"Do you suppose Mrs. Tremayne would let you marry someone like me?" he demanded.

"If I were to tell her everything, I could make her understand. I know I could."

"Drucilla, be reasonable. Charlotte Tremayne has never known what it's like to go hungry or homeless. How could she possibly understand what drives people like us?"

"You don't know her. She sets a great store by her family background, that's true. But she isn't heartless. She's fond of me, and she would want me to be happy."

He shook his head. "She would want her granddaughter to be happy—a very different matter. The moment she knows you're not her granddaughter . . ." He stood looking down at her, the line of his jaw hard. "She'll have you arrested for fraud. We'll both end up in prison. Not a pleasant prospect, is it?"

"I don't care about that . . ."

"Then I'll have to care, for both of us, until you come to your senses." He put his arm around her, led her to a small sofa, and forced her to sit down beside him.

"You want me to marry Radford Seaton?" Hot tears stung her eyelids, but she forced them back.

"You want me to say it? All right, damn it. I want you to marry him, and leave Newport with him and make a new life for yourself. I'm afraid you weren't cut out for the role of an adventuress. Sooner or later, you'll have an attack of conscience and confess the truth to Charlotte Tremayne. And believe me, my dear, she'll show you no mercy."

His words, cool, logical, beat at her brain, but she pushed them from her. "Are you afraid for me—or for yourself?" she lashed out.

And when he remained silent, she went on, her voice rising and taking on an edge of hysteria. "You don't care about me. You never have."

He put a hand on her arm, but she shook it off. From their first meeting, he had dominated her, controlled her actions, and now she felt that he was pushing her into the arms of another man.

"You've used me . . ."

"Drucilla, please, get hold of yourself and . . ."

"Even that first time you made love to me, it was only because . . ." Her face burned with shame, and she had to force the words past the tightness in her throat. "You wanted me to go along with your plans, and when every other persuasion failed, you . . ."

His lips tightened, and she saw the hard lines at their corners. "You believe that of me?" His voice was very quiet.

He got to his feet, and stood looking down at her, his hands jammed into the pockets of his jacket.

"It's true, isn't it?" she cried.

He took a long breath, and the silence between them was cold, frightening. Then he said lightly, "You underestimate yourself, Drucilla. You always have. I made love to you that first night for the same reasons any man would have done. You looked very lovely, and, then, too . . ."

"Go on."

"You were more than willing, as I recall. In the face of such—ardor—how could I have resisted?"

It did not matter that there was an element of truth in his words, that she had indeed offered herself to him. She heard the mockery in his tone, stripping away her pride, leaving her with only rage to sustain her.

She sprang to her feet, and his face blurred before her eyes. She drew back her arm and struck him across the face with all her strength.

"I hate you, Kevin Farrell. I hope I never see you again."

He put his hand to his cheek and rubbed it thoughtfully. There was a sardonic look in his eyes and in the half-smile he gave her. "In that case, there is no reason you shouldn't marry Radford Seaton, is there?"

He turned and left her without a backward glance.

Seven

SHE called out, "Kevin!" and started toward the closed door, then stopped, knowing that there were no words to bring him back. Because he had hurt her she had lashed out at him in anger, and now she had driven him away.

She stood in the hotel room, in the waning light of late afternoon, swept by a sense of desolation. Although he was gone, the room still held wounding memories of him, of his stay here. There was the washstand, with his straight razor and shaving mug on it, the strop hung on a nail above. And the wide bed with its rumpled sheets where, less than an hour ago, he had made love to her, had possessed her with tenderness and passion.

She went to the bed and sank to her knees on the floor beside it, her fingers clutching at the sheets, as if trying to take hold again of the brief time when they had been joined together in shared ecstasy.

She had known Kevin for such a little time, only a few months. Now she could not imagine going on without him. Alone, she would never find the courage to go on with this dangerous venture, to keep up the pretense that she was the Tremayne heiress.

He had changed her life in so many ways; she would never be the same again.

"There's no reason you shouldn't marry Radford Seaton," he had said.

Loneliness engulfed her. After the death of her father, she had loved no one. She had lived among the children at the County Farm, the actors in the stock company, but always she had felt like an outsider, for her existence had mattered to none of them. Her brief friendship with Beth had ended in tragedy, and she had been more desolate than ever. Until one night, a stranger with dark gray eyes had found her in the rain, and had taken her away, into a world she had hitherto only dreamed about.

Now he had left her, and her sense of loss grew until it became a physical thing; she wanted to give way to tears, and found she could not. Instead, when she got to her feet, she saw that the room was swaying, the walls closing in on her. Her hands were icy, and she heard a high, thin humming in her ears.

"I'm going to faint," she thought and welcomed the swirling darkness that began to rise about her. Then, remembering where she was, she thought, "No—I mustn't let myself faint—not here—"

She swayed and caught at the bedpost. A moment later, she started, feeling a hand on her arm. She turned and found herself looking into a pair of green eyes, fringed with pale lashes, and set in a thin, freckled face. A girl about her own age was staring at her with a worried frown.

"Are ye all right, Miss?"

Drucilla saw that the girl had ginger-blonde hair, pulled back under a stiffly starched white cap, and that she wore a neat blue dress, covered by a large white apron. She carried a pile of clean linen, which she now put down on the bedside table, then placed a thin but wiry arm around Drucilla's waist.

"Ye're tremblin' like a rabbit," the girl said. "Ye'd best lie down for a bit."

Drucilla made feeble, struggling motions. "I can't ... I must leave here at once ..."

"Ye can't go anywhere, the state ye're in."

She eased Drucilla down on the bed, then went quickly to the stand that held the basin and pitcher.

"I saw the gentleman leave the room, and I figured this would be a good time to come in and straighten up. I didn't know there'd be anyone else in here."

She poured fresh water into the basin, soaked a cloth, and returned to Drucilla. "It's just as well I came in, though, isn't it, Miss?"

Drucilla let the girl hold the cloth to her forehead.

"Ye're not hurt bad, are ye? There's a doctor here at the hotel, if ye . . ."

"Oh, no. Please. I had a spell of faintness, that's all."

She raised herself to clutch at the girl's arm. Another wave of dizziness enveloped her, and she felt a stirring of nausea. She found these sensations disturbing, for she had always enjoyed excellent health, and the only weakness she had ever known had come from a lack of food. Nevertheless, she wanted no commotion. Bad enough the chambermaid had discovered her here in Kevin Farrell's room, half-dressed and disheveled.

"Promise me you won't call anyone."

"All right, then. But what did he do to ye, to put you in such a state?"

Drucilla set her lips together and looked away.

"Ah, so that's the way of it, ye poor darlin'. No matter how bad a man is, if ye love him, ye'll cover up for him."

Love him? Did she still love Kevin—even now?

"My sister's husband, he is a devil. Used to knock her about somethin' fierce. But she tried to hide her bruises, as best she could."

"But it wasn't . . . he isn't like that."

The girl did not look entirely convinced, but she took Drucilla's hand and patted it comfortingly. Although they were strangers to one another, Drucilla found she was clinging to that bony, work-hardened hand.

"What's your name?" she asked.

"Kitty Nolan, Miss."

"I'm Drucilla . . ." She caught herself in time.

"Drucilla. A fine, elegant name, it is. It suits you."

"If you could stay with me, for a little while, I know I'll be all right. Then I'll get dressed and leave."

Kitty hesitated, casting an anxious glance in the direction of the door. "It's the housekeeper I'm worried about. Strict, she is. Always after us, to make sure we get our chores done, and no idlin' on the job. But there, you don't want to hear about my troubles . . ."

"But I do. Talk to me." As long as Kitty kept talking, it helped to shut out Drucilla's fears. And her strength was coming back slowly.

"What shall I talk about?"

"Anything—your sister and her husband, do they live here in Newport?" Drucilla asked.

"Oh, no. They're back in New York City. I lived with them when I first came over, but I couldn't stand it."

"Did . . . your brother-in-law mistreat you?"

"At first he did, but then I took a stick of kindlin' to him and after that, he kept his distance. But there were other things I couldn't stomach—worse things. In the Five Points, in New York . . ." She broke off and gave Drucilla a shy, embarrassed smile. "Of course, a lady like yerself wouldn't know of such foul places as the Five Points."

"What makes you think I'm a lady?"

"Oh, I can tell. The way ye talk and . . . I don't know, Miss . . . but there's something about ye . . . I'm not askin' how ye came to find yerself here, and in such a state, but I give ye my word, I'll not say anything to anyone about it."

The green eyes were steady and candid. "No," Drucilla said slowly. "I don't believe you would. But we were speaking of you, Kitty, and the Five Points."

"It was enough to make a goat sick, all of us livin' together in a cellar without even a window, and with bottle shops in every other house, and—worse places. A girl couldn't stay decent there." Then she added, "This hotel is like heaven, for all we work long and hard, with that housekeeper nippin' at our heels. Oh, I'd never want to go back to the Five Points."

Drucilla was thinking that if Kevin had not come along that night when she had been thrown out of Mrs.

Baxley's boardinghouse, she might have found herself in a cellar in the Five Points. She pushed away the unwelcome thought and forced herself to sit up; this time the room did not sway before her eyes.

"I'll get dressed and leave now," she said. She did not want Kitty to get into trouble with the housekeeper for neglecting her chores.

But Kitty insisted on helping Drucilla to dress, and as she handled the petticoats, embroidered and trimmed with delicate Valenciennes lace, her green eyes widened; she was obviously impressed. When Drucilla was dressed in her gown of pale blue silk, trimmed with dark blue velvet bows, Kitty stood back and looked at her in awe. "How fine ye are, Miss. But ye must let me do something with yer hair."

Only then did Drucilla realize that her hair still hung in loose tangled masses down to her waist. She certainly could not be seen this way in the hotel lobby. But when she began to fumble with the discarded hairpins, her hands were clumsy. Kevin had taken those pins from her hair and when it had fallen around her face, he had pressed his lips to the silken waves. . . .

"Let me," Kitty said briskly. She worked with quick, deft movements, as she arranged Drucilla's hair into a neat chignon, then helped her to settle her blue chip hat well forward over her forehead.

But Kitty's fingers froze on the brim of the hat, when a shrill voice in the hall called out, "Kitty—where are you?"

The chambermaid left Drucilla and hurried to the door, her thin body taut with fear, her eyes anxious. "It's Annie," she said, over her shoulder. "One of the other maids. I got to get back to my work."

"But wait. I haven't thanked you for . . ."

"I know, Miss. It's all right," Kitty said and threw her a quick, tremulous smile. Then opening the door only far enough to slip through, she was gone.

Drucilla remained standing before the mirror, smoothing a few wisps of hair up under the hat. She was so tired, but at least the peculiar weakness, the dizziness, and nausea were gone.

Had her quarrel with Kevin been the sole cause of those unpleasant reactions? No, she decided, it had been more than that. She had been under great stress during all these weeks in Newport, pretending to be someone she was not, deceiving Charlotte Tremayne, Radford Seaton—all of them. Perhaps Kevin had been right. Perhaps she had been bound to crack—sooner or later.

But she had to go on, there was no escape. She sighed, opened the door, and saw that Kitty and the other maid, Annie, were gone. Now she, too, must leave, and quickly.

On the drive back to Peregrine Court in the twilight, through the quiet Newport streets, now damp and breezy after the rain, she let herself relax. Her lips curved in a wry smile when she thought that, although she had deliberately allowed Kevin to believe she already had a proposal from Radford, that was not the case.

It did not matter, really, for although Radford was undeniably handsome, she was not attracted to him. He was a good companion, intelligent, well-bred, and with a sense of humor. But he had never once stirred her senses as Kevin had done from their first meeting.

She would be seeing him tomorrow, she remembered; he was to take her to an "aquatic picnic," to be held aboard one of the yachts moored in Narragansett Bay. For a moment she thought she might beg off, shut herself in her room, and see no one. But she knew that such behavior would be suspicious, and she had no wish to draw attention from Charlotte Tremayne.

Right now, she would have to concoct a story to explain why she was coming home late for tea. A sudden downpour, and the necessity of taking refuge in a tea shop in town. That was plausible enough, and it would have to do.

By the following afternoon, when Radford came to call for her in his handsome phaeton, she found that she was able to smile and flirt and make the right answers to his pleasantries, but all the time, in the back of her mind, was a dull sense of misery. She could not forget her quarrel with Kevin.

She tried to enjoy the warm, sunlit weather. It was a delightful afternoon, the sky filled with white clouds driven along by the brisk west wind, the front lawn of Peregrine Court like green velvet, accented here and there with marble and cast iron statues, and surrounded by small groves of elm and maple.

They were driving along the road toward the great iron gate, flanked by the two pillars, each topped with its stone falcon. The breeze caught at her ribboned straw hat, and when she turned her head in the other direction, she caught sight of a familiar figure, a girl who was shrinking back against one of the pillars.

Thomas, the liveried gatekeeper, a heavy-set, red-faced man, was shouting, "Get along now, and I'll make you wish you'd never set foot on these grounds. And no more of your lies. The likes of you, saying you know Miss Tremayne."

"But I do know her. If I could only see her for a moment, please . . ."

"Kitty," Drucilla called. "Over here."

Radford, with a puzzled glance at Drucilla, stopped short. Kitty approached slowly and with diffidence. She looked quite different from the way she had yesterday afternoon. Instead of the neat blue uniform and starched white cap and apron, she wore a shabby gray poplin, frayed at the cuffs, and a round, battered straw hat. Her face had a drawn, pinched look, and the green eyes were swollen, as if she had been crying.

"I'm sorry, Miss," she said, with a quick glance at Radford. She shifted a small carpetbag from one hand to the other, as if even that slight weight was too much for her. "I didn't know ye'd be on yer way out . . . I only wanted to . . ." She shook her head. "I'd best be on my way."

"No, wait. Please don't go."

Radford stood up to assist Drucilla, but she was out of the phaeton too quickly for him; she took Kitty's hand, and standing close to her, she caught an odd, overpowering smell. Fish, that's what it was.

"Tell me what happened," Drucilla said.

"I lost my job. And the housekeeper wouldn't give me no reference. I'll be goin' back to New York."

"Why did you . . ." But Drucilla did not finish. She could guess the answer to her question. Kitty had neglected her duties to help her, and the quick-tempered housekeeper had fired her.

"You can't go back to the Five Points," Drucilla said.

"I don't have no choice, Miss." She forced a wan smile. "I'll manage. Only . . . well . . . the money I saved doesn't quite cover the fare back to New York and I was wonderin' . . ."

"You were fired yesterday?"

"That's right, Miss."

"And where did you spend the night?"

"I found an empty fishin' shack, down by Bannister's Wharf. It was snug enough, but the smell of fish was somethin' fierce."

"You must not go back to the Five Points," Drucilla said firmly. She thought quickly, then added, "We have a very large staff here. I'm sure Edith, my grandmother's housekeeper, can find work for you."

Kitty looked across the lawn at the stone mansion with its imposing towers, its glittering windows. "Oh, Miss, I never thought to work in a place as fine as this. Like a palace, it is."

Drucilla turned and called to the gatekeeper, "Thomas, come here. You are to take Kitty to the house, and tell Edith that I want her to be given a job."

"But, Miss Tremayne," the gatekeeper began, "are you sure . . . ?"

"Yes, I am." Never, since she had first come to Peregrine Court, had Drucilla given orders to anyone, for at the back of her mind, she had felt that she had no right to do so. But now, her concern for Kitty was stronger than her own diffidence.

"As you wish, Miss Tremayne," Thomas said. "I could not be sure the girl was telling the truth, saying she knew you. I have to be careful about letting people in here—it's my job to—"

"I understand," Drucilla interrupted. "But now, please do as you've been told."

Kitty looked at Drucilla, with green eyes filled with such passionate gratitude that Drucilla was forced to turn away in embarrassment. Kitty caught Drucilla's hand and pressed it. "I'll never forget what you've done for me this day—I swear I won't."

Drucilla freed herself gently. "It's all right, Kitty. Go along with Thomas, now."

"And what was that all about?" Radford asked, as the phaeton moved briskly down Bellevue Avenue, heading for the wharf.

"I couldn't let her go back to the Five Points," Drucilla said.

Radford looked at her, puzzled. "The Five Points?"

"One of the most dreadful slums in New York. Hundreds of immigrant families are herded together in cellars there, surrounded with every kind of evil. . . ." Her hand flew to her lips, to stem the tide of her words.

"How do you come to know so much about this . . . Kitty?"

"She worked at the Aquidneck House. I was taken ill there, after leaving my dressmaker's suite. She was kind and helpful to me."

"But why should you feel responsible for her welfare? You might have given her a few dollars—but to employ her in your home, isn't that going a bit far?"

How cool and detached he looked, seated there beside her in his elegant fawn-colored trousers, his blue jacket, and embroidered blue waistcoat.

"A few dollars? Enough to pay her way back to New York. Yes, that was all she wanted. Radford, Kitty is a decent girl. And you don't know, you can't imagine what the Five Points can do to a girl like that."

Her voice was unsteady, and Radford put his hand over hers. "You're a strange girl," he said. "Not like any of these other Newport belles."

She felt uneasy, for his blue eyes were studying her with an intensity she had never seen there before. Radford Seaton, for all his conventional background, his light, often frivolous manner, was far from being un-perceptive.

"Don't let's talk about Kitty anymore," she said quickly. "You know, I've never been to an 'aquatic picnic.' I'm so looking forward to it."

"The Mallorys' yacht is certainly something to see," Radford told her. To her relief, he dropped the subject of Kitty, but during the afternoon he was unusually with-drawn. From time to time, Drucilla noticed that he was studying her, his eyes puzzled, thoughtful.

But she was not so aware of his behavior as she might otherwise have been, for she was awed and fasci-nated by the magnificence of the yacht on which the "picnic" was held.

From the reception room, the guests descended by a mahogany stairway to a hall which opened onto a dining salon that might have done credit to any wealthy home. It ran the full width of the vessel, was paneled in light wood, and finished in sky-blue enamel with gold trim.

By the time Drucilla and Radford arrived, several of the guests had already come aboard. The girls wore light-weight silks and the gentlemen natty summer suits. Some were strolling on the deck, while others had gathered in the dining salon, where there was a piano, a long, com-fortable settee, and a round mahogany table laden with platters of food.

Among the guests, Drucilla recognized Radford's two sisters, who had come north with him for the season. She reflected that neither Gwen nor Hazel Seaton looked par-ticularly happy.

Gwen, at twenty-four, was almost surely doomed to the life of a spinster, while Hazel, although only seven-teen, was painfully shy, particularly with members of the opposite sex. And unfortunately, neither girl shared Rad-ford's good looks: where his eyes were a bright blue, theirs were a pale, washed-out shade; and both girls had inherited the strongly defined Seaton jawline, the jutting, aquiline nose, features that gave strength to a man's face, but were no asset to a young woman's.

Later, when she was seated at table, Drucilla was disturbed yet again by seeing the fantastic amount of sheer waste that was a part of this new world in which she now moved. Dozens of rich, elaborate dishes, soft-shell crabs in champagne, broiled fish in white wine, braised pheasant, venison, duckling in burgundy, all to be sampled by the guests who could not possibly finish such a spread. And the yacht, itself, an expensive and elaborate toy, used perhaps a dozen times during the season . . . while families like Kitty's lived in cramped, filthy quarters and were half starved.

But she must not let herself think about Kitty, and certainly she must not mention her again. She regretted having told Radford as much as she had, for, despite the festivities around them, he remained distant, even a little moody.

She was relieved when he brought her back to Pere-grine Court that evening. But when they were together in the sitting room, she was confronted by an unexpected crisis.

Edith, the housekeeper, asked to speak with her, and even Radford's presence was not enough to silence the woman who was plainly distraught.

"Miss Tremayne, I cannot believe it was by your orders that that—impossible young person—was sent to me. She is, of course, quite unsuited for a position in a house such as this one."

"Did my grandmother disapprove?"

"Mrs. Tremayne left for a visit with Mrs. Belmont before the girl arrived, and she has not yet returned. But when she does, I'm sure she will agree that a miserable little creature like Kitty Nolan, reeking of fish, untidy, with no references, is hardly acceptable."

Then, obviously remembering her position, she added more tactfully, "The rest of the staff would be most displeased if I were to make this girl a parlormaid. And she has had no experience in the kitchen, as she admitted herself."

"Very well, Edith," Drucilla said gently. "You need not employ Kitty as a parlormaid, nor in the kitchen."

Edith sighed, plainly relieved. "I was sure you would understand and reconsider, Miss Drucilla."

"I have decided to employ Kitty Nolan as my personal maid."

Edith's eyes widened, and her disapproval was plain in every line of her body. She drew herself up, two spots of color burning high on her cheeks.

"I have been sharing Clarice's services with my grandmother, as you know," Drucilla went on. "With Kitty as my maid, Clarice can go back to serving my grandmother only." She smiled. "At least, Clarice should be pleased with the new arrangement."

Edith opened her mouth as if to make an angry retort, then apparently thought better of it. "As you wish, Miss Drucilla. I will show—Kitty—to her room and explain her duties." She made it clear, by her tone, if not her words, that she resented even that much contact with the newcomer.

After Edith had left, Drucilla turned to Radford. "I'm sure these domestic upheavals must be boring, but I had to settle the matter. Now, may I offer you something? A glass of sherry, perhaps."

But even when they were seated side by side on the dark green and gold sofa, Radford left his sherry untouched and did not look at her. She felt sure that she had displeased him by her unconventional behavior in the matter of Kitty, and she was sorry, for she really liked Radford Seaton. His presence had done much to ease her entry into Newport society, to make her feel that she belonged.

He spoke abruptly. "Drucilla, I'll be going back home in a few weeks, for the season is almost over and there is much work to be done at Seaton Barony."

"I'll miss you," she said.

A curious light came into his blue eyes, and he moved closer to her. "You mean that?"

"Of course I do."

He leaned forward, searching her face, and then he took her hands in his. "We've known each other for only a short time. Perhaps I've no right to expect . . . but I've fallen in love with you, Drucilla. I don't want to return home without you."

Her eyes widened, and she understood. The half-lie

she had told Kevin—that Radford wanted to marry her —was true.

"I said you were different from any other girl I've known and I meant it. You are warm, compassionate, you care about people. Even that miserable waif, Kitty. You're beautiful, and . . ." He broke off, and then his arms were around her and he was kissing her, a long, slow kiss.

She was still for a moment, then turned her face away.

"Please don't be angry." He smiled, and added, "You may slap my face if you like. To preserve the proprieties."

She caught her breath and felt numb with misery, remembering her last meeting with Kevin . . . remembering how she had struck him and driven him away.

"Drucilla, dearest, forgive me. Don't turn away. You must know I care for you. Ever since that first night, at Mrs. Belmont's ball, I have thought of no one else." He paused, then went on with simple dignity, "Seaton Barony is not what it was before the war, but we are rebuilding, and I do not come to you empty-handed. I offer you my name—a proud name—and myself."

To marry Radford and go with him to the South, to begin a new life. Her mind moved swiftly. Kevin would never marry her. After the season, she might not see him again. She had thrown herself at him, and he had repulsed her. He had told her to marry Radford Seaton. Very well, then, why not?

She knew why not. Radford's kiss, tender and ardent, had not moved her at all. She had felt nothing. He would never stir her as Kevin had done. She wanted Kevin with every fiber of her being, needed him, hungered for him.

"I cannot give you an answer—not now."

"But when? We have so little time, and I can't stand the thought of your being miles away—other men around you." There was fierce jealousy in his voice.

"You need not worry about that," she said, still thinking of Kevin.

But Radford, misunderstanding her words, said, "Then you do care for me, don't you?"

"There are a great many things to consider—I can't give you my answer now—there is my grandmother . . ."

"I'll speak with her, of course. I should have done so before asking you to marry me, but I love you so, and the thought of leaving you . . . how long must I wait for your answer?"

"I don't know."

"Your grandmother is giving the last ball of the season, her Harvest Ball. It is two weeks off. Will you give me your answer then?"

She had to be alone, to think, to try to plan ahead. "Yes, I promise," she said quickly. "I will give you my answer at the Harvest Ball. But now . . ."

He rose, and taking her hand, raised it to his lips. Still, she felt nothing for him. Not repulsion, certainly not fear. Simply nothing at all.

After he had left, she remained on the sofa in the darkening room, until one of the maids came in and lit the gas lamps. She was scarcely aware of the girl's presence.

Her "grandmother" had assured her that love must come after marriage, but then, Charlotte Tremayne believed Drucilla was a virgin. Drucilla knew the meaning of love, and the thought of giving herself to another man made her shrink back with distaste.

Radford was handsome, and he was a gentleman; but as she remembered his face, with its fine, patrician features, the sound of his voice, the touch of his hands, she knew that she could not love him. She loved Kevin Farrell and, even if she never saw him again, she would belong to him always.

Then she reminded herself that Kevin had sent her away. He had taken her with the careless passion that was part of his nature, and now he had enough of her. She had served her purpose.

"There is no reason you shouldn't marry Radford Seaton, is there?" She remembered the mockery in his voice, when he had said that.

Kevin was right, damn him. There was no reason to refuse Radford's proposal. And yet . . .

She stood up and smoothed her skirts and walked slowly from the room. She had two weeks in which to make up her mind. Two weeks before the Harvest Ball.

Eight

"MY DEAR, if I had known you wanted a maid of your own, I would have hired one," Mrs. Tremayne said.

She and Drucilla were seated in the library after dinner. A breeze from the Cliff Walk stirred the heavy velvet draperies.

"I had thought," Mrs. Tremayne went on, "you were satisfied with Clarice's services. When we return to New York—yes, I am planning to open the town house there in the fall—I am going to hire an experienced lady's maid for you. Someone suitable."

She emphasized the last two words slightly, and it was plain to Drucilla that she was a little annoyed.

"But Kitty's bright and willing. She can learn quickly, I'm sure."

"The duties of a lady's maid are not simple, Drucilla. She must be able to dress your hair expertly, to take care of your clothes and mend the most delicate fabrics, to iron perfectly, to pack your trunks. Oh, no. It's out of the question."

Drucilla looked at the small, regal woman, who sat

stiffly in her chair, the picture of dignity in her dress of olive-green silk and brocade. The gaslight gave luster to her high-piled white hair, arranged in its elaborate coiffure.

"I am surprised that you hired this girl without consulting me."

"Perhaps I did act rashly," she said, wanting to placate Mrs. Tremayne. "But I did give Kitty Nolan my word, and I can't break it." Then she put a hand on the old lady's arm. "If you would only speak to her, I'm sure you would change your mind."

"Edith told me the girl is most unprepossessing in appearance, and that she is not even clean."

Drucilla's temper flared. "That's not true. This afternoon she was not very tidy, and she did smell strongly of fish, but that was because she was forced to spend the night in a shack on Bannister's Wharf. As soon as she has a bath and a change of clothing, I know she will be satisfactory."

"How on earth did you find such a person to be your maid?"

Drucilla hesitated, then choosing her words with great care, she said, "It was after I'd left Madame Janine's suite at the Aquidneck House. I'd been standing too long for my fitting, and the weather was close and sultry. I had a spell of giddiness in the hallway, and Kitty helped me. She neglected her own duties to make me comfortable. She was fired, without references."

"Edith said nothing about that."

"She didn't know."

Mrs. Tremayne looked thoughtful. "I see. That does put a different light on the matter. But even so, we might just give the girl some money and send her on her way."

"Grandmother, no. Kitty's had a miserable life. I want to do something for her. Something that will really make a difference."

"But my dear, if you have decided to help every homeless unfortunate who has had a miserable life, we will soon find the house crowded with such people."

"But I only want to help Kitty. And it isn't charity.

She will be useful to me. Clarice has more than enough work. And now, with the Harvest Ball, she'll be busier than ever."

She broke off, troubled by the memory of the promise she had given Radford Seaton.

"What's wrong?" Mrs. Tremayne looked at her closely. "You are pleased about the ball, aren't you?"

Drucilla remained silent, and Mrs. Tremayne went on, "The Harvest Ball used to be a tradition here at Peregrine Court. We held one each year, to mark the end of the season. But after my son died, I had no more heart for such festivities. Until now . . ."

"I do understand," Drucilla said. "But . . . grandmother, this afternoon, Radford asked me to marry him, and I promised to give him my answer at the Harvest Ball. He means to speak to you as soon as possible, of course," she added.

Mrs. Tremayne's lined face brightened, and her hazel eyes glowed with satisfaction. "Oh, my dear," she said. "Why didn't you tell me at once? Here we've been discussing the new maid, and all the time you've been keeping this wonderful news to yourself."

Drucilla wanted to change the subject, before she spoiled her grandmother's pleasure by telling her that she planned to refuse Radford's proposal. "But what about Kitty?" she persisted. "I may keep her as my maid, may I not?"

"You've caught me at a weak moment. Yes, keep your little waif, if it pleases you. At least, for the present. But do see that she gets a set of proper uniforms at once. There is a Mrs. Kennicott in town who takes care of these things. Send her there tomorrow."

Kitty Nolan's thoughts were in a turmoil when she returned from town the following afternoon. She could not believe it was only three days since her meeting with Drucilla Tremayne. A fine young lady—and so kind. She had known as much from their first meeting at the Aquidneck House, but even so, when she had come to Peregrine Court, she had never expected to find work here. The most she had dared hope for was that Miss

Drucilla would lend her the fare to take her back to New York. To the cellar in the Five Points, where her sister, Lizzie, lived with her good-for-nothing husband and the children. She had dreaded the prospect, but she had thought there was no other choice.

And then, Miss Drucilla had hired her, not as a kitchen maid, but as her own personal lady's maid. And today, she had gone into town, fine as you please, in the Tremayne's yellow-wheeled trap, to buy a complete wardrobe of the best clothes she had ever owned.

While she waited, Mrs. Kennicott, the dressmaker, had made the necessary alterations on a black poplin skirt, a white shirtwaist, and a small white apron—and those were just for daytime wear. There was a light gray taffeta dress with an embroidered apron for evening. And sturdy cotton undergarments, brand-new and soft against her skin, and stockings, and two nightgowns. Until now, Kitty had slept in the same petticoat she had worn all day.

Now, as she made her way up the wide stairs to Miss Drucilla's room, she still could not believe that she was to be a part of this household. Fine as a palace, it was, with so many beautiful big rooms, all hung with velvet drapes at the windows, and carpeted with thick, soft rugs.

And her own room, in the servants' wing on the third floor, was light and airy and clean. Never had she imagined living in such luxury.

All because she had done a small kindness for the beautiful red-haired girl she had found in that room at the hotel. What had Miss Drucilla been doing there? It troubled her, and she pushed it resolutely out of her mind. Even young ladies from fine families, she supposed, made mistakes where men were concerned. She tried not to remember that when she had first seen Miss Drucilla, she had been naked under a man's bathrobe, that the bed had been rumpled. . . . No, whatever had happened, it hadn't been Miss Drucilla's fault.

She would not think about it, and she would never mention it to Miss Drucilla. Instead, she would devote every minute of her day to serving this young lady who had changed her life with a few words. She would learn what she had to, all the strange ways of this great house.

She was quick and handy, always had been. Now she would learn to dress that waist-length red-gold hair that gleamed like a fine copper kettle; to care for those marvelous dresses, all lace and silk and brocade, and to mend and press them to perfection. But even so, how little to do for someone to whom she owed so much.

"Kitty, how nice you look." Drucilla was seated at her dressing table, and she turned when Kitty came into the room.

"Thank you, Miss," Kitty said.

She watched Miss Drucilla pick up a bottle of cologne and look at the label.

She hesitated, then said, "Something peculiar happened, when I was comin' out of Mrs. Kennicott's house. I met a lady—said she knew ye and wanted to talk to ye but not here at Peregrine Court."

"I don't understand. Did she give you her card?"

Kitty shook her head. "No, but she said to tell ye her name's Baxley, Elvira Baxley, and you'd remember."

The bottle of cologne dropped from Miss Drucilla's hand, shattering against the marble surface of the dressing table, filling the room with the scent of orange flowers.

Miss Drucilla had gone white as the cambric dressing gown she was wearing. Kitty ran to her side. "Are ye all right? Not havin' another one of them spells, are ye?"

Miss Drucilla tried to speak, but no words would come.

"I'll get someone," Kitty said. But Miss Drucilla caught her arm, holding her so tightly it hurt.

"No one," she whispered. "I'll be all right in a moment."

But there was stark, cold fear in her eyes. Kitty freed herself gently, got a hand towel, and cleaned up the spilled perfume and broken glass. She was nearly finished when Miss Drucilla asked, "Where does Mrs. Baxley want me to meet her, if not here?"

"Out on the Cliff Walk, she said. At the top of the Forty Steps. She said she'd be there at eleven o'clock tonight, and would wait 'til twelve."

Miss Drucilla's eyes had changed, the pupils widening until the blue-violet nearly disappeared. Her hands were pressed together tightly, as if she needed to hold herself in to keep from losing control. But when she spoke, her voice was steady enough.

"Very well, Kitty. And now my bath. You may as well learn the routine. Please lay out my dove-gray silk, the one with the lace insertions, and my amethyst earrings, and that pretty watch on the chain. I'll wear that instead of a necklace."

"Yer not goin', Miss. Surely yer not. I didn't like the looks of that woman one bit. Ye can't go out alone to the Cliff Walk to meet such a person."

"I have to, Kitty. Don't worry about me. Now, please start the bath."

"Miss, ye mustn't." Kitty's voice was a wail.

"I don't want to, but I have no choice. Mrs. Baxley is an old acquaintance of mine."

Kitty was mystified. How could Miss Drucilla know an old slut like that Baxley woman? What could they ever have had in common? She did not dare ask any more questions, not when she was so new on the job. But she couldn't let Miss Drucilla go traipsing around late at night with such a person. She didn't know Mrs. Baxley, true enough, but she'd had cause to know her kind often enough when she'd been living in the Five Points. Some were shoplifters, others ran crib houses for the sailors. Smarmy old bitches who'd turn on you and cut your throat for a dollar.

"Let me go with ye, then," Kitty said.

Miss Drucilla hesitated, as if weighing the suggestion. Then she shook her head. "No, Kitty. It's impossible. I must speak with her alone."

Kitty did not pursue the argument but went into the small bathroom that adjoined the bedroom and turned on one of the shining silver taps. A few hours ago, she would have been awestruck by the luxury of the room, with the big tub boxed in mahogany, the floor made of bright-colored bits of tile, laid together to form pictures of waves and rocks and ladies that were made like fish from the waist down, with green tails curving around the rocks. Even the water closet was paneled in mahogany.

But at the moment, Kitty's thoughts were elsewhere, for she was trying to figure out how to keep Miss Drucilla from coming to harm. She was afraid of the Baxley woman, that was for sure. But nothing was going to harm Miss Drucilla. Not if she could help it. She poured fragrant bath salts into the tub, and cudgeled her brain for a solution.

"Well, now, my dear, I didn't think I'd be seeing you again. And here, in this fine place." Mrs. Baxley nodded in the direction of Peregrine Court. She stood leaning her heavy bulk against the side of a wind-twisted tree that overhung the Cliff Walk. In the moonlight, Drucilla could barely make out her features, but in her mind's eye she could see the fat cheeks, the small dark eyes, the pursed lips. The voice was the same. Friendly, even ingratiating, but ready to turn nasty if she did not get what she wanted.

"How did you find me?"

"Why, Miss Reed—I'm sorry, Miss Tremayne it is, now, I saw your picture in the *New York World*, with a lot of other fancy ladies and gents, at a big ball. Given by the Belmonts, wasn't it? And I said to myself, 'that's the pretty red-haired girl used to live here. 'Til she went off with that big, handsome fellow.' I was that pleased, findin' out you'd done so well for yourself. And I thought you didn't have a cent, but there—you never know, do you?"

Drucilla was glad of the darkness that shadowed her face and helped to hide the tremor that ran through her.

"What do you want?" she demanded.

"Did I say I wanted anything? Came to congratulate you on your good fortune, that's all."

"Mrs. Baxley, I mustn't be away from the house too long. So you had best tell me what you want."

"You always did have a high-handed way about you," the landlady said. "I remember when I offered you a lead on work at that concert saloon, you turned up your nose like you was a grand duchess. Of course, I didn't know, at the time, who you really were. Tell me, how did you come to find youself in such a pass? Why didn't you ask your grandmother for . . ."

"That's none of your business. Now, if you've said all you have to say, please go. And don't come near here again."

"Oh, well, if you're going to take that tack." The voice was hard now. "Fact is, things ain't been going too well for me lately. What with the Panic and the banks closing, and all them people out of work, I haven't been having an easy time. So, seeing your picture in the paper, and learning of your good fortune, I thought I'd just come up to see you, and maybe you'd help me out a bit."

"Why should I?" Drucilla knew the answer, but she was determined to stand her ground, hoping that perhaps if she did not show fear, Mrs. Baxley would give way.

"Maybe your grandmother holds the purse strings—is that it, dear? Maybe if I was to go to her, tell her how I tried to help you out after you squandered your last penny, buyin' a dress for your little friend—Beth, wasn't it?—and paid for her funeral as well, she might be generous with a poor woman like me."

"No, you mustn't do that." Even though Charlotte Tremayne did not know the name of her dead granddaughter, her suspicions might be aroused if she heard about the two girls, both the same age, looking somewhat alike, and having lived in Mrs. Baxley's boardinghouse at the same time. Certainly, Mrs. Baxley was on the scent, although Drucilla could not guess how much she really knew. Still, she knew enough to come here to Newport.

Kevin had taken precautions, of course. Since he knew there was a record of Beth Cameron's imprisonment on Blackwell's Island, and a death certificate in that name, he had advised Drucilla to keep her own first name. But, if the Tremaynes' lawyers began an intensive investigation, what might they discover?

If only Kevin were here now, to help her. But, for

all she knew, he might have left Newport right after their quarrel. She had to play for time.

"I have very little money," Drucilla said. "My grandmother pays for my clothes, for everything. But I have jewelry."

She reached up and took the gold and amethyst earrings from her ears, and the gold watch from around her neck. Her hands were shaking, but she managed to control them, until she had put the jewelry in Mrs. Baxley's outstretched palm.

"There's now," the woman said, "I knew you'd be generous. It's only a loan, mind. Until business picks up again."

Mrs. Baxley chuckled, deep in her throat. Drucilla found the sound infuriating. "There are laws against blackmail, you know," she began.

"There's laws against lots of things, aren't there? Think of poor little Beth, hauled off to Blackwell's Island, because there was a bit of a row in that place where she was working."

The wind from the ocean below the Cliff Walk was getting stronger now, driving the clouds before it, so that the moonlight came and went, casting eerie shadows on the dark rocks, the twisted trees. Drucilla pulled her shawl up around her, but she knew that the chill she was feeling came from inside her.

"I'll get along now, dear. It was good seeing you again. For all you wasn't as friendly as you might have been. But, perhaps another time, you'll be in better humor."

"Another time?"

"Well, I do like to keep track of my boarders, especially when they've come up in the world like you. I'm downright proud of you."

The stout woman turned and made her way across the Cliff Walk and started up Narragansett Avenue. Drucilla looked after her, then hurried back to the house.

It was close to sunset, the next day, when Drucilla reined up her horse on the deserted stretch of beach off Bath Road and watched Kevin come toward her. Even after Kitty had taken him her note earlier that day and had reported back that he was, indeed, still at the hotel,

Drucilla had been afraid he might not keep their appointment. Now, seeing him moving with his light stride across the smooth sand, she felt a curious sense of hope; so long as he was here, he would make everything right, she was sure.

He came to her side and reached up and she put her hands on his shoulders; he swung her down beside him.

"I had hoped we'd both be out of Newport before something like this happened," he said. "The damned old harridan. How much did you admit to her?"

Not a word of greeting, not a gesture to indicate what had happened between them in the past. Only cold anger in the gray eyes, and the wide shoulders set a little forward, as if he wanted to charge on Mrs. Baxley herself. He led Drucilla to a small outcropping of sun-warmed rocks.

"I didn't tell Mrs. Baxley anything," Drucilla said. "But I'm sure she knows the truth—Kevin, what are we going to do?"

"I doubt she knows, but obviously she does have some strong suspicions, or she wouldn't have come here."

"What can we do? I gave her my jewelry, the few pieces I was wearing, but I . . ."

"You did what? Drucilla, that was stupid. Jewelry can be identified."

"I had no money. And . . ." She looked into his hard, implacable face. "I was so frightened."

"All right," he said more gently. "It can't be helped now. But she'll be back. A blackmailer always comes back, especially when the victim is as easily intimidated as you were."

"I never wanted any part of this scheme in the first place," she said. "It was your idea." Then, seeing him step away from her, she took his arm, her fingers pressing the rock-hard muscle; he was strong, and nothing frightened him. He had to help her.

"You won't go off and leave me to face this alone, will you?" If only she could have kept her voice steady.

He gave her a cold smile. "You still have the same high opinion of me, don't you?" Then he shrugged. "No, my dear, when they haul us off to prison, we'll go hand in hand."

"Don't, please. How can you joke about something so dreadful?" Her fear turned to anger. "Of course, you've been in prison before, so I suppose it holds no terrors for you."

He did not answer, but the look on his face frightened her and made her long to call back her words.

"Kevin, I'm sorry . . ." she began.

But he cut her off. "You don't understand a damn thing about it. Or about me. But then, it's been a long time since I looked for understanding in any woman. Or kindness." His thin-lipped mouth tightened. His eyes raked her. "What you had to offer you gave me, and most generously."

It wasn't true. She had had understanding to give, love and tenderness and loyalty. But it was always this way between them: he would lash out at her, and she would strike back.

He spoke evenly. "You won't go to prison, and neither will I, if you keep calm and don't lose control."

"But Mrs. Baxley will come back, she'll want more jewelry or money."

He looked away, staring out to sea. The water gleamed like metal in the light of the setting sun, and the clouds were pink and gold and salmon-colored. "I will take care of Mrs. Baxley. She'll make no more trouble for us."

"But how . . ."

"Leave that to me. As for you, I want you to go back to Peregrine Court and act as if nothing had happened. You pride yourself on your acting ability, don't you?"

He took her hand and led her back to her horse. He lifted her and she thought he was going to help her to mount, but instead, he pulled her against him, with a gesture more violent than tender, and his mouth covered hers. Her arms went around him, and she clung to him with all her strength.

But a moment later, he had lifted her into the saddle and stood looking up at her. "Don't be afraid," he said quietly. "You have more strength than you know, my love. It will carry you through whatever lies ahead."

It was as if a cold hand had reached out and touched her. She tried to read the expression in his eyes, but the light from the setting sun blinded her. He struck the horse's rump lightly, and the animal trotted off in the direction of Peregrine Court.

Nine

IN HER bedroom Drucilla was trying on the gown she would wear at the Harvest Ball. A harassed Kitty was helping her, while Charlotte Tremayne sat in a high-backed chair of dark green plush and mahogany, watching critically. Although she had agreed that Drucilla could have Kitty as her personal maid, the older woman made it plain that she still had many reservations about Kitty's aptitude for the position.

Kitty must have been well aware of this, for she was performing her duties with the utmost care, as though robing a princess for a state occasion. She arranged every fold of the honey-colored satin with precision, her pale green eyes narrowed in deep concentration.

"The color becomes you," Mrs. Tremayne said, nodding approval. "It sets off your hair." Then, all at once, she frowned and stood up. "What is to be done with your hair?"

"Is something wrong with it?" Drucilla asked.

"It must be arranged as you will have it the night of the ball," the old lady replied. "With the wreath." She turned to Kitty and demanded, "Why haven't you shown me the wreath?"

"It wasn't ready when I went to get the dress. The dressmaker told me those satin leaves had to be sent up special from New York City, and then sewed onto the band, along with all them pearls and . . . she promised to have it ready in time for the ball, though."

"I'm afraid that won't do." Mrs. Tremayne turned to Drucilla. "Kitty hasn't had any experience in dressing hair, certainly not for an occasion such as this. I must see her do your coiffure, with the wreath, so I can be sure it's right."

"But grandmother, Kitty has been doing my hair for the last two weeks."

"Not in a new coiffure. The wreath, you see, is to be intertwined with the curls." Her tone made it plain that she did not think Kitty could do this correctly.

Kitty, who had been kneeling, while she arranged the flounces of Mechlin lace that edged the skirt, stood up, her thin body tense, beads of perspiration across her upper lip. "If you please, Madame, I can go over to the dressmaker right now and try to get the wreath. If it isn't finished, I'll wait. I'm sure I can get her to hurry, when I tell her how important it is."

Somewhat mollified by the offer, Mrs. Tremayne said, "You had better go right away. Get one of the grooms to drive you."

"Oh, I can drive the trap myself, Madame. I used to do it all the time, back home."

"Very well," Mrs. Tremayne said. "Only hurry." And after Kitty had gone, she said to Drucilla, "The girl's willing enough, I'll say that for her. And she seems devoted to you."

"Indeed, she is," Drucilla said. "Please, do give her a chance, and don't frighten the wits out of her. I know she'll be a perfect lady's maid in no time at all."

"Very well," Mrs. Tremayne agreed, with an indulgent smile for Drucilla. "Now, I must go downstairs and speak with the caterer. He and his staff have just arrived from New York. And I want to explain how the flowers are to be arranged, too."

"Can't Edith see to that? You should not tire yourself."

Mrs. Tremayne laughed, her hazel eyes bright. "I'm not the least bit tired, my dear. Since you've come into this house, I feel twenty years younger."

Drucilla had to admit to herself that Mrs. Tremayne had changed since their first meeting. Although she still walked with a cane, she did not lean on it so heavily. She spoke with a sharp, decisive tone that belied her seventy-odd years, and there was new color in her faded cheeks, a new lift to her head.

"You look wonderful, grandmother, but I still think Edith could manage the details of the ball."

Mrs. Tremayne shook her head. "The Harvest Ball is special, a tradition here, and this one will be the most splendid of them all. There will be fireworks, and flowers —I do believe I've ordered enough to fill a greenhouse. And a masque to be performed in the topiary garden near the summerhouse. A perfect setting, don't you think so?"

But Drucilla was remembering the garden and the summerhouse and her meeting there with Kevin. She pictured, with unholy clarity, how their limbs had intertwined, how their bodies had clung, joined, and become one. The memory stirred in her brain, tormenting her, as she forced herself to listen to Mrs. Tremayne's glowing description of the masque. Such performances had been popular in Tudor England, the old lady was saying and, therefore, would be most suitable for Peregrine Court.

"The performers are coming from New York—all professionals. There will be special lighting and gorgeous costumes. All with the harvest motif, of course."

It occurred to Drucilla that Mrs. Tremayne would have been quite at home in Tudor England, as mistress of one of the great estates. "I do hope the evening is fine," she went on. "Otherwise, we will have to have the masque performed in the ballroom. It would be so much more charming outdoors."

Drucilla thought that, if Mrs. Tremayne could have managed it, she would have ordered clear skies and a full moon, along with the other decorations for the ball.

She smiled, and Mrs. Tremayne said, "You are pleased, my dear, aren't you? I know I will never be able to make it up to you for all those years of privation, but I will do all in my power to see that your future is a good one." She went to the door, then paused, saying, "Call me as soon as Kitty returns, no matter how late it may be. I must be sure she can do your hair properly."

It was after eleven in the evening when Kitty returned. Nevertheless, Mrs. Tremayne insisted on putting the maid through her paces. Not until she had arranged the coiffure three times over, with every curl in its correct place, and the wreath of russet and honey-colored satin leaves fastened just so, was Charlotte Tremayne satisfied.

The following morning, Drucilla arose early, awakened by the hammering of the carpenters, who were finishing the outdoor stage for the masque. Even after they had stopped, she could not get back to sleep. She moved about restlessly in the wide, canopied bed, thinking about tonight and the ball and what answer she was going to give to Radford.

He was in love with her, she was sure of that. Indeed, his possessive behavior, if she so much as smiled at another young man, made her a trifle uneasy. But he would be a good husband. Kind, protective, adoring.

She tried to picture herself as mistress of Seaton Barony. She had never been any farther south than Kentucky, but she could imagine the tall, white-pillared plantation house on a hill, at the end of a curving drive lined on either side with live oaks that trailed veils of Spanish moss, and the slow-moving yellow creek behind the house. But when she tried to imagine herself seated on the veranda with Radford by her side, the vision blurred. And when she tried to imagine what it would be like to share his bed, to surrender her body to him, to bear his children, she felt a sensation of coldness.

She thought of Kevin, his mouth claiming hers, before he had lifted her onto her horse, at the end of their last meeting. Kevin was not gentle as Radford was, not respectful, certainly not adoring. He was hard and selfish, and he could be cruel at times.

She understood the reasons for his harsh outlook on life, his cynicism, his brutality. He had been shaped by the terrible pressures of his early years, the famine in Ireland, his mother's death. Later, he had told her, he had spent a year in the British Navy. "Lord knows, their own seamen were not treated decently," he had said, "but being an Irishman, I was singled out for particular hell. I deserted when we made port in the West Indies. It was that, or I'd have smashed the skull of one of the officers and been hanged for it."

Another time, when she had asked him his reasons for leaving the Pinkerton Agency to go into business on his own, he had revealed an unexpected side of his character. "The work was interesting enough, and paid well. But when Pinkerton sent us to Pennsylvania to shoot down unarmed strikers who wanted no more than a living wage, I knew I had to quit." He had looked faintly embarrassed by his own scruples.

Would she ever understand Kevin? Then a bitter smile curved her lips, for she knew that it didn't matter whether he was good or bad, kind or cruel. He was hers. If she never saw him again, he would still be a part of her—always.

She turned and buried her face in her pillow, but sleep would not return, although it was still early. It was lucky that Charlotte Tremayne's room was at the opposite side of the house; Drucilla hoped that she had not been awakened by the carpenters.

She pushed back her blankets and got out of bed. She would not call Kitty to help her dress, for the poor girl must be worn out, after having made the trip to get the wreath, and then having to set and reset Drucilla's hair under Mrs. Tremayne's sharp scrutiny.

She stripped off her nightgown and stood for a few moments, letting the cool, salt air that blew in through the window caress her body. She ran her fingers lightly over the smooth skin of her high, rosy-tipped breasts, her slender hips and thighs. No man except Kevin had ever seen her this way. No other man had ever possessed her body. How could she give herself to Radford, with-

135

out loving him? How could she belong to anyone but Kevin?

She had to see him once more. She did not care about the risks now, there was no time to think of such things. She could go to him and tell him . . . what would she tell him? How could she make him understand?

"I'll find a way," she assured herself, and she went to the closet to find a dress. Nothing fancy. The lilac muslin would do, with a shawl over her shoulders.

Less than an hour later, she brought the surrey to a stop in front of the Aquidneck House, turned it over to the care of a hotel stableman, and went into the lobby. It was not yet seven, and the desk clerk was yawning behind the reservation desk.

"Please tell Mr. Kevin Farrell that Miss Tremayne wishes to speak to him here in the lobby. It is important."

"But, Miss Tremayne, I . . ."

"It's early, I know. But I must see Mr. Farrell at once."

The clerk shrugged. "I'm sorry. Mr. Farrell checked out late last night. He might have waited until noon today, and it wouldn't have cost him a penny more, but he was set on leaving."

Drucilla's fingers gripped the edge of the oak desk, as she struggled to keep calm.

"You're quite sure?"

"Yes, Miss." He consulted a slip of paper. "Here's a copy of his receipt. Checked out after midnight, last night."

"Did he leave a forwarding address?"

Once again, the clerk checked. "No, I'm afraid not."

"Thank you," she said and turning, she made herself walk slowly across the lobby, return to the surrey, and drive off.

Kevin was gone. He had left Newport without a word, without a good-bye. Perhaps he had gone West, or maybe he had left the country. Why not? Nothing to hold him now. She set her teeth, fighting the urge to cry, swallowing against the knot of pain in her throat.

Mechanically she guided the horse on the route back

to Bellevue Avenue. The early morning fog was wet against her cheeks and, even with her shawl around her, she found the damp air raw and penetrating. A stiff breeze blew in from the ocean below the Cliff Walk. She thought, vaguely, that after the wind had blown away the fog, it might be a fine day. And perhaps a beautiful, clear evening for the Harvest Ball.

She was close to Addisley Park, the estate of the Eastbourne family, when she became aware of the babble of many voices. A moment later, she saw the crowd lining the Cliff Walk. Everyone was peering over in the direction of the rocks, and several of the hardier ones were making their way down the steep side of the cliff. There were servants, wearing the maroon-and-gold Eastbourne livery, townspeople, and fishermen. She wanted to keep going, to get back to Peregrine Court and her room, to shut herself away and try to come to terms with the news of Kevin's departure. But the horse slowed, then came to a halt, and tossed his head, nickering nervously in the midst of the crowd.

She heard a young girl, in a maroon dress with a white apron over it, saying, "Horrible. Never seen nothin' like it. Poor woman must have been goin' along the Cliff Walk and lost her footing on them slippery stones."

And a man, big and heavy-set, also wearing the Eastbourne colors, said, "I sent Jeff to the stable for a blanket to cover the poor soul. He'd best shake a leg if he knows what's good for 'im."

"When do you think it happened?" the maid asked.

"Sometime during the night. Couple of them fishermen saw the body at first light."

"Awful thing," the maid said. "But she should've known better, a stout old lady like that clamberin' around by herself."

It was as if a cold hand brushed Drucilla's face. She leaned over the side of the surrey and asked the heavy-set man, "Who was she? Does anyone know?"

He looked up, startled. "No, Miss—she's not from our place, and none of the townspeople know her, either." Then he added politely, "I'll help you get your horse through this crowd, if you like."

"Not yet. But could you hold him for me, please?"

And without waiting for an answer, she climbed down over the side of the surrey and moved into the crowd.

She pushed her way through the crowd lining the Cliff Walk and began the treacherous descent to the rocks. Few women were equally daring; mostly, the men were going down. One young man in a stained blue workshirt and jeans reached out and gave her a hand.

The bottom of her lilac skirt was soaked and her kidskin slippers were ruined, but she hardly noticed.

"Don't look, Miss. It's a nasty sight for a lady to see . . . " the young man was saying but she ignored him.

She was not conscious of his further warnings or of the excited chatter of the people around her. She was only aware of the face that was turned up to the sky, the familiar face with its heavy jowls, small, pursed mouth, heavy eyebrows. And the fat, shapeless body in the black bombazine dress. Mrs. Baxley. The skin of her face and hands cut and bruised from the fall down to the rocks, the graying hair plastered against the scalp with dried blood.

Drucilla pressed a clenched fist against her mouth, to stifle the scream that was rising from her throat. Mrs. Baxley's face, her dress, even her jet earrings were crusted with salt spray.

She was pushed aside, with the others, when the big heavy-set man in the maroon livery came down the steep incline carrying a coarse blanket. He covered the body, pulling the blanket up over the face. "The police have been sent for," he remarked to no one in particular. "They should be down here, soon."

Drucilla made her way back to the top of the Cliff Walk, where someone had fastened the horse's reins around a wind-stunted tree. She got back into the surrey, brought the whip down with more force than usual, and the animal moved forward at a trot, while people scattered to either side of the avenue.

She heard a few of the men swear in protest, but she did not look back. She had to reach Peregrine Court, quickly, because she could feel the waves of panic licking at the edges of her mind, and she was sure she could not keep control much longer.

It was as if she drove through some landscape in a nightmare, terrifying, unfamiliar. The "cottages," massive buildings of brick and stone and marble, were dim, threatening shapes.

Mrs. Baxley was dead. A greedy old woman, cold and unscrupulous, but she had not deserved to die. Not that way. Murdered. For the first time, she let the thought come, for there was no holding it back. Murdered by Kevin Farrell.

Above the sound of the wind and the waves breaking against the rocks, she heard Kevin's words during their last meeting.

"I will take care of Mrs. Baxley. She'll make no more trouble for us."

She pulled the horse to a stop and bowed her head over the reins, as wave after wave of nausea racked her.

Then the spasms passed, leaving her weak and drained.

Kevin, whom she had loved and trusted. She had given herself to a murderer. But she was not without guilt, either, for she had agreed to his scheme, driven by the weaknesses in her own character. By her passion and her desire for wealth and position. True, she had tried to talk him out of the scheme, but now she found herself asking whether she had been motivated by a sense of right and wrong or by fear. Perhaps Kevin's icy recklessness had been the only real difference between them.

She had to be alone, to think things through, to decide what she must do now. But even after she had returned to Peregrine Court and climbed the stairs to her bedroom, she found that this was not to be. Kitty was waiting in her room, her thin, freckled face anxious.

"Miss Drucilla, thank goodness yer back. Yer grandmother isn't up yet. Where have ye been?"

"I can't talk about it—not now. Please leave me alone, Kitty."

"Are ye sick?"

She shook her head. "Just leave me alone," she repeated.

Kitty hesitated, then nodded. "Yes, Miss. When yer ready for breakfast, ring and I'll be right up with it."

"No breakfast."

"A nice cup of tea, then." She looked at Drucilla more closely. "Yer dress is soaked at the hem, and yer shoes. Here, now, let me get them off. Please. Or yer liable to take cold."

Drucilla let Kitty help her off with her dress and shoes, to get her into a robe and slippers.

But after Kitty had left the room, Drucilla was still unable to think clearly. She knew only that Kevin had murdered Mrs. Baxley and had gone off alone. She sought for possible alternatives. Could Mrs. Baxley's death have been an accident? Perhaps the woman had been roaming around on the Cliff Walk in the dark and had slipped on the wet, slick rocks. Why would she have been out there, unless she planned to meet someone? No, not someone—Kevin Farrell.

He had been clever enough to meet her away from Peregrine Court, far down at the other end of Bellevue Avenue, opposite the Eastbourne estate. Perhaps he had lured her there by promising to pay her off in exchange for her silence.

Drucilla closed her eyes, but she could not shut out the pictures that formed behind the tightly pressed lids. Mrs. Baxley, waiting, and Kevin, walking up behind her with his light, pantherlike step. And pushing her over the edge of the cliff, down onto the rocks below. Kevin, returning to the Aquidneck House and checking out.

"Late last night," the clerk had said. "He could have waited until noon today, and it wouldn't have cost him a penny more, but he was set on leaving."

He would know well enough how to cover his tracks. A freight train west, perhaps, or down to New York, and a ship bound for Europe, or even the Far East.

She wanted to hate him, but she could not. She, too, was guilty. She had fallen in with his scheme, knowing from that first evening on the height overlooking the Hudson, when he had spoken of passing her off as the

Tremayne heiress, that it was wrong. But she had been swept away by her love for him and had not had the will to refuse.

Now, forced to be brutally honest with herself, she knew that not only love had caused her to agree to the plan. She had wanted money, security, position. These last months, here in Newport, had given her everything she had ever daydreamed about, as a child, back at the County Farm, as a chambermaid in the hotel in Cincinnati, and later, touring with the stock company. Always, she had believed in some secret place in her mind that she was destined for something better.

And now, because of her daydreams and desires, a woman was dead. Not a good woman, certainly. Small-minded, greedy, bullying. But Mrs. Baxley had not deserved to die in that horrible way.

While Drucilla lay across the bed, her robe half-open, her hair falling loosely about her face, the morning fog lifted, and the September sunlight came streaming into the room. She found it obscene that she should be lying here, in this luxurious, high-ceilinged room, with its velvet drapes and great canopied bed, its thick rug and marble-topped dressing table, while Mrs. Baxley's body lay under a coarse gray blanket on jagged black rocks. Or had the police come by now and taken it away?

She heard the voices of the servants from the garden below her window. They were going on with the preparations for the Harvest Ball, as if nothing unusual had happened. The news of the death might have reached them by now, but they would not be overly concerned; neither, she imagined, would the owners of the "cottages" along Bellevue Avenue. Attempts had already been made to close off the Cliff Walk not only to tourists but to the townspeople of Newport. Now they could point out that the Cliff Walk held dangers for those who were not familiar with it.

"No, not there. Get it higher." She recognized the voice of the gardener, and she rose and went slowly over to the window. She leaned on the sill and watched him and a helper fastening a string of lanterns between the two trees.

She could not bear it any longer. And she certainly could not face the Harvest Ball tonight. How could she dance in a gown of honey-colored satin and lace, when only a few hours ago she had learned of Kevin's desertion and of Mrs. Baxley's murder?

She went to the closet and, after a few minutes of frantic searching, she dragged out her old carpetbag. It had been pushed all the way to the back of the closet, behind the row of fine silk and satin and brocade dresses.

She took one of the dresses, the first that came to hand, folded it and put it into the carpetbag. Then, crossing to the dresser, she found underclothing, cambric chemises and drawers, and a nightgown, all neatly ironed and folded by Kitty. She stuffed them in on top of the dress. She would take no jewelry, nothing valuable. She had no right to the Tremayne jewelry.

She would get away from Newport as quickly as she could. After that she would make plans. Perhaps she could find the stock company of which she had been a member back in Ohio. Or maybe she would head west to the mining camps. It wasn't important. She would find work someplace and until then . . .

She started violently when she heard the familiar, firm knock at the door. A moment later, Charlotte Tremayne was in her bedroom, dressed in a smart morning costume of blue-gray silk, her white hair piled on her head with the usual neatness and precision, every wave in place. But there was a worried frown between her brows.

"Kitty said you did not have any breakfast," she began. Then she stopped short, and stared at the open carpetbag on the bed, the white camisole in Drucilla's hands.

"What on earth are you doing?"

"I'm leaving. I was going to write you a note."

Charlotte Tremayne went to her and drew her down on the edge of the bed, then pulled up a chair directly in front of her.

"Now, suppose you explain what this is all about."

"I can't stay here any longer."

"But surely you must have some reason." Then she smiled. "It's because of Radford's proposal, isn't it? I had not thought you were the sort of girl to panic over a proposal. If you don't wish to marry him, tell him so. Or, better still, say you need time to make your decision."

"I've made my decision. I can't go to the ball, and I won't speak to Radford at all."

Mrs. Tremayne's eyes flashed, and her head went up. "Were you planning to leave a note for him, also?" she demanded.

Drucilla had not even thought about that, for the shock of discovering what Kevin had done had wiped all thoughts of Radford from her mind.

"Such conduct is unworthy of you," Charlotte Tremayne said. "Your mother was a weak, impulsive creature, but you are different. Remember, you are a Tremayne."

"Yes, of course. A Tremayne." She felt hysterical laughter welling up, and she tried to hold it back, but without success.

"I fail to see what I have said to amuse you. You are a Tremayne, no matter what your mother was."

Drucilla realized that her cheeks were wet, and she wiped her eyes absently with the back of her hand.

"Isobel wasn't my mother. I'm not a Tremayne."

The room was very quiet. She became aware of the sounds of hammering from the garden below, the voices of the servants making preparations for tonight.

"Do you know what you are saying?"

The old lady's cheeks had gone pale, and her whole body recoiled, as if from a blow.

"Dear Lord," Drucilla thought, "why did I tell her? And in this way? Such a shock at her age . . ."

But after a long pause, Charlotte Tremayne recovered her balance—to a degree. Although her voice was unsteady, her eyes did not flinch but met Drucilla's squarely.

"Go on," she said. "Tell me all of it."

"I lied. I needed money, and I got the chance to pretend I was your granddaughter, and I took it." She remembered what Kevin had said to her that afternoon in his room at the Aquidneck House. "You're not cut out for the role of an adventuress." And he had warned

143

her that she had better marry Radford and get away from Peregrine Court, before she broke down and confessed.

She would not involve Kevin; he deserved it, but she could not, even now, be the instrument of his downfall. She refused to ask herself why this was so.

"But the photographs," Charlotte Tremayne was saying. "And Isobel's jewelry. Where did you get them?"

Drucilla said, "You still want to believe I'm your granddaughter. But it's no use. I can't go on deceiving you any longer. I knew your granddaughter, her name was Beth. She left me those family photographs and the pawn tickets for the jewelry."

Mrs. Tremayne closed her eyes for a moment, then opened them again, and said, "My granddaughter is dead, then."

Drucilla nodded, too miserable to speak.

"You were a close friend? Yes, I suppose you must have been, since she left you her possessions."

"Yes, a close friend."

"And Kevin Farrell?"

"He believes I am your granddaughter. She had just died when he came to the place where we had been living. I had no money, nowhere to go, and—I thought it would hurt no one if I pretended to be the girl he was searching for. Those photographs and the jewelry helped to convince him."

Mrs. Tremayne's eyes were hot with anger. "I should have known. That first time I spoke with you, you said certain things that made me wonder, but I needed to believe you were Horace's daughter. You don't understand, do you? You're filled with your own sense of guilt right now. But I have had to live with guilt for many years. And you gave me a chance to make restitution. Now, you have taken that chance away."

"I . . . was desperate. I didn't mean to hurt you. I only . . . but I don't expect you to understand. You can't imagine how people like me have to live."

"Suppose you tell me. Who are you, really?"

"My name is Drucilla Reed. My father was Asa Reed.

He was a schoolmaster in Ohio. My mother died when I was born. . . ."

She went on to tell Charlotte Tremayne about her early years, about the County Farm, and the hotel in Cincinnati, and the stock company she had toured with. But when she got to the part about Beth, she knew she would have to lie. She had hoped she might be through with lies, but she had hurt Charlotte Tremayne too much already.

"Beth had consumption, like her mother," Drucilla said. "But she did not suffer at the end. Believe that. She only grew weaker day by day until one evening she fell asleep and never woke up again."

Charlotte Tremayne made a short, strangled sound and pressed her handkerchief to her lips. "And was buried in potter's field, no doubt. My granddaughter, Horace's child, is lying in a nameless grave."

Drucilla reached out and put a hand on the older woman's arm. "No. You must not think that. It isn't true. Beth is buried in Greenwood Cemetery. I couldn't put up a fine headstone, as you would have done, but she did have a decent burial. I bought her a white silk dress, because white was her favorite . . ."

Drucilla swallowed, struggling to control herself.

"I find it hard to believe that a girl in your circumstances would have spent her savings on such things."

"I suppose you do. Now that you know about me, you must think I am different from you, from all these fine people here on Bellevue Avenue. But let me tell you this: I'm not ashamed of my family. My mother was a preacher's daughter, and my father was an educated man, a good man. I'm only ashamed of myself, for disgracing him this way. He would have been shocked by the things I've done. But—he would have tried to understand, because that's the kind of man he was—"

Then, remembering that she was in no position to lose her temper, she said quietly, "If you'll let me leave, I'll never trouble you again. If you want me to, I'll sign a paper saying I'm no relation of yours."

"And where will you go?"

"Why should you care? Now that you know I'm nothing to you."

"That's not quite true."

Drucilla looked at her blankly.

"These weeks you've been here at Peregrine Court you have come to mean a great deal to me. You have given me the drive to pick up the threads of my life, to open my house to people, to go out into company again. You have brought youth and beauty and warmth into a house that had become a mausoleum." She smiled ruefully. "I'm not feeling sorry for myself. I was alone, but that was my doing. I broke up Horace's marriage. I was so sure I was doing the right thing. I was always so sure I was right. Now I know better. If not for me, Horace might be alive today."

"I don't understand," Drucilla said.

"That first afternoon you came here, you told me that your father—that Horace never came to look for Isobel after she ran away. But you were wrong, Drucilla. He stayed here for a few weeks, drinking himself into a stupor. Yes, he drank heavily. He had been doing so since his college days.

"But that time, after he sobered up, he went to find his wife. I tried to stop him, but I couldn't. He wrote to me from California, telling me that he had found her, that she was carrying his child. He wanted to bring her home. But she would not return here. They quarreled, and he started drinking again. A few weeks after the letter from Horace, I received another, this time from a priest in Sacramento. He informed me that my son had gotten into a brawl, in one of the saloons there. He was stabbed to death."

Drucilla understood what it was costing Charlotte Tremayne to tell her such things. "I'm so sorry," she said. "I didn't know."

"That's right, you didn't. But my granddaughter would have known."

"Perhaps Isobel didn't tell her."

"Perhaps. I tried to believe that. But there were other things. You said your mother had seen to it that you got a proper education, even though you were touring with a theatrical company. That she bought books for you. That did not sound like the Isobel I knew. She cared nothing for books. She often said that a pretty face and a good figure were all any girl needed."

"But you accepted me as your granddaughter."

"I wanted to believe you were." She smiled sadly. "There are times when we disregard what our reason tells us, because of other, stronger needs."

Drucilla thought about Kevin. She had known the kind of man he was, but she had shut her eyes and followed him blindly into this disaster.

But perhaps it was not too late to salvage something from the wreckage. Her freedom, at least.

"I know I've no right to ask for any consideration from you now, but if you will only let me go, I'll never trouble you again."

"I'm afraid it isn't that easy."

Charlotte Tremayne was set on prosecuting her, then. She would be charged with fraud and sent to prison. No more than she deserved but, nevertheless, fear, like a thick strangling fog, began to smother her. She wanted to beg for mercy, but the words would not come. She still had the remnants of her pride.

"Are you going to send for your lawyer now?"

"Mr. Pollock? What on earth would I want with him?" She shook her head. "No, Drucilla. No one will have to know the truth—if you will do exactly as I say."

Ten

"YOU WILL stay here at Peregrine Court, as my granddaughter," Charlotte Tremayne said quietly. "And tonight you will go to the Harvest Ball, exactly as we planned."

Drucilla, completely bewildered, said, "But I've just told you about myself. How can you possibly want me to stay?"

"You have told me more than you know." She gave Drucilla an enigmatic little smile. "You will do as I say. As for Radford's proposal, you must, of course, do as you think best. You do know my feelings, however."

"Why are you doing this?" Drucilla demanded. Then her eyes widened. "It's because you don't want another disgrace in the family, another open scandal, isn't it?"

"You are a suspicious young lady. Perhaps you're not entirely wrong, though. When Isobel ran away from my son, after less than a year of marriage, the gossips in Newport had a field day. And, although no one except Mr. Pollock knows all the circumstances surrounding Horace's death, there was a good deal of speculation at the time. No, I should not care to see the name of

Tremayne dragged through the newspapers again."

Drucilla nodded. "I understand," she began, but Mrs. Tremayne interrupted her.

"Do you? I think not. There is something else, far more important than my dislike for scandal, that makes me want you to stay. Don't you realize that I've become fond of you during the months you've been living here?"

"But surely, you can't be fond of me now that you know I'm an impostor."

"But you're not an impostor any longer. I know who you are. You've told me the truth. And, if you hadn't made your confession now, you'd have done it another time."

"How can you be so sure?"

"I've met a few adventuresses in my day. Lola Montez—a great beauty, but with no more moral sense than a cat. Mrs. Frank Leslie, divorced from her first husband and married again. And likely to repeat the process a few more times, unless I miss my guess. And those sisters, Victoria Woodhull and Tennessee Clafin. They have old Commodore Vanderbilt eating out of their hands, with their mystical mumbo-jumbo. Psychics, indeed. Adventuresses, one and all. But you—" Mrs. Tremayne shook her head. "You're far too impulsive, Drucilla, too much the romantic to make a first-class adventuress. And you have a sense of right and wrong. That's enough to disqualify you at once."

Was there a trace of amusement in the hazel eyes, peering at her from under those drooping, wrinkled lids?

Charlotte Tremayne stood up. "Now, ring for your maid and have some tea, or better yet, a good solid breakfast, if you're up to it. This will be a long day, and an even longer night."

"Mrs. Tremayne, what can I say?"

"You can, for pity's sake, stop calling me Mrs. Tremayne. You've been calling me 'grandmother' all these weeks, and I've grown used to it."

In later years, when Drucilla looked back and remembered the night of the Harvest Ball, her memories would always be vague and confused. She would be able to isolate small, vivid pictures in her mind, but there would be many blanks. . . .

She would remember the big golden moon, round and full, suspended between heaven and earth. Dozens of twinkling lanterns were strung between the trees.

Chrysanthemums, asters and bittersweet, in huge gilded baskets. Festoons of purple grapes draped over arbors constructed especially for the ball. Gilt-dusted sheaves of wheat and ears of corn.

She would recall the miniature theater that had been constructed near the summerhouse in the topiary garden. The actors moving through the elaborate masque, to the music of an orchestra that played appropriate Renaissance music. All the performers had been transported from New York, along with scenery and costumes, for this one night.

And Radford beside her, an elegant figure in his suit of black broadcloth, with narrow trousers, an embroidered plum-colored waistcoat, a fine ruffled shirt.

She would remember the fireworks, showers of silver and gold, green and purple. And Radford's arm around her, his eyes looking down into her upturned face.

"You promised me an answer tonight, Drucilla. You haven't forgotten, have you?"

She shook her head. He drew her closer still as another display of fireworks burst into a rainbow shower overhead. She turned away, her eyes dazzled by the glare, and saw in her mind the face of Kevin Farrell. Gray eyes under dark heavy brows. Hard, thin-lipped mouth, curved in his characteristic smile, sardonic, knowing.

Radford turned her back to face him. His voice was soft, urgent. "Please say you'll marry me. I can make you happy, I know I can."

"Say 'yes'," she thought, "and let him kiss you and, in a little while, he'll take you away from Newport, away from the memories of Kevin—and of Mrs. Baxley's body, sprawled on the rocks below the Cliff Walk. Away to a place called Seaton Barony, where it is always warm, the air soft and fragrant. Where you will be secure and safe. A new beginning. A new life, and the old Drucilla gone forever."

"Say it," he pleaded. Another explosion, and the sky blazing with green and gold. "Say it," he repeated.

"Yes," she heard herself saying. "I'll be your wife, Radford."

Then the trip back to New York City, the tall, narrow townhouse in the fashionable Murray Hill section reopened, and Charlotte Tremayne, in her glory, making plans, elaborate preparations for the wedding, to be held at Grace Church, and the reception.

The smiling guests, many of whom Drucilla remembered from Newport. Theodora Seaton, an imposing figure in mauve-colored glacé silk, heavy with braid and shiny bugling. And Radford's sisters, plain, spinsterish Gwen, and shy Hazel, embracing her, telling her how happy they were to have her as one of the family.

Charlotte Tremayne, in dove-gray satin, saying, "You will come to Newport next summer, my dear." The hazel eyes bright with unshed tears, the cool, wrinkled hand touching her cheeks for a moment. "Of course, grandmother," Drucilla said. Impulsively, she put her arms around the old lady. "I love you, grandmother," she said.

The dock was a bustle of activity, with trunks being loaded aboard the *Gryphon*, the coastal steamboat that was to take Radford and Drucilla from New York to Charleston. Bands played and banners waved and snapped in the crisp fall breeze. Theodora Seaton and her daughters had come to see the newly married pair off, but they planned to remain in New York for a few weeks longer, to replenish their wardrobes for the coming winter season. Even Theodora admitted that there was no place in Charleston to compare with New York's fashionable Ladies' Mile.

Once aboard the boat, Drucilla was impressed by the opulence of her surroundings: the carved and brightly painted figurehead that stretched out from the gilded bow, the gilt eagles balancing on golden balls, atop slim white pillars on the forward decks, the enormous crystal chandeliers that hung from the ceiling of the dining salon, which was two decks high and surrounded by galleries.

After an elaborate dinner of several courses, for which Drucilla found she had little appetite, Radford led the way to the upper deck.

"The bridal suite," he said, opening the door of their stateroom. "I trust you'll find it to your liking."

Then, seeing the flush that rose to her cheeks, he added tactfully, "I believe I would like a stroll on deck, before I retire. I'll join you shortly, dear."

Inside the cabin, Drucilla found a wide-eyed Kitty, admiring the new surroundings. Besides an oversized bed, there was a chaise lounge, covered in plum-covered velvet, matching velvet drapes, white enameled walls, and gilt pillars decorated with raised flowers of boiserie.

"I never saw a ship so fine," Kitty said, as she helped Drucilla into her white silk nightgown, then took the pins from her hair and brushed it into red-gold waves.

"Mr. Seaton's a lucky man," Kitty said, before she started for the door, leaving Drucilla in the wide bed, propped up against the pillows.

"Are your quarters comfortable?" Drucilla asked.

"Oh, yes. They're down in the ladies' cabin." She sighed with pleasure. "Good wool blankets and soft linen," she added. "Not like steerage."

After Kitty was gone, Drucilla let herself be lulled by the motion of the ship. Her eyelids were growing heavy, beginning to close. . . .

Then Radford came into the stateroom, and walked swiftly to the bed. Bending, he kissed her, and she felt his hands, warm and seeking, through the thin layer of silk that covered her body.

She pulled away and drew the sheet up under her chin with a swift, instinctive gesture. Radford smiled indulgently.

"I'm your husband, remember?"

She tried to free herself, but his arm imprisoned her. She put her hands against his shoulders and pushed him away. She heard his quick, irregular breathing.

He was drawing the nightgown down from her shoulders, but he stopped when she made a small, wordless sound of protest. "Please, don't be angry," she began.

"I could never be angry with you," he said, cupping her face in his hands. He kissed her again, his mouth warm and ardent. Then he turned, put out the lamp, and in the darkness she heard him moving about.

A little while later, he was beside her. She tried to force her unwilling body to respond, but she could not. Radford was a kind, courteous stranger. While Kevin . . . But she dared not think about Kevin.

She shut her eyes and heard Radford saying, "I'll be gentle, my love."

She went hot with shame and self-loathing when she realized that he attributed her complete lack of response to virginal modesty.

Gradually, his hunger for her overcame his patience, and she, completely unready, cried out in pain. Afterward, she thought that perhaps, from Radford's point of view, it had been just as well. Better that he should think her frightened, inexperienced, than that he should have the least suspicion of the truth.

The *Gryphon* moved swiftly down the coastline, her coal engines throbbing, then stopped to take on passengers at Baltimore. So far, the days had been pleasant, and Drucilla had steeled herself for the nights. If Radford was disappointed by her lack of passion, he said nothing.

Then, two nights after the boat had steamed out of the harbor at Baltimore, a dance was held, and she and Radford were joined by one of his acquaintances from Charleston, who was also returning home to South Carolina.

"This is Ian Mackintosh," Radford said. It was plain to Drucilla that the appearance of a third person at their table was not particularly welcome; and she also sensed that theirs was only a business relationship.

Mackintosh was not a particularly handsome man; he had a long, craggy face and small russet eyes, but he was well-dressed and self-assured. In his early thirties, Drucilla guessed.

"Mr. Mackintosh has a scheme for building cotton mills in the western part of our state," Radford told her.

"It's more than a scheme now, Mrs. Seaton." He looked quite proud of himself. "A bit more capital, and I'll be ready to start building in November."

"Congratulations," Radford said. "Although I'm not sure the mills are the best thing for our state. True, they give employment to the poor whites, who are grubbing away on a few miserable, worn-out acres, but, in the long run, mills and factories will change the South, and not for the better."

"Do you agree, Mrs. Seaton?" Although he appeared to be interested in her opinion, Drucilla saw that he was very much aware of her as a woman.

The bodice of her apple green satin dress was cut very low, and the delicate black lace trimming did little to conceal the curves of her breasts. The width of the skirt, with its billowing overskirt of black lace, emphasized her waistline.

Kitty had had some difficulty lacing her into the dress, and they had both laughed, agreeing that she must not sample all the delicacies served on the ship.

Now she felt uneasy under Mr. Mackintosh's scrutiny, for she was remembering how angry Radford had been, back in Newport, when she had gone to the musicale with another man. She hoped he would not notice the frank admiration in Mackintosh's eyes.

But Radford was still concerned with business matters.

"I might invest in those mills of yours," he was saying, "but only if I could be sure the workers earned decent wages."

"They do well enough," Mackintosh assured him. "I'll go as high as fifty cents a day for a child, and give an experienced hand a dollar fifty. But I'm afraid we are boring Mrs. Seaton with all this talk."

"No, indeed," Drucilla said. "I know so little about

South Carolina, and since it is to be my home, I am most eager to learn more."

The orchestra began a waltz, and Mr. Mackintosh bowed and asked her for the pleasure of the dance. Radford was looking displeased, she thought, but he smiled courteously as they went out onto the floor.

Mr. Mackintosh was an adequate dancer and a far better talker. He was full of interesting information about Charleston and the rest of the state.

"Our own holdings were nothing like those of the Seatons," he said. "No royal charter for the Mackintosh clan. Fact is, my grandfather was an indentured servant, down in Barbados. He built his fortune with his own hard work, and that of his sons. But I grew up on a good-sized plantation. Nothing like Seaton Barony—but fine, rich acres all the same. We were burned out during the war. Now, I've turned my hand to other fields of endeavor."

"Your mills?"

"That's right. If we'd had our own mills during the war, instead of having to try to run our cotton through the Yankee blockade . . ."

The orchestra gathered speed for the finale of the waltz, and, to her surprise, Drucilla realized that she was getting dizzy and quite breathless. For a moment, the salon appeared to be whirling around, and the chandeliers overhead blurred. Her gloved hand, resting on Mr. Mackintosh's shoulder, tightened convulsively.

"Are you all right?" he asked.

"Could we stop, please? The motion of the ship— I'm not used to it."

Or perhaps, she thought privately, Kitty had laced her too tightly.

"Perhaps a stroll on deck would help," Mr. Mackintosh said. "The sea air is most refreshing."

He was right. The damp, salty breeze and the darkness made her feel better almost at once. A sliver of a moon cast soft, welcome shadows.

He took her arm and they strolled along the deck, passing other couples, ladies in brocade and satin, gentlemen in fine broadcloth.

"My husband told me that Seaton Barony was burned during the war, as your home was," she said.

"But the Barony has been rebuilt. I hope you will be happy there, although I should think Charleston would be more agreeable for a young lady. Seaton Barony is isolated. It is surrounded by swamps and perhaps you will find it a little lonely."

"We plan to spend our summers in Newport, with my grandmother," Drucilla said, but nonetheless, she was a little depressed at the picture Mr. Mackintosh painted.

Once more she began to feel dizzy. She had always enjoyed superb health; even back at the County Farm, where so many children had sickened and died, she had escaped illness. She must speak to Kitty about tight lacing.

She started to speak, then swayed slightly. Mr. Mackintosh stopped and put his arm around her waist. "Your first time at sea?"

"Yes. But I don't understand why . . ."

"It takes people this way, sometimes. Nothing to worry about."

"I'd like to go back to the ballroom," she said. She would explain to Radford that she wasn't feeling well.

But Mr. Mackintosh did not take his arm away; instead, he held her more tightly. "Not yet," he was saying. "It isn't often I have the chance to be alone with such a lovely lady. You are very beautiful."

He drew her close, and she caught the smell of brandy. He must have had a little too much to drink. Not wanting to create a scene, she said quietly, "Please don't say any more."

But a moment later, she heard a harsh sound. His arm slackened, and she saw Radford, his face taut with anger, his eyes blazing.

"Let go of her."

"I felt a little dizzy, and Mr. Mackintosh was only trying to help," she began. Some of the other passengers had stopped to stare.

"Be quiet," Radford ordered, in a voice he had never

used to her before. "Go back to the stateroom. At once."

"See here, Seaton," Mr. Mackintosh began uneasily. "Your wife has just explained what happened."

"I heard what you were saying to her."

If Ian Mackintosh had been a little the worse for brandy, he was completely sober now and obviously uneasy. There was something frightening, unnatural, in Radford's cold fury.

"I apologize to you, and to your wife," he said. He turned to go, but Radford's hand closed on his shoulder, and he swung him around. "We will be putting into Norfolk tomorrow morning," Radford said. "We will go ashore then, and settle our business there."

"Dueling has been outlawed for a number of years, and I refuse to take part in any such charade."

"As you wish."

Drucilla was relieved, but only for a moment. Radford unbuttoned his coat, flung it to the deck, and threw himself on Ian Mackintosh. The other man tried to fend him off, but the attack had been too swift. She heard the sickening sound of fists on flesh and bone and saw blood spurting down the white, ruffled shirtfront, as Ian Mackintosh was hurled against the rail.

A woman screamed, a couple of the men came forward to intervene. Nausea swept through her, and she tried to take a deep breath.

Then a short, stocky man in uniform was beside them. The captain.

"We'll have no brawling on my boat." But Radford shoved the captain aside and lunged at Ian Mackintosh again. It wasn't until the captain shouted an order to a couple of his officers, who appeared out of the darkness and flanked Radford, one on either side, that the young man was subdued. Mr. Mackintosh was bleeding freely from his nose, and his lip was split.

"You'd best go to your cabin, sir," the captain said. "One of the passengers is a doctor. I'll send him to attend you."

"Never mind," Ian Mackintosh said shortly, pressing his handkerchief to his face. "I'm leaving as soon as we dock tomorrow morning. I'll continue my journey by train. In the meantime, keep this madman away from me."

The captain nodded. Then, turning to Drucilla, who clung to the railing for support, he asked gently, "Are you all right, ma'am?"

The nausea was getting worse, and the dizziness, but she managed to say, "Yes," and then she turned and fled to the upper deck, to the sanctuary of her stateroom.

Kitty, who had been laying out a freshly pressed night-gown and robe, turned to look at her. "I didn't expect ye back from the dance so soon." Then, pale green eyes widening with alarm, "Are ye all right?"

"Unlace my stays—quickly—" Drucilla began. But before Kitty could obey, she was at the basin, leaning over, clutching the sides of the washstand, her body wracked with a spasm of nausea.

Kitty put an arm around her for support, and, when the distressing episode had passed, the maid helped her off with her dress and loosened her stays, saying, "I never should have laced ye so tight, ma'am. I'll let out the waist of the dress as soon as I've got ye comfortable."

"Don't worry about it, Kitty," Drucilla said. Kitty soaked a handkerchief in cologne and pressed it to Drucilla's temples. "It's so good to have you here," Drucilla said. "You are always there when I need you. Remember that first time, at the Aquidneck House . . ."

The first time. The afternoon with Kevin, when the rain had lashed against the windows, and he had held her and. . . .

Somewhere in the back of her mind, an unwelcome, a frightening thought stirred to life and would not be put aside.

"Kitty—maybe it wasn't the tight lacing that made me sick."

And it could not have been the fight between Radford and Mr. Mackintosh either, for she had been feeling dizzy before that.

Kitty put a firm, work-hardened palm against Drucilla's forehead.

"No fever. Maybe you've had too much of that fancy food."

"I ate very little today." Indeed, she remembered now that at breakfast, faced with the enormous "steamboat breakfast" of beefsteak, piles of buckwheat cakes swimming in butter and syrup, ham, sausage, fried potatoes, and hot biscuits, she had begun to feel queasy, and had taken only coffee.

Now, she went back over the past weeks, counting, calculating. It could not be so. It must not be so.

But suppose it had happened, that night in the summerhouse. Or the rainy afternoon in Kevin's hotel room. All those times when she had come to him on the warm tide of desire, had given herself with a hunger that matched his own. Now, she might be carrying his child. For only a moment, she felt a mindless, primitive joy.

Then reason returned. Kevin was far away. He had killed and fled. She might never see him again. And she was another man's wife.

"Are ye feelin' poorly again? Maybe I'd better call Mr. Seaton."

Drucilla clutched her arm. "No, Kitty. Radford must not know."

"Know what?"

Then, as she looked down at Drucilla, understanding came into her pale green eyes. She had never mentioned the afternoon of their meeting when she had found Drucilla in Kevin Farrell's room, half-naked and hysterical. Indeed, Drucilla had not spoken of it until a few minutes ago. But now, they were both remembering.

"How far along would ye be?"

"I'm not sure. About two months, I think. Oh, Kitty, what am I going to do?"

Eleven

"I WISH we could stay here in Charleston longer," Drucilla said. "It looks very lovely."

After she had turned to catch a last fleeting glimpse of the *Gryphon* in Charleston harbor, the carriage had whirled them away through the city, along streets lined with fine old houses of rose-colored brick, with balconies of wrought iron as delicate as fine lace and high-walled gardens, fragrant with the mingled scents of wisteria and honeysuckle.

"I've been away from Seaton Barony too long as it is." Radford, seated beside her in the carriage, spoke with cool politeness, but with a finality that made Drucilla lapse into silence. Since the night of the ball on board the *Gryphon*, when Radford had attacked Ian Mackintosh, Drucilla had sensed a change in her husband's attitude. Although he was still courteous, he had turned cool and remote. He had not made love to her during the few remaining nights of the voyage and while, in one way, that had been a relief, it had troubled her, too; Radford's lovemaking, although it did not stir her senses, had provided a bond between them; now they were strangers. And soon she would have to tell him she was pregnant. She would have to convince him that he was the father of her baby.

Now, late on this September afternoon, she sat beside him in the hired carriage, and even the parasol she held over her head did little to protect her from the heat; the sun blazed down, and the air was heavy and sultry. She hoped she would not be sick again before they arrived at the plantation.

The carriage had left the city, and now it swayed and came to a stop on the bank of the Cooper River; the slow-moving water looked black in the shade of the overhanging trees.

Radford got down and helped her to the ground. He paused to go over to the open cart that had followed their carriage from the dock, carrying Kitty and a mountain of baggage. Charlotte Tremayne had insisted on providing Drucilla with a wardrobe so elaborate that she was sure she would never be able to wear half the garments. He gave directions to the black driver of the cart, who started unloading the trunks.

Meanwhile, Drucilla stared at the river in surprise. "You said you had your own boat—but this one is so large," she said, looking at the long craft moored at the landing.

Radford smiled faintly. "Before the war, many Low Country planters had boats like this one. It's made of cypress, the same as those trees growing over there. Three great logs, one for each side and the third for the bottom and keel. It's much more practical to travel by boat than by carriage, particularly when the rain makes the roads through the swamps impassable."

When Radford had helped her on board, she discovered that the boat also had two movable, collapsible cabins, which had been set up, one for herself and Radford, the other for Kitty and some of the smaller pieces of baggage.

Kitty, wide-eyed and silent, let one of the huge black crewmen help her into the boat. There were six crewmen in all, the biggest, most powerfully built men she had ever seen, and nattily dressed in identical white straw hats with long ribbons attached, red flannel jackets and wide-bottomed white cotton trousers.

Radford led Drucilla to the small cabin at the stern, and she sat down on the wide, cushioned bench, spreading her Swiss muslin skirt carefully around her, and loosening the ribbon that fastened the collar of her bodice. Radford took a seat beside her, and she felt the boat begin to glide forward.

One of the black crewmen raised his voice in a kind of chant. She could not understand the first words, for his dialect was completely unfamiliar. But then, the rest of the crew joined in with:

"Ro—o—oll, Jordan, roll."

"It helps them to keep the stroke," Radford explained. "We used to have our own slaves to row this boat, of course, but Mother has hired these free blacks and got them to wear the same sort of clothing the slave crews wore. She wants everything at Seaton Barony to be as it used to be."

"Even the plantation house?"

"It has been rebuilt. Some of the furniture that was destroyed can't be replaced, of course. But Mother plans to import similar pieces from France and England."

"Won't that be very expensive?'

"No need for you to concern yourself, my dear. Mother always manages to get what she wants."

"But how?"

"She is a most resourceful woman."

Drucilla wondered if Theodora Seaton's obvious matchmaking activities back in Newport had been typical of that resourceful disposition. Radford had married her because he loved her, she was sure of it; but had there been a more practical motivation on Theodora's part? Drucilla knew nothing about the size of the marriage settlement, but she was sure that her mother-in-law had found the arrangement satisfying.

What sort of life awaited her in her new home, with these people who were still strangers to her? She shivered. Twilight was coming on swiftly, and she saw the great, ancient-looking trees leaning over the river, trailing veils of gray moss. Mist rose from the river banks and drifted on the heavy air. She moved close to Radford. "Those trees look so strange, almost menacing in this light."

"They're live oaks," he said, "and that long, trailing stuff is Spanish moss. We've a whole avenue of them leading up to the house and more along our creek. And there's palmetto and honeysuckle and . . ." He slapped at a mosquito that had lighted on his cheek. "Now these —they're the real danger here."

"Mosquitoes?"

"They carry malaria. And yellow fever, sometimes. But the fever season's about over now."

Drucilla shuddered. Ever since she had discovered that she was carrying a child, Kevin's child, she had found herself thinking not only of her own safety and well-being, but of the baby's, too. Was it that way with all pregnant women? she wondered.

"Don't look so troubled, my dear." Radford put a hand on her arm, and she was grateful for his presence, finding it comforting in this unfamiliar place.

"We will go north every summer, to escape the danger of fever. To your grandmother's home in Newport, if you like."

"Yes, but are we to live at Seaton Barony all the rest of the year?"

"Where else would we live?"

"I thought perhaps a house in Charleston. At least there we would have neighbors close by."

"Afraid you'll be lonely with only your husband for company?" The hand on her arm was not comforting any longer; his fingers had tightened, and she could feel the tension inside him.

"Of course not," she said. "It's only that I'm used to—"

"You're used to having men like Ian Mackintosh flirting with you—if that is all it was."

"What else could it have been?" She pulled her arm away. "I only met him that night. You introduced us, remember?"

"I know the circumstances of your meeting," Radford said. "But you didn't lose any time in throwing yourself at him, did you? Leading him on, letting him forget you are my wife."

"You've no right to say that. Perhaps I shouldn't have gone up on deck with him, perhaps he should not have —but you were worse than he was. You might have killed him. I think if he had not left the boat the next morning, you would have."

"And I would have been within my rights," Radford said evenly.

Her eyes widened in disbelief. "You can't mean that."

"I can and I do. You have a great deal to learn about our way of life down here." His eyes held hers. "Take my grandfather, for instance. He killed a man in a duel, not far from where we are now."

"What had he done—the man your grandfather—"

"He had been too attentive to a young lady, my grandfather's fiancée. He took her riding in his carriage, without a chaperon. They returned after dark."

"And that was all?"

Radford nodded.

"And the girl?"

"My grandfather did not marry her, of course."

"But why? I mean, perhaps it wasn't her fault."

"No man takes liberties with a woman unless she offers him some encouragement. My grandfather was quite right to break off the engagement. Had they already been married, it might have been much worse for her."

"He would have killed her, too, I suppose." Drucilla's voice was unsteady.

"It has happened down here, more than once."

She looked away, out at the river. Gray mist. Gray-green moss. The riverbank losing shape and substance, like a landscape in a dream.

Radford could not be serious. He was trying to frighten her, that was all. But she remembered the way he had attacked Ian Mackintosh, the madness in his face at that moment. What kind of man was he?

"You belong to me, Drucilla. Never forget that."

She pressed her lips together to keep from crying out:

"I don't belong to you. I'm carrying another man's child."

But she could not, dared not. For there was that other life growing inside her.

"You've been cold toward me, since our wedding night," he was saying. "I thought you were afraid. Or shy. I could have understood that. But now, I wonder." He looked at her as if seeing her for the first time. "What was your life like before you came to Newport? During those years, when your mother was out west, touring in those mining camps? I have a right to know."

When she remained silent, he took her by the arms and shook her. "Answer me," he demanded.

"Let go of me. If you have so little faith in me, why did you marry me?"

He made a harsh, half-incoherent sound, and his arms went around her. He pressed her back against the seat. "I wanted you for the same reason any man would. You're beautiful . . . your body . . . the way you move . . . the way you look at a man. . . ."

He crushed his mouth down on hers and she felt the hot, driving hunger in him. He buried his face in her hair.

"You're mine. Never forget that."

She closed her eyes. The words were not frightening, but the way he said them sent a coldness through her. He did love her, but as strong as his love, stronger perhaps, was his jealousy. If he had been driven into a killing rage because of the trivial incident with Ian Mackintosh, what would he do if he knew about Kevin Farrell and the child she carried?

She had to get away. Out of this boat. She had to run off, anywhere. But there was no escape, and the boat continued to glide along the dark river, into a world of mist and shadow.

Throughout the autumn and winter, Drucilla remained at Seaton Barony, in the great, rambling white house surrounded by live oaks. For the first few weeks, she and Radford were alone there; then, early in October, Theodora Seaton returned accompanied by Gwen and Hazel.

"I'll have to tell them now," Drucilla said to Kitty, one evening, as the maid stood behind her, dressing her hair for evening. "Radford's been so busy, out there in the fields, he hasn't noticed. But Theodora will." Only that afternoon, her mother-in-law had looked at her sharply, when she had gotten up from the luncheon table and hurried upstairs, white-faced and sick.

"Tell them, then," Kitty said firmly. "It won't be the first time a baby arrived in the seventh month." Then seeing Drucilla's blank, bewildered look, Kitty said, "Ye married Mr. Seaton in September. Tell them the baby's due in June. When it comes earlier, well—such things happen. A fall, a shock, a bumpy carriage ride—who's to know?"

"But, Kitty—"

"No 'buts' about it, ma'am. Everybody on the *Gryphon* was talkin' about the daft way he took on, because ye went for a stroll on deck with another gentleman. Crazy jealous he was."

"I know," Drucilla whispered. "But even so—"

She broke off, hearing a knock on the door. A moment later, Radford was in the room. "Not dressed yet?" he asked.

"Kitty has only to put on my gown," she said quickly.

"Mother said you weren't feeling well this afternoon." Radford had not returned to the house for luncheon; he had eaten in the fields, with the overseer, as was his custom.

"I'm not used to the climate yet, that's all. It's so warm and sultry for October."

He smiled indulgently. "Our Low Country weather does take a bit of getting used to. Perhaps you would rather have dinner here in our room, with me."

"I'm perfectly all right now," she began, then catching a swift, meaningful look from Kitty, she said, "It would be pleasant, perhaps—just the two of us."

But when the tray had been brought and uncovered and she caught the rich, heavy smells of ham and gravy, she turned her face away.

"Drucilla, my dear—what is it?" Radford came to her side and put an arm around her. His eyes were troubled. "I think perhaps tomorrow I should take you into Charleston. There are a number of good doctors there."

"No—I don't need a doctor—"

Her voice was shrill with fear. *A doctor would know how far along her pregnancy was, wouldn't he?* "I think you do," Radford said firmly. "Doctor Lucas is—"

"I don't need a doctor—I know what's wrong with me—I'm going to have a baby."

His arm tightened around her, until she felt that she could not breathe. Then he pushed the tray aside and drew her to her feet. "Are you sure?" His voice shook and his eyes blazed with a look of mingled wonder and pride. "Drucilla, are you absolutely certain?"

"Yes, Radford."

He picked her up and carried her to a sofa, close to one of the tall, jalousied windows; sitting down, he held her cradled against him, and stroked her hair. "Why didn't you tell me sooner?"

"I don't know—I wasn't sure—"

He tried to kiss her, but she turned her face away.

"What's wrong? You want the baby, don't you?" And when she remained silent, wracked with shame and guilt, he said, "You mustn't be afraid. Mother will be here, and Aunt Sallie will take care of you, when the time comes. She's delivered dozens of babies, black and white. She helped bring me into the world, and my sisters too."

Aunt Sallie was an old black woman, one of the few who had stayed on, even after she had been given her freedom. "Of course, if you want a doctor from Charleston—"

"No—I'm sure Aunt Sallie will be fine," she said.

"Then that's settled. Now, if you're feeling up to it, I'll have Kitty help you on with your gown, and we'll go downstairs and tell Mother."

"Must she know right away?"

"She'll be so pleased," he said. "This is what she's wanted, what we've all wanted—a son to carry on the Seaton name."

167

Theodora Seaton, more realistic than her son, was prepared to accept the fact that her first grandchild might be a girl, but she was, nevertheless, pleased with Drucilla. "I hope to see half a dozen grandchildren here at Seaton Barony," she said.

Seaton Barony. In the long, dreary months of autumn and winter, Drucilla tried to learn to like her new home. But it was lonely, shut off from the world. Accustomed to living in cities—Cincinnati, New York, Newport—the isolation of the plantation, deep in the swamps, was almost more than she could bear. Here, the rain fell steadily for days on end. Even on clear days, when she went walking along Palmetto Creek, she heard only the cries of the quail, the snipe, and the killdeer, who swept down with a high, thin, wailing cry that sounded half-human. Sometimes she caught sight of an opossum, high in a persimmon tree, or a raccoon scrambling through the tall weeds.

Radford, although he was loving and indulgent, had to spend much time away from the house, in the fields or away on business trips, sometimes to Charleston, sometimes to the western part of the state.

Often, even when he was at home, he and his mother would shut themselves away in her office at the rear of the house to talk business. Drucilla knew that Theodora was planning to invest in cotton mills, to be built in the upcountry to the west; that she was selling off some of the lumber from the plantation. She spoke of hiring an engineer from the North, or perhaps from England, to supervise the rebuilding of the complex arrangement of locks and canals, ditches, dams, and gates that were necessary for the growing of a rice crop.

Even when these matters were discussed at the dinner table, Drucilla was excluded. She was Radford's bride, and she would give him an heir to the plantation. As far as Theodora was concerned, that was all that was required of her.

Gwen and Hazel made occasional trips into Charleston to attend parties or musicales, but when Drucilla suggested that she might go along, both Radford and his mother protested.

"A woman in your condition does not show herself at such functions," Theodora said firmly.

"I wasn't planning to dance," Drucilla said. "But surely I could attend a musicale—"

"It isn't done." Theodora set her jaw, her iron-gray curls quivering slightly. "And if it were, you still could not undertake such a strenuous trip. You must take care of yourself, my dear."

If it had not been for Kitty, Drucilla sometimes thought she would have gone mad during those months of her pregnancy. They talked for hours, in Drucilla's room or on walks along the creek. It was a relief to be with the one person here at Seaton Barony who knew the truth about her. Not all of it, of course. But enough.

And Drucilla listened with interest to Kitty's stories about her own life, of her work in a bleaching factory in Lancashire. Her sister had already emigrated and eventually managed to send her the passage money for the steerage trip to New York.

"It was a shock, though, I can tell ye, seeing the Five Points for the first time. A regular hellhole, beggin' yer pardon, ma'am. And if it hadn't been for you, I'd be back there now. And on the streets, more'n likely."

"You have enough to eat now and a clean bed to sleep in," Drucilla conceded. "But you must be very lonely here."

A few times, Theodora Seaton had suggested that a black maid be found for Drucilla and that Kitty might be sent back North.

"I need Kitty. I want her with me." On that point, Drucilla was adamant.

"The girl might be happier in the North, among other white servants. And I must say, I don't think it's proper for you to spend so much time with her."

Drucilla bit back the urge to lash out and tell her mother-in-law that Kitty was far better company than either Gwen or Hazel. Gwen, with the shadow of spinster-hood overtaking her, was making desperate, last-ditch efforts to find a suitable husband: a middle-aged widower with a flock of children, perhaps.

Once, at the dinner table, Gwen had pleaded with her mother to allow her to go to work. "I received excellent grades at Miss Forster's Academy," she said. "And I would enjoy being a governess, or a teacher in a girls' school."

If Gwen had suggested dancing naked in a waterfront tavern in Charleston, Theodora could not have been more outraged.

"No lady in the Seaton family has ever worked for a living and none ever will."

In desperation, Gwen said, "You ran Seaton Barony after father was killed, you dealt with the factors and the overseers, and you—"

"That was entirely different," Theodora said. She rose from the dinner table, indicating that the conversation was closed.

As for Hazel, although only seventeen, she was painfully shy, the result of her mother's powerful and dominating personality. She replied to nearly every remark put to her with a nervous, high-pitched giggle that set Drucilla's teeth on edge.

Kitty Nolan did not mind the loneliness of the plantation, so long as she could serve Miss Drucilla. Late in March, when Mr. Radford was leaving for New York on business, something having to do with those cotton mills he and his mother were forever talking about, she heard him say, "I don't like to leave you now, Drucilla. But, the baby isn't due until June, and I'll be back long before that."

Kitty, who was folding linen in the adjoining dressing room, heard her mistress say, "You must go, of course."

"I was right," Kitty thought. "He doesn't suspect a thing."

"And you don't mind having Aunt Sallie deliver the baby? If you'd rather have a doctor, I'll get you the best one in Charleston."

"No—I want Aunt Sallie, I really do."

Clever of Miss Drucilla. The short-sighted old black

woman had likely been a good nurse in her day, but now she wasn't too sharp. She wouldn't be likely to notice if the baby was a bit large for seven months.

"Besides," Miss Drucilla said, "I'll have Kitty with me. She's always taken good care of me."

More than you know, Miss Drucilla, Kitty thought. *Ye never did guess what I did for ye, back there in Newport. Ye wouldn't be married to Mr. Radford today, if it hadn't been for me.* She went on folding the dainty nightgowns, the lace-trimmed beribboned camisoles, and smiled with satisfaction. *Some people might think it was a sin, what she did, but the sin was hers, and she would gladly answer for it. And she would take care of Miss Drucilla again, when the baby came. Hadn't she helped to deliver two of her sister's babies?*

Kitty put a hand up and wiped her forehead; although it was not yet April, the weather had turned hot and sultry. Even that old dragon, Theodora Seaton, admitted the heat was unseasonable. Kitty had been perspiring all day, and now her dress clung to her, and her hair drooped in lank wisps under her neat white cap.

But a moment later, she felt cold. Her teeth were chattering. What the devil was wrong with her? Shivering like this when the sun was blazing in through the window, when she'd been sweating like a pig only a minute ago.

She'd be glad when they got back to Newport in July. A fine, healthy climate that had been. Here, the smell of the swamp often came into the house, heavy and unpleasant.

During the first week of April, Kitty knew for sure that something was wrong with her. She had a headache that wouldn't go away. It was getting worse every day. One moment she'd feel as if she were burning in the fires of hell, and the next, she'd be icy cold. Leola, one of the kitchen maids, gave her a mixture of herbs to drink, but it didn't help much.

Miss Drucilla noticed that there was something wrong, but Kitty put her off, saying that she had eaten some pork that must have been spoiled.

She couldn't get sick, not now, not with Miss Drucilla

171

only a few weeks from her time, and no one except that old black woman to care for her.

Kitty was ironing in the kitchen when the pain in her head grew worse, much worse. She was doing up the delicate frills on one of Miss Drucilla's pretty nightgowns, and for a moment, she felt that a metal band was closing around her skull, crushing out sight, making the room lurch.

She caught the smell of scorching lace, and managed somehow to take the iron and put it back on the stove. Mustn't scorch Miss Drucilla's lovely things. She caught at the edge of the stove, then slumped to her knees.

After that, everything was blurred, voices coming and going, faces appearing and fading away.

She heard Theodora Seaton saying, "We can't keep her here in the house . . . the old overseer's place, down by the creek . . ."

She was being wrapped in a blanket, and lifted by a powerful black man. He carried her outside. She heard the creaking of wagon wheels.

Then Miss Drucilla was there, clutching a wrapper around her swollen body, and her eyes, the color of violets they were, filled with tears.

"You can't take Kitty away. I won't let you. I'll take care of her."

Kitty swallowed, her mouth horribly dry. "I'll be all right, Miss Drucilla. A touch of fever, that's all."

And then, she heard Theodora Seaton say, "Malaria, that's what it is. Early in the season for it, but there have been other cases reported, upriver, and a few in Charleston. It's this unseasonable heat, I suppose."

"Let me go with her. Please, let me go with her."

"Drucilla, you are in no condition to nurse anyone. You are carrying Radford's child. How can you even think of risking your baby, and for the sake of a servant girl?"

Even in her agony, Kitty noticed the reference made by Theodora to the child. Not Drucilla. She wasn't concerned with her daughter-in-law, but with the child. You'd think it was going to be a prince, the way they took on. If they knew the truth . . .

And it came to Kitty, through the black haze that was enveloping her, that if she remained in the great house, she might, indeed, cause Miss Drucilla to take sick. Or, in the fever she might rave, as people did. Might say what she would not otherwise have said, that the baby was not Radford Seaton's child.

"Please, Miss Drucilla. She's right. I mustn't stay near you now. Don't worry. I'll be well soon."

The black man was lifting her carefully into the wagon, and then Leola was clambering in beside her.

"Please take good care of her, Leola." Miss Drucilla's voice.

Then darkness.

The cabin down by the creek was close, stuffy. Kitty, when she was able to see anything, saw a candle guttering on a table near the bed, and Leola, her head wrapped in a clean white turban, leaning over her. Making her take some kind of bitter medicine. Kitty swallowed it obediently, but it wasn't helping.

Sometimes, she thought she was back in Lancashire, in the bleaching factory, where the temperature sometimes went over a hundred and thirty degrees. But she had to hurry and finish her work, because the foreman had a heavy hand and wouldn't stand for shirking.

Then she was back in the steerage, with the smell of vomit and worse around her. And the ship plunging so that she thought it would be broken to bits.

Then Newport. The air was fresh and cool in Newport. Not cool, but icy cold. Her body shook and her teeth chattered. And the black girl was putting more blankets on her and forcing the bitter-tasting medicine between her teeth.

And now, at last, Miss Drucilla was with her. She shouldn't be there, but it was so good, seeing her.

"You may go outside and get some air, Leola. You look exhausted."

"I'm all right, ma'am. But you shouldn't be here at all. Does Mrs. Seaton know you're here?"

"Do as I say."

And Leola slipped out of the room, leaving only Miss Drucilla with her.

"It's not a fit place for ye, here."

"Don't talk, Kitty."

"I've got to. I wanted to be with ye . . . when the baby came . . ."

"You will be. You've got to be."

Kitty shook her head. She was burning up, but the black haze that had clouded her mind had lifted. "No, I won't. But ye'll need someone ye can trust. Ye've been so good to me . . . I wanted to be there to help ye, like always."

"You always have," Miss Drucilla said. "Ever since that first afternoon, at the Aquidneck House. Remember?"

Kitty smiled. "An' later, too. When that old devil came to threaten ye. She'd've bled ye white. But I stopped her."

"Who? I don't understand."

"Mrs. . . . Baxter . . . Baxley . . . that was it. Out there . . . on the Cliff Walk."

Miss Drucilla was lifting her head, holding a cup of water to her cracked lips. "That first time ye went out to meet her on the Cliff Walk . . . I followed ye. I wouldn't have let ye go out there with the likes of her. I was close by. I heard—"

"Then you knew the truth about me. You knew I wasn't—"

"I knew ye were the finest, sweetest lady I ever met. Then right before the Harvest Ball, I was comin' back with that wreath. All them satin leaves—so pretty—"

Miss Drucilla took her hand, and bent over her. "You were coming back with the wreath. What happened then?"

"Seen 'er again, hangin' around. Said she wanted ye to meet her again, that night."

"You never told me."

"Never told ye. I went to meet her though. Told 'er if she didn't leave ye alone, I'd kill 'er. She laughed. Said she'd get every cent ye had, or see ye in jail. I hit 'er, then. Didn't mean to—but the rocks were slippery, and her so big an' clumsy, she lost 'er footin'—she went right over the edge of the Cliff Walk—"

Miss Drucilla's eyes widened, and she said something Kitty didn't understand. But that wasn't strange, what with the buzzing in her head and the weakness creeping over her. "Not Kevin," Miss Drucilla was saying. "You killed Mrs. Baxley. It wasn't Kevin at all."

"I ain't sorry I killed her. She'd have got ye put in jail," she said. And I owed ye so much, Miss—"

The pain in her head was bad now, and the room was getting dim, but Miss Drucilla was holding her hand, pressing it against her own cheek, cool and soft.

"Ye were so good to me, Miss Drucilla. The only one that ever was. I—"

She saw the red-gold waves coming nearer, brushing against her burning face, like the light of the sun. Then the sun faded. Disappeared. Darkness rushed in and she gave herself up to it.

Drucilla sat quite still, unable to move or even to think clearly. Kitty had killed Mrs. Baxley. Then why had Kevin left Newport so suddenly? It didn't matter. He wasn't a murderer.

She did not know how much time had passed before she heard Leola saying, "Mr. Radford, it wasn't my fault. She came and sent me away. I didn't want to let her stay in here—"

And then Radford was beside her, his hand on her shoulder. He was looking down at Kitty, and then he said, "Good Lord!" He drew the blanket over Kitty's face.

"Don't do that," Drucilla cried out. "You'll smother her."

"Come with me, now," he said. He was trying to lift her away from the bed.

"No," she said. "I've got to stay here with Kitty."

"But, my dear, can't you see? There is nothing more to be done for Kitty." He shook his head. "Poor girl, it would have been better if mother had sent her back up north, as she wanted to."

"But she'll be all right. She has to be."

Radford shook her lightly. "Drucilla, Kitty is dead."

"No, she can't be."

He raised her to her feet and put his arms around her. She let him lead her out of the cabin; her movements were like those of a sleepwalker.

"I returned less than an hour ago," Radford was saying. "Mother thought you were asleep, but when I couldn't find you—when we searched the house and you weren't there, she told me about Kitty, and I guessed —Drucilla, don't look that way. She did what she thought best."

"She had no right to move Kitty down here, as if she had been a sick animal. She had no right—"

"She had every right. You are carrying her grandchild—"

Drucilla bit down hard on her lower lip, to keep back the hysteria that threatened to overwhelm her.

"Come now, I'll take you back to the house. Leola can do what needs to be done for Kitty now."

"No, I don't want anyone else to touch her. Let me go back to her, please, Radford."

"For pity's sake, Drucilla—she was only a servant. She—"

She loved me. She killed to protect me. She did not say the words, but only twisted free from Radford's arm and started back for the cabin. He seized her around the waist, and she struggled to break his hold, but he was far too strong.

He lifted her off the ground and started back toward the house, holding her in his arms, ignoring her efforts to get away from him.

They were almost as far as the front veranda when she cried out.

"What is it? Did I hurt you? I didn't mean to."

For a moment, the pain that clutched at her insides made it impossible for her to speak. Theodora came running out onto the veranda, followed by Gwen and Hazel.

"She wouldn't come with me," Radford said. "I didn't mean to hurt her. I swear I didn't."

Theodora took a quick look at Drucilla who, as the

pain ebbed, had slumped back against Radford's shoulder.

"Get her upstairs," Theodora said. "And you, Gwen, call Aunt Sallie. I think the baby's coming."

"It can't be," Radford said. "It's too soon." His voice was unsteady, and Drucilla saw the fear and guilt in his face.

She wanted to reassure him, but she knew she could not—unless she told him the truth.

Twelve

RADFORD carried her into the house, and she heard Theodora giving orders.

"Hazel, go to the kitchen. Tell Bessie I want hot bricks and flannel. Enough to line the cradle. The baby's much too early. It will have to be kept warm. Radford, take Drucilla to the bedroom."

"There's no time, Mother. And she's in terrible pain. The library—"

"Even a premature baby seldom arrives within minutes," Theodora said. "And your child must be born in Grandmother Ogeron's bed."

Drucilla remembered that, when she had first arrived here, Theodora had told her about the bed in the master bedroom. It had been brought from France by Radford's maternal grandmother, along with her trousseau. Since then, all the Seaton babies had been born in that bed.

Drucilla buried her face against Radford's shoulder, biting back a cry as another pain began. She wanted to protest, but stronger than her anger at Theodora for making such a point of tradition at a time like this, was her fear of what lay ahead. She had been counting on

Kitty to see her through this ordeal. Aunt Sallie was old and a stranger. They were all strangers, even Radford.

The bed in the master bedroom had a high, carved headboard and footboard and four massive posts, as thick as columns, supporting a faded red and gold canopy. The posts were elaborately carved and to Drucilla's tormented eyes, the carvings looked like the faces of demons; their mouths seemed to twist and writhe, their eyes were narrow with menace.

When Radford put her down on the bed, she reached out blindly, and he took her hand. She saw that sweat was streaming down his face, and soaking his shirt, so that it clung to his chest and shoulders.

"I'm sorry," he said. "The baby's coming early, and it's my fault."

Even through the fear, she felt sorry for him. "It's not," she said. "Don't blame yourself. It's—"

She pressed the back of her free hand against her mouth, and her teeth sank into her own skin. The pain helped her to regain a measure of control.

The baby was not early. Perhaps it might have come a few days later, if she had not gone through the shock of Kitty's death, and then her struggle with Radford. Impossible to say. But her baby was arriving on time.

Aunt Sallie came in, carrying a basket, from which she took a pair of scissors, a ball of twine, and a pile of clean, white cloths. A few moments later, Bessie, the cook, came in with the hot bricks wrapped in flannel and began to line an old wooden cradle. Drucilla had not noticed the cradle being brought in, but she was sure it must be the cradle that had held all the Seaton babies.

Another pain gripped her, starting at the small of her back and closing around her like the jaws of a trap. She screamed, and her fingers tightened on Radford's hand.

"You'd better go now, Radford," Theodora said. "This is no place for a man."

"I can't leave Drucilla like this."

"Don't be foolish. The baby will be fine. I'll see to that."

The baby. That was all Theodora cared about. She

waited until the pain slackened, then let go of Radford's hand. She wished that they would all leave her.

But later, as the night wore on, and the pains became worse, she was grateful for Aunt Sallie's presence. The woman was old and wizened, but there was comfort in her hands. Drucilla was sure that she was doing everything she could to speed the birth.

But the torment went on until Drucilla was stripped of courage and dignity, until she cringed like a frightened animal each time a pain began. She felt a growing weakness, a languor stealing over her.

"I'm going to die," she whispered. At that moment, the thought of death was comforting.

"Nonsense," Theodora said, and there was steel in her voice. "You must fight, girl. Bear down as hard as you can. You're not trying hard enough."

Drucilla turned her face away. Kitty was dead. Kevin was gone. She would never see him again. There was nothing to fight for, and she was so tired.

The sky outside the tall French windows turned from black to gray, then to soft pink and gold. Even at dawn, the air was already humid and although the window was only open a little way, she was sure she smelled the swamp, rank with decay, breeding death. Death for Kitty. And now, she was going to die, too.

Theodora bent over her, took her by the shoulders, and shook her hard. Drucilla was startled by the strength in those small white hands. "Don't give way. Fight. You must. I chose you for my son because I thought you had courage. You can't fail him now. This baby is important to him, to all of us."

Theodora had chosen her as if choosing a brood mare. Damn Theodora Seaton. She wanted to free herself from those strong fingers, to scream that this baby would not be a Seaton.

Not a Seaton . . . It was Kevin's child, fighting to be born. She would never see Kevin again. He would never know about the child. But she would have something, a part of him to love.

The pain was tearing at her, forcing a scream from her throat, and her whole body arched upward. Aunt

Sallie was doing something to her, hurting her. But the pain did not matter now. She was fighting, as hard as Theodora could have wished. Fighting to bring Kevin's child into the world.

Andrew Horace Seaton, named for Radford's father, and for Horace Tremayne, was born a little after sunrise; he was a large baby, strong and healthy. Drucilla wanted to nurse him, but Theodora insisted that a lady in her position must have a wet nurse, and a black woman was found at once.

The baby took on weight rapidly, and by the end of his first year, his hair had changed from a fine blond fuzz to dark ringlets, and his blue eyes became gray . . . Kevin's son.

Radford was pleased and proud. It seemed to Drucilla that after Andrew's birth, both Radford and Theodora were more obsessed than before with the need to increase the Seaton holdings, to rebuild the fortune they had lost after the war, and to make it even larger.

Theodora did not try to hide the fact that she was using Drucilla's dowry to finance many of her ventures: the mills in the upcountry, three of them; the new equipment for the cultivation of the rice crops; the wages for the black laborers who now worked the Seaton acres.

Drucilla did not care. Both Theodora and Radford were shrewd about business matters. It was enough for her that she had her baby to love and care for.

In June, when Andrew was three months old, the Seatons made their annual trip to Newport. She was moved by Charlotte Tremayne's delight on seeing young Andrew for the first time. Even when Charlotte was alone with Drucilla, she made it plain that she considered the baby her grandchild. "Thank you for giving him my son's name," she said. "He is a beautiful child. You must be proud of him."

Drucilla nodded, and then Charlotte asked, "Tell me, my dear, are you happy? I know you had doubts about marrying Radford, but now all that's past, isn't it?"

"Of course, grandmother," Drucilla said quickly.

"Radford is a kind and devoted husband."

True enough, as far as it went. And she had no wish to burden Charlotte with her misgivings about her marriage. She was Radford's wife, and she owed him loyalty.

But Radford was not an easy man to live with, particularly now that they were back in Newport. When she appeared at balls, picnics, dinners and yachting parties, men flocked around her; marriage and childbirth had not dimmed her beauty. Her body had taken on new and seductively rounded curves, and she no longer worried that her hips might be too narrow. Her skin was creamy and flawless, and the brisk, salty air here in Newport gave her face a warm, rich glow; her red-gold hair shone like molten copper.

Although Radford seldom left her side, there were looks from other men that told her how desirable she was. She was careful to avoid the slightest suspicion that she was having a flirtation, and at times she had to be cold, even rude, to a persistent admirer.

One day, late in August, when she and Gwen were driving back from the dressmaker, Drucilla learned, for the first time, the reason behind Radford's unnatural possessiveness.

"He's that way because of Lucy Huger," Gwen said. Then, seeing Drucilla's puzzled look, she went on. "Radford was away, in the cavalry. It was close to the end of the war then. Lucy's family lived a little way up-river from Seaton Barony. She was so pretty. And my brother was crazy in love with her."

"He couldn't have been more than seventeen."

Gwen shrugged. "I guess our young men grow up faster than the Yankees. So many quadroon girls right there, for the taking. Of course, white ladies weren't supposed to know about such things." She gave Drucilla a wry smile. "We weren't allowed to read French novels or look at naked statues. But our men could keep their mistresses right under the same roof with us. And a boy who hadn't paid a visit to the slave quarters by the time he was sixteen was thought to be unmanly."

Drucilla looked away, trying to conceal her shock at Gwen's words. "We were talking about Lucy Huger," she reminded Gwen. "Was Radford engaged to her?"

"No, but—they had an understanding. She kept writing to Radford, until close to the end of the fighting, when hardly any letters were getting through. Then her family moved into Charleston. They'd lost nearly everything, you see. And there was this Yankee major stationed in Charleston with the army of occupation, and we heard he was paying court to Lucy. Some folks said she'd even let him—I don't know for a fact, but there was a lot of talk. Thank goodness the major married Lucy and took her back home with him before Radford returned."

"Why do you say that?"

"Because otherwise, I think Radford would have killed him."

"He never told me," Drucilla said.

"Does that surprise you? He has the devil's own pride. But now that you know, maybe you won't mind when he acts jealous. You're so pretty. Just like Lucy was. But it's more than that. You have something that gets men excited, drives them crazy—"

"You have no right to say such a thing to me."

Gwen put a hand on Drucilla's arm. "I'm sorry," she said. Her face pale, with its heavy jaw, flushed. "I guess the truth is, I'm envious of you. If only one man, any man, would look at me the way Radford looks at you—"

Gwen lapsed into silence, and did not speak for the rest of the drive back to Peregrine Court. Drucilla supposed she should be grateful for the insight her sister-in-law had offered; it did help to explain Radford's behavior, at least in part.

"But he's not going to keep me a prisoner on Seaton Barony for the rest of my life," Drucilla told herself. "I'm not to blame for what another woman did to him. I've got to make him understand that."

As always, the Newport season ended with the Harvest Ball, but this year, the day of the ball dawned gray and cloudy and before noon, torrents of wind-driven rain were hurled against the oriel windows of Peregrine Court, so that Charlotte Tremayne decided, reluctantly, that the festivities would have to be held indoors. She sent the servants hurrying about. They opened the heavy doors between the ballroom and the dining room and laid the tables for the buffet supper. They polished the already gleaming floor of the ballroom, and decorated the musicians' gallery with masses of red and yellow leaves.

"And instead of the fireworks, we will have more autumn leaves dropped from the gallery to float down at the end of the evening."

Although everything went beautifully, Drucilla felt subdued, pensive, as the evening wore on. At supper, she and Radford joined a group who discussed the closing of Jay Cooke and Company the day before.

"Other banks are closing, too," said John Pettigrew, a stout gentleman from Charleston, who had also brought his family to Newport for the summer. "Why, there's talk of closing the New York Stock Exchange."

"I doubt that," Radford said. "Even back in 1869, the Stock Exchange remained open."

"This could be worse than Black Friday," Pettigrew insisted. "I've heard that President Grant hotfooted it up from Long Branch."

"Grant should never have been re-elected," Theodora put in. "There were enough scandals, his first term in office, to make it plain the man's either incompetent or dishonest. Probably both. Black Friday . . ."

"This will be a hell of a lot worse than Black Friday —begging your pardon, ladies. I expect we'll all feel the repercussions back home. Your textile mills, Radford. You'll need capital for expansion and where's it to come from?"

"I'll manage," Radford said calmly.

Drucilla was puzzled by Radford's obvious lack of concern. Then she remembered that Radford had her dowry to draw on. She was pleased that her money was of help to him, but she was sometimes troubled by the number of business ventures that must be draining that generous marriage settlement.

The conversation went back to a discussion of the faults of President Grant, and Drucilla's attention wandered, for she was thoroughly familiar with the Southern opinion of the man who had been instrumental in smashing the Confederacy.

She studied Hazel Seaton's dress, a striking creation of dark-red satin, with an intricately draped skirt and bustle, trimmed with silver brocade and seed pearls. Such a gown would have been dazzling on a tall, elegant brunette, but it overshadowed Hazel's delicate coloring. Her hair looked mousy, in spite of repeated rinses with camomile, and her skin was far too pale in contrast with the rich, deep color.

"I wish I had dared to suggest a touch of rouge," Drucilla thought. But she had known that such a suggestion would have shocked Mrs. Seaton.

"I think it's vastly romantic, don't you, Drucilla?"

"Forgive me—I didn't catch Mr. Pettigrew's last remark," Drucilla said, in answer to Hazel's question.

"Why, Mr. Pettigrew was speaking of the revolution down in Cuba. And the men who are running guns to the revolutionists. They must be quite daring. Slipping in past the Spanish gunboats to deliver their cargoes."

"I'm afraid you get your notions from those foolish novels you're forever reading," said Theodora.

"Indeed, there's nothing romantic about this business," Mr. Pettigrew said. "A gun-runner who falls into the hands of the Spanish forces is subjected to barbaric treatment."

Radford said, "I don't think that's a subject to be discussed before the ladies, John."

"Quite right, of course," Pettigrew agreed. "I wasn't thinking."

"But there is profit in this Cuban business, isn't there?" Theodora asked. "I believe that a number of Charleston businessmen own interests in those ships carrying supplies to the rebels."

John Pettigrew shrugged. "It's a risky venture, for the

owners as well as the captains. We'd have done better to annex Cuba years ago."

"But why?" Drucilla asked. "We have so much land in the West, and much of it unsettled. Why do we need more?"

"Cuba is close to the mainland of the United States. If we don't move in, some other power will, should Spain lose control there. Besides that island is valuable. The climate is far better suited to the growing of sugar cane than even Louisiana or Mississippi."

"They don't need paid labor, either," Radford said. "Slavery has not been abolished in Cuba."

Drucilla wanted to say that was unfortunate but thought better of it.

"If the revolutionary forces win, it won't be long before slavery is abolished," John Pettigrew said. "More's the pity."

After supper, Radford and Drucilla returned to the ballroom, just as the music was beginning. "You're looking very lovely tonight," he said, taking her in his arms for the waltz. "I like the color of your gown—lilac, isn't it?"

She nodded, remembering the purple dress Kevin had bought for her, the day after their first meeting.

"What's wrong, Drucilla?" Radford asked.

"Why do you think there's anything wrong?"

"You've been unusually quiet all evening, a little depressed, I believe. And just now, you looked quite downcast."

She forced a smile, but later, at the end of the ball, when she stood beside Radford, watching the autumn leaves drifting down over the ballroom, her depression grew, and a tightness gripped her throat. She did not want to leave Newport, for she would miss Charlotte Tremayne. And she dreaded the thought of another year, immured at Seaton Barony, now without even Kitty for companionship.

She wouldn't let that happen, she decided. They would get a house in Charleston, one of the handsome townhouses near the Battery, with a piazza to catch the breezes from the harbor, and a high-walled garden. She would shop on King Street, and attend the theater, and make friends with other young married ladies, who would come to tea. There would be parties and musicales, too. She was only nineteen, too young to be shut away on an isolated plantation, miles from the nearest neighbor. She would have to make Radford understand that.

But when he came to her room, after the ball that night, it was plain that he was in no mood for talk. He dismissed her maid, Emmaline, a quadroon girl brought from Charleston, and when Drucilla protested that the maid had not finished brushing her hair, Radford picked up the brush, and ran it lightly down the red-gold waves.

His face was reflected in the mirror over the dressing table; the hot, hungry look in his eyes had become familiar to her, and she was not surprised when, after a few moments, he tossed aside the brush and began to explore her body.

"It's late," she protested. "After three—"

"I know the time." He pushed her white satin nightgown off one shoulder, and his fingers caressed her skin.

"Strange how you can dance all evening and then become tired as soon as we're alone."

When she remained silent, he twisted one hand into her hair, turning her head so she was forced to look directly at him. "Perhaps you find the presence of other men stimulating. Is that it?"

She had done nothing that evening to provoke his jealousy, and the injustice of his words made her angry. But she forced herself to speak quietly. "Please let me go."

When he did not respond, she tried to pull away and felt a searing pain at the roots of her hair. She cried out, and he let her go.

She tried to tell herself that he had not hurt her intentionally, but there was something in his manner tonight, a kind of barely masked hostility, that made her afraid. He must not know he frightened her, she decided; in her days at the County Farm, she had learned that a bully with superior strength could sometimes be faced down—if one refused to show any fear.

"I'm going to bed now," she said, standing up. She started toward the bed, but he grasped her wrist.

"Not yet, Drucilla." His voice was a soft drawl. "I know you're tired. The social life here in Newport can be taxing. But we'll soon be back home, and you can rest."

"I don't want to go back to Seaton Barony. I—thought—"

"Go on, my dear."

"If we could buy a townhouse in Charleston," she said. "Your business takes you away from the plantation so often, and I—"

"You get lonely, is that it?" He put an arm around her waist and jerked her body against his. "You can't wait for me to return, can you?"

She knew she had chosen the worst possible time to bring up the subject of the townhouse, but he was unwilling to let it pass.

"And what will you do to keep yourself occupied in Charleston, when I'm away in New York, or New Orleans?"

"Gwen and Hazel could stay with me, and Andrew—"

"Andrew has a nurse, and a nursery maid to care for him. As for Gwen and Hazel, I didn't know you enjoyed their company."

"I could make friends. I could give teas and suppers, I could shop and go to the theater."

"Unescorted? Or are you planning to find an escort when I'm away, some susceptible male who prefers the company of a married woman? Not that you'd have any trouble that way, a woman as lovely as you."

He held her against him so tightly that she found it hard to breathe. Then, reaching out with his free hand, he ripped open the buttons on the bodice of her nightgown. His fingers cupped her bare breast, then tightened, biting into the soft flesh, bringing tears of pain to her eyes. She set her teeth, refusing to make a sound.

Then, just as she thought she might faint, he let her go. As if nothing unusual had happened, he said, "I don't care for your idea about the townhouse. We won't talk about it again."

"I can use my own money—" She would not submit without a fight.

"A wife has no money of her own, you know that. Your dowry belongs to me, to use as I see fit." He laughed softly. "You belong to me." His eyes were fixed on her naked breasts.

"When I come home to Seaton Barony, I want to find you waiting for me. A man has a right to expect that much from a loving and dutiful wife. But then, perhaps no one ever taught you what the duties of a wife should be—certainly not your mother, who ran away from her own husband and—"

"Stop it," Drucilla cried. "You have no right—" If Radford had been drunk, she might have found it easier to overlook his behavior, but she knew that he had not had that much to drink tonight. "I'm not going to let you talk to me this way. Since we've been married, I haven't looked at another man. You're sick with jealousy, not because of anything I've done but because—"

"Go on."

"It's because of that girl, that—Lucy Huger." She wanted to call back the words, but it was too late. For a moment, she thought he was going to strike her.

"What the hell do you know about Lucy?"

"Only what Gwen told me." His lips were pressed together, and there was a fine white line around them. Gwen had also said that Radford had "the devil's own pride."

"Listen to me," Drucilla pleaded. "I think I understand how you must have felt, you were no more than a boy, fighting in a war, with an army that was facing certain defeat. You came home and expected to find Lucy waiting. But she was gone, and you felt betrayed. But you can't punish me for what she did to you." Remembering how she had felt when Kevin had left Newport last summer, without even saying good-bye, pity for Radford stirred inside her. "I want to be a good wife to you, but how can I when you treat me this way? Don't you see—"

"I see that you are overwrought. That you're making a great fuss over nothing. Even if I were foolish enough to indulge your whim and buy a townhouse, I don't think you'd be in any condition to spend the winter in Charleston."

"Why not?"

"Because it's likely that you'll soon be pregnant again. I'm surprised it hasn't happened already. Don't look so distressed, my dear. I want sons. Half a dozen if possible. It shouldn't be a problem with a woman like you. I do believe you became pregnant the first time I slept with you." One corner of his mouth turned down in a smile, cold and sardonic. "Mother thought you'd be a good breeder—she has an instinct about such matters. When we used to buy female slaves back before the war, my father valued her opinion highly."

Drucilla's cheeks flamed, and her voice shook with anger.

"I'm not a slave," she said. "Nor a brood mare. And if you have some notion that you can keep me pregnant and hidden away at Seaton Barony . . ."

"I can. And I will. And there's nothing you can do about it."

He lifted her off her feet and carried her to the bed.

Until tonight, she had always submitted to him, had even taken pleasure in satisfying his needs. Afterward, she had lain in his arms, and he had stroked her hair and murmured endearments. At those times, she had felt tenderness, even affection for him.

But tonight was different, he was different, and she could not let him take her. She fought him, even when he pressed her back on the bed, even when he tore off her nightgown and looked at her body in the lamplight.

"You're made to bear children," he said. "You'll give me more sons."

She tried to free herself, but his arm was heavy across her breasts. She began to sense that her struggles only excited him. She made herself lie still and submit to her husband, to a man who had become a brutal, pitiless stranger.

Thirteen

WHEN DRUCILLA awoke, the sunlight was streaming in between the heavy, rose-colored drapes. She tried to move, felt a dull aching, and realized that her body was bruised; then she remembered—and stifled a cry.

She turned her head and saw that Radford was asleep, with one arm flung across her body. She looked at him, disbelieving. Was he the man who had used her without pity, only a few hours ago? The hard lines were gone from his face now; his lips were parted slightly, and his breathing was quiet and even. He looked young, vulnerable, but remembering what he had done to her, she was repelled. Slowly, carefully, she began to inch away.

His eyelids fluttered, and he murmured something. She caught her breath and made herself lie still, but it was too late. His eyes opened, and held hers.

"Drucilla . . ."

"Let me go." When he moved his arm and she began to raise herself, the sheet slid from her naked body. He was looking at the livid marks on her arms and breasts now, and he said, "I did that to you."

When she remained silent, he said, "Forgive me."

"How can I? How can I stay with you, after—"

"You're my wife."

"That does not give you the right to use me as you did."

"I know," he said, his voice filled with remorse. "But try to understand."

"What is there to understand?" She tried to get out of bed, but he put a hand on her arm.

"Listen to me, please. Ever since that first night— our wedding night—I hoped I could make you want me. I told myself that it would take time for you to learn to enjoy—that part of marriage. But you never wanted me, not once. All those months at Seaton Barony, every time I came to you, you tolerated me, but that was all. Then, last night, when you said you didn't want any more children, I went a little crazy, I guess. A man has a right to expect his wife to want his children."

Her head throbbed, and the sunlight hurt her eyes. She lay back, but not before Radford had slid his arm under her shoulders. His embrace was gentle, and she did not try to draw away.

She closed her eyes and tried to think clearly in spite of the pain in her head. Radford was within his rights when he said he wanted more children. Any man with property wanted sons to inherit. But she knew, also, that he hoped to use her pregnancies to hold her a prisoner, to keep her shut away from contact with the world outside Seaton Barony. And this she would not allow.

She could leave him, of course. And maybe Charlotte Tremayne would give her, and Andrew, a home here at Peregrine Court. But she felt sick, thinking of the scandal that would surely follow when Radford fought to claim the baby; in cases where a wife deserted her husband, he had a legal right to claim the child, for such a desertion would mark her a fallen woman.

She might tell Radford that Andrew was not his son, but then she would have to brand the child a bastard before the world; she could not possibly burden the child with such shame. And what about Charlotte Tremayne? She was too old to weather another scandal.

And once she began to reveal the whole truth about Andrew, Kevin Farrell would be involved. Charlotte had forgiven her for her deceit, in claiming she was the Tremayne heiress, but the old lady would have no reason to be equally kind to Kevin. She could, if she wished, have him tracked down and made to pay for his part in the impersonation scheme.

Drucilla knew that if she left Radford and tried to keep her baby, she would destroy too many others, and she did not have that kind of ruthlessness in her nature; indeed, she found it hard to hate Radford for what he had done last night, for she tried to understand the dark forces that drove him.

She lay still, with Radford's arm around her, and she felt his lips brush his cheek. "I'll never hurt you again, I swear it," he said.

She did not answer, but she resolved that, somehow, she would find a way to escape from the isolation of Seaton Barony to Charleston and make a life of her own.

It was Theodora who made is possible for her to do so. They were seated around the dining room table, after dinner. They had been back on the plantation for a week, and Drucilla decided she must risk Radford's displeasure by bringing up the matter of a townhouse.

"There are several for sale," Theodora said, "and it would be an excellent chance for the girls to spend the whole season in Charleston, instead of traveling back and forth." She did not have to add that it would be a good opportunity for her daughters to go on with their husband-hunting.

"But Drucilla needn't go with them," Radford said.

Theodora sipped her coffee and nibbled at a piece of Bessie's rich poundcake. "It would not be quite proper for two unmarried young ladies to live alone, even with servants in the house, but with Drucilla for a chaperon, it would be perfectly acceptable."

"Why can't you stay with them in Charleston?" Radford asked his mother.

"I have far too much to keep me busy here."

By now, Drucilla knew her mother-in-law well enough to understand that, although she allowed Radford to help in the running of the plantation, she preferred to have a free hand.

"I suppose you want me off in Charleston with Drucilla and the girls, so you can go on expanding the rice acreage here, replacing all the machinery at ruinous prices. Forgive me, but you're not being practical. We're competing with Louisiana now, and few of the other planters around here are willing to do so."

"They lack capital," Theodora said calmly.

She was adamant about restoring the plantation to what it had been before the war and, unless Drucilla missed her guess, her mother-in-law would make a tidy profit on rice, in spite of the competition and the expense of the new machinery.

Drucilla never ceased to marvel at Theodora, with her rustling taffeta skirts, her lace-trimmed, wisteria-scented handkerchiefs, her bobbing gray curls, and her soft, sweet voice. Who would guess that behind this façade was an aptitude for business as keen as any man's, a ruthless determination to get her own way at all costs. She was set on rebuilding the plantation so that it would be as close as possible to what it had been before the war; the rice crop would flourish; the men who rowed the Seaton barge upriver would continue to wear the traditional livery; the army of house servants would be meticulously trained. Furniture would be imported from Europe, along with fine oil paintings, statues, and crates of leather-bound books. Drucilla knew, of course, that her money was making these extravagances possible, in a time and place where many women like Theodora were working in their own fields or living on the charity of relatives.

But since they had returned from Newport, Theodora had spoken of other plans. She wanted Radford to go into politics.

"We've had black savages and carpetbagging Republicans running our state long enough," she said. "If you are in Charleston for the winter, Radford, you can make the right connections, entertain the right people. The next election isn't so far off."

A few weeks after that discussion, Theodora found a fine old townhouse that had belonged to a wealthy Low Country planter who had been killed in the war. His fortune had died with him, his womenfolk had gone to live with kin in New Orleans, and they were pathetically grateful to be able to sell the house for much-needed cash —and not to a family of carpetbaggers, but to one of their own kind.

Like so many Charleston townhouses, the place had been built for privacy; the gable end fronted on the sidewalk, and a veranda was attached to each story, screened from the sun, and from the view of passers-by, by ample wooden lattices and fragrant trellised vines. The high-walled garden provided seclusion, too; but to Drucilla, it was a welcome change from the isolation of Seaton Barony.

Radford showed her the city on a drive down to the waterfront. They took an open carriage, for the sunlight was warm and pleasant even now in early November, and Radford pointed out the fine homes that lined the Ashley River and the labyrinth of wooden piers and wharves running along the inlets nearby. "Some people say this section reminds them of Venice," he said.

He turned the carriage down King Street, and Drucilla saw that there were several fashionably dressed ladies shopping along that thoroughfare. Although she was not in need of new clothes, she made up her mind that she and the Seaton girls would come here often.

When they reached the waterfront, Drucilla was surprised to see how busy it was: the devastation of the war had passed, and trade was picking up. Radford showed her the lumberyard he had bought, the cotton sheds and pounding mills that were part of the Seaton holdings. A rice schooner was unloading near one of the mills, and black stevedores were shouting to one another.

There was life and activity here, and Drucilla felt her spirits rising. She liked the clanging of hammers, the rattling of drays—the sounds of a bustling city. Sooner or later, she supposed, she would have to return to

Seaton Barony, but right now, she was determined to enjoy her freedom.

Thank heaven, she had not yet become pregnant again. Although Radford still came to her bed, she suspected that he was intimate with her maid, Emmaline. Once, when she had come back to the house earlier than she had planned, she had found them together in the hallway, and Radford's arm had been around Emmaline's slender waist. The girl had given Drucilla a frightened look and scurried off. Another time, she had seen Radford coming from the servants' wing off the kitchen, and his fair skin had flushed slightly when he realized she had seen him. Still, she knew he was determined that she must bear him more sons.

Although she did not love Radford, she would have been willing, but she knew that Radford would use a second pregnancy as an excuse to keep her a prisoner, and she could not submit to that. Did most men regard their wives as possessions, as instruments for the provision of heirs? She had no way of knowing about such matters, for she had never had a close female friend with whom to discuss such matters.

She thought about Kevin. Even if he had married her, she was sure he would not have regarded her as a means of carrying on his name. But then, of course, he had not come of an illustrious family, and he owned no property.

No, it was more than that. Kevin's lovemaking had been natural, uninhibited; he had been as eager to give her pleasure as to receive it. He would never have taken her against her will; he would never have hurt her deliberately, to prove his power over her. Kevin had not been possessed by jealousy and self-doubt, as Radford was.

"Drucilla, my dear." Radford had put a hand on her arm, and she was drawn back to the present, to the bustle and clatter of the docks. "I had no idea you would find all this so fascinating. Most ladies take little interest in commerce."

"Your mother does."

Radford laughed. "Mother is unusual in that way. Tell

me, how do you feel about this notion of hers, that I should go into politics?"

"I think you would do well," she said. "Your family is well-known and respected, and if there is a chance that the Democrats will return to power in the next election—"

"There is, I'm certain of it. The people are fed up with the carpetbaggers and ex-slaves who are running our state these days. Just as this whole country is becoming fed up with Grant and his crooked crew. One scandal after another: the Salary Grab Act, the Crédit Mobilier—"

"But some people say that President Grant was not directly involved in those scandals, that he did not even fully understand their implications."

"Then he's not the man to run the country. He's unfit to be president." Radford's face was cold with anger.

"I didn't mean to question you," Drucilla said. "But if I am to learn, we must discuss these things."

He smiled. "There's no need for a woman to understand politics."

"But if you are going to be a politician, I must understand, I must be able to share your interests. I want to, Radford."

He put an arm around her. "Perhaps you're right," he conceded. And she knew that she had pleased him. "But I'm afraid you're going to be busy enough, having to entertain my supporters, without taking on the extra burden of studying politics and economics."

Her father had believed that a woman's mind was equal to a man's, and that both sexes should receive the same education. But she could not say this, for Radford believed that she was the daughter of Horace and Isobel Tremayne, and he must never learn the truth. So she contented herself with saying,

"Please give me a chance. I'll try to be a credit to you, if you'll help me."

"Very well. Next week, we'll be attending the wedding of Miss Victoria Field, and you'll get your first chance."

"A wedding's not a political rally," she protested.

He laughed. "That's the first thing you must learn: any social gathering can be important to a politician. Miss Field is a cousin of Wade Hampton, one of our most revered military leaders during the war. He'll be the next Democratic candidate for governor, you wait and see."

The wedding Radford had mentioned had been only the first of an endless round of social activities that lasted through the winter of '73 and into the spring of the following year. Drucilla quickly became aware that South Carolina was in a state of ferment, and political and social changes were in the air.

At Radford's suggestion, she began to read the *Charleston News and Courier* regularly, and during the late afternoon hours, when they sat together on the vine-shaded veranda, Radford discussed what he thought to be the most important items. She became familiar with the important issues in South Carolina politics, and although her opinions sometimes differed from his, she tried not to contradict him.

She discovered that he had strong views, not only on local affairs, but also on events abroad, particularly when national honor was involved. He was furious over the affair of the *Virginius*, an American steamer running guns to Cuba.

The *Virginius* had been captured by the Spanish gunboat, *Tornado*, off the coast of Cuba, and all fifty-three men on board the gun-runner, including its American captain and several other American citizens, had been shot.

"And our government in Washington was satisfied with an apology from the Spanish government. It's a disgrace, a damned outrage."

"But if those men were aiding the rebels, didn't the legal government have the right to—" She fell silent as he glared at her.

"Spain does not have the right to control the destinies of Cuban planters, anymore than Washington had the right to control the internal affairs of the South."

She realized that she had blundered. Of course, Radford would equate the struggle of the Cuban slave-holding planters with the South's recent war.

"But I thought the rebels wanted to abolish slavery in Cuba."

"A few perhaps. But most are planters whose economic survival depends on the use of slaves. They simply want to be free of Spain and to run their own affairs."

"Well, at any rate," Drucilla put in, hoping to change the subject, "it's as well you didn't invest in one of those gun-running boats, like the *Virginius*."

"A risky venture," he agreed. "There are safer ways to make money these days. However, some of our friends don't agree. John Pettigrew, for instance."

"Surely, Mr. Pettigrew doesn't plan to take part in a gun-running expedition," she said, remembering the stout, middle-aged planter who had first discussed the Cuban problem at the Harvest Ball. Since moving into Charleston, she had become quite friendly with Pettigrew's wife, Letitia; indeed, she and Radford and the Seaton girls were supposed to attend a party at the Pettigrew estate next week.

Radford laughed. "John's not about to try to take a boat into Havana harbor, my dear. But he has sold a steamer to a captain who plans to do just that."

"But who would be so reckless, after the incident of the *Virginius*?"

Radford shrugged and said, "One of those dashing adventurers that Hazel finds so vastly romantic, at least between the covers of a book."

"Oh, Radford—really!" Hazel had come onto the second-story veranda.

Radford could not resist teasing his younger sister, and Drucilla often intervened, knowing how shy and vulnerable Hazel was. "You must not mind your brother," she said. "He wasn't speaking seriously."

"Oh, but I was," Radford said. "You must try to look particularly well turned out when we go to Pettigrew's oyster roast, Hazel. Who knows, my dear, perhaps you'll catch the eye of one of those dashing gun-runners."

Hazel's face went a deep pink. "I shouldn't know what

to say to such a man," she murmured.

"And besides, I hardly think Mr. Pettigrew would invite such a person to his home."

"Not for a formal dinner, perhaps—but you've never been to a Carolina oyster roast, Drucilla. There'll be a tremendous crowd, tables on the lawn—and political speeches afterward. You'll see."

On the morning of the oyster roast, the Seatons set out before noon. Although it was still March, the weather was already warm, even a little sultry. Drucilla was glad she had worn a cool dress of dainty muslin, and she knew that she looked pretty when she saw Radford's eyes lingering on her appreciatively. She spread the lilac muslin skirt carefully around her, and raised her parasol over her head. Hazel and Gwen took their places in the seat opposite, and the black coachman cracked his whip over the backs of the sleek bays.

"It's important to be on time for an oyster roast," Radford said. "The idea is to get the oysters out of the coals and onto the table while they're piping hot. Of course, I don't know whether a Yankee girl can fully appreciate these rituals—"

"Radford, how dare you?" Gwen's pale eyes flashed with annoyance. "Drucilla's not a Yankee any longer. She's one of us now."

Drucilla was touched by her sister-in-law's swift defense. She wanted to belong, to be a part of this new way of life on which she had embarked when she had married Radford. But somehow she knew that she could never be "one of us" in the way Gwen meant. Even though slavery had been abolished, she saw too many injustices around her. And she knew that men like her husband and John Pettigrew were only waiting until they could regain control of the state through political means; when that happened, she wondered whether the blacks would be in a much better position than they had been before the war.

Already, she had heard stories of bands of "Redshirts" who galloped into the polls to frighten and intimidate black voters; she knew that while people like the Seatons insisted the ex-slaves were unfit to vote, they were also opposed to free education for black people. She knew better than to put forth her views about the problems she saw around her, but she could never share the feelings of the family she had married into. She could never really be one of them.

She was gripped by a curious sense of depression, and as the carriage moved along, heading for the Pettigrew estate on the Ashley River, she looked at the streets without seeing them.

She had not belonged in Newport, either. Always, ever since her father had died, she had had the feeling of being an outsider, belonging nowhere.

With a flutter of panic, she wondered if she would ever find a place where she really belonged. She made herself put the thought aside. Nothing would stop her from having a good time today.

The oyster roast was as elaborate as Radford had told her it would be. Servants had dug pits and set up ovens out on the wide lawn. Long tables stood in rows under the oak trees. When the Seaton carriage drove up, the lawn was already crowded with ladies in bright silk and embroidered muslin dresses. They held their lace-trimmed parasols carefully to protect their complexions from the sun. The gentlemen wore suits of good broadcloth or light wool, with embroidered waistcoats and silk cravats.

Letitia Pettigrew, her pale blonde beauty enhanced by her rose-colored faille dress, with its ecru lace ruffles, hurried forward to greet the new arrivals. Drucilla stared at the long cypress wood tables that had been spread across the lawn for a quarter of a mile, and was even more surprised when Letitia remarked that she had carpenters standing by with extra cypress lumber to add new tables if needed.

At noon, the servants started the fires and the pits were soon aglow with hickory coals. More guests kept arriving, until, at one o'clock, John Pettigrew blew a hunter's horn from the steps of the red brick mansion, as a signal for a host of small black boys to begin pouring barrelsful of oysters on the live coals.

Drucilla took a seat next to Radford, thinking that she would have preferred chairs to benches, for any lady would have been most embarrassed, should a gentleman catch a glimpse of her leg, above the top of her shoe.

As soon as all the guests were seated, the Pettigrews' butler appeared with his assistants, carrying silver pitchers of whisky punch for the gentlemen, and eggnog with a dash of nutmeg and a little Barbados rum for the ladies.

Pettigrew rose and proposed a toast, first to his friends and neighbors gathered here, then to Wade Hampton, the hero who, in spite of the Southern defeat, was still worshipped by so many of his fellow Carolinians. It was too soon to speak directly of the next election, but the cheers that greeted Hampton convinced Drucilla that Radford might well be right in assuming the man could become the next governor of the state. As for Radford himself, he was hoping to win a seat in the state legislature.

After the toasts, the feasting began and went on for almost an hour. Drucilla realized that, for many of the guests, this was a rare treat. Certainly, few had managed to do as well during Reconstruction as Radford Seaton and John Pettigrew.

When the guests got up from the long tables, some wandered over to the creek behind the house for a stroll, while others found seats under the shade of the trees. "There'll be another feast in a few hours," Radford told her.

"Good heavens," she said, "I wasn't planning to eat again for the rest of the day."

"You mustn't say that. No one makes a terrapin stew like the Pettigrews' Sukie."

The sun was overhead now, and the air was heavy and humid.

"Do let's go inside the house," Hazel suggested. "I want to lie down for a bit." The midday siesta was still a custom in this semitropical climate.

But inside the hallway, Letitia drew Drucilla aside.

"Those new paper patterns from Madame Demorest have arrived," she said. "Perhaps you'd like to come into the library and see them. And you, too, Hazel—"

"I'd rather take a nap, thank you," Hazel said. "I'll see them later, if I may."

After the glaring sunlight outside, Drucilla found it hard to see in the darkness of the library. But after a moment she caught sight of John Pettigrew and another man at the far end of the room.

"I'm sorry, John," Letitia said. "I didn't know you were in here."

"Quite all right, my love," he said. "We were just leaving."

"If you're quite sure," Letitia said.

"Yes, indeed, Mrs. Pettigrew. Your husband has been promising to show me that new Arabian mare he has bought."

Drucilla looked at Pettigrew's companion. She heard the familiar voice, and for a moment she could not move. She tried to take a deep breath, but her tight lacing prevented it. In an effort to get control of herself, her hand gripped the delicate ivory handle of her parasol. There was a small, snapping sound.

She could not take her eyes from the man who stood beside John Pettigrew: taller than his host, powerfully built, with wide, heavy shoulders; straight black brows over gray eyes that narrowed slightly when he saw Drucilla.

"Mrs. Seaton, may I present Kevin Farrell."

Kevin kept his face carefully expressionless. He was leaving it to her, to pretend they were strangers if she wanted to. But she said quietly, "Mr. Farrell and I have met."

She caught the surprise in the expressions of both the Pettigrews. Then Letitia's glance shifted, and she cried out, "The handle of your parasol—you've cut yourself—"

Drucilla's hand gripped the handle so tightly that Letitia had to work her fingers loose. "It's bleeding," she said. "How on earth did you—"

"Allow me," Kevin said quickly, taking out his handkerchief. He wrapped the linen square around her hand. "That should do it. It's no more than a scratch."

He kept his hand on hers a little longer than necessary; his touch sent a swift, hot tide surging through every nerve in her body.

Abruptly, she drew her hand away. She thanked him with formal politeness, and the two men left the library.

"Sit down, my dear," Letitia said, taking the paper dress patterns out of their brown envelopes and spreading them on the polished mahogany table. "I declare, Madame Demorest has done a great service to our Southern ladies, with these paper patterns. I do believe half the dresses being worn here today have been remade from the outmoded ones, and all thanks to these patterns. Luckily, the new skirts are so much narrower than those we wore before that it's possible to cut out the really faded parts. Not that you have to worry about such things, Drucilla." Letitia rattled on, and Drucilla tried hard to listen, but her emotions were in a turmoil.

There had never been a day when she had not thought of Kevin, wondered where he was. Every time she held little Andrew in her arms, and buried her face in the child's soft, black ringlets, she had hungered for Kevin. Lying beside her husband at night, she had forced herself not to remember Kevin. She had told herself that she would never see him again and that, with the passing of the years, she would forget him. And now . . .

"Really, my dear, I shouldn't have expected you'd know a man like Mr. Farrell."

Drucilla made her voice casual. "Indeed?"

"I mean—he's not quite—"

"He's John's friend, isn't he?"

"Not really. A business acquaintance. He bought a steamer from John. An old blockade runner."

Letitia was interrupted when Sukie, the cook, tapped on the library door, and there was a hasty conference about some problem in the kitchen. "Forgive me," Letitia said. "I must leave you, but do look at the patterns, and choose the ones you'd like for yourself."

But after Letitia and Sukie had departed, Drucilla remained seated in the quiet library, fingering the brown paper envelopes, not seeing them.

What did Kevin want with a boat? He had been in the

British Navy and had deserted—she remembered that much. But why should he buy a steamer from Pettigrew now?

She caught her breath sharply, remembering a conversation she had had with Radford. About the fighting in Cuba. John Pettigrew was negotiating the sale of a boat to a man who was going to run guns and supplies to the rebels.

Kevin.

Fourteen

"RADFORD, please don't go out tonight."

The Seatons had returned to the townhouse near the Battery and, after a light supper, they had gone out onto the second-story veranda to get the breeze from the harbor. But, instead of taking a seat, Radford announced that he was going to a political meeting at Marcus Thorp's law office on Broad Street.

"I'm sorry, my dear," he said. "But Mr. Thorp's an important man in our Democratic organization here. Wade Hampton has promised to attend the meeting, and Pettigrew will be there. It's important for me to make an appearance."

"May I go with you?"

"I'd like nothing better, but there won't be any ladies present. This is serious business, Drucilla."

"I don't want to be alone." There was desperation in her voice.

"Gwen and Hazel are right here," he said patiently.

But Gwen, who was rocking in a chair opposite Drucilla's, said, "I, for one, plan to retire early. I should think you'd be sleepy, too, Drucilla, what with the heat, and all that food at the Pettigrews'.'"

If only she were able to sleep; but her nerves were taut, and she knew that if she went upstairs now, she would lie wide-eyed in the darkness.

"I'm not the least bit tired," she said.

"Then why don't we look at those new patterns Letitia loaned you?" Hazel suggested. "It's not too soon to choose a few dresses for summer."

"I don't want to look at patterns. I have closets full of dresses now, more than I can ever hope to wear. For heaven's sake, Hazel, don't you ever think of anything but clothes?"

Hazel's pale blue eyes filled with tears. Her sister-in-law had never spoken to her so harshly before. She fumbled for her handkerchief and sniffed audibly. "Very well. I'll take the patterns up to my room and look at them there."

Drucilla felt ashamed. "I'm sorry, dear," she said. "I didn't mean to snap at you."

"You've been cross all evening," Hazel said reproachfully. "I declare, I don't know what's wrong with you. You scarcely said a word on the drive home from the Pettigrews', you sulked all through supper, and now you go into a perfect tizzy-fit because I've asked you to look at patterns."

"I have a headache," Drucilla lied.

"Then I should think you'd want to get to bed early," Radford said. He bent and his lips brushed her cheek. She reached up and clung to him, not out of love, but because of her desperation, because she did not want him to leave her. She wanted to cry out to him, "Stay with me. Keep me safe."

Safe from what? Her own treacherous feelings, the tormenting need that had begun the moment she had seen Kevin. But she only said, "Try to come home early, won't you?"

"I wish I could." He disengaged himself gently from her embrace, but his eyes lingered on her. For evening, she had changed to a pale blue silk, with a low, rounded neckline that revealed the swell of her breasts. "You look so lovely tonight." He broke off, conscious of the presence of his sisters. "Meetings like this go on and on. Even within the Party, there is much disagreement on important issues." He shook his head. "There are times I wish I hadn't listened to Mother's suggestion about my going into politics."

Theodora did not make suggestions; she issued royal edicts, Drucilla thought.

"You must not wait up for me," Radford was saying. And a moment later, he left the veranda. Drucilla picked up her fan and began moving it back and forth rapidly, but the air was heavy, and even the breeze from the harbor did not help; she would not be able to sleep tonight.

She listened to the sound of Radford's carriage driving off, and then felt the warm velvet darkness, like a tangible weight, settling around the house.

"Shall I get you a cup of camomile tea?" Gwen asked.

"Whatever for?"

"Your headache, of course. Or perhaps you'd prefer spirits of hartshorn."

"My headache's almost gone."

"You're sure, dear? You seem so edgy."

She breathed a sigh when the girls withdrew at last, and she was left alone on the veranda. The warm night air was rich with the scents of honeysuckle and wisteria. She closed her eyes and tried to collect her thoughts.

Kevin was here in Charleston, but he was going to Cuba. He must not go. She remembered sitting here on the veranda only a few weeks ago, and listening to Radford speak about the capture of the *Virginius* and the shooting of the crew.

She also recalled the stories in Horace Greeley's *New York Tribune*, shocking accounts of the atrocities committed by the Spanish forces against captured rebels.

"Something must be done for Cuba," Mr. Greeley had written. Perhaps—but not by Kevin. Let others go and carry arms, fight and die. Not Kevin.

She could not sit still another moment, so she went into the house and up to the nursery, where Andrew lay asleep. She could not resist picking him up. He made a few fretful sounds, then, sensing his mother's presence, he relaxed. She held him and rocked him, her lips brushing his thick, black curls. He was nearly a year old now, a sturdy, handsome boy.

She put him back in his bed and pulled the netting around it, then tiptoed out. She paused in the hallway; it would be useless to go to bed, so she went downstairs and into the high-walled garden. She sat down on a bench under a live oak, brushing away the trailing veils of moss.

Tension still gripped her, so that, when she heard a faint, rattling noise at the garden gate, she started and gave a little cry.

"Not yuh be skeered, please, ma'am."

She saw a pair of round eyes peering through the heavy, ornate iron work of the gate. "Is yuh Miz Seaton, please?"

It was the high, piping voice of a small black boy. She went to the gate and said, "I'm Mrs. Seaton. What do you want?"

"Come fuh give yuh dis."

He handed her a note through the bars of the gate. Even before she opened it, she knew.

THE BULL'S HEAD TAVERN. GADSDEN'S WHARF.

There was no signature, but she knew. She must not go. She must send the boy away, tear up the note, and go to bed. If necessary, she would remain in the house until Kevin's boat had sailed.

But it must not sail. He must not go to Cuba, into that hell of violence and killing. She would have to go to meet him and tell him so. She would have to find a way to dissuade him from this crazy scheme.

She said to the boy outside the gate, "Get me a closed carriage, and tell the driver to wait at the end of the street. I'll be ready in a few minutes."

There was still time to change her mind, she thought, as she stood in front of the hall mirror, putting on her bonnet, wrapping a light shawl around her shoulders. But she knew that she would not change her mind. She tried to reassure herself. Radford would not be back for hours. She would meet Kevin at the tavern, talk to him, and then return home.

The Bull's Head Tavern was a noisy place, close to the waterfront. The gray-haired driver looked scandalized at letting a lady out at such a place, but she did not care. She paid him and hurried inside.

Once she was through the door, however, she hesitated. She had been inside such places before, on the riverfront in Ohio and Kentucky, when she had toured with the stock company. But she had changed since those days, and now she was repelled by the sight of sailors and their women, drinking, quarreling, fondling each other openly. She knew that she was drawing attention, for she looked different from the other women, in her pale blue silk dress, simple and obviously expensive, her neat, dark blue bonnet and fine cashmere shawl.

She drew back when a man approached her, a stocky, red-haired sailor in a striped jersey shirt. "Would you be Mrs. Seaton?"

She nodded and he said, "Come with me, if you please. I'm Tim Cleary. First mate on Captain Farrell's boat, the *Medea*."

Somewhat reassured, she took his arm and let him lead her through the crowd; she got many curious looks, but no one bothered her. Beyond the taproom was a short passageway with a door at the end. Inside, Kevin was waiting for her. "Thanks, Tim," he said. "Now you can go and get down to serious drinking."

Even after Tim Cleary had shut the door behind him, Drucilla could still hear the raucous laughter and the shouting from outside.

"Not what you're used to," Kevin said, as if reading her thoughts, "but it's private." Then he fell silent and stood looking down at her. "I've missed you, love." He reached out to embrace her, but she drew back. Laughing softly, he said, "How's your hand?"

"It's better—"

He took the hand in his, looked at it, then pressed his lips against her palm. His tongue traced the cut, warm, caressing. She shivered.

"Here, sit down and have a drink." On a round oak table was a bottle of brandy and two glasses; he had been drinking from one. Now he poured her a drink and when she hesitated, he said, "Go on. It'll steady your nerves."

"There's nothing wrong with my nerves. I hadn't expected to meet you at the Pettigrews' today—naturally I was surprised. And when Letitia told me about the boat you bought from John—that's why I came to talk to you. You can't go to Cuba. You can't."

"Who told you I was?"

"Radford said John Pettigrew was selling his boat to a gun-runner—"

"Ah, yes. Radford. You lost no time in taking my advice, did you? I'd only just left Newport when you and Seaton were married. I'm sure your 'grandmother' and Radford's mother were both delighted by the match. Two fine old families, united." He raised his glass. "It's not too late to toast the bride, is it? Long life, happiness. And love. You do love him, don't you, Drucilla?"

"Of course. . . ." Her voice faltered.

"Say it."

"I love Radford."

"Is that why you broke the handle of a perfectly good parasol when you set eyes on me this afternoon? Is that why you came here tonight? Why you—"

"Stop it, Kevin. Please."

"Why you trembled like a schoolgirl when I touched you a moment ago?"

"I only came here tonight because—Kevin, you mustn't sail for Cuba. I know you're planning to go, but you can't. There are other ways to make money—without risking your life."

"But none of those other ways interest me at the moment."

"You must be mad. They shot the crew of the *Virginius* —Americans as well as Cubans."

"I had no idea you took such an interest in foreign affairs. Do you think it's quite ladylike?"

"Stop it. I can't stand the thought of you going into a war and—"

"I don't plan to go into combat, love. I'm taking the *Medea* on one quick voyage. A highly profitable trip."

"But if something goes wrong—if anything happens to you—"

He put down his glass and peered into her face sharply.

"You *do* care, then." There was an intensity in his look, his voice, that startled and confused her.

"You know I do. Get rid of that boat. Or use it to haul lumber or rice."

He shook his read. "The *Medea* is a fine, swift vessel. She was built to run the Yankee blockade. Why, it would be a disgrace to put her to hauling lumber or rice. Now love, we've talked long enough. The night will be half-over before I've got you on board."

"I don't understand."

"Yes, you do. That's why you came here. Don't deny it. And don't be ashamed of your feelings."

"I'm married—"

"You can marry a dozen men for all I care. You still belong to me. You always will."

Kevin rowed her out to the *Medea*, across the dark waters of Charleston Harbor, under a cloudy sky, where only a few stars glowed faintly. She did not speak, but sat opposite him, watching him row. She had a sense of the inevitability of this moment, of what she was about to do. Kevin was right; she belonged to him. Even if Radford had not gone out tonight, leaving her alone, she would have come to Kevin sooner or later.

She looked up to see the *Medea* rising up out of the water, heard the waves lapping against her sides. Kevin made a signal to the man on watch, who helped Drucilla aboard.

She was startled, for she had thought she and Kevin would be alone; the presence of the sailors on deck made her uneasy. They would surely be thinking she was a fancy girl, paid by their captain for a few hours of pleasure. She was thankful for the dim lighting on deck, only a few lanterns.

Kevin put an arm around her to steady her, as he led the way. "Careful," he said once, pulling her aside. "That hatch is open—they all are. The rest of the cargo is still being carried on board."

"At this time of night?"

"We don't want to advertise the purpose of our voyage. The rebels have agents here in Charleston, but the Spanish do, too."

"It's dangerous, then. Why must you do it? Can't you give up the whole idea? It's not too late—"

He silenced her, turning her face to his and kissing her mouth. "Hush, my love," he said. Then, "Come along, now. Down these steps. Careful. . . ."

Kevin's cabin was small, and not nearly so fine as the stateroom she had shared with Radford on their honeymoon voyage aboard the *Gryphon*. There were no velvet drapes, no gilt and enamel walls, no fine Oriental rugs. She breathed the mingled odors of fresh paint, polished brass, and kerosene from the lantern that swung overhead with the motion of the ship. Even at anchor, the *Medea* swayed gently on the night tide.

She took off her blue bonnet and her cashmere shawl, and a moment later, Kevin caught her in his arms and held her against him; he kissed her closed eyes, her mouth, her throat, with fierce hunger.

"I've missed you. I never thought—I wouldn't have believed. Lord, how I've missed you."

"Not enough to stay with me in Newport. You left without a word and then—"

"And then, in New York, I read about your marriage to Radford." He looked away for a moment. "You were right to marry him, of course. He's given you the kind of security I never could. Not only money. A home. A respected name. A position in society down here in Charleston."

And night after night wtihout love, she thought. Giving myself to Radford out of a sense of duty. Pretending that Andrew is his son. But she knew she could not say these things to Kevin, not now.

He was kissing her again, a long, lingering kiss. Then he held her away for a moment. "That's a most becoming dress," he said, "but if you're not out of it in two minutes flat—"

She began to open the buttons of her bodice, then glanced at the swinging lantern. "Don't make me turn it off," he said. "I want to look at you. I haven't looked at your body for so long."

A few minutes later, when she lay beside him in the narrow bed, he traced the soft curves and shadowy little hollows with his fingertips. Her skin gleamed like warm ivory in the lantern's fire; her red-gold hair was a cascade of molten fire.

"You're a woman now," he said.

"I haven't changed."

"Oh, but you have. And I like it. You've filled out here a bit. . . ." He pressed his lips against the roundness of her hip. "And here, too, I think. . . ." His tongue moved slowly along the inside of her thigh. "And . . ."

He spread her legs, and she made a sound of protest when she sensed what he was going to do; he had never done that before.

"Don't be shy, love," he said. Again she gave a cry, but this time because he was arousing her in every nerve, every fiber of her body, using his lips, his tongue, his fingers. Probing deeply . . . withdrawing. . . . Her hands moved, grasped his hair.

Her body felt warm, pliant, responsive to every touch. "Wait," she gasped. "Not that way . . . I want you to. . . ."

He moved, and now he was over her, and her fingers pressed into his back, drawing him down to her, into her.

But even when he was inside her, he delayed, moving with slow, hard thrusts, but stopping to kiss her throat, her shoulders, her breasts, until she could stand it no longer, until she encircled him with her long, slim legs and arched her hips. Until there was no holding back for either of them. She heard his harsh breathing, then her own voice, sobbing with joy, with complete fulfillment.

They rested, and then made love again. And again. After the long months of separation, he could not get enough of her. And her need matched his own. How had she lived through the months of emptiness? Nothing that had happened during those months had been real or meaningful.

Except the birth of Andrew. She had been resting in Kevin's arms, completely relaxed, when she remembered Andrew. Kevin's son. And she thought that perhaps, if she told him about Andrew, he might not go away. If he knew he had a son, perhaps he would not be willing to risk his safety so lightly.

"Kevin."

"Yes, love? Are you ready again? So soon?"

"It's not that. It's—there's something I haven't told you. While you were away I—"

"Go on."

"I have a baby. A little boy."

His eyes went bleak for a moment, and she was angry with herself for having broken, even slightly, this perfect thing they had shared tonight.

"I knew," he said quietly. "John Pettigrew mentioned it. He also said Radford plans to go into politics. That he and Pettigrew and some of the others were going to be at a political meeting tonight. Otherwise, I would not have sent that note. After all, you'll have to go on living with your husband after I'm gone."

After I'm gone.

But he must not go. "About the baby," she began again.

"All right, you have a baby. There's nothing extraordinary about presenting your husband with a son, is there?" But she heard the bitterness in his voice. He cared enough to be jealous, but not enough to stay with her.

"Does he look like his father?"

She wanted to cry, for she felt that the beauty of this night was slipping away, and she hated herself for it. She could not try to hold Kevin by appealing to a sense of duty. If he did not love her enough to stay because of her, she would not tell him the truth. And yet—

"Yes," she said, quietly. "He looks exactly like his father."

"Radford must be a proud man. And I suppose Theodora is pleased, too."

"It means a great deal to both of them. A boy, to carry on the family name. One day he'll be master of Seaton Barony."

Kevin said nothing. He lay staring moodily at the swaying lamp overhead. She reached out and put her hand on his chest, stroking the hard, heavy muscles. For a moment, he did not move; he did not look at her. She raised herself and pressed her parted lips against his shoulder. His skin was damp and tasted of salt. "Please, Kevin," she whispered. "Please. . . ."

Slowly he smiled, reached up and pulled her down on top of him. He stroked her breasts until the nipples were hard and tingling. He did not take his eyes from her face, even as he grasped her hips and positioned her above him. When she understood what he wanted she said, "It doesn't seem—right—this way—"

He laughed. "You insist on the missionary position?"

"The what?"

"A sailor told me once that the missionaries who went to some of those South Sea Islands to get the natives to wear clothes and worry about their immortal souls, insisted there was only one proper position for love-making. The man on top and the woman underneath."

Drucilla could not help smiling. "How silly. But—how had the islanders been doing it before?"

"The man crouched down on his haunches and the woman—at least, that's what this sailor told me." They were both laughing now, and he was holding her against him. Her long hair swept over his face, and he raised his head to kiss the perfumed waves. "I think I like this better."

His voice was deep and a little unsteady, and his eyes held hers. He did not stop looking into her eyes, as once again, they became one, giving and receiving total pleasure.

It was only a little before dawn when Drucilla returned to the townhouse near the Battery. She went in through the garden and upstairs to the bedroom. She hesitated, then opened the door slowly, noiselessly. The bed was smooth, untouched. Radford had not come home yet, which did not surprise her, since he had said the meeting would go on all night. She suspected that although these political meetings might start in a private home or office, they ended in one of the more elegant barrooms in the city.

She turned on the gas, and by the soft light from the white china globe, she took off her bonnet. The silk of her dark blue bonnet was damp and spotted with sea spray, after the trip across the harbor.

She had promised to meet Kevin again, tomorrow night. No, tonight, for it was already a new day. As she looked at her face in the mirror above the dresser, she thought how it had changed in a few hours. She saw the soft, rich color in her cheeks, the little smile that curved her mouth. Pressing her lips together, she felt a slight swelling, for Kevin had kissed her hard, holding her in his arms back there on Gadsden's Wharf. Pressing his mouth to hers as if he could never get enough of her.

She cupped her breasts in her hands, pressing them through the thin silk of her dress, and closed her eyes, letting herself bask in the sheer pleasure of her senses.

She did not hear the footsteps on the carpeted stairs, the bedroom door opening.

"Drucilla."

Radford stood in the doorway behind her, his face flushed, his blue eyes glazed. There was a looseness about his mouth. He had been drinking more than usual. He started forward, swayed, and grabbed for the doorknob. "Drucilla, honey. Sorry. Home so late. Don't be angry."

"I'm not angry."

"Sweet Drucilla. Sweet . . ." His voice was thick, the words slurred. "And pretty. So pretty . . ."

"Hush, now. You'll wake the house."

"Don' want to wake anyone. Want to sleep."

He got to the bed, and lay down on it, fully dressed. His eyes closed and a moment later, she heard his even breathing.

Thank heaven. If Radford had been sober, he could not have failed to see that she was still wearing the blue dress she had worn at dinner, that her bonnet and shawl were flung carelessly across the dresser. At this hour of the morning.

She put on a nightgown, but could not bring herself to lie down beside Radford. Instead, she curled up on the chaise longue at the other end of the room and fell asleep almost at once.

Radford did not come down to breakfast that morning, and at noon, he was still in the darkened bedroom. When he appeared in the garden, after lunch, he looked pale and drawn. Drucilla, who had been watching Andrew playing among the shrubbery, looked up at her husband in surprise. He had a good head for liquor and even when he had gotten drunk before, he had been well enough the following morning.

She offered him a cup of strong, black coffee from the silver pot on the table beside her. He swallowed it, then drank another.

Of course, she did not mention his condition when he had come in early that morning. No matter how drunk a gentleman might become, a lady pretended not to notice; it was a husband's right to get drunk, and a wife's duty to be calmly oblivious, Theodora had once told her.

"Aren't you going to ask how the meeting went?"

"I hope it was successful," she said.

"It was. I'll run for the legislature in the next election, and I haven't the slightest doubt I'll get a seat. The Democrats will make a clean sweep, this time."

"That's good," she said, as she watched Andrew tussling with his black-and-white puppy.

"You aren't very interested, are you?"

Then, without giving her a chance to reply, he said,

"I believe I'll go upriver to Seaton Barony this evening. My mother will want to know about the meeting."

She caught the note of reproach, but she did not care. All that morning, she had been trying to figure out some way to get to see Kevin tonight. She had considered and rejected a dozen schemes. Now, without any effort on her part, Radford had given her the perfect opportunity. She felt a twinge of guilt, but it passed. All that mattered was being with Kevin for a few more hours.

She tried not to remember how short a time they would have together. He had not told her when he would sail, and she had not been able to bring herself to ask.

She must not think about his sailing for Cuba. She must be grateful for whatever time they had.

"Do you want to go upriver with me?" Radford asked, his eyes fixed on her face.

"Your mother wants me to stay here with Gwen and Hazel."

"Ah, yes, I was forgetting. You must play the chaperon."

She thought she heard a note of irony in his voice. "It was your mother's idea," she reminded him.

"And you've never really liked Seaton Barony, have you?"

"I've tried. It's a beautiful place but it's so far from everything."

"Yes, of course." He went over to Andrew, picked him up and swung him high. The baby crowed wtih pleasure. "I hope my son loves the plantation as I do. It will be a part of his heritage."

That evening, after Radford had departed for Seaton Barony, and Gwen and Hazel had retired, Drucilla slipped out of the house, hailed a closed carriage and by midnight, she was once again aboard the *Medea.* There was more activity on the boat tonight than there had been last night. The men were working quickly, their bodies shining with sweat in the lantern light as they got the crates on board and into the hold.

"You're leaving very soon, aren't you?" Drucilla asked Kevin.

"Yes, love."

"When?"

"Must we talk about it now?" He led her to the stern but she stopped at the top of the steps leading down to the cabin.

"Isn't there anything I can say or do to make you change your mind?"

But his face had that obstinate look she had come to know so well. She moved aside, as Tim Cleary led a working party forward to one of the hatches.

"If it's money you need, I can—"

"The money's important. But there are other considerations."

She stared at him in surprise. "Surely, you're not one of the rebels. Cuba's not your country."

"I don't care a damn which side wins. If the Spanish forces needed supplies, I'd sell to them."

"Then why must you go? Tell me."

He sighed impatiently. "Drucilla, you mean more to me than any woman I've ever known. I didn't realize that, myself, until I came here to Charleston and saw you again. And last night—" He put his hands on her arms, and she closed her eyes.

"Now," she thought. "He's going to say he loves me. That he'll stay with me."

"But I don't think any woman can understand certain things about a man. I have to go to Cuba. If it wasn't Cuba, it would be somewhere else. But it will always be somewhere else."

Her eyes flew open, and she fought back the tears of disappointment. "You're right," she said. "I don't understand. I thought you hated the sea. You deserted from the British Navy, you told me so."

"I did. And I'd do the same thing again, under the same circumstances. But I like the sea—always have—and here aboard the *Medea*, I'm in command. I don't have to take orders from some pompous little bastard in a gold-laced coat whose only claim to authority is his family's ability to buy him a commission."

"Were they all like that?"

"No," he said quietly. "Some knew their business, and a few were fair-minded. But there was one young lieutenant who informed me that he hated all Irishmen on general principle, and that he'd break me before the voyage was over. I took it as long as I could, then, when we were in the West Indies and I saw my chance, I deserted."

"And after that?"

"I stayed alive and I kept moving."

"But you can't go on like that the rest of your life. You have to settle down sometime."

"Listen," he said. "Most men do settle down, sooner or later. They marry, raise children, put down roots on a piece of land and make it their own. But some of us can't. I can't."

"But last night I thought—"

"Last night was a time I'll never forget. I'll take the memory with me to the end of my days. Believe that, Drucilla."

"And will a memory be enough for you?"

"It will have to be. It's the way I'm made. Don't ask for more than I have to give."

There was a finality in his voice that made it impossible for her to say anymore. She turned her face away and stared out at the blackness of the sea, and listened to the soft lapping of the waves against the side of the boat.

"Come down to the cabin now," he said. "Let's make the most of what we have." He drew her into his arms, but she held herself rigid. Then, after a moment, her need overcame her pride. She melted against him. "I love you so," she said.

Footsteps came along the deck, and Kevin released her gently.

"Yes, Tim, what is it? I told you I wasn't to be disturbed."

"Sorry, sir. But this here gentleman, says he's from Mr. Pettigrew, and I figured—"

Drucilla turned and screamed. Radford stood there, his eyes hot with fury, his mouth a narrow slit. Kevin stepped in front of Drucilla.

"Radford, listen to me, please," Drucilla began.

But Kevin interrupted smoothly. "Seaton, your wife and I are old acquaintances. She found out I was here in Charleston and came on board to say good-bye—"

"You're a damned liar," Radford said. There was a bright, glassy look in his eyes that made Drucilla wonder if he had been drinking again. Then she realized with a start that he had not been as drunk as he had appeared to be, when he had come into the bedroom at dawn. Not too drunk to notice the dress, the bonnet and shawl. And to wonder and to brood.

He had never intended to go to Seaton Barony at all. He had waited for her somewhere and had followed her here tonight.

"I was the one who found Drucilla—Mrs. Seaton—in New York and brought her back to her grandmother, you see. So naturally, she wanted to see me again, to—"

"You're a damn liar. And she's an unfaithful little slut. I know her kind. Quiet and ladylike and then, when a man turns his back for an hour—"

"That's enough," Kevin said. He took a step forward. "Now, get off my boat."

Drucilla knew that Kevin was only controlling himself for her sake, because after he was gone, she would have to go back and live with Radford. "Tim," Kevin said, when Radford made no move to go, "take this gentleman forward, and, if he's in no condition to handle a rowboat, have one of the crew get him back ashore."

"I'll toss him over the side, if you say the word, sir," Cleary said.

"That won't be necessary. I think Mr. Seaton's a bit the worse for drink, that's all."

For the first time, Drucilla saw that Radford was carrying a flat, rosewood box under his arm. He opened it, and the light of one of the lanterns caught the gleam of metal. Two long-barreled pistols lay on a bed of velvet. "Take one," Radford said, holding out the box to Kevin. "As the injured party, I have the choice of weapons."

"Dueling pistols?" Kevin shook his head. "Come now, Seaton, you know as well as I that dueling's been outlawed for years and even if it hadn't been, I'm damned if I'd take part in any such nonsense."

"If you don't know how to handle a pistol—"

"I do," Kevin said. "But you're out of your mind if you think I'm going to fight you. You are drunk. Or crazy. In either case—"

Radford lifted one of the pistols out of the case, then he slid the case with the other pistol across the deck with his foot. "Pick it up."

Kevin ignored him. "In either case, you'll be safer without these." He bent, picked up the case with the pistol still lying inside, and with one quick movement, he threw it overboard, into the waters of the harbor.

Then he walked up to Radford, so that Radford's pistol was pointed directly at his chest. Drucilla did not dare to make a sound or even to move.

After that, everything happened so quickly she only got a series of confused and terrifying impressions. Kevin, lunging forward, and the roar of the explosion as the gun fired, and the harsh smell of smoke. Kevin's shirt had been burned away and there was blood on his arm. Now she did scream, but no one paid any attention. Kevin went down, and she thought for one sickening second that he'd been killed but he was moving, getting hold of Radford around the knees, and then both men were struggling, panting like a pair of animals.

Then Kevin was hauling Radford up again, and smashing him against the bulkhead, holding him there, using the uninjured arm to slam his head against the hard surface.

When he released Radford, Kevin stood for a moment, weaving slightly, looking down with surprise at his own blood. The bullet had only grazed his arm, even Drucilla could see that, but she felt sick, thinking of what might have happened.

Radford fell to his knees, shaking his head as if to clear it. "Get him off the boat, Tim," Kevin said, turning to Drucilla.

"It's all right," he said. "Don't look so frightened. It's over now."

But Radford did not rise. Instead, she saw him crawl across the deck on his knees, and then the pistol was in his hand again. He was getting to his feet, shakily, and although the pistol wavered for a moment, he regained control and aimed.

She heard Tim Cleary swear, and then she saw him pick up a heavy wrench that was lying beside the open hatchway. But he'd be too late. He wasn't close enough to Radford to stop him. Then the wrench made a swift arc through the air and caught Radford on the back of the head.

She watched as Radford dropped the pistol and staggered backward, his hands seeking something to grip, to regain his balance, but there was nothing and he went back into emptiness, into the open hatchway, and a moment later, she heard a sickening thud.

Kevin turned away, looking at Cleary, and it was as if, for the moment, she was not there at all. "Come on," he said to Cleary. There were other men milling around now, drawn by the sound of the pistol firing. She tried to follow Kevin, but he pushed her away. "Let me go to him," she said.

"Stay back." And, to one of the sailors, he added, "Keep her here."

Arms were holding her, and she could not free herself. She could not struggle long, and she slumped back against the man who restrained her. What was taking Kevin so long down there with Cleary? Why didn't he come back and speak to her, tell her—?

And then he was coming up out of the hold. His head and shoulders emerged first, and she saw the torn place on his shirt and the bright blood.

The sailor who had been holding her released her now, at a nod from Kevin, who took her by the hand and led her down to his cabin.

She looked at the blood, still oozing slowly from the wound in his arm. It should be cleaned and bandaged, she thought. It was easier to think about Kevin's wound than about Radford. For terror was growing inside her, and a sickening suspicion.

"Can I go down to him?"

Kevin shook his head. "Radford's dead," he told her. "His neck's broken."

Fifteen

SHE swayed, and would have fallen, but Kevin caught her around the waist with his uninjured arm, and half-led, half-carried her to his cabin, where he put her down on the bed. She was shivering, although the air in the cabin was warm and humid.

"Here, drink this." He tried to hand her a glass of dark, thick Demerara rum, but realized she could not hold it in her fingers. He had to put it to her lips. "Go on, drink it," he said.

It burned and she gagged and coughed.

"Now, can you listen to me?"

She nodded. "I want you to stay right here. I'll get back as quickly as I can." He forced the rest of the rum into her, and she managed to get it down. Then he rose.

"Where are you going?" she asked.

"Lie down. We'll talk when I get back."

Her head was spinning with shock and the powerful drink he had given her, but she noticed that his arm was still bleeding. "Your arm. Let me—"

"Tim can take care of it."

Then she remembered. "What happened to—Radford. It wasn't Tim's fault." She found it hard to speak her husband's name. "I'll see Tim's not punished. I'll tell them—"

"You'll tell—what are you talking about?"

"The authorities. I'll tell them exactly how it happened."

"For the love of Christ, Drucilla. You can't tell anyone anything. Don't you see that?"

"But I've got to—I—" She tried to rise, but he forced her back on the bed.

"Be still," he said gently. "Close your eyes and try to sleep. That rum should do it."

But after he had gone, although the rum had made her lightheaded and the cabin was a blur, she did not lose consciousness. She did not sleep. Long shudders wracked her. She gripped the blanket and waited for Kevin to return.

When he got back, he was no longer wearing the blood-stained shirt; he was stripped to the waist, and there was a clean white bandage over the wound on his arm. He was talking quietly, saying things that made no sense. Something about an accident.

"Radford's body will be found at the foot of the steps leading to one of the wharves. It will look like an accident."

As he went on talking he found a clean shirt, and put it on. "It will appear to be a dockside killing. My men took care of everything. Stripped him of his wallet and all his valuables and tossed them into the harbor. Men are robbed and beaten for far less every night down there."

Drucilla began to understand, and, for the first time, she thought about the others: Theodora. Gwen. Hazel.

"His mother," she said. "It will be horrible for her. And his sisters—"

"Not nearly so horrible as the truth would have been."

Drucilla sat up and gave a strangled cry.

"Stop that. And listen to me. If you told the authorities the facts, I'd get off scot-free, and so would Tim. But you'd suffer."

"I deserve to suffer."

He sat down on the edge of the bed and took her cold hands in his. "No, Drucilla. You aren't to blame. You did not know he would follow you here tonight and try to kill us."

"I should have realized. He's always been half-crazy with jealousy. Even on our honeymoon. He challenged a man who had only flirted with me. And then, when the man refused his challenge, he beat him—he would have killed him, I think, but the captain—"

"In that case," Kevin cut in, "you've no right to blame yourself."

"Radford's dead—he's dead—" The trembling started again.

"You didn't want him to die, and I didn't either. But I'd have killed him myself before I'd have let him shoot us down. And no law in the world would have blamed me."

"Then why must we hide the truth?"

"Because of the scandal. If the truth were known, your reputation would be lost. You'd be destroyed."

"I don't care about that."

"Maybe not for yourself. But what about your son? That's right, Drucilla. Think of how it would be for him. Hearing his mother called—you know what they'd call you."

"Yes, I know." She remembered Mrs. Belmont's ball, that first season in Newport. Those two girls who had been so cruel, who had said such vicious things about her because they had thought she was the daughter of Isobel Tremayne.

"It'll be hard enough for the boy, having to grow up without his father. At least, you can spare him the shame of an open scandal. Let him grow up proud of his name, proud of his mother. That can mean a lot to a boy. You do see that, don't you?"

She nodded, her throat tightening. Kevin thought Andrew was Radford's son, and yet he was concerned for the child.

"All right, then. That's settled. But you have to do your part, and it won't be easy. You'll have to go back to your house and get in without being seen. Tomorrow, maybe even the next day, you'll have to behave as if everything is perfectly normal. Wait a minute. They'll ask where Radford is, won't they? His sisters. The servants."

"He said he was going upriver to Seaton Barony."

"That's all right, then. But what about his mother? Was she expecting him to arrive at the plantation today?"

Drucilla shook her head. "Last night, when he came in, I had just got back home. He was drunk, and I thought he hadn't noticed I was still wearing my dress, that my bonnet and shawl hadn't been put away. But he had noticed. Or maybe he realized what he had seen when he woke up. He didn't say anything to me, but he must have waited and followed me here. He never had any intention of going to the plantation—he only wanted to throw me off guard."

"So he won't be missed either at the house or at Seaton Barony for a few days, and by then, they'll have—"

"Yes, I understand."

"When the body's found, you may have to identify it. No one will think it's strange if you break down. But you must not say anything that will make anyone suspect Radford's death was not an accident." He put his arm around her and drew her head down against his shoulder.

"Where will you be?" she asked.

"I'm sailing for Cuba tomorrow. But even if I stayed, it would be too dangerous for us to meet again before I sailed. You can see that, can't you?"

"I'm afraid," she said. "Without you, I won't be able to do what I have to do."

He stroked her hair. "You'll be all right. Drucilla, you're not the scared girl I found in the rain that night back in New York. You're a woman, and you have more strength than you know. You have a child to protect. Only you can do it."

She winced. It was still not too late to tell him about

Andrew, but she knew she could not. She would have to let him sail and stay on here alone.

On the dock, they stood locked in an embrace; she clung to him and willed the moment to go on and on. But too quickly, he disengaged her arms. She opened her eyes and saw that dawn had come; the sky over the harbor blazed red and gold, and across the burnished surface of the water, she looked out at the hard, dark outline of the *Medea*, riding at anchor.

She did not watch Kevin go. She could not. Instead, she kept her eyes fixed on the boat, a black, inexorable shape against the sky.

"You are a young lady of property now," Marcus Thorp told Drucilla. They were seated in Thorp's law office on Broad Street, and the lawyer was finishing his description of the nature and extent of Drucilla's property.

Although the first meeting had taken place a few weeks before, the Seatons' lawyer had asked Drucilla to come in again, at her convenience, so that he could give her a more complete explanation of her inheritance from her late husband.

The plantation belonged to Theodora, for it had been left to her by Radford's father, who had died in the early days of the war. But all the property that Radford had purchased in his own name now passed directly to Drucilla. She sat in the large, old-fashioned office, across the desk from Mr. Thorp; the windows were open, but the room was hot all the same. It was already May, and Charleston was baking in an early heat wave. Drucilla, in her mourning dress of heavy silk, shifted uncomfortably in her chair, and fanned herself, hoping the meeting would be over soon. But Mr. Thorp went on, describing the textile mills, together with the workers' cottages and company stores, in the western part of the state; the lumber mills here in Charleson, the warehouses down on the waterfront, as well as railroad stocks, shares in a tobacco company. "Then there are a few small shops on King Street—"

"Please, Mr. Thorp. I can't take all this in right now. I've never known much about business matters."

"You can learn," he said. "Not right away, perhaps, but little by little, as your mother-in-law did. In the meantime, you needn't fret; I'll handle the details of managing the property. As I have done for the Seatons all these years."

Drucilla had liked Marcus Thorp from the first meeting. Although he must be in his fifties, his face, under the thick shock of silver-white hair, was ruddy and youthful, and his eyes were kind.

"Now then, what are your plans, if I may ask? Will you be going to live with Theodora at Seaton Barony? Or will you remain in the town house, here in the city?"

"I have no plans."

"Understandable, after such a tragedy, of course. It takes time, my dear, but you'll pick up the pieces of your life. May I say something, as a friend?"

"Of course."

"Don't bury yourself out at the plantation. A house, even one the size of Seaton Barony, can have only one mistress. You must think about making a new life for yourself."

"A new life?"

"You're a young woman, and a very beautiful one. You should think about marrying again. Not for a while, of course, but after a decent interval. You've a son to think about. A boy needs a father."

Kevin had said that. She turned her face away, and tried not to think about Kevin, off in Cuba.

"Forgive me," Marcus Thorp said. "Perhaps it is too soon to speak of such matters. Tell me, will you spend the summer with your grandmother in Newport? A fine, healthy climate they have up there."

Drucilla shook her head. "My grandmother won't be opening the house at Newport this summer. She told me, when she came down here for the funeral, that her doctor has ordered her to go abroad. She's to take the waters in France, at Aix-les-Bains; her rheumatism has been troubling her this year."

"I see. But you're not planning to spend the summer

here in Charleston. It would be unwise. Too much fever about."

She nodded, remembering Kitty's death. "No, I won't stay here. Theodora has arranged for all of us to spend the summer at a hotel in the mountains in North Carolina. Near Asheville."

"The very thing," Thorp said enthusiastically. "Secluded and quiet, of course—nothing like Newport. But the mountains are magnificent, and the air is bracing. It will do that boy of yours a world of good, and you, too, my dear."

Drucilla did not care where she spent the summer. She was still shocked and dazed by Radford's death, and by Kevin's departure. Now Kevin had gone to an island where a bloody war raged. The newspapers here in the United States described the savage guerrilla attacks and the brutal reprisals by the Spanish forces, omitting none of the unpleasant details.

On her drive back to her town house, Drucilla closed her eyes against the fierce glare of the sun; the air was already heavy with the heat of the approaching summer. Only in the high-walled gardens was there any hint of coolness. Gwen had told her once that the houses of Charleston, with their heavy, hurricane-proof tiles, wide piazzas, fretted iron-work, and jalousied doors and windows, had been copied from those in the West Indies; surely, even Barbados, where many of the oldest Charleston families had originally made their fortunes, could not have been much hotter than this, Drucilla thought.

She wanted to get back to the house, to strip off her close-fitting mourning dress and her veiled bonnet, and put on a cool muslin wrapper. But when she was inside the dim hallway at last, she heard voices from the parlor, and realized that Gwen and Hazel were engaged in one of their frequent squabbles.

"Mother says that if the crop's good, there's no reason we can't go to London for the winter season next year," Hazel said. "Think of it, Gwen: London, Paris, maybe Rome."

"I suppose you find the thought of a European tour vastly romantic." Gwen's tone was sarcastic. At twenty-six, she had abandoned her attempts to appear flirtatious and girlish; she was a confirmed spinster, in speech and manner.

Now, catching sight of Drucilla, she called, "Do come in, dear, and have some of this lemonade. I'm sure you need it after that drive."

Drucilla joined Gwen and Hazel, taking a seat near the window. The lemonade was cool and tart, but she wished she could have slipped upstairs unnoticed; she did not want to become involved in an argument between her sisters-in-law.

Gwen said, "Don't you know why Mother wants to drag us off to London? We'll be out of mourning then, and she can parade us around to balls and concerts and theaters. And keep trying to find husbands for us."

"Gwen, really."

"You know it's true, Hazel. But I won't do it. I won't go to London and that's final."

"What else is there for us? Young ladies must marry—"

"I'm not a young lady," Gwen snapped. "I'm an old maid. Even Mother must know that. You still have a chance, Hazel, or you would if you didn't get flustered every time you have to speak to a man. Go with Mother, by all means, if you want to. I'm sick of being put on display, the way they used to do with those quadroon girls at the auctions."

Hazel gasped, then gave a nervous giggle. "Oh, my dear, what a dreadful thing to say. Whatever will Drucilla think—"

"Drucilla's got good sense. She knows I'm right." Gwen got up and began pacing the floor, her stiff black skirt rustling around her. "I never wanted to get married, not really. I've always found the thought of marriage most distasteful."

"She's overwrought, Drucilla," Hazel said. "And no wonder. This heat and all the preparations for our trip to Asheville. Gwen, dear, do let me get some eau de cologne to rub on your forehead."

"I don't want eau de cologne. And I don't want you fluttering around me. Just because I express an honest opinion, you act as if I'm having an attack of the vapors. I simply said what I felt."

"But—if you don't marry—what will you do?"

"I'm not sure. I only know that although most women are suited to marriage, born to be wives and mothers, I wasn't. I don't want to share a bed with any man, or bear his children, or— Oh, for pity's sake, Hazel. You think marriage is the same in life as in those silly novels you're forever reading. One chaste kiss on the brow, and a lot of pretty speeches. But there's more to it than that. For the woman, marriage means serving a man, submitting to his animal needs, and going through pregnancy and childbirth."

Hazel gave a little cry, like the squeak of a rabbit in a trap. "You should not say such things—it's indecent—" Then, rallying a little, she added, "Besides, how can you possibly know about marriage?"

"Because I've read some books besides those nonsensical things that clutter your bookshelves. Books Father brought back from France and Germany. My French is excellent, and my German is tolerably good, you know."

"Mother said we weren't supposed to read those books."

"Mother may control the purse strings and choose our clothes, but she can't control our thoughts. Not mine, at any rate."

Drucilla looked at her sister-in-law with admiration; she had always known that Gwen was bright, but she had never guessed that beneath the prim exterior, she was so spirited.

Hazel rose and, lifting her skirts, fled from the parlor. "I won't listen," she said, disappearing into the hallway.

Gwen smiled. "I trust I haven't shocked you, too, Drucilla."

"Don't be silly. As a matter of fact, I agree that a young woman should be free to marry or not, as she chooses."

"Much good may such notions do me, as long as Mother doles out every penny. I suppose she will go on trying to marry me off, until even she's forced to admit it's hopeless. And then, she'll spend the rest of her life making me miserable and blaming me for my single state." She gave a harsh little laugh. "Oh, it's different for girls like you, Drucilla. You're so beautiful —so—men are naturally attracted to you, and they want to make you happy, to give you everything—"

"Perhaps," Drucilla said, quietly, remembering her stormy marriage, her frequently bitter clashes with Kevin. "But even for me—" She broke off abruptly.

"I know," Gwen said. "Radford was free to come and go as he pleased, to do what he liked. And when he wanted Emmaline, he—" She drew a sharp breath, and her face flushed. "Oh, forgive me," she said, with genuine distress. "I never meant to—"

"I guessed the truth about Radford and Emmaline," Drucilla said calmly. "I suppose even a war wasn't enough to change that particular custom down here."

Then, to relieve Gwen's painful embarrassment, she said,

"Hazel asked you what you would do if you did not marry. What would you like to do?"

Gwen shrugged. "It doesn't matter, does it? But if I could do as I pleased, I'd open a school for young ladies. I'd make a good school mistress, I know it. And I would be able to teach them, perhaps, that there is more for a girl than learning to flirt and primp and catch a husband. I would—"

"Go on," Drucilla urged.

"I have a good knowledge of languages, not only French and German but Latin as well. And I could hire suitable teachers for those subjects in which I'm not especially proficient. Music, dancing, sketching. Oh, but what's the use? If Radford had lived, perhaps he would have understood—at least a little—and helped me, but now—"

"I'll help you." Drucilla hadn't planned to say the words; they had come, unbidden, to her lips. But she was not sorry. "I have so much, more than I'll ever need. Marcus Thorp was telling me only this afternoon about all the property that is now mine. I'll give you what you need to start your school and hire your teachers. We'll go and talk to Mr. Thorp about it. He might even know of a house that would be suitable."

Gwen's pale eyes glowed, and her face grew pink; she looked almost pretty in her enthusiasm. "You really mean it?" Then she said, "Oh, but I couldn't possibly allow you to pay for the school."

"Why not? Radford would not have wanted you to drag out your whole life, trailing after your mother, putting up with her temper and her snide remarks. Wasting your abilities. And there is nothing disgraceful about teaching school, no matter what she may think." Drucilla was remembering her father and his dedication to teaching.

"Mother will never forgive me. Or you, for helping me."

"I'll risk her displeasure, if you will," Drucilla said.

Gwen put a hand on Drucilla's arm. "I will—oh, I will. And I'll never forget this. I'll pay you back. Not only in money, although as soon as the school begins to make a profit you'll get your money back, I promise. But—if there is ever anything I can do for you—" Her voice shook, and Drucilla was afraid she might cry. But instead she said, "Let's go to see Mr. Thorp tomorrow. And ask him to help me find a house."

Theodora stormed and argued, but to no avail.

"Marcus thinks it is a perfectly sound idea," Gwen told her mother.

"Drucilla probably influenced him," Theodora shot back.

"Marcus Thorp is old enough to be Drucilla's father, and he adores his wife," Gwen said.

"A man's age doesn't keep him from being silly at the sight of a pretty face," Theodora said.

"I think it was wonderful of Drucilla to want to help Gwen," Hazel put in. "I think—"

"I don't remember having asked for your opinion," Theodora said. "And, by the way, since we'll be leaving tomorrow, you had better check and make sure that Bessie has prepared that cucumber face wash for you. It's too bad you're so sallow, Hazel. Perhaps the change

236

of air will improve your complexion."

Having shaken what little self-confidence her daughter could muster, Theodora was, for the time, satisfied.

Drucilla sighed, as she looked ahead to a summer of bickering and arguments, but at least she knew she had done what she could to free Gwen from a lifetime of servitude to Theodora. She briefly considered refusing to go to the resort, but she knew she could not. Theodora had been looking forward to spending the whole summer with Andrew, and Drucilla hadn't the heart to deprive her of the child's company. Andrew was all Theodora cared about now. Andrew, and Seaton Barony.

The summer was every bit as difficult as Drucilla had anticipated. She tried to concentrate on the loveliness of the surroundings: the crisp, cool mountain air; the beauty of the rhododendron and laurel in full bloom; the majestic, somber balsam and cedar trees that added their own splendor to this uncultivated land; the pale blue of the mountains, against the deeper blue of the sky. She took long walks up the winding pathways, or played with Andrew in the shade of the trees.

Although the hotel guests had an active social schedule, the Seatons were not expected to attend the dances, musicales and picnics, because they were in mourning. Drucilla was aware that some of the gentlemen looked at her with more than respect and compassion; she had no doubt that there were a few who would have been pleased to cheer her and try to make her forget her loss. But she treated them with a cool, distant politeness that discouraged any advances, and even Theodora could have found no fault with her behavior in her newly widowed state.

Kevin was rarely out of her thoughts. Seated in the grove of cedars, watching Andrew throw stones into the pond, or take his first steps across the grass, she was tormented by the child's growing resemblance to his father; by her longing to have Kevin here with her, to share these moments.

She tried not to listen, when the hotel guests occasionally discussed the latest news from Cuba, described in vivid and often horrifying detail. There was a strong movement in Washington to get President Grant to recognize the justice of the rebel cause; but Hamilton Fish, Grant's Secretary of State, was firmly opposed to giving any support to the revolutionists, and so far, his influence had prevailed.

While the gentlemen on the hotel veranda might discuss the pros and cons of the rebellion. Drucilla could think only of Kevin and pray for his safety. She reminded herself that he was not involved in the fighting, that he was only being paid to deliver his cargo. He was too self-absorbed to become personally involved in the rebel cause. Hadn't he told her he would as soon sell arms to the other side, if they had wanted to pay him?

At night, lying awake in her bed, she would stare at the silvery moonlight that filtered in through the curtains; she would breathe the scent of the damp grass and the mountain flowers, and her whole body would come alive, would ache for Kevin's touch. At such times, she relived every moment of their night aboard the *Medea*; she felt his hands, his lips on her naked flesh, and she turned with a sob to bury her face in her pillow.

Hazel Seaton spent the summer lost in the novels she had brought along; she sighed over romantic adventures of Bertie Cecil, glowingly described by the daring lady novelist Ouida, in her popular *Under Two Flags*; daydreamed about next year's trip to London and wondered if she might meet a dashing aristocratic young officer there. She had dismissed Gwen's distressing talk about the realities of love and marriage.

Gwen kept busy collecting specimens of the local plants and flowers, drying them and classifying them for her albums and notebooks. She reviewed her Latin grammar and made plans for the housekeeping arrangements of her school.

Early in September, a letter arrived from Marcus Thorp, who had found a house on the Battery in Charleston that was up for sale. He had examined it carefully and found it to be well constructed and large enough for Gwen's purpose. Gwen was eager to leave for Charleston at once, but Theodora, as usual, raised objections.

"I hope you don't expect me to go traipsing back to Charleston before the end of September. It's still far too hot down there."

"There's no need for you to come, Mother."

"I don't like the idea of your traveling around the country by yourself. It's not proper."

"Really, Mother," Gwen said, "I'm not going to California, only back to Charleston. And," she added, with the ironic smile that was becoming characteristic these past months, "I have never had to worry about fending off the attentions of gentlemen. I'm quite safe."

"If you had made more of an effort to be pleasing to gentlemen when you were younger, you might have found a husband. You would not have been forced to spend your life as a school mistress. I certainly gave you every opportunity—"

Drucilla, unable to listen in silence any longer, said,

"I will go to Charleston with Gwen, and Emmaline can accompany us."

"The town house is closed," Theodora said. "The servants won't be expecting you."

"I can take the dust sheets off the furniture myself," Drucilla said, trying to restrain her irritation.

"As you please." Then a shadow passed over Theodora's firm features. "You won't take Andrew, will you? The mountain air is better for him than the heat down in Charleston. Why, he must have grown two inches this summer. You will let him stay, won't you?"

Whatever feelings Drucilla might have toward her mother-in-law, she could never question the older woman's love for Andrew. "Of course he must stay," Drucilla agreed.

Gwen was delighted with the description of the house Marcus Thorp had found. It was built of brick that had mellowed to a soft rose-color in the salt air of the harbor. The three-story, rectangular building dated from shortly after the Revolutionary War, Thorp said. The paneling inside was rich and beautiful with the patina of age, and although some of the cornices and window trim had cracked, they could be repaired. "There's a high-walled garden below the piazza, perfect for your young ladies to take the air in, without being observed from the street," Marcus told Gwen. She had insisted upon going straight to his office, as soon as she and Drucilla had arrived in the city.

"It sounds perfect. Let's go to see it at once. That is, if you're not tired from the trip, Drucilla."

"No, but I would like to go to our house, and let the servants know we're back. We'll have to air the rooms and remove the dust covers. Why don't you and Marcus go to look over the new property, and Emmaline and I can go on home."

After dropping Gwen and Marcus Thorp off at the brick building on the Battery, Drucilla ordered the coachman to take her to the townhouse, by way of the harbor. "At least there will be a breeze," she told Emmaline.

The harbor was busy, in spite of the heat, and Drucilla caught the rich mingled smells of coffee, spices and salt. Black stevedores, naked to the waist, their skins glistening with sweat, bent under their burdens. Wagons rumbled down to the docks to discharge their cargoes or pick up crates of incoming goods.

It was sunset now, and the sky turned a rich rose while the water flamed with reflected color. She looked out over the harbor, and her breath caught in her throat. "Stop the carriage," she called to the coachman.

He obeyed, and she stood up, shading her eyes with one hand. She knew little enough about boats, but the outline of the *Medea* had burned itself into her mind that dawn when she had stood looking out to sea, after Kevin had left her.

Emmaline looked up anxiously. "Anything wrong, Miz Seaton, ma'am? Do you want your smelling salts?"

Drucilla shook her head and, a moment later, was out of the carriage and hurrying down the dock. She almost collided with a tall, tanned young man wearing a blue jacket and an officer's cap.

"Please," she said, grasping his arm. "That boat out

there. Yes, that one." She pointed across the harbor. "That is the *Medea*, isn't it?"

He looked startled; his eyes moved over her, taking in the high-necked black dress, the wide hat with its heavy mourning veil. Then he whipped off his cap. "Yes, ma'am," he said, with a New England twang. "That's the *Medea*, all right. She came into port yesterday, with less than half her crew aboard. Good thing for Tim Cleary he had smooth weather or he never would've brought her in at all."

"Tim Cleary? But—where was Captain Farrell?"

"I don't know, ma'am. Cleary's over at the Bull's Head Tavern." The young officer put out a hand to detain her. "Wait, ma'am. The Bull's Head is no place for a lady like you and besides, Cleary's been drinking steadily since he—"

She shook him off, without waiting to hear the rest. Tim had brought the *Medea* back, but without Kevin. All the fears she had been fighting down since Kevin's departure now welled up in her. Her heart was beating thickly as she returned to the carriage. The driver helped her in, then got back up on the box. She ignored Emmaline's puzzled look, and made herself speak with a calmness she did not feel.

"Take me to the Bull's Head Tavern—quickly."

Sixteen

DRUCILLA found Tim Cleary slumped over a whisky-stained wooden table in the back room of the Bull's Head. His shirt was open, revealing the heavy mat of red hair on his massive chest; his blue eyes were bloodshot. At any other time, she would have feared this drunken giant, for she knew well enough the violence of which he was capable, but now it did not seem important. She put a hand on his shoulder, and he turned to look up at her.

"Get outta here, girl," he said. "I didn't ask for a girl—this is all I need—" He picked up his glass and drained it.

She did not take her hand away, but shook him. "Look at me. I'm Drucilla Seaton. Tim, please."

He blinked rapidly, and the bloodshot eyes focused. "Oh, Lord," he said. "Mrs. Seaton—"

"That's right." She took a seat opposite him. "Kevin didn't come back with you?"

"No, ma'am. He didn't come back."

She had had some faint hope that the officer she had

questioned back there on the dock had been mistaken; now that hope was gone.

"Where is he?"

"In Cuba." Tim reached across the table and his huge hand, covered with reddish hair, closed around her arm in a painfully tight grip. She winced but kept her eyes fixed on his face.

"Ye've gotta believe me, there wasn't no way I could've got him outta that place. Bloody fortress they got up there—"

Her fear grew until it blotted out everything else. She gripped the edge of the table, willing herself not to give way to hysteria. She was remembering the crew of that other gun-runner, the *Virginius*. All of them shot by the Spanish forces in Cuba. The American captain along with the others.

"Kevin's dead," she whispered.

Tim shook his head. "No—don't think that. He's alive. Leastways, he was when I sailed away from that hellish island."

Anger flared up inside her. "Alive? And you left him there?"

"There wasn't no other way, I'm telling ye. I swear, I'd've tore that garrison apart stone by stone if I could've." He peered into her face. "Get outta here, Mrs. Seaton. Forget about Kevin Farrell. There's nothin' anybody can do for him, now."

He picked up the bottle and poured himself another glass of whisky, sloshing the liquid over the top. Drucilla's hand shot out, and she sent the glass crashing to the floor.

"No more of that, Tim. Not until you've told me everything."

Brief anger flared in his eyes, then faded. "All right," he said slowly. He stared down at the spilled whisky, watching the amber drops trickle along a crack in the floor. It was plain he could not bring himself to look at her.

"The voyage went smooth as ye please. Good, sound boat, the *Medea*. We anchored in a little cove, on the eastern end of the island, it was. A place that was controlled by the rebels."

"Go on," she said.

"The plan was to form two shore parties, and leave the rest of the crew on the boat. We were to take the arms and supplies overland. I had one of the rebels to lead me and my party. I didn't even know where he was takin' us, but we made it all right. A command post up in the hills, it was. Delivered this stuff to this big black man, Cap'n Antonio Maceo. Regular settlement he's got up there. His men have their wives and children there with them. They're a mixed batch, them rebels—runaway slaves, small planters, bandits. And they got lawyers, businessmen—even a few scholars and poets. All they got in common is they're willin' to die to get their freedom from Spain."

Drucilla forced herself to be patient and let Tim tell the story in his own way, but she could only think about Kevin. What was happening to Kevin?

"I stayed on the boat with my men. And I waited there for Cap'n Farrell, like he'd ordered me to. Only—he never came back."

"Then how do you know he's alive?"

"One of the rebels, a girl named Pia, got word to me. She's no more'n fifteen, but like I say, they've got all kinds fightin' down there. She does the laundry for the Spanish officers at the garrison in Oriente province. Way up in the mountains, it is. She saw the soldiers bring in Kevin. They'd ambushed his party and, from what she could make out, they'd killed the others. A regular damn massacre."

"Why—didn't they kill him, too?"

"Because he's the only one who can give them the information they need. They're holdin' him for questioning."

It took a second before the full meaning of his words struck her. Then she remembered the stories she had read in the newspapers, about the brutal tactics used by the Spanish in questioning prisoners. Her body went rigid, and her skin was bathed in icy perspiration.

"He knows the names of the Cuban exiles here, who're

putting up the money for the arms. And the names of their contacts in Havana." Tim's voice was flat, expressionless, but she could see the tension in the set of his shoulders, the hard lines around his mouth. "He knows the locations of the rebel outposts in the hills— and where they're supposed to move, if it gets too hot for them where they are."

"But surely he must have told them what he knew— he's not one of the rebels. He told me before he sailed that he didn't care which side won."

"I know. It's hard to figure. But this little girl, Pia, she heard some of the soldiers talkin'. They were sayin' that the Cap'n wouldn't give Colonel Ramón Martinez— he's the garrison commander—one word of information. They were—" He broke off and wiped his lips on the back of his hand. "They were makin' bets on how long he could hold out."

She began to tremble uncontrollably. "He may be dead now. They might have—"

"Not Kevin Farrell. He's strong, you know that. And stubborn. He'll hold out for a long time, but the things those bastards can think of, to do to their prisoners . . ."

She gave a cry and shut her eyes as if to blot out the vision that arose, horrible and vivid: Kevin's body, strong and clean, swift and ardent in lovemaking. Tortured now, perhaps mutilated. The vision was ugly, obscene, but she could not escape it.

Suddenly a movement on the other side of the table, and she heard Tim get up so quickly his chair overturned. "Don't," he said, coming to her. "I never wanted to tell you—there, now—"

She stood up and reached out to him, and pressed her face against his chest, not minding the reek of whisky and sweat. He held her, a little awkwardly, patting her shoulder. "We've got to get him away from there—Tim, we've got to—"

He took her by the shoulders and held her away. He was not nearly so drunk as she had thought. "Now listen to me. Be still and hear me out. It can't be done. Don't ye think I'd have tried if there was any hope at all? But there ain't. That's why I've been sittin' here ever since I came ashore yesterday. Tryin' to get drunk enough not to think about it. Like I told ye, that garrison's armed like a fortress. Stone walls. Big guns mounted up on top. Ye'd have to raise an army, and even then—"

"But we've got to do something." She cast about in her mind, frantically. "The Seaton name is a respected one in this state. Surely, there must be someone—a congressman, a senator, who would use his influence—"

"Ye'd have a better chance with one of them Spanish officials."

"You're not making sense. Kevin's a prisoner of the Spanish. Why would one of their own officials raise a hand to help him escape?"

Tim laughed sourly. "For money, Mrs. Seaton. Pia told me that's one reason the rebels are tryin' to get free of Spain. Because the government is so crooked—some of those high-up Spanish officials only take those posts in Cuba to make their fortune. They don't do a thing for the people, and they go back home in a few years, filthy rich from bribes. But, hell, it would take a fortune for what you want to do. Getting a prisoner out of that garrison. Why, where'd ye get that kind of money?"

Drucilla's mind worked swiftly. When Marcus Thorp had told her about the extent of her holdings, she had been indifferent. Indeed, the only use she had found for her property was to give Gwen the money for her school so she could get out from under Theodora's control.

But she could also use her property to raise money that would buy Kevin's way out of Cuba. "Listen to me," she said, gripping Tim's arm. "I can get the money. I have a great deal of property: mills, stocks, my town house—I'm a wealthy woman."

He looked at her, hope dawning in his eyes. "But even if ye can lay hands on enough money, and it might take thousands, we'd have to move fast. Because—"

He did not finish but Drucilla knew what he meant. If they did not reach Kevin soon and get him out of Cuba, it might be too late.

"I'll go straight to my lawyer," she said. "I'll get the money. But then you'll have to take me to Cuba. You will do it, won't you, Tim?"

"Wait a minute," he said. "You're sure ye want to risk it? Havana's safe enough, right now, and some of the plantation country to the west, but even so, it's a tricky situation down there. Looting and burning."

"I don't care. I'm going. It will be safer if I offer the bribe. You've worked with the rebels, and your identity might be known. But I'll be there as a wealthy American widow, with no interest in the war. You can remain offshore aboard the *Medea*, and when Kevin's free—" Her voice faltered. Suppose she could not buy Kevin's freedom? Suppose there was no official ready to undertake so great a risk, no matter how large the bribe might be?

"It's a chance in a million," Tim said.

"I don't care." In the face of danger confronting Kevin, she felt oddly calm, in control of the situation. "He told me, once, that I had more strength than I knew," she said. "Maybe he was right."

Tim looked at her closely. "You're quite a woman, Mrs. Seaton."

"Drucilla," she said. "We're partners now, Tim. How soon can we sail?"

"Dependin' on how soon you get the money, I'd say a couple of weeks. Take me that long to get a full crew and make a few repairs. If we can sail in two weeks, we ought to get there in time." He took her hand in his huge one and gripped it.

As it happened, there was no need to wait for the following day to speak to Marcus Thorp. Drucilla returned to the town house to find that Gwen had invited the lawyer to dinner.

"It was the least I could do, considering Marcus found that perfectly splendid building for the school," Gwen said, as the three of them were finishing the meal in the high-ceilinged dining room. "It's not much of a dinner, of course; the cook wasn't expecting us."

"Delicious, I assure you," Thorp said.

But afterwards, when the three of them were seated in the garden having their coffee, and Drucilla told Marcus what she wanted him to do, he was startled and reluctant.

"Forgive me, my dear, but what you're suggesting is quite impractical. Given time, several months, or a year, I could get you what the property is worth. But in a matter of weeks, I could not sell the mills, the warehouses, anything, without your taking a considerable loss. I would need time to find the right buyers. Now, John Pettigrew might be interested in those warehouses. And he'd surely offer you a fair price. And there are certain northern business syndicates I know of that might want to buy the textile mills—if you're foolish enough to want to dispose of them now, when they are becoming so profitable. But all this takes time and patience, my dear."

Drucilla clenched her hands in her lap and pressed her lips together. She looked at the white-haired lawyer, calm and composed, an elegant figure in his pale gray broadcloth suit and dark gray satin vest. His voice droned on, as he explained the difficulties of disposing of her property to raise the needed money. He paused, from time to time, to take a sip of the strong, black coffee.

To Drucilla, it had an air of unreality: the quiet moonlit garden with its high, mossy stone walls, its live oaks stirring in the light evening breeze, the carefully tended flowerbeds and sweet-smelling shrubs.

Somewhere in the eastern part of Cuba, in a mountain range called the Sierra Maestra, Kevin was shut away in darkness. Hurt, perhaps dying.

"I must have the money, and quickly. Twenty-five thousand at least. More, if possible."

Gwen put her coffee cup down in her saucer. "Drucilla, what's wrong? You were perfectly all right when you left Marcus and me this afternoon. Now you're beside yourself. You scarcely touched your dinner. And now, these demands for money. Surely you can tell us why you need such a sum."

Drucilla looked from Gwen back to Marcus. Could

she trust them? She had never had a trusting disposition —not since her days at the County Farm. She had learned to hide her feelings, to share her hurts and fears with no one. But now she began to realize that she could not simply disappear from Charleston; that she would have to offer some explanation for her leaving. And there was Andrew. He would have to be cared for until she got back.

"My dear," Marcus was saying, "I have taken care of the affairs of the Seaton family for years now. I'll do all I can to help you. But you must be frank with me —and with Gwen."

Drucilla hesitated, drew a long breath, then said, "I am leaving Charleston. I must go to Cuba at once, and I must have money to take with me, a great deal of money."

"Cuba? But what reason would you have for going there?"

"A—friend of mine is in serious trouble." Completely inadequate, but how else was she to say it? "He's been imprisoned by the Spanish forces there. I've been told that I may be able to get him out, but it will take money. A large bribe."

Gwen and Marcus exchanged glances. "It's quite true there are corrupt officials in Cuba who'll do almost anything for a bribe. Indeed, the corruption of the Spanish colonial government is well known and it is one of the reasons this war is being fought. But your friend— Why are they holding him in prison?" Marcus asked.

"That's not important. If you'll only—"

"Indeed, it is important. I have a few contacts in Washington. If you'll give me all the information you have, I can set the wheels in motion, and it may be possible to help your friend—"

"But that will take time, won't it?" Drucilla asked.

"I'm afraid so."

"I have no time. Unless I get him out quickly, they'll kill him."

"I see." Marcus was frankly curious, but his good breeding would not permit him to demand any more information than she was willing to give.

"Unless you help me raise the money, I'll have to turn my affairs over to another lawyer," she said with determination.

"Drucilla—Marcus is trying to help you— We both want to help you."

"There is no need for you to get another lawyer," Marcus said, with quiet dignity. "If you insist, I will sell some of your property at once, although, as I've already pointed out, you'll take quite a loss. As for the rest, you can get loans using your railroad stocks for collateral. And the textile mills as well. I'll get you the best terms I can."

Drucilla's throat tightened, and her eyes burned with unshed tears. She had always liked Marcus Thorp and now she was moved by his obvious willingness to help her. "Please do what you can."

"Trust me," he said, rising from his chair. "And Drucilla—once you have the money, you'll be needing the names of contacts among the officials down there —unless you already have them."

"No—I hadn't thought about that."

"I'll see what I can do. If possible, I'll supply you with letters of introduction, through some of my contacts here in Charleston. But you must promise me one thing."

"What's that?"

"Promise you won't leave Havana. It's fairly safe there, you see. Business as usual. But the back country, that's quite a different matter. Give me your word you'll do nothing reckless."

"I promise," she said.

After Marcus had left, Drucilla and Gwen sat in silence. Gwen was the first to speak. "What can I do?" she asked. "I owe you so much. If there is any way I can help, tell me."

"You can smooth things over with your mother. When she returns from Asheville, I'll be gone. I want you to tell her as little as possible. Tell her—" But her mind was too confused, too filled with thoughts of Kevin, to be able to cope with the problem of Theodora.

"I'll say you've decided to take a trip. It's perfectly natural. Many young widows seek distraction in travel. I'll say you've gone to the West Indies. That'll be the truth." Gwen smiled, but her eyes were still troubled.

"And she'll take good care of Andrew, I'm sure of it."

"You know she will," Gwen said. "She'll spoil him, of course. But she'll be delighted to have him with her at Seaton Barony."

Andrew. It hurt to think of leaving her small son this way, without seeing him one more time before she sailed. But she would be back soon.

"I'll only be gone a short time," she said, as much for her own benefit as to reassure Gwen. "I'll be back in time to spend Christmas here in Charleston with all of you."

But even as she spoke, a bell tolled deep in her mind, and fear moved inside her. The rising moon had an icy radiance that made the shadows in the corners of the garden look black and menacing. She was seized with a sense of looming danger.

But she put such thoughts away at once. She would do what had to be done to save Kevin's life. Nothing, no one, not even her own fears, would stand in her way.

Seventeen

KEVIN Farrell lay face down on the narrow cot. He raised his head and squinted up at the harsh yellow glare that came through the small, barred grille set high in the wall. The oil lamp had been lit in the corridor outside his cell. The heat that had pressed down on him like a thick, damp weight was receding now; the stone-walled cubicle would be chilly in a little while.

Would tonight bring sleep? Or would he be taken out by the soldiers again, and brought upstairs to the orderly room for questioning? They usually questioned him at night, sometimes for a few hours, often until dawn.

He tried to shift his position, to ease the aching in his muscles, but his wrists and ankles were shackled to the cot. From the day they had brought him to the garrison, he had been kept in solitary confinement. How long had it been? A month? Perhaps more? Hard to keep track of the passing days. There had been times, for hours on end, when he had lain in a stupor, hot and parched with fever, his senses disordered.

Tonight, however, he was alert. Unbearably so. They had not taken him upstairs for questioning for the past five days. He closed his eyes and pressed his face into the thin, straw-filled mattress. The minutes crawled by.

Colonel Ramón Martinez, the garrison commander, always allowed Kevin enough time to recover from the last interrogation before questioning him again. The colonel did not want to kill him; not until he had extracted the desired information from him.

Kevin forced himself not to remember those sessions upstairs in the small room next to the colonel's office, nor to speculate on what new agonies they might inflict on him tonight.

Instead, he made himself remember the beginning of the expedition to Cuba. Everything had gone smoothly, at first. . . .

He had come ashore in a small fishing boat, and met his contact in Havana, a member of the rebel forces, who gave him a map and verbal instructions. "Memorize the map and destroy it," the Cuban had ordered.

When Kevin returned to the *Medea*, anchored some distance outside Havana harbor, he had sailed for the eastern end of Cuba and anchored in a cove in rebel-held territory.

There he and Cleary and their parties had gone ashore at night and split up. Cleary went to the headquarters of Antonio Maceo, while Kevin and his men took their part of the arms shipment up La Plata by flatboats, to a barren, rocky area where the only vegetation was coarse cactus. There he had gone ashore, and had been supplied with wagons and mules for hauling the crates of arms, and with a horse for himself, a big black stallion. "An excellent animal, señor," one of the rebels had told him. "We stole the beast from one of the finest plantations on the island."

With four crewmen to drive the wagons, he had gone on to the village of Santa Clara, in the foothills of the Sierra Maestra, to wait for the courier who was to pay him the remaining half of the sum agreed upon. After that, he would continue up the slopes of the Pico Turquino, the highest mountain in the Sierra Maestra, to deliver the weapons to the headquarters of the rebel army in this sector.

Diego Barbosa, the mayor of the rebel-held village of Santa Clara, greeted him warmly. "You may have to wait a few days for the courier," he said. "There are Spanish patrols throughout Oriente."

"I've waited in worse places," Kevin assured him. Santa Clara and the surrounding countryside were lush and beautiful, with lemon trees, pineapple plants, and banana and regal wild palms that towered as high as eighty feet, their fronds deep emerald against the dazzling blue of the sky.

Barbosa showed him the village, built on the ruins of an abandoned sugar plantation. There were guards, for, as Barbosa explained, an attack might come at any time. But there was also a primitive hospital, a number of workshops and storehouses, cultivated fields where the people raised their own food, pens for livestock.

"We are not savages here," Barbosa said, seeing Kevin's surprise. "We fight when we must, and we fight well, the women beside the men. But that will pass. We are building a new world here in Cuba."

Kevin had examined the weapons in the storage sheds, the machetes and the daggers made of native indigo wood; with these, Barbosa had led his forces against the well-trained, well-equipped Spanish troops.

"You look doubtful, señor," he said.

"It's not my concern. I'm being paid to deliver arms. That's all."

"But you think we're fools, throwing our lives away in an impossible cause."

"I hope not," Kevin said. He couldn't help liking Barbosa and admiring his courage. "I hope you get that new world you're fighting for."

"We must," the man said simply. "And we will—all of us, fighting together."

"You don't appear to have much in common with the others here," Kevin said. "Runaway slaves, bandits, illiterate peasants. You're an educated man."

Barbosa smiled, his white teeth lighting his lean, dark face with its deep-set eyes. "*No importa*," he said. "True,

I was educated in Spain. I studied the law. But when I returned home, I soon discovered that law—justice did not exist for the mass of the people here. I saw dishonest officials stripping small landholders of their property, in return for bribes from the wealthy planters. I discovered that slaves were still being smuggled in. The law here forbids their importation, although it is still permitted to own slaves. I saw the owners of sugar plantations living like kings in Havana, yet never visiting their land and giving complete charge to overseers. As my own father did."

"You could have done the same," Kevin said.

Barbosa shook his head. "There are things a man may not do, if he is to call himself a man." He gave Kevin a long, searching look. "You understand, señor?"

Kevin shrugged. "I once gave up a good job back in the States because I didn't want to shoot down unarmed strikers."

He looked away, embarrassed at sharing this confidence. He caught sight of a young woman walking down to the stream at the edge of the clearing where he and Barbosa were standing.

She was tall and statuesque, with skin the color of honey. She had the delicate features Kevin had seen on many of the quadroon girls here in Cuba, and she carried herself with superb animal grace. Kevin, watching the sway of her rounded buttocks, the sinuous movement of her hips, the thrust of her large, firm breasts against the thin cloth of the single garment she wore, felt a need that was purely physical and painfully urgent.

"Her name's Guadalupe. She's a good fighter, and she dances beautifully. You'll see her dance at the fiesta tomorrow night."

"Fiesta?" He could not take his eyes away from the girl's body until she disappeared into the shrubbery that lined the banks of the stream.

"Sí, Señor Farrell. We are fighting a war, but we have time for other things." He laughed. "We Cubans always find time for dancing."

"And the girl—Guadalupe—"

"She belongs to no man here in the village—in case

you were wondering. She gives herself to whom she will. If she should take a fancy to you, señor—"

He broke off as a boy came running across the clearing.

"The courier has arrived," the boy said. Kevin forgot about Guadalupe.

But the following night, at the fiesta, he saw her again. She danced the *zapateo* and the *caringa* with magnificent abandon. Kevin did not know whether Barbosa had spoken to her about him, but she threw him sidelong glances every time she and one of her partners moved close to the place where he was seated. Her eyes were large and dark. Kevin could not look away.

When it was close to midnight, the dancing stopped and she came to sit beside him, to feast on roast pig and yams, baked fish, pineapples, calalú seasoned with amaranth and spices. She reached for a cup of wine, and her body brushed his. In the firelight, her skin looked like deep, burnished copper.

"More wine, señor?" He shook his head. She gave him a long look. Then she stood up and held out her hand. He rose and followed her into the shadows, away from the crowd around the fire.

In the velvety darkness, she stripped off her skirt and blouse and tossed them aside. His body was on fire, his mouth went dry, and the blood began to hammer in his temples.

"I'll be leaving at dawn," he said.

"I know, señor. But it is a long time until dawn."

She dropped to the grass in one smooth, graceful movement and a moment later he was beside her. He felt the warmth radiating from her body, enveloping him. She gave herself freely, with the same fierce sensuality she had shown in the dancing.

Later, she lay in his arms, and he stroked her hair. "We are all grateful to you, for what you are doing," she said. "Those weapons you bring mean much to our cause."

"Is that why you came here with me tonight?"

She laughed, and drew his face down against her

breasts. "You are far too modest, if you believe that, señor."

During the journey up the slopes of the Pico Turquino, Kevin rode at the head of the wagons, mounted on the black stallion. Four of his crewmen followed, two mounted on the seat of the largest wagon, and one on each of the others. The roads were narrow, and they had to move slowly. The sunlight slanted down through the banana trees; brightly colored birds—parrots, hummingbirds, green pigeons—swooped and wheeled overhead; flowering vines, with purple, red and blue blossoms, spilled down over the rocks.

Jack Bailey, a big, rangy youngster, drove the first wagon in the line. Kevin heard him humming a fragment of a tune that had been played at the fiesta last night. The boy had given his age as nineteen when he had signed on for the voyage, but Kevin had suspected he had added a few years.

The sun was growing hotter now, for it was getting past noon. It would have been pleasant to make camp for a few hours, but Kevin decided it would be better to keep going. He had his money now, stowed away in a belt inside his shirt. It remained only to deliver the crates of weapons to the outpost atop Pico Turquino, then come down the other side and return to the *Medea*. The men would be eager to get their shares.

Kevin turned the stallion into a narrow ravine, and the rest of the small cavalcade followed, the wagons jolting and swaying. A waterfall splashed down from the rocks on one side, throwing glittering spray high into the clear sunlit air; the sound of the falling waters echoed from the rocky sides of the ravine.

Kevin did not hear the horses above them until the Spanish troopers were at the far end of the ravine. He looked up, saw the white and gold of their uniforms, and the hard glitter of their carbines, raised to fire. He wheeled the stallion around. More troopers were blocking off the other end of the ravine, through which he and his men had entered.

He dropped from his horse and drew a pistol from his

belt. The crewmen behind him leaped down from the wagons. They were far outnumbered by the Spanish troopers, but that did not stop them from putting up a fight. A few minutes later, it was over. Two of Kevin's men lay dead, another coughing his life out. Jack Bailey had not been hit, and neither had Kevin.

The troopers galloped down into the ravine and dismounted. Kevin and Bailey were forced back against the rocks, opposite the waterfall. The dying man was making terrible strangling sounds, and Kevin tried to get to him, but one of the troopers rammed the barrel of a carbine against his chest.

Others smashed open a few of the crates in the wagons.

They showed the contents, guns, ammunition, bayonets, to their leader, a tall young man with a broad, fleshy nose and yellow eyes. "See, *Teniente*," one of them said. "Weapons, all new. We can make use of them, no?"

The expression on the lieutenant's face did not change. He looked from Kevin to Bailey, as if weighing their relative usefulness. Then he raised his riding crop and pointed to Bailey.

"That one," he said. Two of the troopers seized the boy and brought him to the lieutenant.

"You were taking these weapons to the rebels," the lieutenant said. "Where is their camp?"

Bailey looked at Kevin. Only Kevin knew the directions for reaching the camp. The sailor at the rear of the wagons made a last, strangling sound and then was still.

"You will answer me. At once." The lieutenant's voice was hard.

"I don't know—" Bailey began. The troopers ripped his shirt away, threw him down on the grass, and then, as Kevin watched in silence, one of them took a mule whip from the lead wagon. The whip was six feet long, braided, heavy.

Two of the other troopers crushed Bailey's wrists down into the grass with their heavy boots, holding him immobile.

Kevin wanted to look away, but he could not. The

trooper holding the whip raised it high over his head and brought it down across Bailey's back. A red line appeared from his shoulders to his ribs. His body jerked convulsively, but he did not cry out. The whip slashed down again and again.

He screamed and writhed. "I don't know," he cried. "I swear. Captain Farrell—don't let them—"

"Stop," Kevin shouted. "Stop, damn you. He's telling the truth. He doesn't know anything."

The lieutenant signaled to the trooper, who put down the whip. "Bring the other one here," he ordered. Then, looking down into Kevin's face, he said, "He called you *Capitán*. You lead this rabble?"

Kevin hesitated, then, hearing the boy's tortured breathing, he said, "Yes. I'm their leader."

"*Bueno*. Then you can tell us—yes, you can tell us a great deal, I think. Tie his hands. He goes with us."

The troopers searched Kevin, found the money belt, and removed it. Then they lashed his hands together behind him with rope. It cut into his wrists. "And the other one?" a trooper asked, kicking Bailey's prostrate body.

"He's of no use to us," the lieutenant said.

Half a dozen troopers closed in on Bailey, swinging their carbines. Kevin heard the thud of the carbine butts against flesh and bone, heard Bailey's agonized cries.

Then Kevin lunged forward, fighting to free himself from the men who held him, using his head, his feet, his shoulders, cursing, panting. He caught a glimpse of something flashing down alongside his head; one of the men had struck at him with a carbine. The sunlit ravine exploded into a shower of blinding colors; the jarring pain brought him to his knees. The man struck again, and Kevin was falling into darkness.

It was late afternoon of the following day when Kevin entered the garrison of San Rafael. During the long march, the troopers had not given him any food and barely enough water to keep him going. When he had fallen, they had gotten him back on his feet with blows and kicks. His bound wrists were raw and bleeding and his arms, twisted behind his back, were numb.

Once, when the troop had halted to drink from a stream and refill their canteens, the lieutenant had ridden over and demanded, "Where were you taking the weapons?"

Kevin had not answered, and the lieutenant had shrugged.

"As you wish, *Capitán*. We'll find out what we want to know when we get you to San Rafael."

The inside of the garrison was cool after the heat of the mountains. Kevin's jaw throbbed from the blow he had taken, back in the ravine; the side of his face was swollen. His body was bruised and aching, too. But his thirst made his other discomforts unimportant.

The troopers pushed him along a maze of stone corridors, then made him halt before a massive wooden door. The lieutenant knocked and went inside. Kevin tried to swallow but his throat was parched.

After a few minutes, the lieutenant came out and led Kevin into the room. Some of the troopers followed.

Kevin saw a heavy-set man in his forties seated behind a wide desk of inlaid, polished wood. The man wore a handsome, spotless white and gold uniform. He had dark hair and a deeply lined face.

"I am Colonel Ramón Martinez," the man said. "And you are Farrell. An American?"

Kevin licked his cracked lips and stared at a decanter of pale yellow wine that stood on the colonel's desk. "That's right," he said.

"You suffered some hardships on your way here?"

Kevin did not answer.

"Regrettable. Now, I trust you are prepared to spare yourself any further discomfort by telling us all you know."

"I know nothing—"

Martinez looked at him, with shrewd, searching brown eyes. "You were carrying a large sum of money, señor. Paid to you by the rebels for a shipment of arms you smuggled into Cuba."

Kevin shook his head. "I didn't bring them into Cuba."

"Indeed?"

Kevin's mind worked quickly. "I came to Cuba to take a job as an overseer on one of the plantations. I—didn't like the work—so I quit."

He paused. Martinez did not speak.

"I met a man in Havana. He asked me to deliver a load of supplies to a town here in Oriente."

"You did not know what supplies you were carrying?"

"I didn't care. The pay was good."

"He paid you on the spot, in Havana?"

"That's right."

"And the other men who were with you?"

"He hired them, too."

Kevin swallowed. He ran his tongue over his cracked lips.

"Thirsty, Señor Farrell?"

"Yes."

"Untie his arms, and pour him a glass of wine," Martinez ordered. A trooper obeyed. Hot knives of pain jabbed his muscles as he moved his arms, but he was able to hold the glass. He forgot everything else, as he gulped the cool, dry wine. He drained the glass, and the sensation of relief from the tormenting thirst was exquisite. He had not eaten for nearly two days, and he felt a bit lightheaded but able to think clearly all the same. He had talked his way out of tight places before; he could do it again.

Martinez stood up, and came around to the front of the polished desk. He was a tall man, almost as tall as Kevin, with a thick neck and broad, heavy shoulders. He spoke in quiet, well-modulated tones, and Kevin recognized the precise accents of Castilian Spanish. Martinez smiled faintly.

"So, you met a man in Havana who paid you to transport supplies across the island. What was his name?"

"Muñoz—Mendez—I don't remember. Something like that."

"And where did you meet him?"

"In a cafe, near the harbor."

"The name of the cafe—"

"I don't recall—"

"And you were naive enough to accept the job without

261

demanding to know what you were carrying? At a time like this, when Cuba is being torn apart by revolution?"

"I needed the money. I've already told you—"

Martinez did not raise his voice, but his heavy-lidded brown eyes were as cold as those of a lizard. "What you've told me, Señor Farrell, is a pack of lies. But in a little you will speak the truth. All of it. And you will beg me to listen to you." The colonel turned, took a cigar from a carved mahogany box on his desk. One of the troopers lit it for him. Kevin smelled the rich scent of fine Havana tobacco.

"Lieutenant Sandoval has told me of an unpleasant incident," Colonel Martinez said. "The death of a young man back in that ravine where you were taken prisoner."

The memory came back to Kevin, vivid, obscene. The waterfall splashing down on the rocks, glittering in the sunlight, and Jack Bailey, stretched on the ground, screaming.

"Your men clubbed him to death." Kevin had to make an effort to keep his voice steady.

"*Ah, sí. Que lástima.* My men are a hot-tempered lot. But, Sandoval said that before the young man died, he called to you. He addressed you as *Capitán* Farrell."

Kevin pressed his lips together.

"Don't be stubborn," the colonel said, drawing on his cigar. "Do you recall telling Sandoval that the young man knew nothing?"

"I don't remember."

"I think you do. I also believe you were telling the truth. Your men knew nothing, but *you* know a great deal. You were their leader. You hired them yourself, back in the United States, to bring a shipload of arms to Cuba."

"That isn't true. I've already told you—"

"You are a mercenary," Martinez interrupted. "One of many who find it profitable to smuggle arms to the rebels. Without your kind, those bastards couldn't go on fighting."

Kevin remembered the village of Santa Clara, the storage sheds with their primitive weapons, machetes and daggers of indigo wood.

"We're going to cut off the supply lines to the rebels. Then we're going to round them up and wipe them out. Does that thought distress you, *Capitán* Farrell?"

"I don't give a damn one way or the other. This isn't my country."

"But there are those in your country who would like to see the power of Spain destroyed here in the Caribbean. You are greedy, you Americans. Cuba is a rich country. Sugar, coffee, tobacco. If this island were to fall into the hands of a gang of ignorant, disorganized rebels, America would step in fast enough. Manifest Destiny, your politicians have called it."

"I don't know anything about that."

Martinez leaned forward. "Listen to me, señor, and listen well. You are in our hands. Your rebel friends cannot help you—even if they wanted to. You have two choices. Tell us everything you know, and you will be given a prison sentence. Six months in the marble quarries near Havana, perhaps."

Kevin raised his eyebrows. "Not a particularly appealing prospect, Colonel."

"All things are relative," Martinez said. "Consider the other choice. If you remain silent, we will tear the truth out of you. Make no mistake, *Capitán* Farrell. We can do it. My men know a number of ways to make a man talk. Sandoval, here, is an expert. I think he enjoys his work."

"I've no doubt of that," Kevin said. He remembered how Bailey had been flogged at Sandoval's orders. Remembering, he felt a hot current of anger. Bailey, who had said he was nineteen, but might have been younger. Clubbed to death afterward, like a dog.

"*Bueno*," Martinez said crisply. "You know, now, what you may expect if you are foolish enough to remain silent."

Outside the windows, with their iron grillework, Kevin saw that the sun was going down. The sky was turning golden, and the high-ceilinged room was cool with the fragrant twilight air. But Kevin had started to sweat. There was a metallic taste on his tongue.

Martinez put a hand on Kevin's shoulder. "I am a

soldier, señor—not an inquisitor. But I have my orders. To put an end to this rebellion by any means necessary. I would prefer to meet these rebels on the field of battle, but they hide, they move about in the forests, in the mountains. To destroy them, I must know where they are, what their contacts are, in Havana, in the villages of the back country. You will give me that information."

Tell them, then. Take six months in their damn quarry. Tell them and be done with it. Serve your sentence and get off the island. Back to the States. Back to Drucilla.

Kevin looked past Colonel Martinez, and out at the twilight sky beyond the iron grillework. He thought of Drucilla's slender, curving body. Eyes that were the color of violets. Red-gold hair that had brushed his face in a soft, perfumed cascade, when she had bent to kiss him that night in his cabin aboard the *Medea*.

He had never before allowed himself to admit how much she meant to him . . . how much a part of his life she had become. He didn't want to love her . . . or any woman. To love another human being was to offer a hostage to fortune.

"I'm waiting, señor. What is it to be?"

Tell them everything. Tell them about the rebels in Santa Clara. Barbosa and the rest of them. Women, children, too. The contacts in New York and in Havana. Why not? He had been paid to transport weapons. Not to be a damn martyr for a cause that wasn't his.

"You are trying my patience," Martinez said.

"I—" Kevin jammed his hands into his pockets. "I have nothing to tell you."

Kevin looked away from the colonel, and over at Lieutenant Sandoval, who was smiling; his yellow eyes narrowed as they flicked over Kevin's body. Moving swiftly, Sandoval came to Kevin and closed a hand on the prisoner's arm, while a trooper took Kevin's other arm; between them, he was led into the next room. It had a low ceiling and small, barred windows, and was unfurnished except for a narrow table and a few high-backed chairs. The rest of the troopers came into the room.

One of the troopers ordered Kevin to push the narrow table to the center of the room and, when he had obeyed, told him to strip. His fingers were clumsy as he unbuttoned his shirt and unfastened his belt. The stone-walled room was damp and chilly.

Two of the troopers threw him down across the table and tied him to it, fastening his wrists and ankles with rawhide strips. He heard the men moving about, their booted feet noisy on the stone floor. He was able to turn his head and saw that someone had brought in a bucket of water. Sandoval was holding a long whip, like the one they had used on Bailey. Kevin watched as Sandoval dipped the end of the whip into the bucket. "Wet leather cuts deeper," he said. "Did you know that, *Capitán?*"

The night breeze from the barred window trailed icy fingers over his body.

The lieutenant flicked a drop of water off the end of the whip. An uncontrollable shudder ran through Kevin's body.

He caught the rich smell of cigar smoke. Martinez had come into the room. The colonel walked over and stood next to the table. "You can still change your mind," he said.

Sandoval brought the whip down on the back of one of the tall chairs. The impact sounded like a rifle shot. Kevin's body jerked upward against the rawhide bonds that held him.

"Let us start with the money you were carrying when you were captured," Martinez said. "Who paid you? And where was the payment made?"

"I've told you—a man in Havana—"

"Oh, no." Martinez's voice was soft, reasonable. "If you had been paid off back in Havana, what would have prevented you from going aboard your ship, and returning to the United States? The rebels are not so foolish."

Kevin pressed his forehead against the surface of the table and closed his eyes. "Once again. Where were you paid that money?"

Tell them about Santa Clara, hidden in the depths of the forest, on the site of the ruined plantation. Tell them. They'll go there and round up everyone. Diego Barbosa. And the girl who had lain with him on the night of the fiesta. Guadalupe. They wouldn't kill her right away. They'd have other uses for her strong, splendid body.

Kevin heard the whip whistling through the air, and a moment later, a line of fire tore across his back. From somewhere in the room, he heard one of the troopers begin to count. *Uno . . . dos . . . tres . . . cuatro. . . .* With each blow his senses reeled, shattered by the pain. But he did not lose consciousness. Sandoval was an expert, as the colonel had warned. After each stroke, he came back to his full awareness, in time to feel the force of the next stroke. The scent of the colonel's cigar was rich and pungent.

He did not scream at the first blow, or the second. It was not until he heard the trooper count off the tenth that he lost control. The pain spread from his back and shoulders up into his brain, so that he felt as if the whip were tearing apart the very core of his being. He heard his own wordless animal cries. When the whip cut into the same strip of flesh twice, the agony was unendurable.

Then he was floating in a hot, red-streaked darkness, the world falling away beneath him. He could still hear the crack of the whip, and feel his body jerking spasmodically, but his mind was detached, drifting. . . .

Someone dashed a bucket of cold water over his head and shoulders. Consciousness returned. Colonel Martinez was bending over him. Kevin turned his head and looked into the cold, heavy-lidded brown eyes. "Enough?" he asked.

Kevin had to fight to draw air into his lungs. He was panting, so that it took a moment before he could get the words out. "I have—nothing—to tell you—"

"You are mistaken. You have a great deal to tell me, and you will talk. One way or another."

They used the whip on him again, and their fists and their boots. But at dawn, when two of the troopers carried him out of the room, down a flight of stairs, and into a cell, he still retained enough consciousness to know that he had not betrayed anyone. He was past feeling pride; he only felt a faint surprise that he was still alive, that he could still think—after a fashion.

He heard one of the troopers say, "He has much strength, this one."

And the other answered, "*Sí*, Paco. But our colonel will break him, all the same."

A month had passed since then. Maybe longer. There had been nearly a dozen sessions of interrogation. And still, he had not broken.

Now, as he lay in his cell, he knew he would not sleep. His eyes were fixed on the grille in the cell wall, his ears straining to catch the sound of boots in the corridor.

He made himself close his eyes, and let his mind drift. Back to Charleston . . . back to Drucilla. . . . She would be sitting in her garden now, perhaps . . . cool and beautiful . . . wearing a purple dress. . . . He had bought her a purple dress that day after their first meeting in New York. And a small hat with purple plumes. He had taken her driving under the leafy green trees in Central Park. . . .

He heard it now, the sound of booted feet ringing against the stone floor of the corridor. His body went rigid, and his insides twisted.

Maybe it was only a guard, making rounds. Maybe the footsteps would go past his cell.

They stopped outside his cell door. A key grated in the lock.

He wanted to hide, to find a dark corner and crawl into it and hide like a terrified animal. But he was shackled hand and foot, and there was no place to hide.

Eighteen

DRUCILLA stood before the mirror in her spacious bedroom at the home of the Cardonas in Havana; she looked at her reflection with pleasure. Her gown of purple satin, cut very low in front, revealed the full curves of her breasts; the skirt flared out around her, and was half-covered by an overskirt of pale lilac net. Her eyes glowed deep violet. Kevin had liked seeing her in purple. That day, back in New York, he had taken her to the Ladies Mile and had bought her a beautiful purple dress.

She must not think about that now. She was here in Havana for one purpose only, and she must not let herself yield to weakness or sentiment; she must not even allow herself to think how much she loved Kevin, or she would not be able to bear the thought of what was happening to him.

"If the señora will be seated, *un momento*, I will complete her coiffure."

The tall, thin black woman who had been provided by Luisa Cardona to act as Drucilla's maid during her stay here was well-trained and skillful. Drucilla seated herself, and while the woman's hands moved deftly, arranging the gleaming, red-gold hair in elaborate waves and curls, Drucilla's thoughts went back to Kevin.

Why had he become so much a part of her, drawing her into what might prove a dangerous intrigue? Why couldn't she stop loving him? From that first night, when he had lifted her out of his carriage, on the rise overlooking the Hudson, when he had carried her into the grove of trees and made love to her, she had known that she belonged to him. In that one reckless hour, she had given him, not only her body, but her mind and her soul. From that hour, there had been no turning back.

She knew that she had to save him, to get him out of that terrible place where he was being held. If she failed, there would no longer be any purpose to her existence.

Tonight, she was to be entertained at a ball, here in the Cardonas' luxurious house; she was to meet Havana society and to begin the long, careful arrangements that would lead, if all went well, to Kevin's freedom.

In spite of the revolution, Cuba was enjoying unprecedented prosperity in this, the fourth year of the fighting; and the wealthy Creoles of Havana did not stint on their entertainments. There were theater parties, banquets, fiestas, and tonight the ball, given by Santiago and Luisa Cardona to introduce their American guest to society.

In the week she had been staying with the Cardonas, she had found Havana to be an exciting but somewhat disturbing city, a curious blend of gaiety and violence, of fantastic luxury and terrible poverty; in the last few days, she had ridden through the narrow streets in the Cardonas' fine carriage, attended by bewigged footmen and postilions, and drawn by the spirited horses that had been bred on her host's own plantation. She was fascinated, and a little dazed by all she saw: the soldiers, everywhere, in their straw hats with red cockades; the fine shops filled with marvelous displays of jewelry and silver, of millinery and rich fabrics, perfumes and leather boots. Luisa Cardona pointed out the many squares and parks; the most fashionable was the Paseo, which, on Sunday afternoons, was crowded with the carriages and volantes of the wealthy Havanese.

In the course of these rides, Drucilla saw, too, the countless cafes where the soldiers and their women sat smoking and enjoying *refrescas*: ices, sherbets, *limonada* with rum. She noted fruit stands piled high with pineapples, oranges and bananas.

Havana was never quiet. Drucilla's ears were assailed by church bells, by the clatter of horses' hooves and the rumbling wheels of volantes and ox carts, by the cries of the pedlars and the sellers of lottery tickets, the music of guitars and the trumpets of soldiers at their drills.

Drucilla had been in Havana only a few days when her hostess, Luisa Cardona, had mentioned the ball. "A celebration," she explained, her dark eyes sparkling in her plump, still pretty face. Then, seeing Drucilla's bewildered look she added, "You are thinking of this dreary war, no doubt. But that is of no real importance: an uprising of disorganized rabble. It will be crushed. Meanwhile, the sugar grows, as always. Last year's harvest here on our island was the largest we have ever had. Seven hundred and fifty-five thousand tons. And Santiago expects this year's harvest will be even greater."

Like most of the Havanese ladies, Luisa Cardona preferred to spend all her time in her splendid home in Havana; the overseers could take care of the running of the sugar plantation, with an occasional visit from her husband. Having presented Santiago Cardona with eight children, Luisa felt she had quite enough to keep her occupied.

Drucilla had obtained a letter of introduction to the Cardona family from her lawyer, Marcus Thorp.

"Since you're determined to make this trip, at least I will know you are safe and well cared for in Havana," he had said. He explained that he had had business dealings with Santiago Cardona before the Civil War; that, indeed, Señor Cardona had been his guest in Charleston.

"The Cardonas are among the oldest and wealthiest families on the island," he told her. "At their home, you will meet everyone of importance in Havana."

She felt deeply grateful to Marcus Thorp for providing her with an entree into this otherwise closed society, although at this moment she was not sure how she was going to proceed. Now, as the maid put the finishing touches to her toilette, arranging her hair in loose, shining ringlets over her shoulders, and fastening the soft curls into place atop her head, Drucilla, in spite of her elegant appearance, began to feel frightened and out of her depth.

The Cardonas were not in sympathy with the rebel cause, although some of the owners of the smaller plantations were. But their home provided a gathering place for all sorts of people, and she must somehow make the right contacts.

She told the Cardonas that she was in Cuba seeking a change of scene, and implied that she would go on to some of the other West Indian islands. Under other circumstances, she might have felt guilty at such a deception; but Kevin's life was at stake, and she would let nothing stand in her way; she would use any means at her command to help him.

She thought of Tim Cleary, waiting aboard the *Medea*, which lay anchored off one of the tiny islands that surrounded Cuba; Tim would do his part, but it was up to her to buy Kevin's way out of the garrison at San Rafael. In the meantime, she dared not let herself think about what might be happening to him behind those stone walls.

"What jewels will the señora wear tonight?" the maid was asking.

"The diamonds," she said. It would do no harm for her to flaunt her wealth, for it was her strongest weapon in the struggle that lay ahead.

The Casa Cardona, like most of the Creole homes in the city, was built around a patio; the air was heavy with the mingled scents of heliotrope, mignonette and oleander. These flowering shrubs were silver now in the moonlight, and the waters of the fountains sparkled coldly. During the early part of the evening, couples had strolled around the patio, and Luisa had introduced

Drucilla to these raven-haired, dark-eyed beauties and their escorts. Drucilla caught the glances of the men, ranging from admiration and interest to frank lust; they were obviously impressed by the contrast of her red-gold hair, ivory skin, and violet eyes the coloring of their own ladies. Even in that wealthy assemblage, the Tremayne diamonds were impressive, sparkling on her bosom, in her ears, in her shining hair.

She knew that these Havanese gallants were interested in the fact that one so young, so lovely, and so wealthy, was a widow. She intercepted numberless meaningful looks, and she was aware that these gentlemen were surprised and disappointed when she favored a nobody, a young journalist from the *London Times*, with the first dance of the evening.

Bartholomew Oakes was not a particularly skillful dancer, although he managed to lead Drucilla through the opening figures of the *contradanza* with dogged competence. In reply to her questioning, he told her that he had been assigned by his newspaper to report on the rebellion in Cuba, and that he had recently returned from a trip into the back country, where the guerrilla fighting was hottest.

"Wasn't it difficult to get official permission to go across the island?" she asked, making her voice casual. "I have been told that much of the island is under martial law."

"That's true," he said. "But if one approaches the right official and provides him with—shall we say—sufficient incentive, such things can be arranged."

Although Oakes was a young man, his long, thin face was shrewd and a little cynical; he had a large, sandy mustache, and short-cropped hair; his blue eyes were direct and intelligent. He did not dress with the casual elegance of the young Creoles; but he was well turned out in his dark blue suit and fawn-colored waistcoat.

Drucilla deliberately missed a step in the complicated figure of the dance, looked up at Oakes, and said, "I'm not familiar with these Cuban dances. I wonder, Mr. Oakes—perhaps we might take a turn about the patio."

The moon was a large silver disk in the sky above

the deserted patio. Drucilla gave Bartholomew her arm, and for a little while they strolled in silence. Then she said, "You must have had some fascinating experiences in the course of your travels about the island."

"Fascinating, yes. But unpleasant, some of them. This war's like every other, an ugly, brutal business."

"Do you think the rebels have a chance of winning?"

"I doubt it, Mrs. Seaton. They're good fighters, but they've had heavy casualties and they lack supplies and organization." He smiled apologetically. "Surely, you're not interested in the progress of the war here."

"But you're wrong. I have certain interests in Cuba."

Oakes showed no surprise. A number of Americans had business interests on the island; a few owned plantations.

"It's true enough some of the sugar estates have been burned by the rebels," he said. "But most of them are still untouched. And highly productive. Why, last year's harvest—"

"Yes, I know. Luisa Cardona told me there was a record crop."

"True enough. Besides, this rebellion can't go on much longer. General Jovellar, the present Captain-General, is completely ruthless in his methods of suppressing the activities of the *guerrilleros*."

"You know this Captain-General?"

"I've met him, yes."

"Is he the official you spoke of—the one who gave you permission to visit the countryside, where the fighting is going on?"

"Well, no." He looked puzzled by her obvious interest, but flattered, too. "Why do you ask?"

She stopped in front of the fountain and turned to face him. "Mr. Oakes, would you give me the name of the man, the official who—"

"I don't understand," he said. "If you have need of a contact in the government, surely Santiago Cardona would be pleased to help you."

"I can't ask him," she blurted out. "The Cardonas mustn't know."

The journalist held up a hand. "Now, just a minute.

Am I to understand that you're in some sort of difficulty? That you need help from a government official?" She nodded, and he went on, "That sort of help can be expensive, Mrs. Seaton."

"I don't care about the expense."

"In that case, I suggest you go to Don Miguel Altamonte. He's with the quartermaster department. He gives out contracts for Army supplies to those merchants who are willing to grease his palm."

"But you said he got permission for you to travel across the island—"

"True enough. You see, these officials come from Spain, to serve here in Cuba for relatively little pay. They go home wealthy, most of them, because of the bribes they manage to collect in return for using their influence. A merchant can't unload a cargo of wine here in Havana without paying off. A foreign journalist like myself can't get the slightest cooperation unless he offers a suitable bribe. The greater the service, the more money is extorted. I suspect that your need is rather unusual, since you can't discuss it with the Cardonas."

"It is," she said simply.

"Then may I give you a word of warning? Be careful. This Altamonte is powerful, but he's slippery as an eel. If you could bring yourself to tell me what you want from him, perhaps I—"

She shook her head. "It's good of you to be concerned, but I can't tell you anything more."

He shook his head. "Very well. But if you should run into trouble, I'd be honored if you'd call upon me."

"Thank you," she said. "You have already helped me, more than you will ever know."

Don Miguel Altamonte was an obese man, with a fringe of black hair around a shiny, pinkish bald head. His white suit was dark under the arms, and his face glistened with sweat. Bartholomew Oakes, who had driven her to the residence of the government official, had remained in the volante at the foot of the avenue of mangos leading up to the house; Drucilla had insisted she must speak to Altamonte in private.

Now, seated in a pleasant, candlelit room at the rear of the house, she heard Altamonte say, "What you ask of me, señora, may be impossible."

"I was told you are a man of great influence, Don Miguel."

He smiled, showing small, yellow teeth. "You flatter me. Of course, I will do all in my power to help so beautiful a lady as yourself. Still . . ."

She tried not to notice that his eyes flickered over the curves of her breasts, beneath the thin silk of her gown.

"I'll pay whatever you ask."

"Ah, but you see, it's not a question of money alone. True, I can help a merchant to get a government contract. On occasion I can even assist in getting some foolish, hot-headed boy from a good family out of Cuba, after he has disgraced himself by showing sympathy for the rebel cause. But this man you speak of, a gun-runner, a man who is valuable to the Spanish forces because of the information he can give them . . . I fear I can do nothing for you."

Drucilla stood up. "Then I am sorry I've wasted your time to no purpose," she said, trying to keep her voice steady.

He reached out and put a plump hand on her arm. "*Por favor*, there is no need to be so hasty. Sit down and let us consider what may be done."

She drew her arm away and sank back into her chair.

"This man, this *Capitán* Farrell. He means a great deal to you."

"I should think that would be obvious, considering the sum I've offered you for his release."

"It is, indeed, a generous offer. But consider, your *Capitán* Farrell may not even be alive. Forgive me, but you must face facts. He was taken to San Rafael in August, and it is now late September."

"He's got to be alive. You can't make me believe—"

"Calm yourself, señora. Very well, let us say you are right. He still lives. Even so, he may be in no condition to make an escape, over dangerous country, to Havana."

Seeing her bewildered look, he went on, "Colonel Martinez, who is in command of the garrison at San Rafael, is a formidable man. He has been questioning *Capitán* Farrell for many weeks. Farrell may now be too badly injured to travel—he may have gone mad—"

Drucilla gave a sharp cry, then pressed her hand to her lips. She must not give way to emotion, not in front of this soft-spoken, gross man who was Kevin's link with survival.

"You can make inquiries, find out if—if—"

"It will cost a great deal even to make such inquiries."

"I've told you, I'll pay whatever you ask. And more, much more, when Kevin Farrell is brought here to Havana."

"And you have means for getting him off the island?"

"That's right."

Don Miguel Altamonte sighed. The silence grew, lengthened until Drucilla had to dig her nails into her palms. From the garden, she heard the soft murmur of doves, the rustling of the hot breeze in the leaves of the mangos.

"*Bueno*," Altamonte said at last. "I have always been tenderhearted where the ladies are concerned. And one so young, so lovely as you—" He shrugged. "Come back in a week, señora. I should have news for you then, if we are lucky."

But it was three weeks before Don Miguel Altamonte was able to inform Drucilla that Kevin Farrell was, indeed, living, and might even be capable of traveling to Havana. And it was mid-November when she received a message from one of Altamonte's servants that she was to accompany him to his master's residence at once.

She had to go alone this time, for Bartholomew Oakes was away on another of his trips, this time to Camaguey province, where the rebels were launching an offensive. She had found the company of the young English journalist pleasant, and she had drawn security from his presence on her visits to Altamonte. But now, she was far too excited by this summons to Altamonte's house to think about Oakes.

Perhaps Altamonte would give her the long-awaited news that Kevin had been helped to escape from San

Rafael, that he was being taken across the island to Havana. Altamonte had agreed, reluctantly, that Farrell could stay hidden in an abandoned farm building on his property, while Drucilla made the necessary arrangements for getting the *Capitán* off the island.

"No more than a few days, you understand," Altamonte had warned. "And I am taking a terrible risk, even so."

"A risk for which you're being well paid," Drucilla had reminded him coldly.

"There are some risks beyond price, señora," he had said. He had wiped his face with a silk handkerchief. His uneasiness was genuine and was outweighed only by his greed.

The servant who brought her the message escorted her to a volante, drawn by two white mules; mounting up onto the box, he cracked his whip, and the mules started off. The driver kept his eyes fixed on the street and did not speak to Drucilla.

She sat back in her seat and raised her parasol over her head. She had not had time to change and still wore a simple pale blue muslin afternoon dress, embroidered with small white flowers.

At sunset, the driver turned the volante into the long avenue of mangos leading to the Altamonte house, on its hill overlooking Havana. The trees cast purple shadows on the dew-soaked grass; the air was heavy with mignonette and heliotrope; against the rosy sky, the white doves wheeled and swooped before settling down in their marble dovecot for the night.

The driver helped her down and struck the huge, iron knocker; a moment later, the great door swung open. It took a moment for Drucilla's eyes to adjust to the dim light in the hallway, so that she could see, not Altamonte's major-domo, but a soldier, like those she had seen drilling in the plazas of Havana.

"This way, if you please," he said, and she sensed that it was not an invitation, but a command. She followed the soldier down the hallway to Miguel Altamonte's study. Had he tricked her, betrayed her? She did not dare think about the consequences to Kevin if he had.

The soldier knocked on the study door, then opened it, and stood aside to let Drucilla enter. In the light from the windows, she could see a man, in the white and gold uniform of a Spanish officer; he was seated in Altamonte's tall, carved chair, but he rose at once, as she came through the door.

He inclined his dark head politely. "Señora Seaton? Allow me to introduce myself. I am *Capitán* Julio Vargas, of the Army of his Most Catholic Majesty."

"But I had an appointment with Don Miguel. He sent me a message."

"No, señora. It was I who sent the message."

"But where—"

"Don Miguel Altamonte has been recalled to Spain. His ship left Havana harbor two days ago. At that, he's fortunate. Without his family's influence, he would be facing a firing squad."

She fought against the rising panic that threatened to sweep away all reason. Her plans had failed. Kevin was not on his way to Havana. He would die in that terrible place.

The room blurred before her eyes and she swayed forward. Then she felt a hand beneath her arm. She was dimly aware that Captain Vargas was leading her out of the room, onto the marble balcony that overlooked the magnificent gardens. She leaned against him, for the strength had drained from her body.

As she did so, she looked up at him and saw something flicker in his black eyes. She knew, as surely as if he had spoken, that he was aware of her, not as a conspirator, an enemy of Spain—but as a woman. Her spine stiffened and she knew she was not beaten yet.

Nineteen

"WHAT, exactly, is your relationship with Kevin Farrell, señora?"

Vargas stood with his back to the ornate iron railing and studied Drucilla. Whatever she had seen in his eyes a few moments ago was gone. His voice was courteous but impersonal.

"We're—friends."

"Indeed?" One corner of his mouth lifted in a faint, ironic smile. "It would be better if you were quite honest with me."

"This is an official interrogation, then." She tried to keep the fear out of her eyes, but her throat went dry.

"Don't let your imagination run away with you," he said.

"I've heard about the way Spanish officers interrogate prisoners."

"No doubt. But you are a woman."

He took a step closer to her and, looking up at him, she realized for the first time how handsome he was. Although only a little above medium height, he had wide shoulders and a narrow waist and hips. His hair was blue-black, and he wore sideburns. His eyes, fixed on hers, were so dark that the pupil and iris appeared to be one. The mouth was full-lipped, but there was nothing weak about it. She guessed that she would not be able to deal with Captain Vargas as she had with Altamonte.

Maybe she would not be able to deal with him at all. Perhaps, within the next few hours, she herself would be in a prison cell.

"Please, sit down, and try to compose yourself," he said. "My orderly will bring us wine." He left her for a moment to give the order, then returned, and stood at the railing again.

"You have been very foolish," he said. "Did you really think it would be so easy to help a valuable prisoner escape from San Rafael?"

She did not answer. The orderly brought the wine and placed it on a small table, with two goblets. It was sweet but potent, and she felt new courage flowing into her as she drank. She would find a way to save Kevin yet.

"Well, señora? You have not answered me."

"Altamonte said he could get Captain Farrell out. I offered him a great deal of money, and he assured me it could be done." She looked up questioningly. Vargas shook his head.

"Don't waste your time," he said. "I do not make such arrangements."

"Perhaps you don't understand how much money is involved. I am prepared to offer you—"

He held up his hand. "Please, let us not pursue this. As it happens, I am the eldest son of Don Raúl Vargas." Seeing her blank expression, he smiled. "You are a newcomer to our island, so you cannot be expected to understand. I am not one of those who came to Cuba to enrich myself through the kind of trickery employed by Miguel Altamonte. My father's plantation is one of the largest on the island. I do not say this to impress you, señora. Merely to show you the futility of your offer."

"I've offered you nothing," she said.

"You were about to." He shook his head. "You have failed, Señora Seaton, and you must accept that fact. There is nothing for you to do but return to your own country."

Her hand began to tremble, and she put down the goblet with a sharp clicking sound. "Don't be afraid," he went on. "You will suffer no unpleasantness. I myself will escort you to the next ship leaving Havana. In the meantime, you have nothing to fear."

She was not afraid for herself, however. "I won't go," she said stubbornly. "Not while Kevin Farrell remains at San Rafael."

"You must care for this man very much," he said.

"Yes."

"That is unfortunate," he told her evenly. "Because there is nothing you, or anyone else, can do to save him. Unless—"

He was studying her closely. His dark eyes moved over her, and she became aware that her light muslin dress, far more revealing than anything she had worn back in Charleston, accented the lines of her body. It was a dress meant to be worn in the afternoon, when she was taking the air in the patio, with Luisa Cardona. But she had not wanted to take the time to change when she had received the summons to Altamonte's house early this afternoon. She had not even put on a hat, but had thrown a delicate, white lace veil over her hair.

Her feelings were still numb, after the shock of learning that her scheme had failed; that Miguel Altamonte had been sent back to Spain, and that she was alone, at the mercy of this implacable representative of Spanish power here in Cuba.

But, she reminded herself, he was also a man. She knew the effect she had on men. She could not help but know. And here in Cuba, where her coloring made her stand out from the other women, she had drawn admiring glances wherever she had gone. Now, on the balcony overlooking the garden, warm with the colors of sunset, fragrant with flowering shrubs, she found herself wondering with a curious, unnatural calm, exactly what she was prepared to do to win Kevin's freedom. The answer came, swift and instinctive. Kevin was her life. If money would not save him, she would use other means.

She leaned forward a little in her chair and, with a seemingly artless movement, she took the delicate lace veil from her hair. In the last rays of the setting sun, the copper-gold waves blazed with fire. She raised her wine glass and took another sip, then looked at Captain Vargas. His dark eyes narrowed and his lips parted slightly.

"You puzzle me, Señora Seaton," he said. "You care very much for *Capitán* Farrell. And yet, you had a husband, back in your own country."

"I—knew Captain Farrell long before I was married."

"And now you have come to Cuba and you say you will not leave without this man. But what means, other than money, have you?"

She rose in one graceful movement and moved toward him.

"Of course, you are a very beautiful woman. And one who is capable of great love."

She stood before him, trying to steady herself. He was going to touch her now. To kiss her, perhaps. She fought down the instinctive fear. This man was a stranger. Well-bred, outwardly courteous, but, she suspected, capable of violence, even cruelty. There was something in his eyes, in the set of his full-lipped mouth. . . .

"Tell me, are you personally involved in this revolution?"

She was startled by his question, it was so completely unexpected.

"Well?" he demanded.

"No, of course not. What does a war between Spain and an army of Cuban revolutionaries have to do with me?"

He shrugged. "There are a few foolish idealists in your country who have espoused the rebel cause. And some abolitionists in America who are not satisfied that the slaves have been freed in your own South. They hope that if the rebels win here, our plantation owners will also be forced to free their slaves."

"I don't believe in slavery anywhere," Drucilla said frankly. "But I've never been involved in any sort of abolitionist movement. Neither has Captain Farrell. He came here with those guns only because he was being well paid to do so. He told me."

"He appears to have undergone a change of heart since then." Vargas shook his head. "I think he is a fool but I can't help admiring his courage. And yours, señora."

"You're quite wrong about me. I'm not brave. I only—" Her voice shook. "Please, Captain Vargas. I beg you— don't force me to leave Cuba without—at least, let me go to him—let me see him. I'll do anything you ask. Anything—"

"What possible good would it do for you to see him? You would only distress yourself to no purpose." He shook his head. "No," he said. "I will not take a bribe, no matter how large. I respect your *Capitán* Farrell for his devotion to what he thinks to be his duty. But you must understand I am no less devoted to my own cause. I am an officer, señora. The men of my family have served the rulers of Spain for longer than your country has existed. I will do nothing to help an enemy of Spain to escape."

Disheartened, desperate, she looked away. What would it be like to go back to Charleston, to face the long, empty years without Kevin? To look at Kevin's son, and know each time the full measure of her defeat?

"There may be a way for you to help Farrell. If you are willing."

The words cut through the fog of misery that surrounded her. "Anything. I'll do anything you wish."

"Suppose—with the consent of *Capitán-General* Jovellar, I could take you to San Rafael. A difficult journey for a woman, and dangerous in wartime—"

"I don't care about the danger."

"Very well. Perhaps if you were to see Farrell alone, talk to him. Perhaps you could persuade him that his resistance is useless."

"I don't know. I'm not sure I could—"

"He must love you very much. What man could resist the pleading of a woman who has been willing to risk so much for his sake? I do not know what is between you. I do not ask."

She looked past Vargas and down at the garden where the shadows had drained the color from the flowers and the grass. Kevin had never said he loved her. Not in words. But when their bodies had been joined, he had told her without words that he cared for her, that she was a part of him.

"If I can persuade him to talk, what then?" she asked.

"He could be removed from San Rafael. Transferred to a prison in Havana perhaps. For a short sentence. Then, he would go free."

"Oh, but another prison—"

"He would not be questioned there."

"Tortured, that's what you mean."

"A regrettable necessity in wartime."

"It's barbaric—no civilized country would—"

"I will not debate that with you. A woman cannot be expected to understand such matters." He took her arm and led her back to her chair, then seated himself opposite her. "Well, what is your answer?"

"I'll go, of course. When can we leave?"

"Within a few days, I should think. It will be necessary for me to detain you here in the meantime."

"But the Cardonas, what will they think when I—"

"I'll tell them as much as they need to know. Santiago Cardona is loyal to Spain. He will understand."

He smiled at her. "You need not look so uneasy. You are in no danger from me. I am not the sort of man who would force myself upon a woman. Certainly not a woman like you."

"What sort of woman do you think I am?"

"A lady. A great lady, for all your indiscreet behavior. Sensitive . . . gentle . . . a little too impulsive, perhaps . . . and very beautiful. This *Capitán* Farrell—he is to be envied, in spite of his present situation."

Drucilla's body ached by the end of her first day on horseback. The roads across Cuba were bad; in places, they were nonexistent. From time to time, the military escort that accompanied her and Captain Vargas had to dismount, to cut away the thick green undergrowth with machetes.

For the first two nights, they slept at ranches, commandeered by Vargas without ceremony. After that, they slept in the open, with two of the six soldiers on guard at all times.

"I told you it would be no pleasure trip," Vargas said, when he helped her to bed down outdoors for the first time. He had fixed her blankets close to a high out-cropping of rock, and had showed her how to wrap herself in more blankets, to keep warm, for as they began to go up into the hills, the nights were damp and chilly. "Only two more nights of this," he said, as he rolled himself up into his own blankets, close to her side. "Then, San Rafael."

The ground was hard, in spite of the blankets, and she shifted, her leg muscles aching. In the darkness, she heard Vargas ask, "Is anything wrong?"

"No, only—I'm not used to riding astride."

"But you did tell me you were an experienced rider."

"It's different, riding sidesaddle along one of the roads outside Charleston."

"You come from Charleston? You have a family there, perhaps?"

"My husband's family. My mother-in-law lives on Seaton Barony. A rice plantation."

"Your mother-in-law. She knows of your trip to Cuba?"

"She only knows I'm traveling in the West Indies." She had spoken without thinking, and she felt a swift current of fear. "But there are others who know where I am. My lawyer. And my sister-in-law. If they have no word from me, I assure you, they will make inquiries."

She heard Vargas laugh softly. "You are afraid you, too, may be imprisoned in San Rafael?"

"I've thought of it, yes."

"And yet you came. Without hesitation. You are a most unusual woman. But you need not be afraid. You are in no danger. I have given you my word."

She turned her head to look at him. She could make out his features in the flickering firelight. "I have no choice but to trust you," she said.

"You're quite right," Vargas said. "And now, you'd better go to sleep. We still have two days' hard riding ahead of us, before we reach San Rafael."

Kevin Farrell had not yet finished the tasteless mixture of cornmeal and water that was his breakfast, when the trooper, Paco, came for him. The tin dish dropped from Kevin's fingers, and his breathing become unsteady; he felt a thrust of pain in his ribs, where Lieutenant Sandoval had kicked him, a few nights before.

"On your feet," Paco ordered. "Come with me."

For the first time since his imprisonment, Kevin was permitted to bathe, and was given a shave. "What's the occasion?" he asked Paco. "You getting me fixed up for a firing squad?"

Paco laughed. Unlike the other troopers, Paco would, on occasion, exchange pleasantries with him. "No firing squad, *Capitán*. You have visitors."

Poca handed him a change of clothes, clean shirt and pants. "Get dressed, and be quick about it."

Kevin obeyed. Visitors, he thought. An official from Havana, impatient with the way the interrogations were going. Maybe this new arrival would have a few ideas of his own. Although there was damn little Sandoval hadn't thought of.

Twenty

DRUCILLA had changed from the clothes she had worn on the journey—a man's close-fitting riding breeches, leather boots, and a white cambric shirt—to the blue muslin, the only dress she had with her. She was aware of the troopers' glances but, in the presence of Colonel Ramón Martinez and Captain Julio Vargas, the soldiers confined themselves to swift, furtive looks.

When she heard footsteps in the hall outside the colonel's office, she caught her breath and began to rise; Vargas, who was seated beside her, put a restraining hand on her arm.

"That will be Farrell, now," Martinez said. "You may talk to him in here, if you like. Perhaps your methods of persuasion will be more effective than ours."

A tall young lieutenant with hard, yellow eyes gave a short laugh; it was a harsh, ugly sound.

The colonel went to the door, motioning to the troopers to follow him. "My men will be on guard outside," he told her. "It would be most unwise for *Capitán* Farrell to try to bolt."

She watched the colonel and his men leave the room.

Although she had longed to see Kevin, now that the moment of their meeting had come, she was afraid. Vargas put a hand over hers.

"You must not lose heart now, señora," he said. "Remember what is at stake."

A moment later, a guard pushed Kevin into the room, with such force that he stumbled; he grasped the back of a chair and regained his balance. He put up his arm quickly to shield his eyes from the afternoon sunlight that streamed through the heavy iron grillework of the windows.

Drucilla's throat constricted. How long had they kept him shut away in darkness?

"Kevin."

At the sound of her voice, his arm dropped to his side. "Drucilla. They said I had visitors but—"

He broke off as soon as he saw that she was not alone.

Julio Vargas rose and said, "I'll be outside, if you need me."

"Thank you, Captain Vargas," she said automatically. But she was no longer aware of him; she only waited until he was gone, then ran across the room and flung herself into Kevin's arms. She pressed her body against his, holding him to her, searching his face, as if to reassure herself that he was the man she remembered . . . the man she loved.

There was something in his eyes that she had never seen there before.

His face was thinner, the flesh drawn tightly over the cheekbones. There was a livid bruise on his jaw, a cut under one eye, and a long, raised white scar running from chin to temple.

"Oh, Kevin. Tim told me what these—these—what they were doing to you."

"Is Cleary safe? They didn't get him, too, did they?"

She shook her head, then hesitated.

"Don't be afraid to talk," he said grimly. "These walls are stone, at least a foot thick. Tell me, where's Tim?"

"He brought the *Medea* into Charleston harbor, and I found him at the Bull's Head Tavern. He told me you'd been captured. I came as quickly as I could, with Tim.

He's aboard the *Medea* now, anchored off the coast on the other side of the island."

"But you—why didn't you stay in Charleston? You must have been out of your mind, coming here."

"I had to come. When Tim told me, when he made me understand—" The long strain had brought her to the edge of hysteria. "I won't let them hurt you again! I won't! I'll get you out of here!"

Tears ran down her face, and he took her in his arms.

"Don't cry. Don't, love." He held her against him and stroked her hair. "Hush, now." He led her to the high-backed horsehair sofa in a corner of the room, and drew her down beside him. She tried to hold back her tears, but it was no use. He cupped her face in his hands and smiled, with a trace of the old, familiar mockery. "Can this be the girl who told me, on our first meeting, that she never cried?"

"Don't you dare laugh at me, Kevin Farrell. And don't blame Tim for bringing me to Cuba. Surely, you didn't think I could stay away. Once I knew where you were, and what they were doing to you, no one could have stopped me."

She fumbled in her pocket and found a handkerchief and wiped her eyes.

"Tim's given to exaggeration. He had no way of knowing what was happening to me."

"But he did. A girl named Pia, a laundress for the garrison, is a rebel spy. She got word to him about where you were. She said they were . . ." Drucilla swallowed against the sickness that rose inside her. . . . "that they were making bets, these Spanish soldiers, on how long it would take before they made you talk."

She could not go on. She took his hand and pressed her lips against it, and as she did, she saw the bruised flesh that encircled his wrist. She stifled a scream.

"I'm a valuable prisoner," he said. "They have to keep me chained at night. Although how the devil they think I'd get out of here, I don't know. Those walls out there are ten feet high, at least; even if I got out of the building I'd never make it over the wall. . . ."

"I know. Tim told me. That's why I made him bring me

back with him. I thought I could get you out with bribery. I almost did, too, but Altamonte, the Spanish official who was making the arrangements for your escape, was discovered and recalled to Spain. That was when I met Captain Vargas. He got permission for me to come here."

"And who is this Captain Vargas?"

"He's the officer who was with me when they brought you in."

"Oh, yes. And exactly what did you have to do to get Vargas to help you?"

"We made a bargain."

His face went dark with suspicion. "What kind of bargain?"

"An—arrangement. Kevin, I can get you out of here."

"What kind of bargain?" he repeated. His hands gripped her arms, his fingers hurting her. "Answer me, Drucilla."

"Not the kind you're obviously thinking about."

"All right, then. What were the terms of this arrangement? You must have offered him something."

"Kevin, back in Charleston, you told me you didn't care which side won this war. Tim couldn't explain why you were holding out, refusing to give the Spanish the information they want. I can't understand, either."

His eyes were remote. "There's no need for you to understand."

"Tell me, please."

"I can't. Not without sounding like a fool or an idealist—and you've known me long enough to realize I'm neither."

He looked toward the closed door, then back at Drucilla.

"So that was the plan. Bring you here, have you plead with me to talk and get my freedom." He smiled. "Captain Vargas must be a romantic, in his way—"

"Kevin, listen to me—"

"It's no good, Drucilla. It won't work."

"But why can't you tell Martinez whatever he wants to know? You're not a rebel. You have no stake in this war, except money. You said so yourself."

"That was a long time ago," Kevin said. "Things can happen to a man . . . It isn't easy to talk about, not even with you." His eyes were filled with self-mockery. "I've always been a selfish man—I haven't changed altogether. But I can't sell out the men and women who trusted me. I lived among them, you see, and I talked with them. I even . . . no matter. I can't let Martinez find them and slaughter them."

"What about you? How much longer can you hold out?"

"We Irish are a stubborn lot. Besides, there's a chance the rebels will take this garrison; they're strong here in Oriente. With the right weapons, and enough men, San Rafael can be taken."

"But what will happen to you in the meantime? Kevin, I won't let you do this." Her voice was trembling. "I know you—don't love me. But that isn't important anymore. As long as you're safe and free, that's all I care about."

"Stop it." His voice was harsh, almost angry. He took her in his arms and held her against him. "You mustn't think—I can't let you go believing that. I do love you, Drucilla. I never wanted to. But I do."

A warm tide swept through her. Now, at last, he was saying what she had longed to hear all these years. She pressed her face against his shoulder. She heard him saying, "These weeks I've been here, I've had time to think. To remember. In my cell at night, when I couldn't sleep, I thought about you. I remembered so many little things. That first time I came into your room at the boarding-house in New York. You were afraid of me and trying not to show it. And those afternoons I took you riding in Central Park. That purple dress you wore, with all those frills—"

"You could think about things like that—here?"

"It helped keep me sane. I felt you with me in the darkness. I talked to you, sometimes. . . ."

"But now I'm really here, and I won't leave without you. Kevin, tell them what they want to know. We can leave here together, and Captain Vargas and his men will take us back to Havana. I'll wait for you while you're in jail. Then we'll go home together."

"I'm sorry, love. I can't."

"But if you care anything about me—"

"That's got nothing to do with it. I want you to leave San Rafael at once. Get back to Charleston as soon as you can."

"Without you? Why should I go anywhere without you? You're all I have."

He drew away and looked down at her. "Have you forgotten that you have a son in Charleston?"

She hadn't meant to tell him, but he was leaving her no choice. Her eyes held his. "That's right," she said. "I have a son. Your son, Kevin. Andrew is your child."

He flinched as if she had struck him. The color drained from his face. "I don't believe it."

"I swear to you, it's the truth."

He took a long breath, let it out, then said softly, "You wouldn't lie, would you? Not about this."

"No. Not about this. I was pregnant when you walked out on me back in Newport. I didn't know it, of course. I didn't find out until Radford and I were on our honeymoon. I was two months along by that time."

"I never thought—I wanted you and I took you, and I never considered the possibility that you might have a child by me. I'm sorry."

"I'm not. Andrew's part of you. The first time I held him in my arms, I was so proud and happy."

"A son—my son." Kevin's voice was unsteady. "Tell me about him."

"He—he's tall for his age. A big, handsome boy. He has thick black curls and—and a stubborn mouth. Like yours. And a disposition to match. When I left him, he was starting to walk."

"Where did you leave him?"

"With Theodora Seaton. She adores him."

"That night, aboard the *Medea*, when we were talking about him—why didn't you tell me then?"

"I couldn't have used Andrew to hold you, when I thought you didn't love me. But now—" Her eyes pleaded with him. "Now everything's changed. Andrew needs his father."

"Not a father like me. What would I have to give him?"

"Everything that matters. Love, and pride and strength

—I want him to be like you, Kevin. And—I need you, too."

"We'll be together again, after I get out of here. You've got to believe that."

His arms encircled her, and he bent her back on the couch. She felt the hardness of his body, pressed against hers; his mouth taking her lips in a long, slow kiss that deepened, that possessed her. She drew his bruised face down against her breasts. She could feel the hunger in him, the hard, urgent need. The world fell away, and she forgot where they were, forgot the high stone walls, the barred windows, the soldiers stationed outside the door.

There were only the two of them in a warm, sunlit place of love and joy. His fingers shook a little as he began to undo the buttons of her bodice. She closed her eyes. He was going to make love to her. And after that, he would not let her leave without him.

Then she gave a little cry, as he pushed her away. His breath came quickly. "I want you. But not like this. If I take you now, I won't be able to do what I must do."

He stood up. His hands were closed into hard fists. His face was like granite. She watched him turn and walk swiftly to the door. He flung it open. "Captain Vargas," he called.

The troopers raised their carbines but Vargas thrust them aside and came into the office.

"What is it, señor?"

"I want you to take Mrs. Seaton out of here," Kevin said. Even now, in the coarse cotton pants and shirt of a prisoner, there was something commanding about him. "Get her back to Havana, and put her on the first ship going to Charleston."

Drucilla ran to Kevin and tried to put her arms around him, but he thrust her away. "Kevin, please—I won't go alone. I won't go until you promise me—"

He looked past her, directly at Julio Vargas. "No promises," he said. "And no arrangements. You can tell Martinez I said so."

"Don't be a fool, señor. Why should you sacrifice yourself for these rebels?"

"That's my business," Kevin said evenly. "Are you going to tell Martinez, or shall I?"

Drucilla saw the reluctant admiration in Captain Vargas's eyes. "I understand," he said. "It's too bad you chose the wrong side. Our army could use a man like you."

But Kevin was looking at Drucilla again. "You'd better go now," he said quietly.

"No—I won't go—let me stay, please—"

"You'll take care of her, Captain Vargas?"

"She'll be safe with me. I give you my word," Vargas said.

"Then take her. *Now*."

Vargas put a hand on Drucilla's arm, but she struggled until he had to put one arm around her waist and the other under her knees and lift her off the floor. She kicked and writhed, twisting against him. Through her tears she saw Kevin's face. His mouth was set in a hard, thin line, and his gray eyes were bleak and desolate.

Drucilla and Vargas left the garrison of San Rafael less than an hour later, accompanied by the military escort he had brought from Havana. They rode down the slopes of the Sierra Maestra, through the green rain forest with its tree ferns stirring in the light breeze. Flocks of red and green parrots flew overhead, screeching. The cavalcade moved steadily down to the lower, drier levels of the mountains, where huge, curiously shaped cacti cast their grotesque shadows on the rocks. The sky turned from bright blue to gold, then to the soft purple of twilight.

Time had no meaning for Drucilla. She kept her eyes fixed on the trail ahead, seeing Kevin's face, as she had seen it those last moments, through her tears. She wasn't crying now, but there was a hard ache in her chest.

What were they doing to him now, in that terrible place? A thousand unspeakable images formed and shifted in her mind. Now that he had refused to yield to her persuasions, Martinez would be more than ever convinced that force was the only method of getting the information he needed.

A few times Captain Vargas tried to speak to her, to comfort her. But she ignored him.

When they made camp the first night, and Vargas tried to persuade her to eat some of the stew his orderly had prepared, she pushed the dish aside. Vargas seated himself on a broad flat rock, close beside her. "You must eat, or you won't have the strength for the journey back to Havana."

"Why don't you leave me here?" she asked tonelessly. "I'm of no further use to you."

"Drucilla, listen to me." She was startled out of her lethargy by his tone and the use of her given name. Always, before, he had called her Señora Seaton. "Right now you are sure your life is over. But later, you will see you are wrong. Farrell is doomed, but you—"

She turned on him fiercely. "He's not. I won't believe that."

"He is finished," Vargas said quietly. "But you must go on and make a new life. You are young and you have courage, and you are beautiful." His dark eyes moved from her face and lingered on her high, rounded breasts, clearly outlined against the thin cambric shirt. She drew away from him and he smiled. "Don't be afraid," he said. "I'm a patient man."

"Captain Vargas—"

"Julio," he said. "Formality is out of place in such primitive surroundings." He put her dish back into her hands. "My orderly takes great pride in his cooking," he said. "You must not offend him."

For the next two nights, they camped along the trail, but late on the afternoon of the third day, they reached a small inn beside the Rio Cauto. "Now you can have a hot bath and a change of clothes," he said. "And a comfortable bed to sleep in."

When he helped her down from her horse, he held her against him for a moment; she felt the strength in those steely arms, the hardness of his chest.

Upstairs, in her room, Drucilla luxuriated in a tin tub filled with hot water. The innkeeper's wife, a stout motherly woman, waited on her and even managed to find a piece of perfumed soap for her to use. If the woman was curious about the red-haired *americana* who traveled in a man's riding clothes with a troop of Spanish cavalrymen, she did not ask any questions. She and her husband were plainly awed and a little frightened by their guests.

For the first time in days, Drucilla was able to scrub herself all over and wash her hair. She changed back into the blue muslin, then went out onto the veranda that ran along the back of the inn, with the second-floor rooms opening out onto it. In the warm, late afternoon sunlight, she brushed the heavy red-gold waves of her hair until they fell in damp shining masses down to her waist.

A sound made her wheel around. Julio Vargas had come out of his room, next to hers, and he stood looking at her, the sunlight glowing on his handsome, olive-skinned face with its full sensual mouth and dark eyes.

She turned to go back inside, but he put a hand on her arm. "I didn't think you'd want to dine downstairs in the taproom with the soldiers," he said. "I told the innkeeper to have our dinner served here."

The innkeeper's wife set a small table out on the veranda, overlooking the slow-moving river with its black frieze of towering royal palms. After a dinner of freshwater prawns, *guisado de pollo*, and black bean soup flavored with rum, Drucilla and Julio sat over coffee and brandy. The rising moon turned the river to silver, and a breeze rustled the leaves of the palms.

"It's so peaceful," Drucilla said. "It's hard to believe—" She broke off and stared down at the river.

"Hard to believe Cuba is at war? It can't last much longer, this rebellion."

"You don't think the rebels have any chance of winning, do you?"

"None," he said. "We have had these uprisings before, many times. A few malcontents, a handful of runaway slaves—it never comes to anything. Your own president has refused to recognize the rebel government here."

"But Kevin said the rebels would overrun Oriente. That they would take San Rafael."

He smiled faintly. "Farrell only said that to make it easier for you to leave him." He reached across the table and put his hand over hers. "Come now," he said, "don't grieve. He made his choice. You did all you could for him. Now you must think of yourself, of your future."

She wanted to take her hand away, but something made her hesitate. Julio Vargas wanted her. She had known that from their first meeting. But now, with every other avenue of escape closed to Kevin, a plan began to take shape in her mind; a plan that depended on Vargas. She felt her spirit shrink away, but she forced herself to consider the plan, to examine it carefully.

She could not go back to Charleston but would have to remain in Havana, free to come and go as she pleased, to mingle with government officials, with Cubans in all walks of life, to make contacts with the right people, and there was only one way to do that.

"My future," she said softly. "And what is that to be?"

"I'll put you aboard a ship for the United States—for Charleston, if possible."

"I have nothing to go back to in Charleston," she said. "My husband's family doesn't care about me. And I have no family of my own."

She stood up and went to the railing of the veranda. He followed her, as she had known he would. "You are quite alone then."

"That need not concern you," she said. "Indeed, you have been more than kind, and I'm grateful."

He put his hands on her shoulders, and turned her around to face him. "I want more than your gratitude, Drucilla. Let me help you to forget the past. Let me—"

He drew her to him, tentatively, ready to release her if that was what she wanted. But she let herself relax against him, and his mouth found hers. When she still offered no resistance, his arms tightened. She opened her lips, and his tongue explored the moist softness of her mouth. To her surprise she felt a swift stirring along her nerves, as the warmth of his body enveloped hers.

He lifted her into his arms and carried her through the French doors and into her room. He put her down on the bed.

She had been ready to give herself to Vargas on the day they had first met, in Altamonte's house, if that would have insured Kevin's escape. Why should it be any worse now?

297

Let him do what he wanted with her. She would not let herself think or feel.

He undressed her, his fingers opening buttons, untying ribbons with a quick skill that told her he was a man of considerable experience. She did not close her eyes. She watched while he took off his heavy leather belt, his white and gold tunic, and riding breeches.

He was not a tall man, but his chest was wide, his hips lean. She saw the heavy muscles across the flat abdomen and down along the thighs. It was the body of a young man in superb condition, a man who spent long hours on horseback.

She cried out, in spite of herself, when he came to lie beside her and she felt the first touch of his naked body against hers. She tried to draw back then, but his arms encircled her, and his voice was deep with passion. "*Querida.* My beautiful Drucilla."

She forced herself to remain still now, while his hands explored her body. His mouth lingered on her breasts, and his tongue played with the nipples until they stood out, hard and erect. Strange, she thought, how the body has a will of its own. She heard him laugh with masculine pride and satisfaction. "I knew it," he said. "A woman like you needs a man. No, don't turn your head away. I want to see your face, your eyes."

He had not turned down the oil lamp beside the bed, so that she was denied the darkness in which to hide her shame. She told herself it did not matter. But when his hands parted her thighs, his fingers stroking, probing, she could not stop herself from crying out, "No—I can't—" and knew that it was no use.

He was above her now, his eyes hot, his lips parted. He entered her with one swift thrust, then moved with long hard strokes. She felt a brief, tenuous response within herself. Then it disappeared. She forced herself to embrace him, to submit to him. She heard the harsh sound of his breathing as his movements quickened, his urgency mounted to a kind of violence. His hands were not gentle now, as they gripped her, bruised her. She couldn't stand it any longer, she couldn't. . . . He reached his climax and a few minutes after, he moved off her.

The violence was gone now. He put his arm under her shoulders. "I'm sorry," he said. "I wanted it to be good for you, too."

"But I—"

"No lies, *querida*. I should have waited longer, given you time to— But—there will be other nights."

He raised himself and his dark eyes searched her face. "You will stay with me, won't you? I'll give you anything you want. The finest house in Havana. Servants. A carriage. Dresses from Paris. Jewels."

There was only one thing she wanted: Kevin's freedom. She looked away. Julio said quickly, "Do not misunderstand, *querida*. I know you're not a woman to be bought. You are, perhaps, wealthy in your own right."

"I did have some money, left me by my late husband. It's gone now, though. Those bribes I paid to Altamonte," she lied. There was still a tidy sum on deposit with a reliable merchant in Havana.

"*Pobrecita*," he said. "My poor Drucilla. So generous, so brave . . . and so foolish. You need a man to look after you. I ask no more, for now. In time, you will come to love me. I will make you love me." Flushed with his recent conquest he said, "Even a little while ago, you were not entirely cold to me." His white teeth flashed in a smile. "I understand you better than you suppose."

Fear gripped her. Surely, he could not have guessed at her real reason for giving herself to him.

"Your marriage to the unfortunate Señor Seaton. Was it an arranged marriage?"

"You might say that," she conceded.

"And then Farrell came along. No, don't turn away. We must speak of him, this one last time. He is an adventurer. Handsome enough, after his fashion, I suppose. A strong man, surely, and of great courage. I don't know how you met him, or what was between you. I don't wish to know. With me you will have a new life. You will be happy."

After Julio had fallen asleep, she got up and stood at the window, the moonlight turning her naked body to a silver statue. She would never forget Kevin, never stop loving him. Even if he died. But he would not die in San Rafael. She would prevent it.

It was dawn before she slipped back into bed beside Julio.

Twenty-one

"I'VE found someone who'll help you, Drucilla."

Bartholomew Oakes spoke softly, although there was little chance of being heard by the other guests, who had gathered around the dancers at the center of the patio. The night air was reverberating with the drums, the chachás, the maracas of the hired black musicians while the dancers moved through the swift measures of the balbúl, an African dance of frank sexuality, raised to an art by the incomparable grace of those lithe bronze bodies.

"Come with me, Bart," Drucilla said, leading the way through the tall French doors that opened onto the morning room, with its fragrant plants and caged tropical birds.

"Now tell me, quickly."

Drucilla had renewed her acquaintance with the correspondent from the *London Times* upon her return to Havana; Oakes was a frequent guest in the magnificent house Julio had leased for her.

On his first visit, she had told him her reason for coming to Cuba; the failure of her attempt to bribe Altamonte; her fruitless journey to see Kevin at San Rafael. And its aftermath.

"I couldn't let Julio send me back to Charleston, you see."

The reserved young Englishman had looked embarrassed.

"Yes. I see. And now you want me to help you contrive to get Farrell out of San Rafael. It's risky. Now that you and Vargas—that is—if he were to find out what you're doing, he might not stop with having you deported."

"I don't care."

Finally, after all his warnings had failed, Oakes had agreed to help her. "At least, if I act as go-between, there will be less danger for you."

Now, after nearly a month, he had come to tell her his efforts had been successful. "The man I talked to is a rebel leader from Oriente. His headquarters are close to San Rafael. He didn't want to become involved, but when I mentioned Farrell's name, his whole attitude changed. He knows Farrell personally, and he's perfectly aware of what he and his people owe Farrell for keeping silent."

"When can I see this man?" Her voice shook with eagerness.

"Now, Drucilla, get hold of yourself. You're not going to meet Barbosa at all. I'll handle the details."

"But why should you?"

A faint flush came to his thin, intelligent face. "I've had occasion to see the—work—of men like Colonel Martinez. I know what they're capable of. Once, I visited a rebel village in eastern Cuba that had been conquered by the Spanish troops. I saw what was left of their victims, and I'm not likely to forget. That would be enough, more than enough, to make me help you, even if I didn't—" The warmth in his blue eyes told Drucilla the rest.

"Oh, Bart, my dear. But you must understand that Kevin and I—"

"I understand." He cleared his throat and ran a hand over his short-cropped sandy hair. "Now, I have to know where Farrell's boat is anchored. And how much money you can provide. Diego Barbosa says he needs not only guns but explosives as well, because to take San Rafael, they'll have to blast their way through the outer walls."

"Diego Barbosa," she repeated. "You sure he can be trusted."

"I'm sure."

From outside in the patio, she heard the furious beating of the drums. The dance was drawing to its climax. Swiftly, she gave Oakes the information he had asked for. Then, finding no words with which to thank him, she reached up and touched her lips to his.

After that night, time dragged by, as the year of 1874 drew to a close. Christmas was celebrated with all the enthusiasm of these volatile Havanese. There was dancing and feasting, and the cafes were crowded. Drucilla, sitting with Julio in a cafe, drinking wine and watching the merrymakers, felt her heart contract with pain. She had told Gwen Seaton she would be back in Charleston in time to celebrate Christmas. Did Andrew miss her? Or had Theodora taken her place in the child's affections?

Vargas put a hand over hers. "*Querida*, are you tired?"

She shook her head. It was better to be out among people, under the blazing sun and the brilliant sky, than alone with her fears. The nights were worst. She had become accustomed to Julio's lovemaking; at times, she could even respond, could lose herself in the violence of his passion. But afterward, when he slept beside her, she lay wide-eyed in the darkness. Or fell asleep to be tormented by terrible dreams.

On Christmas Eve, she wrote to Gwen Seaton, the only member of Radford's family with whom she could feel any real kinship. She tried to keep the letter bright and pleasant, describing Havana, the house in which she was living. She mentioned her "friendship" with a young Army officer, Julio Vargas, knowing that Gwen, although a spinster, would read between the lines. "Give Andrew all my love. Kiss him for me and. . . ." She had to fight back the tears before she could finish the letter.

She wrote also to Charlotte Tremayne, at the spa in the south of France. Julio, who promised to post the letters for her, glanced curiously at the French address.

"My grandmother," Drucilla explained. "She is staying in France indefinitely. The climate is beneficial. Better for an old lady than Newport, particularly in winter."

"Even down here we have heard of Newport. Your grandmother is a lady of wealth and position, then?"

"She's as proud of her family as you are of yours," Drucilla said. She saw no harm in telling Julio about the Tremayne history, omitting the fact that she was Charlotte's granddaughter only by adoption.

They went to midnight Mass together and returned for a night of feasting that lasted almost until dawn, when the last of their guests left the house. Exhausted, she fell asleep quickly, only to be caught up in a nightmare. She saw Kevin's tortured face, heard him crying her name. She tried to get to him, but a wall rose between them, a wall that grew to a fantastic height, until she could no longer see him or hear him. She beat at the stones and screamed.

She woke to feel Julio's arms around her. She rested her head against his chest and let him stroke her hair. "All those rich dishes at the party—and all that champagne—" she managed to say. "I had a nightmare, who wouldn't?"

Although he accepted her explanation, and murmured words of comfort and tenderness, she knew that she would not sleep again that night.

The following day, Julio told her that he would have to leave Havana. "The rebels may be mounting a new offensive," he said. "I've been ordered into Oriente."

Would the attack of the rebels on San Rafael be a part of that offensive? Fear clutched at her, and Julio, misunderstanding the cause of her distress, said: "Don't be afraid, *querida*. I promised to take you to the carnival ball, and I will. Buy yourself a new dress. I want you to look beautiful for me when I return."

On the evening of the masked ball, one of dozens that would precede the Lenten season, Drucilla had not yet received word from Bartholomew Oakes about Kevin. Julio was still away, but she had obeyed him and ordered a dress from one of the finest dressmakers in the city, and now her maid was helping her into it. The dress was of amber satin, encrusted with gold embroidery and tiny seed pearls. The skirt was looped up over an underskirt of pale gold moire with ruffles of black lace. The maid was wide-eyed with admiration. *"Que hermosa! Que linda!"*

Drucilla heard swift hoofbeats on the street outside and then the opening of the downstairs door. She ran out of the bedroom and leaned over the heavy, wrought-iron railing. Julio had returned for the ball, as he had promised, but he did not come rushing upstairs, as he usually did, to greet her; instead, he went along the down-stairs hall and out onto the patio.

Captain Julio Vargas was a troubled man, that evening. The cold, unimaginative courage that had made him an excellent officer, did not serve him now. His love for Drucilla was equal to his pride in possessing such a woman; he could not let her go. He could not lose her now. But he would lose her, unless he did this thing, so out of keeping with his character. All during the ride back to Havana, he had wrestled with his decision: to tell the truth and face a life without her, or to lie, and keep her always.

He turned, hearing the rustle of her skirts, the quick, light footsteps. How lovely she was, how desirable, standing there in the soft purple haze of early twilight.

"Julio, I'm ready." Seeing his blank look she said: "The masked ball. Don't you remember?"

He came to her then and kissed her, his arms tightening around her. She was warm and pliant in his embrace.

"She does love me," he thought. "If it were not for the memory of that other love . . ."

He took her arm, and they walked to a bench under a flowering pomegranate tree.

"The fighting," she said. "Was it very bad?"

"We had our share of losses. The rebels fought like demons. Drucilla, listen to me. This war will be over soon. After that, I'm going to resign my commission. My father is dead, my brothers live in Madrid. I want to take charge of Villanueva, my family's plantation." He took her hands and went on quickly. "I want you with me. Not as my mistress. You were not made to be a mistress— a camp-follower. I want you to marry me."

"Julio, I can't—I—"

"Because of him? Because of a romantic infatuation with a common adventurer?" Anger welled up in him. *Say it, then, and be done with it. It is for her good, as well as yours.*

"Be quiet and listen," he said. He felt her hands begin to tremble in his, but he went on, his voice hard and inexorable.

"We rode into Oriente to smash the rebel offensive. They're good fighters, I'll admit that. They took a number of towns. And they captured the garrison at San Rafael."

He saw her eyes blaze with swift hope.

"No, Drucilla. Farrell won't be coming back to you. He's dead. He was killed in the fighting."

"You're—sure?"

"Yes, *querida.*" He waited, expecting her to weep, to give way to hysteria. But she made no sound; her face was a set, white mask.

"So you see," he went on, "whatever you may have felt for this man, it's over now."

"Yes, it's over. There's nothing left now. Nothing."

"But there is. I've asked you to become my wife. I did not make much a proposal lightly. You see, I've made inquiries about the Tremayne family."

"Did you?"

"Yes, and I know now, I had no right to take a woman from such a family for a mistress. But all that will be forgotten. You will be respected, you will be received into the best society in Cuba—you will have everything—"

She had begun to laugh, softly at first, then on a shrill, rising note. Hysteria, as he had expected. He took her in his arms and held her, until the laughter changed to tears, and she pressed her face against his chest. He lifted her and carried her upstairs. He would say no more about marriage tonight; he would give her time to get control of herself.

A few days later, when Bartholomew Oakes came to the

house, to tell Drucilla of the success of the escape plan, he found that the shutters were closed, the house silent. Oakes had returned only the night before from Manzanillo, where the rebels had driven off a detachment of Spanish cavalry in a fierce battle.

The old mulatto woman who answered his knock was surprised when he asked to speak to her mistress. "But, señor, have you not heard? They were married three days ago, *el Capitán Vargas* and the *americana*. They have left for Spain on their wedding trip."

For Kevin, there had been intervals of consciousness, then long, confused times when he had drifted in a feverish delirium. He awoke now, still burning with fever. Someone was lifting him, and pushing a cup against his cracked lips. Water. He swallowed, then gagged. Not water, but something bitter. He was still in San Rafael, then, and Lieutenant Sandoval had found a new way to torture him. "Bastard," he whispered.

"You must be feeling better, Captain."

That wasn't Sandoval's voice. He opened his eyes. "Tim?" Then he felt the familiar rise and fall, and was seized with hope. "We're at sea?"

"That's right. Here, drink the rest of this. It's quinine. For the fever. We'll be back home soon."

"Home?" It was hard for Kevin to speak; his jaw throbbed and there was a sharp, knifelike pain in his ribs.

"We'll put in at Key West," Tim said. "I'll find a doctor for you there. Christ, Kevin, you look like you were trampled by a team of horses."

"I feel like it, too." Kevin tried to smile but his face hurt too badly. He swallowed the rest of the quinine.

"Tim, what happened? How did I get to the boat? I can't remember much. . . ."

He tried to draw together the shattered fragments of memory to make a coherent pattern. He could remember the last interrogation.

He had heard some of the troopers talking among themselves about a rebel offensive, and Sandoval had been more brutal than usual, as if determined to get the information before it was too late. Kevin could remember being knocked down on the stone floor, and kicked in the ribs, in the stomach. And Sandoval's voice, coming from somewhere above him. "That beautiful lady who came to see you here—you remember her, *Capitán*?"

Kevin had fought for breath, unable to answer.

"When I'm finished with you this time. you'll be of no use to her or any other woman—you understand?"

He had seen the booted foot draw back, and from somewhere, he had found the strength to roll over on his side, so that he was facing away from Sandoval, and the pain exploded at the base of his spine.

"Careful, Lieutenant," Colonel Martinez said. "Smash his kidneys and we'll have a corpse on our hands."

The troopers had turned him over on his back and were holding him immobile. He had known he could not keep silent now. He had wanted to tell them, but he couldn't get the words out.

Then he had heard a sound as if the world were exploding around him, and the troopers had let him go. Later, there was the crackling of rifle fire outside.

The troopers had left him, and a little while later, he was being carried into the open air. He had smelled the wet earth and the trees. He was somewhere in the mountains. More rifle fire, men cursing and shouting. Then unconsciousness.

"Tim, how did I get back here?"

"I'll tell you all about it later." Tim said. "Try to sleep now."

The next time Kevin awoke, he was sweating; his body was soaked, and he knew the fever had broken. In the early morning light, he saw, not Tim Cleary, but a girl with enormous dark eyes and smooth olive skin. Her black hair was braided and looped up on her head.

She wiped his face with a wet cloth. Her touch was light and careful. "Shall I call Señor Cleary now?" She asked.

"Wait," Kevin said. There was something familiar about the girl's features, although he was sure he had never seen her before. "Who are you?"

"Maria Barbosa," she said. "Diego Barbosa was my brother."

Kevin jerked away from her soothing touch. "Was?"

"Diego was killed in a skirmish with the Spanish troopers, while he was bringing you out of the Sierra Maestra. His men carried you the rest of the way to your boat."

She stood up. "Señor Cleary said to call him when you regained consciousness."

When Tim came into the cabin, Kevin demanded: "I want to know what happened. All of it."

"Not much to tell. Barbosa sent a man to the boat. Told me to stand by, that they were going to attack the garrison in force and get you out. I had my doubts, but I waited, and they brought you to the boat."

"But what about Maria?"

"Barbosa's messenger made a deal with me. After they got you out, I was to go around to the western end of the island, and anchor outside the harbor. His sister would be brought out to the *Medea*. It was a tricky business. The Spanish had her under surveillance."

"And Drucilla—what about Drucilla? She's not still on the island?"

"Drucilla's safe enough," Tim said dryly.

"Where is she?"

When Tim remained silent, Kevin sat up, ignoring the knife-thrust of pain under his ribs. "What happened to her?"

"She—well, the fact is, she married one of them Spanish officers. They left for Spain on a honeymoon. Now lie down, will you?" He put a hand on Kevin's shoulder. "Damned if I know why she did it."

Kevin lay back on the pillow. "I think I know," he said. She had pleaded with him that day at San Rafael to do whatever he had to do, to be released. She had even told him the truth about their son. And he had remained unmoved. Or so it must have appeared to her. "How do you know she's married?"

"I told him, señor," Maria said. "All Havana knew about the beautiful, red-haired *americana* who had lived with *Capitán* Julio Vargas as his mistress, the splendid entertainments in their house—"

She had been his mistress then, before she had become his wife.

"The wedding was magnificent. The Vargas family is very important in Cuba and very wealthy."

"Julio Vargas." Kevin remembered now the arrogant, good-looking young officer.

"She may have had her reasons," Tim began.

"I don't want to discuss it."

"She loved you," Tim persisted. "And if you ask me—"

Something in Kevin's face made him stop.

When Tim spoke again, it was a ship's officer addressing his captain. "We'll be putting in at Key West soon. I'd better get back up on deck."

Kevin turned to Maria Barbosa. "What are you going to do after we get to Key West?" he asked.

"There are many Cuban refugees there," she told him. "I will have a place to stay. Don't concern yourself about me."

But he could not let his own personal misery make him forget the debt he owed Maria's brother.

"I am concerned," he said. "And if there's anything I can do at any time, you have only to call on me."

The doctor who attended Kevin in Key West had been recommended by the friends of Maria Barbosa, in whose home Kevin was staying. A stocky, white-haired man, he shook his head as he examined Kevin. "You're lucky to be alive, señor." His face hardened. "Anyone who is a prisoner of the Spanish army is fortunate if he survives."

His fingers were skilled, but Kevin had to set his teeth to keep back a cry, as the doctor did his work. "No serious internal injuries," he said. "A fracture of the collar bone, but that's mending." He changed the dressing Tim had applied to Kevin's back, and swabbed the cuts with a stinging liquid.

To distract him, Tim said, "You know, Captain, you've still got the *Medea.* And a crew. I've been thinking, there's money to be made, trading with some of them islands down there."

"Not Cuba," Kevin said.

"Of course not. I don't care if I ever see Cuba again. But there's Jamaica and Barbados. A lot of them planters are importing modern machinery for their sugar plantations."

Kevin smiled wryly, knowing that Tim was talking this way not only to take his mind off the doctor's ministrations, but off his bleak thoughts about Drucilla.

"I'll think about it, Tim. Mightn't be a bad idea at that."

Twenty-two

DURING the first weeks of Drucilla's marriage to Julio, she moved through a blurred gray landscape, a part of her mind numb with grief. It was as if she had sustained some terrible physical injury that left her dazed, wounded, but without feeling in the lacerated tissues. The pain would come later.

She moved like a mechanical doll through the elaborate wedding ceremony in the cathedral in Havana. During the voyage across the Atlantic, she spent much of her time in her cabin. Sometimes, late at night, Julio was able to persuade her to come up on deck for a walk; she clung to his arm, and he was perceptive enough to say little, to leave her to her thoughts.

Kevin was dead, and Drucilla was sure she would feel nothing ever again, except the ache of emptiness. If Julio Vargas, for some inexplicable reason of his own, wanted her for his wife, so be it. If he felt a need to possess her, she submitted, without desire, without repulsion. But more often than not, he contented himself with lying at her side, holding her in his arms, and talking softly to her, when she was unable to sleep. Impersonal talk, about his boyhood on his father's great, sprawling sugar plantation, of his boyhood friends, the young Santovenias, whose own plantation was closest to Villanueva—half a day's ride away. He told her of learning to ride, to shoot, and added: "It was a good life. I'm thankful my father believed in raising his children on his plantation, not in Havana or abroad, as so many Cubans do."

When Drucilla and Julio reached Madrid, they stayed with his family, and she met an endless procession of Vargas relations: his younger brothers and their wives and children, his uncles, aunts, and cousins. Although they were surprised that Julio had chosen to marry *una americana*, they were impressed when he spoke of her family background: the Tremaynes of Newport and the Seatons of South Carolina. They treated her with punctilious courtesy, and she was grateful for the language barrier, which precluded all but formal conversation.

Then Julio took her on to Paris, and here she found herself coming alive again. Although only a few years had passed since the Franco-Prussian War and the siege, the French capital had regained its lighthearted atmosphere. Julio escorted her to world-famous restaurants, to theaters and operas and the ballet; he took her riding in an open carriage on the wide boulevards. His pride in her was plain to see.

He showered her with gowns, in the rich, heavy fabrics that were in vogue that season, gowns that were intended to make their wearers look like the ladies in paintings by the old masters: brocades, interwoven wtih silver and gold; satins with raised velvet designs; silk embroidery encrusted with silver and pearls. A diamond-and-sapphire ornament, in the shape of a butterfly, for her hair. A dozen bonnets, decorated with plumes, flowers and lace. A magnificent lilac satin opera cloak. Dozens upon dozens of sheer silk and lace nightgowns.

Each night, when they returned to their hotel, he made love to her, gently, circumspectly at first; then with a curious blending of violence and tenderness that she gradually came to accept.

And at last, during their final week in Paris, on a night

when the moonlight flooded their bedroom, she found with a shock that her body was reawakening under his hands and lips and tongue; felt the spiraling excitement, and let it carry her along, until she cried out and clung to him, moving, matching her rhythm to his, coming to climax.

Afterward, she was moved by his obvious pleasure in having caused her to respond completely. From that night on, he could not get enough of her. She half-expected to become pregnant as a result of her honeymoon, but when she did not, a part of her mind was relieved. She had no immediate desire to bear Julio's child. Not yet. Perhaps not ever.

By the time Julio brought Drucilla back to Havana, the revolution was nearing its end. The wealthy exiles in New York, who had financed the rebel cause, were beginning to withdraw their support, seeing that, for the time being, the cause was lost. General Arsenio Martinez Campos arrived from Spain with twenty-five thousand men as reinforcements. In February of 1878, a truce was signed at Zanjón, promising that the rebel leaders would be permitted to leave Cuba.

But long before that, Julio, according to his promise to Drucilla, had resigned his commission in the Spanish army, and had turned his attention to the business of running one of the largest plantations on the island: Villanueva, near the port of Cienfuegos in the western part of Cuba.

Although it was the custom of many Cuban planters to turn their plantations over to the care of overseers, and to live in Havana, or abroad, Julio had different ideas. He was convinced that even the most reliable overseer could not look out properly for the interests of the owner. Furthermore, he had countless plans of his own for improving the production of the plantation.

"My father was a fine man, but old-fashioned in his methods," Julio explained to Drucilla shortly after their arrival at Villanueva. "True, the plantation has always been profitable, thanks to our fine Cuban climate. All the same, with new machinery, we will be able to produce twice as much sugar as we do now, and it will be of higher quality."

Drucilla listened with interest, as he went on to explain that, with the old-fashioned machines, the sugar had to be produced in loaves; whereas, with the new centrifugal machinery, consisting of an iron cylinder with a metal drum inside, connecting with a steam engine, it would be possible to convert the sugar at once into the clear, loose, dry, fine product now in demand.

"With these new machines, I shouldn't think you would need many slaves," Drucilla said hopefully.

"What nonsense, *querida*. Of course we'll need slaves to harvest the cane, to care for the cattle. And as house servants. But, forgive me, this talk must be boring to you."

"Not at all," Drucilla said. "And I'm sure I could learn about the workings of the plantation, if you would be patient and explain them to me. Perhaps you have some books I could read."

He threw back his head and laughed, but fondly. "Books? What need has a beautiful woman for books?"

But when she managed, with some difficulty, to convince him that she liked to read, he shrugged and gave in to this peculiar preference, adding a library to the house. Most of the planters' wives spent their days gossiping with friends, visiting Havana, or riding on their plantations. But if his wife wanted books, she should have them. He directed the young French architect he had hired to design a library, and he sent to New York, Boston, London, and Paris for fine leather-bound volumes.

That was only the beginning, however. Julio had the interior stonework of the plantation house replaced with marble: white, green, and rose-colored; he imported some of the marble from the nearby quarries on the Isle of Pines, off the Cuban coast, and some from as far away as Genoa. Crystal chandeliers took the place of the simpler wrought iron fixtures; drapes of raw silk were hung at the windows, and Oriental rugs were put down on the floors.

Like many Cuban houses, the original plantation house had been built along the lines of a fortress, with heavy doorways studded with knobs and decorations, and large windows without glass, but with iron bars. Julio had the bars removed and glass windows installed, and Drucilla admitted the effect was far more homelike; but she winced when Julio explained that the bars had been protection during the early part of the last century, when Villanueva had experienced its first—and only—slave uprising.

Seeing her reaction, Julio said: "You need not fear an uprising now. I've taken measures. The slaves are housed in *barracones*—one-story barracks—instead of the little huts where they lived in my grandfather's time. Family ties between slaves make for trouble. Now, I have the males and females kept apart in small cells. The *mayoral*, Ruiz, lives inside the compound, and the *contramayoral*, the assistant overseer, sleeps inside the *barracones*. The gates are locked at night. Then, too, we have the dogs." He went on to tell her with some pride, that the Cuban dogs, bred to hunt slaves, were the fiercest in the West Indies.

"Why, when there was an uprising in Jamaica, some years ago, the British planters imported our dogs and their handlers. There are none as good anywhere."

From the time they arrived at the plantation, Julio discouraged Drucilla from going to the *barracones* or the mills. "But I want to see for myself the workings of the plantation," she protested.

"The mills are stifling hot. And there is often disease in the *barracones*: *vómito negro*, even cholera."

"Do you have a doctor, or a hospital, to care for the sick slaves?"

He shook his head. "We did have a doctor, an Englishman who was drunk most of the time on cane brandy. He finally drank himself to death, and I have not gotten around to replacing him. But no matter. These blacks put more faith in their own remedies, herbs and such."

Drucilla found the house slaves efficient and well trained. There were several maids, who wore skirts of brightly-colored, stiffly starched cotton; they spoke little, but responded instantly to a gesture from the master for service.

Inez, Drucilla's personal maid, was a beautiful young octoroon with golden skin and hair that was deep chestnut rather than black. Like the other maids, Inez spoke hardly at all, except in reply to a direct question, and she rarely smiled.

The first time Inez had bathed her, Drucilla had been startled and a little embarrassed; even on Seaton Barony, the maids had drawn baths, then left their mistresses in privacy. But Drucilla gradually resigned herself to the custom of her new home.

Julio had installed a separate bathroom with an enormous sunken tub of pale pink marble, fit for a Roman empress. Following the example of the millionaire planter, Justo Cantaro of Trinidad, Julio demanded not only two spouts, one for hot water and one for cold water, but a third for Drucilla's eau de cologne; each spout was in the shape of a fish and was made of solid silver.

Drucilla did not begin to grasp the full impact of slavery until a few months after her arrival at Villanueva. One afternoon, she and Julio had made the long ride to visit Mateo and Carmen Santovenia, their nearest neighbors. Mateo had promised to take them to see his new bulls, recently imported from Spain; like Julio, Mateo not only bred bulls but fought them for sport.

The two couples were riding out to the pasture on a trail that edged the slave quarters. Carmen, an excellent horsewoman, spurred her mare to a gallop, while the other three remained a little behind. Drucilla cried out when she saw Carmen's horse rear up, pawing the air with its forelegs.

A small black child, a girl of about five, skinny and almost naked, had darted out of the underbrush directly into the mare's path. Carmen was too good a rider to be thrown easily; in a moment, she had brought the plunging animal under control. Mateo galloped up to her, and looked down at the child who lay quite still under the blazing, sun-washed Cuban sky. He made no move to dismount. Neither did Carmen.

"Dead, I believe," Mateo said.

An ancient black woman hobbled out into the roadway.

"You should take better care of your charges, *vieja*," Mateo said calmly.

Carmen's lovely face was petulant. "My mare might

have fallen. She might have been injured."

"But she wasn't," Mateo reminded his wife. "So no harm has been done."

She spurred her horse forward, and Mateo kept pace.

Drucilla watched, sick and shaken, as the old woman picked up the child and scurried off into the underbrush with her burden.

"Isn't there a chance the child may be alive?" Drucilla demanded. "Please, Julio, let's find out. Maybe—"

"I saw the angle of the child's neck. Broken. No matter. Every plantation has far too many black girls."

"I don't understand."

"It's quite simple. In the cotton fields of your own South, before the war, female slaves had some value. A female can pick cotton, but it takes a man's strength to swing the machete."

For a moment she was not sure she had understood. Then she cried out: "Julio, you're speaking about human beings."

"Slaves are animals. Come, don't make a scene. Wait, where are you going?"

Drucilla had wheeled her horse around. "I'm going home."

He blocked her way. "You'll do no such thing. The Santovenias are our friends. To ride off without any explanation would be discourteous."

"Discourteous? A child has been killed and you can—"

"Put it out of your mind," he said firmly. "In time, you won't let such things distress you."

She could not put the incident out of her mind, however; and she knew that she would never come to think of people as animals, not if she lived at Villanueva for the rest of her life. She hoped that the talk she had been hearing about the possible abolition of slavery on the island was true; even now, a few plantation owners had freed their slaves voluntarily, and had replaced them with hired laborers. But she knew that Julio would never do that; it would take a decree from the Spanish government to make him give up his slaves.

A few months after the incident at the Santovenias'

plantation, Drucilla was seated in the bedroom at Villa-nueva. She was writing to Gwen Seaton in reply to a recent letter from her sister-in-law. Gwen had written that Theodora Seaton had suffered a mild stroke; that she was recovering; that Hazel had gone to stay at Seaton Barony to help care for her mother and look after Andrew.

Drucilla thought, as she had so often, about sending for her son. Julio knew about the boy, but she had not told him that Andrew's father was Kevin Farrell; like everyone else, Julio had assumed that her child was the offspring of Radford Seaton.

"I long to have Andrew with me," she wrote to Gwen now. "Perhaps one day soon, it will be possible." She had not yet spoken to Julio about having Andrew come to live with them; she knew Julio wanted sons of his own. She lifted her head and put down her pen. Julio was in his dressing room, adjoining the bedroom. Miguel, Julio's new valet, a light-skinned quadroon, was helping his master to dress for the daily ride around the plantation. The boy was plainly nervous; he had recently been ap-pointed to this coveted position, and he was only fifteen.

Drucilla watched absently, as Miguel kneeled to help Julio on with his boots; her mind was still on the problem of Andrew. She heard Julio say: "These boots are a disgrace."

He did not sound particularly angry, only annoyed.

"I'm sorry, señor. I will take them back at once and polish them until they are like glass."

"I should think so," Julio said. Drucilla rose and approached the dressing room door. She saw nothing in her husband's face to warn her of what was going to happen. A moment later, Julio picked up his riding crop and, with one swift, slashing movement, he brought the crop down across the boy's upturned face.

Drucilla flung herself on her husband, clutching his arm. Julio shook her off. The boy, taking advantage of the interruption, started to get to his feet to make his escape.

"Did I dismiss you?" Julio asked.

Miguel was crying, silently, his face streaked with tears and blood. "No, señor."

"You have been given a place of responsibility in this

house," Julio said, in the calm, even tones of a school-master rebuking a careless pupil. "You do not wish to exchange it for that of a fieldhand, do you?"

"No, señor. Please, I beg you—"

"*Bueno*. Take these boots and put them in a fit condition for me to wear. Send them up by one of the other servants. Then report to the *mayoral*. Tell him you are to have ten lashes."

For a moment, Drucilla could not believe what she had heard. She waited for the boy to protest, to plead. But Miguel only said: "*Grácias*, señor."

When the boy was gone, Drucilla thought she was going to be sick. She swallowed and said: "He thanked you."

"Of course. He'd far rather take ten lashes than to be sent into the cane fields at harvest." Julio drew her down on the couch where he sat, and said: "Forget Miguel. Now, since it looks as though I won't be leaving on my ride for awhile . . ."

He took her in his arms and held her against him. He began stroking her shoulders, fondling her breasts. It was not the first time he had made love to her, on impulse, during the day.

Once, when he had come in on her while she was still in the tub, he had dismissed Inez, had lifted her out and pressed her down on the marble floor, her body still slippery with soap, warm and pink from the heat of the bath. To her surprise, she had responded with unusual ardor, for she found such uninhibited displays of passion exciting.

But now it was different; she was repelled by the memory of the scene she had witnessed. "Let go of me," she cried.

He laughed softly, convinced that she was teasing him, as she sometimes did, pretending reluctance only to excite him to greater urgency. Then, when he began to realize that she wasn't playing a game, when she began to beat at his chest with her fists, he stopped. He kept one arm around her, but his other hand stopped moving on her body. "What's wrong with you?" he demanded, his face darkening with anger.

Drucilla was not intimidated. Not this time. "Call Miguel back here at once," she said. "You've got to. The boy is new at his work. He's trying to please you."

"And he will, in time. When he has been properly trained. He's bright enough, for a black." Julio nodded thoughtfully. "He should be. He was sired by my own father."

Drucilla might have been more shocked but, having lived in Charleston, she had heard of such things happening before the War; Gwen had been most outspoken about relations between slaves and masters. But this had happened here in her own home.

"The boy needs discipline, that's all. And the whip is the only teacher a slave can understand."

"I don't believe that," Drucilla said.

"In this case, your beliefs do not matter."

"But Julio, in heaven's name, how can I live in a house where— If it's so bad here, what must it be like for the field workers?"

"Be still," he said. "I'm master here. I give the orders, and I will not be questioned."

He released her and she stood up, thankful for the full skirt that concealed the trembling of her legs. She was seeing a side of her husband that had been hidden from her until now. He had once called her "the queen of Villanueva," but now he had made it plain that he had absolute power here.

"What about me?" she asked. "Suppose I did something to anger you? What would you do to me? What orders would you give?"

He laughed. "Don't be childish. You are my wife. How can you compare yourself to a slave? You are being unfair. Have I ever once treated you unkindly?"

She shook her head. "No, but—"

"Haven't I given you every luxury? I want you to be happy here. I would have spared you this business with Miguel if you hadn't come rushing in to see it."

"But whether I see such things or not, the very fact that they are going on is wrong, dreadfully wrong."

She broke off, filled with despair. She would never be able to make Julio understand her feelings about slavery.

He behaved in the same way as his father and his grandfather before him. Although he had rebuilt the house and installed the newest machinery in the mills, he kept to the old ways in his dealings with his slaves.

"How is it possible for you to admit that you and Miguel had the same father, and then to degrade him as you did?"

"You are speaking of matters you don't understand." Some of the anger had gone out of his voice now. "I've heard that in your country, there are women who meddle in their husbands' business affairs. Who even start businesses of their own, like that spinster sister-in-law of yours. It's no wonder her mother had a stroke."

"That's unfair," Drucilla began. Then she remembered Andrew and the thoughts which had preoccupied her before the incident with Miguel.

"Forget this foolishness," Julio was saying. "Devote yourself to womanly concerns and leave the rest to me."

"I have nothing to do around the house," she pointed out. "I don't even have to give myself a bath or put on my own stockings."

He laughed. "Some women might envy you," he said. He drew her down beside him again. "Listen, *querida*, when you hold your first child in your arms, you will have no time for other thoughts."

"I already have a child," she reminded him.

"Ah, yes. I'd almost forgotten." His dark eyes searched her face. "You miss the boy, don't you?"

"Of course I do."

"I begin to see. That is why you've been so unreasonable about trifling matters. I should have guessed. Would it please you to have the boy here with you?"

"Oh, yes—but—"

"We will send for him at once," Julio said.

She hesitated. "I'm not sure we should right now. You see, Theodora Seaton has cared for him ever since I left Charleston. Now that she is ill, the shock of giving him up might be too much for her."

"As you wish. But when you want me to send for the boy, you have only to ask." He lifted her hand and pressed it to his lips. "I want you to be happy," he said.

She looked at him in bewilderment, thinking how complex, how unpredictable he was: capable of shocking cruelty, but also able to give her tenderness and understanding.

Theodora Seaton recovered from her first stroke, but two more followed, and she was left a bedridden invalid, waited on by her daughter, Hazel. Then, when Drucilla had been married to Julio for five years, a letter came to Villanueva from Gwen, informing Drucilla that Theodora had had a fourth and fatal stroke.

When Drucilla told Julio the news he said, "Now, there is no reason you can't have the boy here."

She had not yet become pregnant by Julio, and she was surprised that, under the circumstances, he would want another man's child in his home. But she soon realized that he was only doing it to please her, as he would have sent for an Arabian horse, or a pet ocelot, had she ever expressed a desire for one.

Even after Andrew arrived, shy and bewildered by the abrupt change in his life, mourning the loss of his grandmother, and a little distant with a mother who was a stranger to him, Julio maintained the same attitude; he was not unkind to the boy but simply ignored him.

Then, one evening, Drucilla and Julio came into the dining room and found Andrew teetering precariously on a chair, reaching for one of the cavalry sabers that were fastened to the wall over the fireplace.

Drucilla gave a little cry of alarm. Julio shouted: "Get down from there at once."

The little boy, startled, jerked his hand away too fast.

"Now, look," Julio said. "You've cut yourself." He seized a napkin from the dining room table. Then, lifting Andrew down, he said: "Let me see that."

Andrew held out his hand. "It's not a bad cut," Julio told Drucilla. "I'll see to it."

He took a bottle of brandy, the first thing he could find, and poured a little over the cut. Drucilla saw Andrew's teeth bite down on his lower lip, but he made no sound although she knew the alcohol must have stung. While Julio tied the napkin around the boy's hand, he asked: "Did you fight with those sabers, señor?"

"Hold still," Julio said sternly.

"But did you?" the boy persisted. "Did you ever kill anyone with them?"

"Andrew, please. Don't speak of such things."

"A soldier must kill in war, that's his duty," Julio said.

"But with a saber?"

"Not often. Pistols were more effective."

"Do you have pistols? Will you show them to me?"

"Andrew—" Drucilla tried to distract the child, but he would not be put off.

"He's a boy," Julio said. "All boys like to hear of fighting." He ruffled Andrew's dark curls. "Such talk is distressing to ladies, *niño*. Particularly gentle, soft-hearted ladies like your mother. After dinner, I'll take you to my study and show you my pistols. And I'll tell you about the war, if you like."

Drucilla wanted to protest, but she realized that this was the first time Julio had shown the slightest interest in her son. She must do nothing to interfere.

After that evening, Julio was friendlier to Andrew. He taught the boy to ride a pony, and promised him a fine horse when he got a little older. Andrew had a lively mind and the precocity of a child raised in the company of adults. He bombarded Julio with questions about the plantation, and Julio took him to see the mills, the fields, even the *barracones*. Every morning, Andrew came back to the house with stories about what he had seen and done.

"Señor Vargas took me into the sugar mills, mother. It was hot in there. Hotter than a furnace. He was afraid I'd be sick, but I wasn't."

Later, Julio told Drucilla that the boy had been very sick indeed but had managed to control himself until they left the mills and he was able to dash away into the relative privacy of a stand of sugar cane.

"He didn't want me to know. And I pretended not to. He has pride, that boy."

Another evening, Andrew told Drucilla he had watched the slaves cutting cane. "One of them didn't work fast enough, and the *mayoral*, Señor Ruiz, hit him with a whip."

Drucilla held the child against her. "Oh, darling, you should not have been allowed to see that."

"It was nothing," Andrew said. "Only a couple of strokes. Señor Vargas says the blacks are not like us. They won't work unless they're beaten. And they must be watched all the time. Otherwise they run away. Do you know what the *mayoral* did to the last runaway slave, after they caught him?"

"Be quiet," Drucilla said. Had she been right to bring the boy here? She looked down into his gray eyes, under the straight black brows. Kevin's eyes. She lifted him into her arms, and pressed her lips against his flushed cheek, against his dark, tangled curls. He permitted this display of affection for a moment, then began to squirm. She let him go and watched him race out of the room.

She told herself that it was natural that a small boy, who had been raised by women, would seek the company of a man like Julio. A man who rode magnificently, who fought bulls with the same cold courage he had shown in leading a cavalry charge; who gave orders and controlled the lives of hundreds of other human beings.

Not everything Julio taught the boy was bad. Self-control, indifference to discomfort, the kind of hardness a boy would need later on. But she did not want Kevin's son to grow up into a replica of Julio Vargas. To look on, unmoved, at the sufferings of the slaves. And yet, she was helpless to interfere. If she turned Andrew's mind against Julio, the boy would be the one to suffer. Julio would not take criticism from her and would certainly resent it from her son.

Twenty-three

THE sound of barking dogs woke Drucilla at dawn. She stirred in the wide bed and reached out her hand. Then her eyes flew open. Julio was not beside her, although the sheets were still warm from his body, and the pillow bore the dent made by his head. After nearly six years of marriage, she had become accustomed to having him beside her when she awoke; often, even if had made love to her the night before, he would turn to her again, when she was only half-awake, would push her nightgown up under her arms and take her once more.

Now, finding herself alone in bed and hearing the ominous baying of the dogs, she sat up. The air was already warm, even at this early hour. Through the open shutters she could see the peaks of the Sierra de Escambray, jagged against the rosy sky. But this morning, she had no time to enjoy the beauty of her surroundings.

She knew that the dogs were taken out by the slave-catchers who had trained them and for only one purpose. There must have been another runaway.

Escapes were more frequent when the harvest was at its height. She had been shocked when Julio had told her that, at harvest time, the slaves were allowed only four hours' sleep a night and were driven mercilessly for the remaining twenty. Harvest lasted five or six months out of the year.

Some slaves died from overwork, others from accidents in the mills. "It was worse before we got the new equipment," he assured her. "I can remember, in my father's day, that the *mayoral* stood in the mill with a machete, so that if a slave fell asleep and got a hand caught in the rollers, it could be chopped off, and the work could go on without interruption." With the new machinery, such accidents were rare. But he also admitted that mechanization caused the slaves to be treated more as part of the machinery than as mere animals. Indeed, there were more slave revolts in the large, mechanized mills, than in the smaller, more old-fashioned ones.

She heard a sound and turned to see Julio coming in from his dressing room, adjoining the bedroom. He was fully dressed and wearing his riding boots.

"I'm sorry you were awakened, *querida*," he said and strode over to the bed to kiss her. "Try to go back to sleep, if you can. And don't wait dinner for me if I'm late. I'm not sure when I'll be back."

"The dogs—"

"Another runaway." His lips tightened. "There were two of them this time. Ernesto and Felix. Troublemakers, both of them. And cunning. Worked up, I suppose, by all this foolish talk of abolition." He struck his riding crop against his booted leg. "There'll be no abolition for them."

"Must you go along on the hunt?" she asked. "I should think with the dogs and their handlers, and the *mayoral*, it wouldn't be necessary."

"I prefer to go," he said.

"How can you watch men torn to pieces by dogs?"

"They won't be, not these two. They will be brought back and dealt with publicly, at the *barracones*, where the other slaves can watch."

"What will be done to them?" She did not want to know, but something forced her to ask.

"Drucilla, I've told you so often, such things are not

fit for discussion with a woman—certainly not a woman like you. I don't want you to concern yourself." He pressed her hand. "Listen, as soon as the harvest is over, we'll take a little excursion to Havana for a few days. We'll go to the theater—you always like that. And you'll order as many new gowns as you please. And new furniture, too, if you like."

"Stop it," she protested. "I'm not a child. Don't you know after all this time that I'd rather wear the same gown for the next ten years and sleep on straw than to profit by the torture of other people? Innocent people who—"

"Innocent! They're animals—bloodthirsty, treacherous animals. You know what happened in Haiti, don't you? Two thousand whites died—as many as were guillotined in Paris during the Reign of Terror. The French sugar trade was ruined. Plantations were burned, planters slaughtered, and their wives raped. That will not happen in Cuba."

"But don't you see—can't I make you understand—that slaves rebel because they are treated with cruelty? As you are treating yours."

"That's enough. I refuse to discuss it any longer."

He turned to go out but before he could leave the bedroom, the door was flung open, and Andrew burst in, fully dressed, his gray eyes gleaming with excitement. It was unusual for him to enter their bedroom without knocking, to forget his manners so completely.

"Take me along," the boy begged, seizing Julio's sleeve. "Please, señor. I won't be any bother."

"But, niño, this is men's work."

"I'll be a man soon," Andrew said.

"We will have to ride fast to catch up with those black swine."

"You said I was a good rider."

"And you are," Julio said. "But your pony can scarcely keep pace with my Conquistador."

Drucilla felt cold to her fingertips as she listened. Could this be Kevin Farrell's son, pleading to be taken on a slave hunt? "Of course you're not going, Andrew," she said. "Go back to your room at once."

"Do I have to, señor?" Andrew made his appeal to Julio.

Then, in her agitation, Drucilla committed a serious error. She said: "I forbid you to take him, Julio."

Her husband's face flushed and his dark eyes narrowed. The moment the words were out she realized her mistake. She had lived in Cuba long enough, had spent enough time visiting with the wives of other planters, to know that here, on this island, a wife did not forbid her husband anything. She might plead, or cajole; she might use feminine wiles, in bed or out, but she did not give her husband a direct order.

Julio pressed his lips together until a white line formed around them. She looked up at him, fearful of what he might say or do; even Andrew took a step backward. When Julio finally spoke, it was not to her but to the boy. "Come with me," he said.

"Shall I have my pony saddled?"

"No, niño. You can ride before me, on Conquistador. He won't even notice the extra weight."

"You'll let me ride on Conquistador?" The boy was shaking with excitement. He had always admired the huge, black stallion, a powerful, spirited brute feared by the stablehands who were unlucky enough to have to care for him.

"Julio, I beg you, don't take the boy. Please don't." Now, when it was too late, Drucilla was resorting to the very approach that might have won her point earlier.

"Go back to sleep," Julio said quietly. "And don't upset yourself."

But after he and Andrew had left, after she heard the hoofbeats dying away down the avenue of royal palms, the baying and snarling of the dogs growing fainter, she was still unable to make her taut body relax.

She rang for Inez. "Please prepare my bath," she said.

"It's very early, señora," the girl observed. Drucilla saw that the girl's beautiful, golden-skinned face was drawn, as if she had not slept last night, and that her eyes were swollen. And when she helped Drucilla off with her nightgown and pinned her hair up on top of her head. Drucilla noticed that her fingers were shaking.

"What's wrong with you, Inez? Are you ill?"

"No, señora," the girl said.

"But you have been crying. Don't bother to deny it."

"The bath is ready now."

Drucilla sank into the warm perfumed water, but she could not ignore the maid's obvious distress. "If you've had an accident, broken a bottle of cologne or scorched one of my dresses, you can surely tell me. You know I won't punish you."

The girl hesitated, then shook her head. "It's because of Ernesto that I was crying."

"Ernesto." Of course. One of the runaways. But female house slaves were forbidden to associate with the male field hands, without express permission from Julio. Even in the *barracones*, Drucilla remembered, men and women were kept separated, unless the master chose to breed them. Although marriage between slaves was permitted in Cuba by the Church, Julio did not allow it. Neither did he allow religious services for his slaves.

But Drucilla, looking at Inez, knew the octoroon's secret as though the girl had shouted it aloud.

"Maybe Ernesto won't be caught."

Inez soaped a washcloth and applied it to Drucilla's shoulders. "He'll be caught, señora. And killed."

"But Ernesto's valuable. He's strong and clever. The *mayoral* has spoken of making him a driver."

Inez said nothing but her hand shook so badly that she dropped the washcloth into the water. "Señora, you have always been so good—an angel— If you would speak to the master, perhaps, for your sake, he would—" She broke off as if terrified by her own daring.

"I'll talk to him." And this time, Drucilla thought, I won't make demands. I'll humble myself if I have to. The thought was distasteful, but what did it matter, if she could save a man's life? She would do what she could to get Ernesto off with a milder punishment, and Felix, too.

"You must love Ernesto very much," Drucilla said.

"I would marry him, if it were allowed," Inez said simply. "In my heart, I am his wife, already."

Drucilla had hoped to spend the day making plans for

her talk with her husband when he returned, but soon after she was dressed, she saw, with dismay, that the volante owned by the Santovenias was rolling up the avenue. A few minutes later, she was downstairs in the salon, receiving Carmen Santovenia and Beatriz Talavera, a plump, pretty woman in her forties.

Carmen said: "Beatriz is my cousin. She and her husband, Fernando are visiting us, all the way from Spain." She flashed a dazzling smile at Drucilla. "We were not planning to come today, but when we got word of the runaways, Mateo and Fernando came to join in the chase. They're off on the trail now. And we'll keep you company until the men have returned."

Drucilla tried to look pleased, as she rang for a maid to bring refreshments. Then, she sat and made conversation while her guests drank *limonada* and nibbled at squares of *panatela*, the light, brandy-flavored spongecake for which the Vargases' cook was justly famous.

"Beatriz," Carmen was saying, "you should have seen Villanueva before Drucilla came here. A fine, comfortable house, to be sure. But now—" Her expansive gesture took in the rosewood furniture with its silk upholstery, the marble statues, the brocaded wall hangings.

Beatriz nodded. "As fine as any great house I have seen in any of the capitals of Europe," she agreed. As the wife of a Spanish diplomat, Beatriz Talavera was in a position to speak with authority. "Fernando and I have traveled in your country as well," she told Drucilla. "What part of the United States do you come from, if I may ask?"

"I was born in Cincinnati," Drucilla said. "But I have lived in many places: New York, Newport, Charleston." To her surprise, Drucilla felt a wave of homesickness, not for any particular city—perhaps for all of them. For Central Park, where Kevin had taken her driving on that long-ago day; for the Cliff Walk in Newport, with the breeze coming in from the sea; for Charleston, with its gracious old houses and high-walled gardens.

"Ah, Charleston. A beautiful city," Beatriz was saying. "Of course, I have not seen it since your Civil War, but I have been told that it has been rebuilt and that it is thriving. You Americans are such an energetic people."

"Drucilla is not an American any longer," Carmen interrupted. "She is a Cuban, now."

"But of course," Beatriz agreed. "A wife becomes whatever her husband may be. She adapts to his way of life, is that not so? In my own case, for instance, I have had to move about over half of Europe, because of Fernando's position in the diplomatic service."

"You must have had some fascinating experiences," Drucilla said. "Tell me, which of the European cities was your favorite?"

If she could keep Beatriz talking, she, herself, would not have to carry the burden of the conversation; at this moment, she was simply not up to it. Her mind was with Julio and Andrew. Had they caught the runaways yet? She remembered her promise to Inez, to intervene. Could she make Julio listen to her, or would he still be angry after their confrontation that morning?

She realized, with a start, that Beatriz was speaking directly to her. "Forgive me," she said. "My mind in on— something else. I'm so sorry."

"You're certainly not yourself today," Carmen observed. "And you're quite pale. Surely, by now, you're accustomed to our Cuban climate."

"It's not the climate that's troubling me," Drucilla snapped. She had disliked Carmen since that day when she had seen her riding away from the broken body of the slave child, without a backward glance or an expression of regret. But she had to tolerate Carmen's presence in her home, since the two families had been close friends for generations. "It's the business of the runaways," she said.

"But surely you don't fear for Julio's safety; he is with our men, and has the dogs and their handlers along."

"He took Andrew with him," Drucilla said. "I asked him not to, but he wouldn't listen."

"You should be thankful Julio takes such an interest in the boy," Carmen said. "It's not every man who would accept another man's son, and make a friend of him."

She doesn't like me any more than I like her, Drucilla thought.

"For my part, I shouldn't want any of my children to see such a thing," Beatriz said unexpectedly.

"Oh, really," Carmen said. "I do believe you're as foolish as Drucilla, *prima mia*. All this fuss about the treatment of the slaves. But then, I suppose it is only to be expected, since your parents took you from Cuba when you were a baby, and you've lived in Madrid—and places like Paris and London." She named the last two cities with obvious scorn, but Beatriz remained unruffled.

"If you ask me, our Spain is behind the times in this matter of slavery. England, France, the United States have no more slaves. However," she added, fanning herself slowly, "Fernando says that quite soon, the Spanish government, too, will see fit to abolish slavery in her colonies."

"I hope he doesn't talk that way to Mateo," Carmen said. "Or Julio, for that matter. I'll admit these slaves of ours can cause problems, but if they are properly handled, they—"

Carmen broke off at the sound of hoofbeats coming down the avenue of royal palms. Drucilla sprang to her feet and ran to the window to see the small cavalcade of horsemen riding up, with Julio on Conquistador in the lead, and holding Andrew in front of him in the saddle.

She excused herself hastily and hurried outside. The grooms were racing up from the stables to take care of the lathered horses; Andrew's nurse, Luz, a black mountain of a woman in a spotless white turban, was already on hand to take charge of the boy.

Drucilla brushed past her, and ran to meet Julio. He drew rein and sat looking down at her from his horse, his handsome face flushed with exertion, his damp shirt clinging to his wide chest. If he remembered their quarrel, he gave no sign, but got down quickly and swung Andrew out of the saddle.

"*Dios mio*, that was fine sport, Julio," Mateo said, as he tossed the reins of his bay mare to the nearest groom. "But my throat's as dry as dust."

"I've been out of the saddle too long for such exertions," Fernando said ruefully.

Mateo laughed. "The only exercise you diplomats get is dancing with pretty women at embassy balls."

Fernando shrugged. "Not the most disagreeable form of exercise, *primo mio.*"

Drucilla was looking at Andrew, whose face appeared greenish-white in the strong sunlight. There were dark smudges under his gray eyes, and he stood still for a moment, where Julio had set him down. Then he flung himself into Drucilla's arms, and she felt his body trembling.

"Are you ill, darling?" she asked anxiously.

Julio said quickly: "Of course, he's not ill. He had a long, hard ride, that's all. Luz, take him to his room, give him a good meal and a bath. And see he goes to bed early."

He put a hand on the boy's shoulder. "Not sorry you came along, are you, niño?"

Drucilla heard the unspoken challenge, and she was sure the boy had, too. "No, señor," he said, but his voice, muffled against his mother's shoulder, was unsteady.

Drucilla longed to put Andrew to bed herself, and to try to find out what was wrong with him, but she knew that her first duty was to her guests; reluctantly, she gave the boy to Luz.

The men would want rum to drink, and then she would have to see that guest rooms were prepared, where they and their wives could rest and change for dinner.

Inez asked no questions as she was helping Drucilla change, but the octoroon's lovely face was set in a mask of despair. "I haven't forgotten my promise," Drucilla said, trying to comfort her. Inez continued fastening Drucilla's gown. "I haven't had a chance yet—" Drucilla broke off as her husband came in.

His hair was brushed until it shone with blue-black lights, and he smelled of rum and of lime cologne. He dismissed the maid with a gesture.

"Let me fasten these last two buttons," he said. He did so, then touched his lips to Drucilla's shoulder. "Turn around and let me look at you. Superb. Isn't that one of the gowns you bought the last time we were in Havana?"

She forced a smile. "Yes, dear," she said. After their recent quarrel, she realized that if she wanted to help

Ernesto and Felix she would have to be diplomatic. The heat, the long visit with Carmen and Beatriz, and her concern for Andrew combined to make her edgy. But there was something else, far more disturbing.

For the last two months, she had suspected she was pregnant; and now, after missing her second period in a row, she was sure of it. Her waistline was still small, but her breasts were slightly larger and tender to the touch. There was no longer any doubt in her mind; she was going to bear Julio the child he had wanted all these years.

She had hesitated to tell him, awaiting the right moment. She did not like to admit it, even to herself, but she knew that she had put off telling her husband of her pregnancy because of the irrational feeling that so long as no one else knew, it would not be quite real.

It was real enough, though. After Julio had finished fastening the bodice, she could feel her breasts pushing against the fabric. Time enough to tell him, when this terrible business of the runaways had been settled.

"Did you find them both?" she asked.

Julio ignored the question. He took her hands and held her away at arm's length, to get the full effect of her gown. "Yes, I like it," he said. "Those colors are most becoming." The gown was made of silk, in a soft shade of brown, with a pale yellow overskirt. The bodice was cut low in front, and the fullness of her breasts was visible. Yes, soon, very soon, Julio would have to know.

"Please, tell me what happened out there today," she persisted.

"Not now," he said. "Our guests are waiting."

"But I want to know."

"Later," he said. She caught the warning note in his voice, sighed, took his arm, and together they descended the wide staircase.

Heliotrope in silver vases scented the warm air. The dining room table was set with a snowy white damask cloth and laden with ornate silver and fine china from France. The candles in the chandelier overhead glowed down on the shimmering silks and satins worn by the women.

Slaves brought one succulent dish after another and

kept the wine glasses filled. The conversation grew animated. When Beatriz learned that Drucilla had spent a part of her wedding trip in Paris, she began comparing notes with her on the charms of that city. "The operas—the balls—and the restaurants—"

Julio smiled with pride. "I'll wager you won't find such prawns as these in any restaurant in Paris. Our cook makes a special sauce for them. She will tell no one her secret."

"Excellent," Mateo said. "And I'm prepared to do full justice to the dish. There's nothing like a day in the saddle to give a man a good appetite."

Drucilla saw her chance. "Mateo, what happened today? You caught the slaves, didn't you?"

"Julio hasn't told you? Of course we got them. And sooner than we'd thought we would. Those dogs are splendid."

He took a sip of wine, then went on: "There was an accident, however. One of the handlers lost control of his beast. The dog tore that short, skinny black—what was he called?—Felix—to shreds. There was blood everywhere."

He dipped a prawn into the rich, thick sauce and put it into his mouth.

Drucilla gagged. She shut her eyes for a moment. Andrew had seen it all. Dear heaven, no wonder he had been so pale and silent on his return home. No wonder he had trembled against her when she had held him. Her insides began to churn.

"And the other one?" She could hardly force the words out. "Ernesto. What happened to him?"

"He was bitten on the leg. He's locked in a cell in the *barracones* right now." Mateo laughed. "However, there won't be time for his wound to fester."

Julio shot a warning look at Mateo, but it went unnoticed. "Tomorrow, he'll be out of his misery," Mateo said.

Drucilla made a choking sound, and stood up, knocking over her wine glass. One of the slaves came swiftly to blot up the spilled wine; his face was impassive, as if he had not understood a word he had heard.

Drucilla lifted her silk skirt and fled outside into the patio. A moment later Julio was beside her, gripping her arm. His annoyance changed to concern as he looked at her. "You're so pale," he said.

"Leave me alone. I think I'm going to be sick." She had not wanted to tell him this way, but she could not control herself. "I'm pregnant, you see. I'm going to have your baby. And I'm so afraid."

"A baby? You're sure?"

"Yes. Quite sure."

"But what have you to fear? This is wonderful news. Aren't you happy, too?"

"How can I be happy to think of raising a child here?"

His brow contracted. "This business of the slaves again? What has that to do with our child?"

"Andrew saw a terrible thing today—something no child should ever see. And now this baby. Growing up where cruelty is accepted, where human beings are tortured and murdered."

"Hush. *Amada mia*, you must not upset yourself this way. Not now. A woman in your condition must have no worries, no fears." He held her and tried to comfort her. "Please, *mi vida*, what do you want me to do?"

"Let Ernesto live."

He made an impatient sound, but after a moment, he nodded.

"Very well. How can I refuse you anything, now? But," he added, "discipline must be maintained. I can't let that black devil go unpunished."

Drucilla had been prepared for this, and she accepted it although not without a shudder of distaste.

"Now," he said, "let us go back to our guests and tell them that you have made me the happiest of men. You don't mind if I tell them about the baby, do you?"

"Of course not."

Seated once more at the dining room table, Drucilla smiled as she received the congratulations of the guests. She still had mixed feelings about bearing Julio's child, but at least, her pregnancy had helped her achieve her immediate wish: to save Ernesto's life.

"You won't let him off scot-free?" Mateo asked, after

Julio had told them that they would be deprived of seeing an execution the following morning. "If he goes unpunished, it will start a bad precedent for the rest of us. And with all this talk of abolition, we can't let the blacks think we've turned soft. Otherwise, they'll all be running off."

"It's more than talk, this business of abolition," Fernando began. But Carmen cut him short, with an imperious toss of her head.

"Whatever led you to change your mind about having the slave killed?" she asked Julio. "I'll wager that was your wife's idea." She laughed. "Drucilla has the most curious notions about coddling the slaves."

She turned her dark eyes on Drucilla who, not for the first time, sensed hostility in this woman. Until Drucilla had come to Villanueva, Carmen had been considered the most beautiful woman in the vicinity of Cienfuegos. Indeed she was a striking figure tonight, with her blue-black hair gleaming under the delicate mantilla of gold lace. Her gown of flamingo pink satin-de-Lyon, with its underskirt of jade green worked in gold thread and pearls, suited her bold beauty admirably.

"Well, Julio?" she demanded. "Wasn't it Drucilla who saved your Ernesto from his just punishment?"

Julio put her off with a shrug. "I'm too happy tonight to think of such matters," he said. "But to set your mind at rest, let me assure you, Ernesto won't get off completely. Fifty lashes and a hot iron to his forehead will end his urge for freedom. As for Felix, I've given orders that his body is to remain in full view, in the courtyard of the *barracones*, until it rots. Even you, Carmen, must admit that's enough to keep the slaves under control for awhile."

"With all due respect," Fernando said, "you must face facts. Sooner or later, you'll be forced to set your slaves free. Whether or not they'll be better off that way, who can say."

"Drucilla, perhaps," Beatriz said. "You lived in Charleston after the war. What do you think?"

Drucilla hesitated, for she was well aware of the great concession Julio had made in agreeing to let Ernesto live;

she had no wish to irritate her husband now, of all times.

"There are many problems, of course," she said carefully. "Both for the freedmen and their former owners."

"I've heard most of the former slaves in your country are worse off than they ever were on the plantations. The old and the sick cannot take care of themselves. And their former masters are no longer forced to provide for them. They are like helpless children, roaming the countryside, aren't they?" The smug note in Mateo's voice set her teeth on edge.

"There's some truth in what you say," she agreed. "But times are changing. Schools have been established for the freedmen, both in the North and in the South. Not nearly as many as one would wish, but—"

"Schools for those black apes?" Carmen laughed. "They only know how to work and to breed. And they can only be entrusted with the simplest tasks."

"That's not quite fair," Drucilla said. "Norbert Rillieux, a Louisiana mulatto, developed the designs for the new vacuum boilers that are now installed in our sugar mills, and yours, too, Carmen. Those boilers have enabled us to produce far more sugar and of better quality, as I'm sure you know."

"A single example," Julio protested. "It's scarcely proof that the majority of blacks would profit by freedom, let alone education. For my part, I hope I won't live to see the end of slavery here in Cuba."

"Now, Julio," Fernando said, "such changes are inevitable. Indeed, one day, Spain will have to renounce her claim to Cuba altogether. Your island will be an independent nation."

"I helped fight a war to prevent that," Julio said. "And I'd fight another, if necessary."

The candle flames blurred before Drucilla's eyes. In spite of all the sacrifices of the revolutionists, their cause had been crushed. Kevin had suffered and died for nothing. Suppose she had not conspired a second time to help him escape; would he have survived the horrors of San Rafael? Would he have come back to her?

She tried to put these thoughts out of her mind. She was with child by another man. Even if she knew she would never love anyone the way she had loved Kevin, she had to make a good life for herself and her husband, for Andrew and her unborn baby. She had to.

Later that night, when Inez came to help her prepare for bed, Drucilla saw at once that there was no need to tell the girl of Julio's decision; there was a grapevine of information, not only within the house itself, but across the plantation. She was embarrassed, but touched, too, when Inez dropped to her knees and said, "I'll never forget what you have done, señora. Never." She pressed Drucilla's hand to her lips.

"Please, don't," Drucilla said, drawing her hand away gently. "I only wish I could have done more. But I didn't dare pursue the matter, once my husband had agreed to spare Ernesto's life."

"He's a strong man," Inez said, with grief and a curious pride mingled in her voice. "He will be able to bear the lash and the branding. He'll be alive. That's the important thing." She looked at Drucilla and her lips parted in surprise. "Why, what is wrong, señora? What have I said?"

In that moment, Drucilla knew that although she and Inez were of different races, they were alike in a very fundamental way. Kevin, too, had been strong, able to endure much. If only he had lived . . . even if she never saw him again, held him again, only to know that somewhere he was alive.

Then she realized that Inez was still looking at her with deep concern. "I'm a little tired, that's all," she assured the girl.

"Of course," Inez said, as she helped Drucilla on with her nightgown. "It's to be expected, when you are carrying a new life within you."

"You know about the baby, too?"

"*El señor* made the announcement downstairs. Besides, I am your personal maid." She brushed Drucilla's hair into a gleaming, coppery fan across her shoulders.

Drucilla smiled. "At least you learned my secret by natural means. I thought for a moment you might be a witch."

"*Una bruja*? Oh, no, señora."

"I was joking, Inez."

"But in truth, my grandmother had certain powers. She could heal many illnesses with herbs." Inez stopped brushing Drucilla's hair and bit her full lower lip. Then she said: "You've done so much for me already, I do not like to ask another favor. But—would it be possible for me to slip out to the *barracones* to see Ernesto tomorrow? There is a certain salve. My grandmother taught me to make it. It will ease his pain and help the wounds to heal faster."

"It will be dangerous for you. If my husband should find out—"

"Oh, but he won't. We have our ways, señora."

The next morning when Julio, accompanied by his male houseguests, departed for the *barracones* to watch Ernesto's punishment, Drucilla insisted that Andrew should remain behind with her. The boy, much subdued since his experience of the day before, made no protest.

But although Drucilla had her way this time, she was well aware that she was fighting a losing battle; within a couple of days, Andrew was out riding with Julio again, to the cane fields and the mills. She did not know whether her son had seen the mangled corpse of the dead slave, Felix, tied to a post in the courtyard of the *barracones*, and she could not bring herself to ask.

Twenty-four

DURING the following month, Drucilla was denied the state of drowsy contentment that often accompanies early pregnancy, for her mind was in a turmoil. She would have to act quickly, before it became impossible for her to travel; she must get away from the plantation, if only for a while, and take Andrew with her; but she would have to be circumspect in dealing with Julio.

A letter from Charlotte Tremayne helped her to form a tentative plan. Charlotte had written from Aix-les-Bains to say that she was returning from France and would spend the winter in her townhouse in New York City. She said that she missed Drucilla and offered endless advice about the precautions she should take during her pregnancy.

"I do hope they have at least one decent doctor on that island," she concluded. "But I have my doubts."

Drucilla read and reread Charlotte's letter on the day it arrived, and that night, as she lay beside Julio, her mind still raced feverishly.

He made love to her, gently, without a trace of the violence that she had come to expect. Ever since he had learned of her pregnancy, he had kept himself under control, even in their most intimate moments; she knew him well enough to sense the effort it cost him.

Now, having reached his climax, he was drawing away, but she put her arms around him and held him to her. She stroked his back, his lean, hard buttocks, her fingers probing, teasing, until gradually she felt him stiffen within her again. She used her body deliberately, skillfully, to give him the fullest pleasure.

Afterward, she lay listening to his whispered words of adoration. "I could go on making love to you until dawn," he said, "but you must sleep now, *querida*."

"I can't sleep," she said.

He raised himself up on one elbow, and touched her cheek. "Is something troubling you?"

"I received a letter today."

"From one of the Seaton spinsters?" he asked.

"No. From my grandmother. She's leaving the spa in France. Her rheumatism is much improved. She'll spend this winter in her townhouse in New York." Drucilla paused, then went on carefully. "She misses me, Julio."

"Perhaps one day we will visit her," he said. His voice was becoming drowsy. He had gone out to the fields before sunrise that morning. Now, having satisfied his physical needs, he was ready for sleep.

"If I don't go to see her soon, this year perhaps, it may be too late," Drucilla said. "She's old and frail."

"This year? That's impossible. I can't leave the plantation until the harvest is over. Then I must see to the new mill and the installation of the machinery. He put his hand on her belly, now curving outward a little. "In any case," he said, "you are in no condition to make a long trip now."

"I'm sure I could manage, if I left right away," she said. Then realizing that her words were too urgent, her tone too desperate, she went on: "I'm not too unwieldy yet, am I, dear?" She gave a flirtatious little laugh that sounded strained, even to her.

"You're lovely," he said. "But all the same, your idea of going on a visit to New York is quite out of the question."

"I could take one of the maids," she persisted. "And Andrew, and perhaps Luz."

Julio sat up and reached out to turn on the lamp beside the bed. "What are you saying? Travel alone? That may be the custom among some women in your country, but a Cuban wife travels with her husband, or not at all. And in your condition, it would be foolish to attempt such a trip."

"There are excellent doctors in New York."

"And in Havana, too." There was a hard edge of impatience in Julio's voice now. "The doctor who delivered Carmen Santovenia's second daughter was educated in Paris and Madrid, I understand. I'll have him brought here from Havana, if you like. He can stay here the whole month before your delivery. I'll pay him whatever he asks. Does that satisfy you?"

"If I could only have the baby back home . . ." she began, panic mounting.

"This is your home. I've heard that women in your condition get strange notions. But what you ask is impossible. I won't leave Villenueva now. I cannot. And I will not permit you to leave alone."

"Won't you even discuss it? It would mean so much to me to—"

He stretched out a hand to turn off the oil lamp, but she clutched at his arm. "How can I make you understand?"

"I think I'm beginning to. It's Andrew, isn't it? Ever since that day I took him on the hunt for the runaway slaves, you've been taking on about him. No, even before that. You've been looking for an excuse to get him away from the plantation, and now you're using your pregnancy as a pretext. That, and your sudden, overwhelming need to visit your grandmother." His eyes were icy with anger. "When we were in Paris, you never once suggested making the trip down to Aix-les-Bains to see her. Ah, but I'm forgetting. On our wedding trip you were still brooding about Kevin Farrell, and no one else mattered."

He got up out of bed, thrust his arms into the sleeves of his light silk robe, and belted it, with a quick, jerky movement. "I'm corrupting your son, that's it. And, of course,

344

he's far more important to you than I am. His welfare—whatever you conceive that to be—must be placed ahead of your duty to your husband."

"If you'd ever once tried to understand my feelings about slavery—"

"Understand? *Madre de Dios*, what is there to understand? I've catered to your ridiculous notions whenever possible. I even spared Ernesto's life, to please you."

"I know you've tried to be kind," she admitted.

"Tried to be kind? I've treated you like a queen. I've done everything to make you happy. And I've been faithful—I haven't touched a slave woman since I married you. Do you know how rare that is, for a man in my circumstances? I don't even keep a mistress in Havana, as Mateo does."

"I've never accused you of being unfaithful."

"Be silent," he ordered. He paced the bedroom, his hands thrust into the pockets of his robe. "You wanted Andrew here. I sent for him."

He wheeled around to confront her. "You think it was easy for me, having the boy here? Kevin Farrell's bastard, living under my roof."

She cried out, and her eyes widened in shocked horror. "Andrew is—"

"Don't lie to me. Not now. I knew the truth about the boy the first moment I saw him."

"How could you have known?"

"I saw Kevin Farrell that day at San Rafael. Surely you haven't forgotten. I stood quite close to him, when he called me into the colonel's office to give me his answer. *No promises. No arrangements.* Remember?"

As Julio spoke, the scene came back to her, as clearly as if she had witnessed it only the day before. Kevin, pushing her away from him, disengaging her clinging arms, ordering Julio to take her out of San Rafael. She, struggling in Julio's arms until she had been too exhausted to fight any longer. Then the ride down the slopes of the Sierra Maestra, through the rain forest with its giant ferns. Julio, comforting her.

"I knew you still loved him," Julio said. "Even that night at the inn, when you let me make love to you for the first time— You let me." His voice was filled with self-mockery. "As if I couldn't have taken you any time I wanted you. And turned you over to my troopers, afterward. But, no. I wanted you to love me. Does that amuse you, Drucilla?"

"You know it doesn't." She held out a hand in a pleading gesture. "I was grateful to you. And I've tried to love you. But I can't forget Kevin. I'll never forget him, not as long as I live."

"Your honesty is refreshing," he said. She knew that he had never been so angry with her before. Her mouth went dry, and she swallowed against the metallic taste of fear on her tongue.

In the light of the single lamp, in its painted globe, the room stirred with shifting shadows. Julio's face was that of a stranger. She knew she had wounded this arrogant man, had hurt his pride. He would not forgive readily. Perhaps not at all.

"I've loved you as much as a man can love a woman," he said. "When we were in Paris, on our wedding trip, I let myself believe you'd begun to care for me, too. That you had forgotten Farrell. You gave yourself to me with such passion. Or were you pretending?"

"Oh, no. Don't think that of me. You—made me want you that way."

"I see. I was able to stir your senses, then. But your mind—that's always belonged to him. You made a shrine to him there. This mercenary. This common adventurer."

"Kevin Farrell was—"

"Stop. Spare me your account of his many virtues." Julio made an impatient gesture. "He had animal courage. Even a kind of honor." He strode over to the bed. "And he had your love. You married me, but you never stopped loving him."

She hung her head, her hair tangled about her face. She could not deny what Julio was saying.

"I've been too kind to you, Drucilla. Too indulgent. I see that now. I might have kept you as my mistress, until I tired of you, but instead, I married you. I gave you the Vargas name. And all the time, you were mooning over a man who used you like *una puta*—who gave you a bastard child, and then walked out on you."

"It wasn't like that. Kevin didn't even—"

"Be quiet. I don't want to hear his name again."

"How can you be jealous of a dead man?"

He smiled in a way that terrified her. "Dead? How do you know he's dead?"

"You told me so. When you came back from Oriente, that time, you—"

"I lied."

"You wouldn't—not about that—you—" Her words died away. Julio's face blurred before her eyes. The room was silent, but she heard a dull roar in her ears, like the surge of waves on a beach. She was drowning, fighting to breathe.

Then, through the roar, she heard Julio saying, "Yes, Farrell escaped from San Rafael, with the help of his rebel friends. I was afraid he would come for you, and I loved you too much to risk losing you."

"But why tell me now? You think, because we're married, I won't leave you and take Andrew? I'll find Kevin. Wherever he is, I'll find him."

She made a move to rise, but he pushed her back against the pillows, and, putting an arm on either side of her, he said: "You won't go to him. You are my wife and you are carrying my child. You think I'd give you up, now?"

"You have no choice. You can't stop me—"

He drew back one arm and struck her across the face. "You're a fool, Drucilla. You're mine and nothing can change that."

She put a hand to her cheek, and listened to his voice, hard, decisive, implacable.

"Things will be different here from now on. I will make the decisions and you will obey me in everything. You will discipline the house slaves, or you will be made to watch, while I do. You will not interfere with Andrew —I will raise him as I see fit, and you will say nothing."

"You've no right—Andrew's my child." She would not plead for herself, but Andrew was so vulnerable and, with Julio in his present mood, there was no telling what he might do to the boy.

He laughed, a short, hard sound, like the bark of a

fox. "Don't look at me that way, my dear wife. I won't abuse the boy. Or you. That slap was to show you who is master. It won't happen again, unless you make it necessary."

He sat down on the side of the bed. She found it hard to believe that only a little while ago, he had held her with love, had caressed her, and murmured endearments.

"You know," he said, in a brisk, conversational way, "I have nothing against the boy, except that his father was Kevin Farrell. I rather like Andrew. He has spirit and intelligence. And he has shown quite an interest in the workings of the plantation. I think I'll continue taking him out with me, to the fields and the mills. Who knows, when he's grown up, he might make an excellent *mayoral*."

"An overseer? Andrew, an overseer?"

"You surely did not expect me to make him master of Villanueva. Not when you'll give me sons of my own. Oh, yes, Drucilla, you will. And, in time, you will learn what it means to be a dutiful wife."

Twenty-five

AS THE harvest went on, Julio spent less and less time with Drucilla; he passed his days out in the fields, and at night, he often went to the mills, which were kept running until two or three in the morning. It was not necessary for him to do so; many of the other planters relegated the harvesting to the *mayoral* and his helpers; indeed, the Santovenias had recently departed for Spain with Beatriz and Fernando Talavera, for a long-deferred holiday.

Julio, however, insisted upon supervising every phase of the work, even while admitting that Ruiz, the *mayoral*, and Cespedes, the *contramayoral*, were competent at their duties. Ruiz, although he dressed like a dandy in a suit of striped blue linen, a fine Panama hat, and an embroidered silk scarf, had a reputation among the slaves for unspeakable brutality.

Ruiz and Cespedes were never seen without their short-handled rawhide whips, and each carried a pistol. Black slavedrivers assisted the white overseers in driving the gangs out in the cane fields. Nevertheless, Julio, mounted on Conquistador, was everywhere, directing which fields should be cut next, setting the amount of cane to be cut and hauled to the mills on a given day. The slaves were mustered before dawn, by the light of torches, and set to work; at midmorning, they were allowed to pause long enough to swallow a ration of dried fish and rice, then put to work again. The stalks fell under the sweeping machetes, were piled up into creaking ox carts, and taken to the mills.

At least, Drucilla thought, the long hours of the harvest kept Julio away from her much of the time, allowing her privacy in which to make plans. She would not remain here, that much she had known the night Julio had told her Kevin had not been killed at San Rafael. Julio was a fool to think he could keep her from finding Kevin now.

She considered the possibility that Kevin, although he had not died in the attack on the garrison, might have succumbed later to the injuries he had received while a prisoner. But she set her mind firmly against the thought. "He's got to be alive," she told herself over and over again.

Now, since Kevin had admitted he loved her, she knew that nothing could keep them apart. She would take Andrew and go find him, wherever he was.

It did not even matter to her that she was carrying Julio's child. The baby would be born in the United States and would remain with her. The Tremayne money would buy her the help of the most skilled lawyers. No child of hers, no matter who had fathered it, would grow up at Villanueva.

Lying awake at night, thinking over her plans, she found herself, at times, possessed by fear. She would rise from bed and pace the floor, trying to steady herself for what lay ahead. Stronger than fear was her certainty that she could no longer go on living here at Villanueva as the wife of Julio Vargas.

How, she asked herself, had she been able to stay here this long?

The answers came slowly, painfully. As long as she had believed that Kevin was dead, she had been able to tell herself that nothing could matter to her again. She had moved through the days like a sleepwalker. She had even let herself think that she could change Julio, could win some concessions from him for the benefit of the slaves. She had deceived herself, had refused to recognize the darker side of her husband's nature.

But on the night of their quarrel, when he had struck her, when he had told her how he had tricked her into marriage with a lie, she had seen him for what he was. And she could never forgive him. Never.

Her deepest feelings, numbed by her belief that she had lost Kevin forever, now stirred back to life. She could not let herself give way to fear.

Andrew's whole future was at stake. He was only nine years old, but the years would pass swiftly enough, and she was remembering Julio's taunting remark that he would make Andrew an overseer here. She would not let that happen. She felt a new strength flooding through her. What she might not have dared to risk for herself, she would risk for Andrew.

Now, knowing that Kevin was alive, she could let herself remember him again, could let herself relive their last meeting at San Rafael. Now, at last, she understood why Kevin had sent her away, why he had been willing to endure the horrors of that place, rather than to compromise. *No promises. No arrangements.*

She did not have Kevin's kind of strength, perhaps, but she did have a woman's weapons. And she would use them.

Outwardly, she deferred to Julio in everything. She let him believe that she was now the submissive wife he demanded. He still took his pleasure with her, not gently, as he had during the first weeks of her pregnancy, but without cruelty; he possessed her body quickly, almost impersonally; afterward, he turned his back on her and went to sleep at once.

During the first days after their quarrel, she had feared for Andrew. But gradually her fears faded for, although Julio was sometimes short with the boy, he still took him out to the fields each day, and Andrew went willingly. During the hottest part of the afternoon, Julio insisted that Andrew should rest in the shade of the wagons.

351

One evening, at dinner, Andrew told her: "Señor Vargas is going to clear a stretch of forest, so that he can plant a bigger crop next year."

"That won't be until after the harvest," Julio said. "Don't be alarmed," he added to Drucilla. "The clearing and burning will be done at night—I won't take the boy along."

"Oh, but I—" Andrew began, but Julio silenced him at once.

"You heard what I said. We won't talk about it again."

"It's a pity to burn such beautiful trees," Drucilla said.

Julio shrugged. "I cannot concern myself with beauty when I need more space for sugarcane."

"If you fertilized the fields, as they do in the United States—"

"It's cheaper to clear virgin land," he said. Then, turning to Andrew, who was obviously downcast, he said: "You have many years ahead to see these things, *niño*."

The boy brightened but Drucilla knew the thrust had been intended for her, to remind her that Andrew would remain here until he grew to manhood.

Don't bet on it, she thought.

Sometime within the next few months, she and Andrew would be on board a ship, heading for New York. But how? That was her problem. Julio had forbidden her to ride a horse as soon as he learned she was pregnant; even if he hadn't, she could hardly get to Havana on horseback in her condition. And there was also the problem of Andrew, good enough with his pony, but unable to handle a full-sized mount.

That left the volante, the large-wheeled coach that took two horses or, if necessary, a pair of mules to draw it. Not the ideal form of transportation for a pregnant woman either, but she would manage the trip somehow. Not alone. That would be beyond her powers, determined though she was. Suppose the volante should break down on an isolated stretch of road?

It had also occurred to her that she might have to take Andrew away by force, for she knew Julio had driven a wedge between her and her son; she was not at all sure Andrew would go willingly. She did not dare risk telling the child her plans until the last moment.

But who, here at Villanueva, would help her? The slaves might want to, but they would be too afraid of Julio. Even the house servants, who had cause to appreciate her kindness, would hardly take such a risk.

Except, perhaps, Inez.

Drucilla hesitated to draw the girl into her plans, for no punishment Julio might inflict upon his wife would be as terrible as that he would surely mete out to a slave.

One night, after dinner, Drucilla sat in the bedroom, waiting for Inez to answer her ring. Julio, who was preparing to go down to the mills, said: "Where is that girl? She should have been here five minutes ago. You're too slack with the house servants and they take advantage of you."

"I—she's in the kitchen, brewing herbs for a soothing drink for me."

"Why can't the cook do that?" he demanded.

"Inez is the only one who knews which herbs to use and how much of each," Drucilla said, thankful she had been able to think of a plausible excuse on such short notice; she had no idea where Inez might be.

Julio laughed. "Oh, yes. Her grandmother was skilled in the use of herbs, I remember." He appeared satisfied and Drucilla breathed a sigh. She remembered his threat about forcing her to discipline the house servants, and she knew that nothing could ever make her take a whip to another human being.

"Why do you need a soothing drink?" he asked.

"I have trouble sleeping sometimes. The baby kicks and keeps me awake."

"You never told me," he said.

An angry retort came to her lips, but she bit it back.

"I have to leave now," he said. "Unless you want me to stay here until Inez comes."

How dare he try to play the kind, understanding husband now, after what had happened between them?

"I'm quite all right," she said.

It was past eleven, and she was tired, but it was nearly half an hour before Inez finally came to prepare her for bed. The girl was breathless, her usually smooth chestnut

353

hair disordered. "Forgive me, señora," she said. "I did not mean to keep you waiting."

"What delayed you?" Drucilla asked.

The girl looked away. "I was with Ernesto." She scarcely raised her voice above a whisper.

"But the danger," Drucilla said. "If my husband were to find out, you know what would happen."

"I have to see Ernesto. I could not live without seeing him—sometimes. And he needs me, too. We're careful, señora."

"But what about your future? Sooner or later, you'll be caught."

"A slave has no future," Inez said calmly.

"Still, you must think about it sometime," Drucilla said. "Suppose you were to have a child. . . ."

"Señor Vargas would probably sell it," the girl said. "Or it would die of disease or neglect in the slave nursery."

Drucilla hesitated, then said: "It doesn't have to be that way. You and Ernesto could be free to marry, to raise a family. He could work for wages."

"There has always been talk about freeing the slaves here on the island," Inez said. "But it never happens. And if Ernesto and I ran away, we would be caught and brought back. That other time he ran away, he thought to get to Havana, to try to pass himself off as an *emancipado*. Then later, I might have run away, too, and joined him. But you remember what happened."

"I remember," Drucilla said grimly. "But you could go farther away than Havana. To the United States, where you could be free."

Inez shrugged. "We cannot even get away from Villanueva, Ernesto and I. How could we think of going across the sea to another country?"

Drucilla put a hand on Inez's arm and drew the girl close. "It can be done," she said. "The risk would be great, but if you and Ernesto are willing to try, I'll show you a way."

"But, señora, the risk would be great for you also. If Señor Vargas found out, he would do you some harm—"

"By the time he finds out, it will be too late for him to

hurt me—I'm going with you. And Andrew, too."

"This is madness," Inez said. "Why should you want to leave here?"

"I have my reasons," Drucilla said. "Later, I'll tell them to you. Now we must make plans. Money is no problem. I will take my jewels along and sell them in Havana. Then we will take passage on the first ship leaving for the United States."

Inez's dark eyes moved over Drucilla's body. "How can you travel, as you are now?"

"We'll take the volante," Drucilla said. "Ernesto can drive. If we're seen, no one will be suspicious of a lady traveling to Havana with her coachman and maid and her little boy."

"Señor Vargas would look for you. He'd send out searchers."

"I've thought of that, too. I will tell him I am going to Cienfuegos, to visit with a friend overnight. That will give us more than a day's headstart. That should be enough—it has to be."

"And Ernesto, what about him? He isn't a coachman. He's been sent back to the fields."

"We'll start out with Pablo driving," Drucilla said. "Before we leave the plantation, Ernesto will have to take over. I don't want Pablo hurt. Only tied up where he won't be found for a day or so."

"Ernesto can do that, easily. He has great strength."

"Will he be willing to chance a second escape?" Drucilla asked.

"I'm sure he will, señora. I think it is only because of me that he hasn't tried again before this."

The last weeks of the harvest passed, and when it was over, Julio gave orders to clear a great tract of forest on the western side of Villanueva.

Andrew, bitterly disappointed because he was not to be taken along, stood in the doorway of his room; he was already bathed and dressed in his cotton nightshirt. He looked out into the upstairs hallway, where Señor Vargas stood talking with Mother. "I won't be back before dawn," Andrew heard him saying. "You'll be all right, won't you?"

Mother was going to have a baby. Andrew had heard the house servants talking about it. He was a little scared. Would she feel sick when she had the baby? From what he had overheard, he had decided it would hurt a lot. But she didn't act afraid.

"Inez will be here with me," she said.

Andrew backed into his room. He watched Señor Vargas walk past. Then Luz, his fat nurse, put him to bed, draping the mosquito netting around him.

But he couldn't sleep. It was hot, and he kept thinking about the big fire tonight. Maybe if he went out onto the balcony, he could see the fire.

He waited until he heard Luz moving across the floor, in the little room next to his, getting ready for bed. A little later, he heard her snoring.

He got up and went out onto the balcony. He stared in the direction where Señor Vargas had told him the fire would be. Nothing yet.

Then he remembered a certain steep hill, right near the *barracones*. There were a lot of big rocks around the bottom of the hill, and a grove of bamboo on the top. If he could go there, he could see the fire, and nobody would see him.

Señor Vargas hadn't told him not to leave the house tonight. But he knew perfectly well he wasn't supposed to.

Ever since the day when Señor Vargas had taken him on the slave hunt, Andrew had been a little afraid of his stepfather. And he knew that Miguel's face had been scarred by a blow from Señor Vargas's riding crop— he'd heard the servants talking about it once. If he made Señor Vargas angry, would he be punished that way?

He'd be careful. He'd only go as far as the hill. No one would know.

He went back to his bedroom, pulled off his nightshirt, and got back into his clothes. Then he returned to the balcony, to a place where a tree grew so close that he could reach out and take hold of a thick branch. He climbed out onto the branch and scrambled down to the ground.

He felt scared again, when he stood looking down the avenue of palms leading away from the house. But the moon was big and bright tonight. He wouldn't get lost. He knew his way around the plantation by this time.

The house slaves talked among themselves about spirits, devils, with glittering eyes and long claws, who roamed around at night. But Señor Vargas had said that such talk was nonsense. "What would you expect from a pack of savages?" he'd said. Then he had laughed. "All the same, *niño*, it is good the blacks believe such things. It keeps them indoors at night, where they belong."

It was a long time before Andrew got to the *barracones*. The familiar pathways looked strange at night, and the wind made queer, rattling sounds in the palm trees. His legs were very tired. Maybe he should have stayed in the house.

The wooden walls around the *barracones* were high. No one would see him. Besides, most of the slaves were out with Señor Vargas, clearing the stretch of timber. Digging firebreaks. Standing by with buckets of water to keep the flames under control. Señor Vargas had told him how it was done.

There was the hill, right ahead. He clambered up over the big rocks, his legs aching now. Then he threw himself down on his stomach and looked out over the land in the direction where he thought the fire should be. It still hadn't been started. He was sleepy. He had never been up so late before. He closed his eyes. The night breeze was cool on his face and the grass was soft . . . it smelled sweet. . . .

He woke up all of a sudden, and for a moment he could not remember why he was here, under the open sky, with the trees all around him. Then he saw a reddish glare. The fire. He was about to get up to get a better look, when he heard voices close by. Two people talking down below, among the rocks at the foot of the hill.

"You'll do it, then?"

It was a woman talking. Inez. Mother's maid. But what was she doing out here? The house slaves were supposed to stay indoors after dark. Inez was supposed to be taking care of Mother.

"You have to ask?" A man's voice now. Deep, angry. "Of course I'll do it."

"Pablo is not to be hurt. Only tied up somewhere where he won't be found until after we're far away."

"I'll try not to hurt him. But the risk for you, if we're caught—"

"It's our only chance, Ernesto," Inez said. "Think what it will mean to us to be free. Once we're on that ship bound for the United States, no one can harm us."

Andrew flattened himself in the tall grass, forgetting all about the fire. The sky was crimson now, and the wind carried the smell of burning wood. But Andrew hardly noticed.

His eyes were wide and he could feel his heart thumping. Inez and Ernesto were planning to run away.

The fires were still flickering, with a pale light, against the sky. It was almost dawn now. Andrew waited until Inez and Ernesto had left. Then, slowly, he made his way home.

He tried the huge front door. It was locked. Too late, he remembered that all the doors were locked at night. He prowled around the house, shivering in the cool, damp air of early morning, until he found an open window; bracing himself on the wide stone sill, he scrambled up and dropped to the floor inside.

A moment later, he was startled to find himself confronting his stepfather, who was seated at one end of the long, polished dining room table, smoking a cigar and drinking his morning coffee.

Julio was equally surprised. "Where have you been?" he demanded, rising from the table and setting his cup down with a loud clinking sound. "Come here."

Andrew obeyed, and Julio saw that the boy's shirt was torn, and marked with dirt and grass stains; his breeches were in an equally disreputable state.

"How did you get yourself into such a condition?"

Andrew did not answer, but began to tremble; Julio saw the guilty look in his gray eyes and relented silently. The boy had been up to mischief, but Julio remembered that he and his brothers had often been mixed up in one trifling escapade or another during the years that they were growing up.

Julio took Andrew by the shoulder and set him down in a chair.

"Very well, now, tell me. Have you done something you were forbidden to do?"

Andrew nodded, his underlip starting to tremble; he was close to tears.

"Come now," Julio said, "it can't be as bad as that."

"It is, though." Andrew looked about as if seeking a means of escape.

"Speak up."

"I went out last night to see the fire."

"Against my orders?"

Andrew sniffed and rubbed the back of one dirty hand across his eyes. "I didn't go all the way to where the fire was. Only to a hill near the *barracones*. I was tired and I fell asleep, and when I woke up I saw the fire. And then I heard them talking, and I was scared they'd find me but they didn't—"

Julio handed the boy a handkerchief. "Blow your nose," he said. "And stop talking in riddles. Who are 'they'?"

Andrew obeyed, but remained silent.

"All right," Julio said. "You left the house. Without being seen, I presume. How?"

"I climbed down the tree outside my room."

Julio himself had often used the same means of exit as a child.

"And then?"

"I walked to the hill I told you about. The big one with the bamboo trees on top. I didn't go anywhere close to the fire. I only wanted to watch."

"And you fell asleep and had a bad dream, is that it?"

He shook his head. "It wasn't any dream. Señor, it's wrong for slaves to run away, isn't it?" He kicked the chair with one foot. "I mean, they belong to you. Like Conquistador. Or the new bulls you had shipped from Spain."

"Of course. But we weren't talking about slaves." Julio

stopped and peered at the boy. "And there was no run-away last night."

"But there's going to be."

Julio's hand shot out, and he gripped Andrew's shoulder so hard that the boy cried out.

"What are you saying? You're making all this up, aren't you? So you won't be punished."

Andrew shook his head. "I knew you'd punish me if you caught me. But it's true, all the same. About the slaves. I heard them."

Julio relaxed his grip. "I want you to tell me everything you heard."

After the trees had been cleared away, and the stumps and rocks removed, the work at Villanueva began to slacken off. The harvest had been a good one, and next year's should be even better.

Julio Vargas, although he was a hard master, had never denied his slaves the celebration that marked the end of the harvest: the drum dances that went on for three days, with plentiful rations of cane brandy. Drucilla, knowing this from past years, had planned to make her escape during the celebration.

She had been afraid that Julio might object to her request to drive into Cienfuegos and visit with Señora Tacón, the middle-aged widow of a colonel who had served with Julio in the cavalry. But he had given his permission readily. Although it was customary for the master and the overseers to attend the drum dances, the planters' wives did not go to these celebrations. "The dances are bawdy," Julio had explained, during her first year at Villanueva. "And the words of the songs are worse."

This year, Drucilla arose early on the morning of the harvest dance, but she waited until Julio had left for the *barracones* before starting her preparations.

She packed a small trunk and put a bag, containing a collection of small but expensive jewels, into the bosom of her dress.

After the cook had left for the festivities, Inez had slipped into the pantry, and had filled a basket with food: a roast chicken, a ham, fruit, and bread. She added a bottle of brandy and several bottles of water.

Andrew made no comment when Drucilla told him he was to accompany her on the visit to Señora Tacón, nor had he asked to be allowed to go to the drum dance instead. She realized that the boy had been unusually subdued these last few weeks. At times, she was sure he was avoiding her.

She told herself it didn't matter. Once she had him out of Cuba and in New York with her, she would win him back again. And one day, she would be able to take him to his father.

Soon, she thought. *Let it be soon.*

The thought of showing Kevin his son for the first time gave her courage and made it possible for her to carry out the preparations for her flight.

It was midmorning when she descended the stairs and left the house. Andrew was with her, wearing a new blue linen suit, and a round straw hat with blue ribbons. Drucilla looked fresh and cool, in spite of her advanced pregnancy, in a loose gown of pale gray and white striped silk, and a wide leghorn hat trimmed with white flowers. Her gray parasol was trimmed with lace and lined with rose-colored silk.

Pablo, a tall, thin black man in fine purple and gold livery, drew up before the house; Inez was already seated in the volante; she had managed to push the trunk and basket under her seat. Her full, starched cotton skirts were spread out around her, and most of her chestnut hair was pushed up under her turban. She was outwardly composed, but Drucilla saw the fear in her soft brown eyes. She gave the maid an encouraging smile.

Pablo sprang down and helped Drucilla and Andrew into the volante. He handed the boy a stick of sugar cane to chew on. Drucilla had never liked this particular custom. A growing boy should have meat and eggs and plenty of milk, not sweets. But she reminded herself that Andrew would soon learn new customs.

Pablo got back on the front seat, cracked his whip, and the horses trotted forward, along the avenue of royal palms. Drucilla turned to look back at the big, rambling stone house. The sun glittered on the window panes. She felt a pang, remembering that Julio had removed the iron bars and put in glass; that he had ordered silk drapes.

I've treated you like a queen. I've done everything to make you happy.

But he had lied to her about Kevin. He had let her believe Kevin was dead. She could understand, even pity him—but she could not wholly forgive him.

The volante turned off the avenue of palms, and onto a road that led through the stripped cane fields. Close to the edge of the southern boundary was a grove of banana trees. Ernesto would be waiting there.

Usually, Drucilla reveled in the beauty of the plantation, the sunlit acres, the palm fronds glittering like dark green spears against the blue of the sky, the flowers—yellow, purple, red, and white—that spilled over the rocks in incredible profusion. Today, she scarcely saw her surroundings.

From the *barracones*, she heard the sound of the drums, and the cries of the dancers. How could slaves dance and make merry after the backbreaking work of the harvest? How could they forget, even for a little while, the cruelty that was their lot?

Julio might call them animals, but Drucilla knew better. Looking over at Inez, she thought how much courage it had taken for the octoroon to agree to the escape plan. And Ernesto, with the marks of the overseer's whip still on his back; the brand scarring his face, had agreed to risk more punishment, in the hope of gaining his freedom.

The road shimmered in the sunlight and Drucilla leaned forward, squinting a little. There it was. The grove of banana trees. She put an arm around Andrew, who looked up at her in surprise, but continued to chew on his sugar cane.

Every muscle in her body tensed, as she saw Ernesto step out from the shadow of the trees. She shut her eyes for a moment, then opened them again and screamed.

Julio rode out of the bamboo thicket on the opposite side of the road; he was mounted on Conquistador, and was accompanied by Ruiz, the *mayoral*, and half a dozen black slave drivers. Pablo jerked on the reins and brought the volante to a stop; Ernesto gave a hoarse cry and tried to dive back into the grove of banana trees, but Ruiz drew a pistol and shouted: "Stop, right there."

The drivers threw themselves on Ernesto, who fought with astonishing strength, until Ruiz stepped in and brought the pistol down on the side of his head, not once, but three times. Ernesto slumped forward, the blacks supporting his limp body.

"Take him to the *barracones*, and lock him in a cell," Julio ordered. "You, Ruiz—get that black slut down from there."

Ruiz swung Inez out of the volante and, when she tried to free herself, clawing at his face, he dealt her a hard, backhanded blow on the cheek.

Andrew had dropped his stick of sugar cane and was clutching at Drucilla's skirt with sticky hands.

Julio turned his head and told Pablo: "Turn the volante around. Señora Vargas is going back to the house with me."

Andrew threw one terrified glance at his stepfather, then, too frightened to cry, he buried his face in his mother's lap.

Julio did not speak to Drucilla on the ride home; he slowed Conquistador to a walk and kept pace with the volante. His eyes were set on the road ahead. At the house, he remained outside for awhile, talking to Pablo. Drucilla led Andrew upstairs and went into her bedroom, while Luz led the child away. A little while later, Julio joined Drucilla.

"I knew about Inez and Ernesto. Your son was most informative. Of course, he didn't realize that you and he were to take part in this ridiculous plan."

"There was no plan. I was going to see Señora Tacón, as I told you. Perhaps Ernesto had no business being out of the *barracones*, but he—"

"Drucilla, *por favor*. That trunk in the volante, under the seat. Oh, yes, I found it there. And food enough for a week." He paused. "What I don't understand is how you planned to pay the passage to the United States for the four of you."

It was futile to go on denying the truth. Somehow Andrew had overheard enough of the plan to alert Julio.

She tried to comfort herself with the knowledge that her son had not, at least, betrayed her. He hadn't known, or understood that she was involved. And he had not seen anything wrong with warning Julio of the intended escape of a pair of slaves. How could he, when Julio had taught him that slaves were property without human feelings or needs?

"I know you're resourceful, my dear, but I still want to find out what you planned to use for passage money. There was nothing in the trunk to—"

His eyes moved swiftly over her, and then he put a hand into the deep ruffle that edged the top of her gown. He tore the bodice open, and thrust hard, searching fingers into her camisole. He pulled out the small chamois bag, threw the contents on the bed. The diamond earrings Charlotte Tremayne had given her on her arrival at Newport, that first summer. The sapphire-and-diamond butterfly Julio had bought for her in Paris. A pair of fine jade earrings. A diamond-and-ruby bracelet.

He seized her wrist and turned her hand palm downward.

"Then, of course, there's your diamond wedding band. I suppose you were going to sell that, too. It means nothing to you now—if it ever did."

Her mind was whirling and, out of all he had said, she remembered only his remark about Andrew. "He didn't know," she said. "He thought I was taking him on a visit to Cienfuegos."

"That's right. You look puzzled, my dear. It's really quite simple. The night we burned the trees, he slipped out to watch, and he overheard Inez and Ernesto. He didn't betray you. He didn't understand that you were the instigator of the plan. He only caught bits and pieces of the conversation, you see. But after he told me what he'd heard, I watched and waited. I alerted Ruiz and a few of the household slaves. It wasn't difficult."

"You set the slaves to spy on me?"

"Don't play the outraged wife. It doesn't suit you."

"What—are you going to do?"

"To you? Nothing at the moment. Except to keep you here in the house, in your room if necessary."

"And the others?"

"The two blacks? What do you suppose? Death is the only proper punishment for runaways. Ernesto will be flogged to death, as he should have been the first time he tried to escape. Perhaps Ruiz will think of a few other things to do to him, first. And Inez can watch. Then, afterward—"

"You can't kill her. Julio, she's only eighteen—a girl—"

"And as devious as any other female, black or white."

She ignored the implication. "I forced Inez to help me. She was afraid not to."

He smiled. "There's not a slave in this house who is afraid of you, my dear."

His eyes studied her, without emotion. "You look quite pale, my dear. I'd better send Luz in to look after you."

"She's taking care of Andrew."

"*No importa.* I will take Andrew with me to the *barracones*. His reward for being so helpful."

He turned away, and started for the door. "Too bad we must spoil the celebration. But two executions will serve to remind the rest how to behave. There'll be no more escapes from Villanueva." His eyes met hers. "None, Drucilla."

Twenty-six

DRUCILLA went after him, seized his arm, and cried:
"You can't do this—you mustn't—"

He flung her off and slammed the door behind him. She sank to the floor and the room began to spin slowly.

Luz, Andrew's nurse, found her and helped her to her feet. "Please, Señora. The master says you must stay here until he returns."

"But I can't. I've got to go down to the *barracones*. . . ."

"There is nothing you can do," the huge black woman said quietly. "Come, lie down, and I will bring you something to help you rest. A cup of herb tea, perhaps."

For all her enormous bulk and slow movements, Luz was strong. She put an arm around Drucilla and led her to the bed. Then, calling for one of the kitchen maids, Luz told her to bring the tea. "If you can sleep a little—"

"I'd like to sleep—forever," Drucilla said. Her voice sounded weak and drained. For the first time in years, she remembered how Beth Cameron, unable to endure her existence, had taken a bottle of laudanum in Mrs. Baxley's boardinghouse.

How peaceful Beth had looked, lying in her coffin, in her white silk dress. . . .

Drucilla started and pushed the treacherous thought away. She was frightened that it had come to her. She had Andrew to think about. And her unborn baby. And Kevin.

But, she thought in despair, Andrew had become Julio's pawn, a weapon to be used against her. A little boy, lost, confused, drawn to the man he thought was strong and all-powerful. The baby would belong to Julio, too. His own child, to be molded by him.

And Kevin? She would never see Kevin again.

She had no illusions about what her position would be at Villanueva from now on. Julio could, if he chose, keep her a prisoner here in the house. As much a slave as any of those blacks in the *barracones*. He could keep her locked in her room, or even chained in the cellar, if he wanted to. No one would ask questions. No one would interfere. Their nearest neighbors, the Santovenias, were away in Spain.

And after today, no slave, however devoted, would dare to lift a hand to help her. Not after they had witnessed the torture and killing of Inez and her lover.

The drums were silent now. Drucilla heard the wind in the palms; the harsh screams of a flock of parrots flying over the house; the muted voices of the household slaves.

The herb tea did not make her sleep, but whatever it contained made her a little calmer. She closed her eyes afterward, and willed herself to think.

When, a few hours later, she heard the clatter of hooves outside, she was able to get up, to order Luz to bring her a fresh gown and arrange her hair. Julio would not find her cowering in her room.

She went out into the hall and down the stairs to meet her husband, and Luz followed her like a watchdog. She had reached the foot of the stairs when the great front door swung open, and Julio came inside. One look told her something was terribly wrong. Andrew was with him, and Ruiz and Cespedes. And two other white men she knew only by sight. The *maestro de azúcar*, the young French

367

technician, and his assistant, who had been hired to supervise the details of the heating and mixture of the syrup. Julio was giving orders to the men in a hard, controlled voice.

Andrew ran up to her, gave her one terrified look, and then allowed Luz to scoop him up and carry him to his room. Usually, the boy protested against such coddling, but now he acted thoroughly cowed.

Drucilla saw, as she drew nearer, that the French *maestro de azúcar* was holding a revolver—a little awkwardly, as if he had never handled a weapon before. His assistant was equally nonplussed when Ruiz thrust a revolver into his hand.

It was a moment before Julio became aware of Drucilla. Then he said: "There was trouble down at the *barracones*. The black bastards tried to rush us."

"An uprising?" Drucilla asked.

"They're drunk on cane brandy," he said. "And worked up by those drum dances. The dances have something to do with their barbaric African religion."

"What happened?"

"After Ruiz finished off Ernesto and was getting started on Inez, the blacks began carrying on like cattle before a hurricane. Then they moved in on us. We killed a few of them. Then we mounted and rode back to the house."

"They'll come here, won't they?" she asked. Strange, she wasn't afraid. She felt nothing at all.

"Probably not," he said. "We're only taking precautions. They have no guns. What can they hope to do against us?"

"You told me once that there had been an uprising in your grandfather's time. You said there'd never be another—"

"And there wouldn't have been, except for you. I never should have let you talk me into sparing Ernesto's life that first time he ran away. But that wasn't enough. You had to plot with him and with Inez."

He turned away to shout at the young Frenchman. "*Madre de Dios*, Señor Lefevre—that revolver's not a live snake. It won't bite you. Ruiz, show him—and this other one—how to shoot those things."

"Yes, Señor Vargas. But first, we should consider the household slaves. Perhaps they ought to be locked in the cellar."

"Nonsense. A bunch of maids, the butler, and my valet, Miguel? They think they're a different breed from the field workers, you know that. They won't get swept away by the frenzy."

Julio shouted for Miguel, who came hurrying downstairs.

"Close the shutters," he said. "And have the butler bring wine for the men here."

Drucilla looked at the boy, seeing the long scar that marred his otherwise handsome, golden-skinned face. Since that day when Julio had struck him with the riding crop, then ordered him to report for a flogging, the boy had done his work swiftly, efficiently, and in silence. Now Miguel inclined his head and hurried off to obey.

Julio turned back to Drucilla. "You'd better go to your room and stay there."

"I'm not afraid."

"There is no reason you should be. The blacks may set a few fires. They may even damage some of the equipment at the mills. But they're too afraid to try to rush the house."

"Then why did you arm all the men and order the shutters closed?"

"A precaution, nothing more. You don't know these blacks. They'll get roaring drunk, smash and burn the mills, perhaps, and a few of the bolder ones may run off into the hills."

"They did much more than that in Haiti in 1791," Lefevre said. "Shouldn't we send for troops, Señor Vargas?"

"Troops? The nearest garrison's twenty miles from here. By the time the troops arrived, we'd have the blacks under control and the ringleaders hanged."

But Drucilla intercepted the swift look that passed between her husband and the Frenchman, and she suspected that Julio's words were for her benefit.

She turned and went back upstairs, to try to comfort Andrew although she was sure there was nothing she could ever say or do to wipe out the memories of the horrors the child had witnessed today.

It was after dark when the first of the slaves came slipping into the grounds in front of the house. Drucilla had managed to persuade Andrew to eat some bread and butter, and drink a glass of warm milk. Now he was dozing on his bed, tossing fitfully, and mumbling to himself from time to time.

The house was very warm, now that the shutters had been closed. Drucilla had not eaten all that day, but she was not hungry. The heavy, humid air deadened her appetite, and each time she thought about what had happened to Ernesto, her stomach churned. A few times she felt hard thrusts of pain inside.

Was Inez still alive? Julio had said that the slaves had attacked when Ruiz had begun to torture the girl. She had to know what had happened. She left Andrew with Luz and went back downstairs.

Julio was kneeling beside one of the windows. He had opened one of the shutters a little and was firing out into the garden. She heard a hoarse cry. One of the slaves must have been hit. Were they so close, then?

From the other rooms at the sides of the house, she heard more firing.

Ruiz came over to Julio and said: "Señor, perhaps if one of us could get through to the Santovenia plantation, we could get help."

"Mateo Santovenia's in Spain."

"His overseers are there. And they have guns. Shall I try it, señor?"

Drucilla's nerves were no longer numbed with despair, and she felt a shock of fear. Ruiz would not be willing to take such a risk unless he thought it would be more dangerous if they all remained in the house, without reinforcements.

"It's not necessary," Julio said. "After we've picked off a few more of those blacks, the rest will go skulking back to the *barracones*, you'll see. Even in my grandfather's time, when they had their uprising, they didn't dare rush the house."

"In your grandfather's time, there was none of this talk of abolition to stir them up. Also, in those days, this house was a fortress, with an oak door three feet thick and iron bars at the windows."

Miguel came into the room, moving softly as he always did. In the light of the one lamp that was burning in the room, Drucilla saw the scar. Julio's half-brother. Sired by the same man.

"Here is fresh coffee and brandy," Miguel said. "If you and the other gentlemen want food, I can prepare it."

"Where's the cook?" Julio demanded.

"She's hiding in the cellar with the maids. They are very frightened, señor. They are of no use at all."

"And the butler?"

"I can't find him."

"No doubt he's hiding in the cellar with the women," Julio said scornfully. "You see, Ruiz, they're all a pack of frightened cattle. We're in no danger from them." He crouched down again, took careful aim, and a moment later the revolver cracked, and Drucilla heard an agonized shriek from outside.

"But that bitch, Inez, is out there," Ruiz said. "She's urging them on, yelling like a fury. They think she is *una bruja,* like her grandmother was. They think she has powers to protect them."

"That's enough." Julio threw a swift glance at Ruiz. "In a moment you'll have my wife in hysterics, like those women in the cellar."

"I'm not in the least hysterical," Drucilla said. "But Señor Ruiz may be right. Inez is almost white, you know, and a household slave. And since she has joined forces with the rest of them, it may give them courage—particularly if they believe she has some sort of unearthly powers."

"Her powers were not great enough to save Ernesto," Julio said. "Now, enough of this. Go back to your room."

Drucilla went upstairs again and stretched out on the bed. There was a dull pain at the small of her back, her legs ached, aand she felt small, fleeting contractions in the pit of her stomach. "I really should try to eat," she thought, but she was too tired to call for Miguel and ask him to bring her food.

It was quiet outside the house now. She could not hear any sound from the slaves. And except for an occasional shot, the firing had slackened off.

Had Julio been right about the uprising after all? Perhaps the slaves had lost their nerve, and had withdrawn to the *barracones* to sleep off the effects of the cáne brandy. A few of the bolder ones might have gone off into the hills. After all, they had not acted according to an organized plan; the uprising had been set off by the death of Ernesto, and the threat of death for Inez.

Julio had once told her that uprisings rarely happened during the harvest; perhaps the backbreaking work left them too exhausted to do anything but snatch a few hours of sleep at the end of each day. But with the festival, there had been a relaxation of tension, an ample supply of cane brandy, and the drumming and dancing to excite them. And then, abruptly, the festival had been stopped; they had witnessed, instead, an execution of one of their leaders.

And as for Inez, it might be true they thought she was *una bruja*. Drucilla had no idea of the complicated religions that had survived on the passage from Africa to Cuba, that had taken strange, barbaric forms here in the New World. Occasionally, she had overheard gossip among the house slaves about spells for winning the love of a favored male, for rendering an unwanted suitor impotent, for destroying an enemy. Once she had found some small stones and a few feathers arranged in a curious, complicated pattern in front of the stable door. That had been the day after Conquistador had kicked one of the grooms and split the man's skull.

Did the slaves really think that their pitiful spells were strong enough to win over the guns and whips of the master and his overseers? Or were the blacks desperate enough to risk an uprising, even though they knew it would fail in the end, and that the reprisals would be unspeakable? Drucilla realized that she really knew very little about these people who produced such great wealth for Julio, whose labors provided the silk drapes, the rosewood furniture, the fine crystal and silver that made Villanueva a showplace.

She moved restlessly on the bed. She had not changed to her nightgown, but had only removed her shoes and unbuttoned her bodice. Although it was after midnight, the heat had not diminished. The air was heavy. From the pond beside the house, a chorus of bullfrogs filled the night with their monotonous croaking. Maybe it would rain by morning. Maybe by morning, the uprising would be over.

She tried not to think about what would happen then, to the slaves who had rebelled. And to her. She closed her eyes and fell into a light sleep.

Julio was shaking her by the shoulder, leaning over the bed. She gave a violent start and sat up. She saw, through the cracks in the shutters, an odd, pinkish glow. Could it be morning already?

"Get up," Julio said. "We'll have to leave the house."

"What's happening? It was so quiet, I thought the slaves had gone back to the *barracones*."

She heard the crack of a revolver, even as she spoke.

"We've almost run out of ammunition, and those black swine have guessed it, I think. They're back with torches. They're going to set fire to the house."

Drucilla stood up, and he put an arm around her to steady her. "Now listen carefully," he said. "You'll be all right, if you don't panic. We still have a chance. We'll leave by the back way, through the kitchen. The men downstairs will keep firing. You'll go and hide in the woods. I'll get through to the stables, saddle Conquistador, and ride to the Santovenias' plantation. I'll dispatch a man from there to go to the garrison for troops, and I'll bring back the rest of the *mayorales*, with guns and ammunition."

He paused, as Miguel appeared in the doorway, leading Andrew by the hand; the little boy was sleepy, confused, but fully dressed.

"Put a shawl over you," Julio told her. "See that your hair is well covered."

She obeyed without hesitation. Julio was taking a desperate gamble. The uprising might have spread to other plantations by that incomprehensible system of communication known only to the blacks. But this was their only chance, and she would do nothing to slow Julio down. She put on her shoes and fastened them, feeling, as she bent over, a sharp thrust of pain low down in her belly. She ignored it, and a moment later it had passed.

"Miguel will go with you and Andrew," Julio said. "He knows a number of hiding places in the forest. Perhaps one of the caves."

The valet nodded. "I'll see they're safely hidden, señor."

Then Miguel added: "I've heard the talk downstairs—most of the ammunition's gone, isn't it?"

"That's right. There should have been a dozen boxes more, by my count, but—" He shrugged. "No matter. I'll be back by nightfall tomorrow with the Santovenias' men. And the garrison troops will set out as soon as they get our message."

"And then?"

"Need you ask, Miguel? The ringleaders will be hanged; and the rest will be locked up on short rations, until they come to their senses."

Miguel said no more. They went down the back stairway and out through the empty kitchen. The fragrant night breeze stirred in the branches of the cinnamon trees behind the house. Julio stopped and drew Drucilla to him.

"You've never lacked for courage," he said. "In that way, at least, you've never disappointed me. Don't do so now."

"Julio—if only I could—"

"No more talk." He bent and his lips brushed hers. "Go now," he said, releasing her. She turned and obeyed, following Miguel and Andrew along the back of the house, keeping in the shadows.

She stumbled over something. Looking down, she saw the body of a black man, his chest torn and covered with dried blood. She caught the glint of light on the blade of the machete that was beside him. "Take it," she told Miguel. "We may need it, getting through the forest."

She took Andrew's hand, and Miguel picked up the machete. As they cleared the back of the house, she was dazzled by the glare of flames. The front of the house was blazing. She heard the triumphant yells of the slaves. The smashing of glass. No bars on the windows now, to keep them out. Her silk drapes would burn, and the embroidered wall hangings, and the rosewood furniture.

Andrew cried out. She put a hand over his mouth. "Hush," she said fiercely. "They mustn't hear us."

She was blinded for a moment by the red and gold of the flames, and when she looked into the darkness of the trees up ahead, she could no longer see Miguel. She whispered his name, but he did not answer. Had he panicked and run off into the woods without her?

Then Andrew tugged at her hand. "Look," he cried. "Over there—by the stables."

In the reflected glare from the fire, she saw Julio, mounted on Conquistador. He was spurring the large horse forward, as if leading his cavalry troop. He would get through, she thought, with a curious kind of pride. She began moving cautiously toward the wooded area again, and was in among the bushes on the edge of it, when she stopped and stifled a cry.

Miguel had not gone into the woods at all. He had slipped around the side of the house, and now he was brandishing his machete, and shouting to the slaves: "Here—back here—the master's getting away. He's going for troops—this way—"

Drucilla dragged Andrew into a bamboo thicket and pulled him down beside her. She held him against the swollen curve of her body.

The slaves, led by Miguel, ran forward, passing the place where she and Andrew lay hidden. She saw Julio draw his revolver and take aim at Miguel, but at that same moment, another slave struck Conquistador across the flank with a machete, and the horse reared. Julio's shot went wide of the mark. A dozen slaves were slashing at the horse now, and Drucilla winced as she heard the shrill whinnying and saw the stallion go down, its entrails spilling onto the ground.

Julio managed to roll clear and get back on his feet. He fired, hitting one slave, then another. When the revolver was empty, the slaves rushed him, and he struck two of them down with the barrel; then they were all upon him, a dark tide, and their machetes rose and fell. Drucilla heard Julio scream, heard the scream cut off abruptly.

It took all her strength to hold Andrew still, and once again, she put her hand over his mouth. She felt the hot tears spilling down her cheeks.

Miguel, holding Julio's revolver, was urging the other slaves back to the house. And Inez was in the thick of the mob, mounted on a mule, her chestnut hair whipping around her face, her eyes narrow and glittering. Her cotton dress was ripped; her small, golden breasts were bare. Her skirt was bunched up around her thighs, and her long naked legs gripped the sides of the mule. She was screaming words Drucilla did not understand. Only some were Spanish.

Drucilla felt Andrew writhing in her grasp, and then the child went limp. Had she suffocated him? She took her hand away. No, he was still breathing.

She picked him up, and bending low, she moved deeper into the trees. Branches cut her face and arms, drawing blood; and the weight of the child sent waves of pain through her swollen body, but she kept moving, holding his head against her shoulder. Even here in the wooded area, she could smell the smoke from the house.

She hoped that the household slaves, the cook, the maids and the butler, had managed to get out of the cellar. She even found herself hoping that Ruiz and Cespedes might escape, or strangle from the smoke before the slaves could reach them. And the others, too: the young French *maestro de azúcar* and his assistant, who had never harmed the slaves at all. She was sure that the slaves would make no exceptions but kill every white person they could reach.

Then she stopped thinking and simply moved forward like an automaton, until she tripped over a tree root and fell, twisting her body so that she would not hurt Andrew.

She hit the ground and pain exploded inside her. She was going to black out. She heard Andrew whimpering.

"Be still—and don't leave me," she managed to say. "Stay here—don't—"

After that she drifted in and out of oblivion. She felt hands lifting her. She heard Andrew crying. Then his cry was cut off.

"They've killed him," she thought. "Now they'll kill me, too." It didn't matter to her now.

She was in a dark, foul-smelling place. She felt pain again; the same kind of pain she had known when Andrew was born. But it was too early for this baby . . . too early . . . .

She saw a tiny pinprick of light that wavered, then became a candle flame. "Señora, can you hear me?"

"Miguel?"

"You're safe now," Miguel said. "The child, also. I put him farther back in the cave. He's sleeping."

"Why didn't you kill us, too?"

"You can ask that? The fieldhands don't know you. But we do—Inez and the others who worked in the house. That day the master struck me with his crop, you tried to stop him. And when he sent me to the *mayoral* to be punished, you pleaded for me. I heard you."

She tried to speak, but pain gripped her again. Miguel watched her face. "You need a woman with you now. You need Inez. Can you stand it here, with only Andrew, until I can bring her back?"

"Yes—I think so."

"You won't cry out, no matter how bad the pain gets? There may be some stray fieldhands in the woods here. If they find you—"

"I know. I won't make any noise." She hoped she could keep her promise.

Miguel held a bottle of water to her lips and supported her while she drank. "I'll leave this here beside you," he said.

Then she heard a curious sound from the depths of the cave. "*Chui, chui, chui.*" Like some weird kind of bird.

Miguel smiled. "Those are only bats."

"Bats?"

"These caves are full of them. And the floors of the

caves are covered with bat droppings. They turn to dry powder, and they're soft as a feather bed."

So that was the foul odor she had been aware of. She was beyond revulsion now. Still she was grateful when Miguel added: "They're quite harmless, the bats." He rose and said: "I'll go now. I don't know how long it will be before I can bring Inez back with me. The others must not become suspicious."

"Suppose Andrew wakes up."

"I told him that if he moved or made a sound, the field-hands would find you and kill you both."

She shuddered, thinking how terrified Andrew must have been, but she knew that Miguel's action had been necessary. This had been a dreadful time for the child: in one day, his whole world had exploded into a nightmare of burning and killing. He had seen Ernesto flogged to death and Julio cut to pieces by the machetes of the slaves. His home was in flames, and he lay hidden here in this foul-smelling cave with a mother too ill to comfort him. Why had she brought the child to Cuba? Better by far, if she had let Gwen or Hazel Seaton raise him, back in the safety of Charleston.

She sank into a whirling, shifting darkness, coming back from time to time, only to writhe in pain. Finally, she stuffed a corner of her shawl between her teeth and bit down each time she felt the need to cry out. Her body was soaked with sweat.

She heard the chittering of the bats from the back of the cave. Once, she heard a group of noisy, drunken slaves, laughing and shouting to each other, and she held her breath, but they passed by. Heading for the shell of the house, she supposed. Hoping to find some loot that had not been destroyed in the fire. Another time, she heard the frenzied beating of drums and the sound of chanting, in a language she did not understand.

Then she felt a hand on her hair, brushing the sweat-drenched tendrils back from her face. "Inez?"

"I'm here, señora. And Miguel, too. He's back there with Andrew."

Inez was touching her body, with strong, purposeful

378

hands. There was more pain. "It will be over soon," Inez said. "Only a little longer, now."

"It's dangerous for you to be here," Drucilla gasped out, between pains. "If the others find out—"

Inez said. "I went off with Miguel, hand in hand. If the others noticed, they thought we were going to bed down together. That's what the rest are doing—those who aren't still dancing or sleeping off the cane brandy."

Drucilla managed a smile but it froze on her lips. She felt a wrenching, tearing sensation, and clung to Inez.

The last thing she heard was Inez saying, "It was too soon . . . he could not have lived. . . ."

And Miguel's reply. "Better this way . . . it would have been another Vargas. . . ."

Twenty-seven

WHENEVER Kevin Farrell's boat, the *Medea*, docked in New York harbor, he made it a point to visit Maria Barbosa. On this particular spring evening, in 1880, he stood waiting for her, in the showroom of her small but elegant dress shop, at Broadway and Twelfth Street, in the fashionable "Ladies' Mile."

As he stood looking around the room, with its gray and gold hangings, and its thick gray rug, he realized that these visits were no longer made out of a sense of duty. He had felt responsible for Maria, the first time he had seen her in the cabin of the *Medea*, and had learned of the death of her brother; he had brought her to New York and provided the money to set her up in the shop, which now employed three assistants. And he had introduced her to the circle of Cuban exiles who had settled in New York.

This last year, he had come to look forward to seeing her each time he completed a successful voyage to some Caribbean port. She was more beautiful every time he saw her, and he enjoyed squiring her around the city.

She had been sixteen at their first meeting; and he had

been in no condition to respond to feminine charms. Now, however, she was nearly twenty, a tall, shapely young woman with huge brown eyes under thick dark lashes, a smooth olive skin, and full, softly-curved red lips. She had an air of elegance about her and a quiet dignity that sometimes reminded him of Diego.

She had closed the shop a little early tonight, and was changing for the evening, in her living quarters on the second floor. Kevin began to pace restlessly about the shop, feeling out of place among these feminine fripperies: a hat edged with lace and trimmed with artificial rosebuds and pink silk ribbons; a silk cape sparkling with jet beads; shawls and parasols, ivory combs and Japanese fans, all attractively displayed in their glass showcases.

He turned, hearing the soft whisper of taffeta. The curtains at the rear of the shop parted, and Maria came to him saying: "I'm sorry I'm late. I had to say a few words to the seamstresses. Poor girls, they're still at work. I feel quite guilty about leaving them to go out for an evening's entertainment."

"You've earned it," Kevin said. "The shop looks prosperous. And you look very lovely indeed."

Her gown was rose-colored taffeta, trimmed with black lace; it left her shoulders bare and showed the soft, rounded curves of her bosom. Her dark hair was draped with a delicate black lace veil for, although she had been away from Cuba these last five years, she had not abandoned the mantilla. She wore it now without a comb, but with two tiny jeweled pins to hold it in place.

Kevin helped her put on the satin-lined black velvet cape. Then she took his arm, and they went out to the hansom cab he had left waiting at the curb.

Inside, she settled next to him, and he told her: "I have tickets for the performance at Booth's Theater. They're doing *A Midsummer Night's Dream*. Afterward, if you like we'll dine at Delmonico's."

"It all sounds very grand," she said.

"I want tonight to be special."

Her large, dark eyes grew troubled. "That means you're leaving again soon, doesn't it?"

"As soon as we finish loading the cargo," he told her.

"And when will that be?"

"Day after tomorrow."

"I almost wish you were not going, Kevin."

He put his hand over hers and pressed it gently. "Don't concern yourself, Maria. I'll be quite safe—this time."

She drew closer to him. "I don't understand how you can go back to Cuba, even now."

"Conditions have changed. You know that. And you will go back there yourself, one day—when all this is over. I'm sure you must be homesick for the island at times, aren't you?"

"I miss the warmth and the sunlight. The sound of my own language. Many things. But when I remember what happened to Diego and to you—" Maria shuddered. "One does not forget such things," she said.

"I haven't forgotten, either," he said. "That's the only reason I'm taking this cargo to Havana. But don't spoil our evening with such talk. I know you'll enjoy the performance tonight. The players at Booth's are always good, and the scenery is quite remarkable. I'm told the stage equipment is far superior to anything they've had in New York before. Sets can be raised to the stage from below or lowered from above."

"I'm sure it's splendid," she said. "You're so kind to me, Kevin. You always take me to such wonderful places when you're here in town. And you gave me the shop—I never could have managed to save enough for that without you—"

"You've nearly paid me back," he reminded her. "Not that I wanted you to, my dear."

"It was necessary." Her cheeks flushed, and Kevin understood. No respectable young woman could allow a man who was not a relative to set her up in business; not unless she was his mistress. There had never been any suggestion of intimacies between Kevin and Maria.

She was Diego's sister. But she was also a beautiful and desirable young woman. Like most Cuban girls, she had reached physical maturity early. Her breasts were full and rounded, and she held her head high, with calm self-assurance. There was an aura of lush femininity about her that no man could ignore.

At the same time, Kevin thought, there was something childlike in her expression as she looked at her surroundings. She did not behave in the cool, slightly bored way that was fashionable with many of the ladies around her. She was wide-eyed with admiration as she surveyed the walls and ceiling of the theater, which were frescoed and ornamented with fine bas-reliefs in plaster. The seats were luxuriously upholstered to harmonize with the rich carpeting.

The orchestra began to play as she seated herself beside Kevin, and she leaned forward, her lips parted. Kevin was more interested in observing Maria than in watching the play.

After the performance, he took her to Delmonico's at Fifth Avenue and Twenty-Sixth Street and, even after they were seated and he had ordered, he realized she was still under the spell of the play.

"There are fine theaters in Havana, but I have never seen anything like tonight's performance."

A moment later, she broke off and put a hand on Kevin's arm. Although her touch was light, he was surprised and a little disconcerted at his response to this physical contact. "You're sure you will be safe in Havana?"

"I've told you—and you have enough friends among the Cuban exiles to know—the situation is quite different now."

"But you'll be carrying weapons, the same as before."

"Only to the outside of the harbor. They'll be taken off there by fishing boats, and I'll be paid on the spot. I'll be carrying other merchandise, too. Legal merchandise."

She sighed. "You think this uprising will be more successful than the last?"

"I don't know. But I do know that one day—soon—Cuba will be free from Spain. Emancipation is not far off now."

"I don't see the connection—"

"Once the slaves are free, the Cuban planters won't need Spanish troops to keep their workers under control. There'll be no more fear of uprisings. Then even wealthy Cubans with large holdings will have nothing to gain from their ties with Spain."

"Yes, I see that. And they'll be glad to be free of Spanish monopolies, to trade with any country they choose."

"They're trading with the United States already. But it will be easier, once Spain's out of the picture."

"Kevin, I can't think about such things now. I'm afraid for you. You don't know what you looked like, that first time I saw you in your cabin aboard the *Medea*."

"I have a fairly good idea. But, Maria—" He gave her a level look from under his black brows. "Would you rather I had lied to you? Told you I was taking another shipment of machinery to Barbados or Jamaica?"

"No. You must not lie to me, ever. You must always be honest, as I am with you—" She looked away, and her cheeks grew pink. She dropped her menu and bent to pick it up, and he knew she was concealing something. A moment later, when their eyes met, he guessed.

"Maria—"

"Yes," she said quietly. "It's true. I love you, Kevin. I have from the first time I saw you."

"Impossible," he said, trying to make light of her words. "You have just implied I was a battered wreck the first time you saw me."

"Please don't," she said. "You mustn't laugh at me—"

"I could never do that, Maria. But you've got to understand that—"

"But I do understand. I was there, remember, when Tim Cleary told you about—her. I saw how you looked when he told you she had married another man."

"That's got nothing to do with it."

Looking across the table at Maria, he asked himself what he felt for her. He was attracted by her dark beauty and moved by the passion he sensed beneath her quiet poise. She had so much to give a man.

"I'll bet you have half a dozen young men courting you, when I'm off at sea," he said.

"I have received a few proposals of marriage during the last two years."

"From Cubans here in the city, I suppose. Young men from fine *criollo* families like your own."

"They didn't matter to me, none of them."

"Why not?" he demanded roughly. "Because none of them were kicked around in a Cuban prison cell? That's all you really know about me, isn't it?"

"You are all that is good and fine in a man—"

"Like hell I am," he said. "I've done a few things I'd be ashamed to tell you about."

He fell silent. *Why don't I marry Maria? No man could want more. I could sell the boat to Tim, and settle down, here in New York, maybe. Maria and I could have a good life, together. She was made to be a wife, to give a man children. . . .*

A moment later, he was seeing another girl. A girl with red-gold hair and dark violet eyes, who had clung to him in the colonel's office at San Rafael and had pleaded with him. Who had admitted she had borne him a son. Who had cried and fought when Captain Julio Vargas had carried her out of the room.

Damn her. She hadn't waited long to get into bed with Captain Vargas. Maybe she hadn't waited to find a bed, maybe she had lain with him on the ground that first night after they left the garrison together. Then, in Havana, she became his mistress, lived with him in high style . . . married him when he asked her.

He felt a light touch on his hand. "Kevin, please. What is it? Have I made you angry?"

"Not you, my dear."

But there was a long, uneasy silence between them during the ride home. And later, in the gaslit parlor of her apartment above the shop, he hesitated before kissing her good-night.

He had always kissed her before, in an easy, casual way. He couldn't leave without kissing her this time. He bent and touched his lips to her cheek, but she turned her head swiftly, instinctively, and her lips were under his; he felt the soft roundness of her breasts against his chest, and he breathed the delicate perfume of her hair. For a moment, his arms tightened around her. He knew that if he picked her up and carried her into the bedroom, she would give herself to him freely. Because she loved and trusted him.

"No, Maria." He pulled away, then, taking one of her hands, he lifted it to his lips.

In the light from the gas lamp, he saw that her enormous eyes were glistening with unshed tears. But she raised her head a little, and when she spoke her voice was calm, controlled.

"Will I see you again before you sail?"

"I don't think so," he told her. "There's too much to be done down at the docks. But I'll come to call on you when I get back."

The look she gave him, her face lighting with joy and hope, made him feel humble. And a little ashamed.

He dismissed the waiting hansom cab and walked for miles, downtown along Broadway. A light drizzle began to fall, blurring the glare of the gas lights, but the streets were still crowded. A fresh breeze blew in from the river. By tomorrow night or the following morning, at latest, he would be out at sea.

In one way, he found this a comforting thought. No complications, no decisions to be made except those involving the running of the boat.

Why hadn't he proposed to Maria tonight? Or even taken her without a promise of marriage. Once he might have done exactly that, might have seized his pleasure, without any thought of the future. He remembered the softness of her lips, and the way her breasts had felt, pressed against him.

He turned off Broadway onto Houston Street. Harry Hill's Concert Saloon had closed a few years ago. The huge red-and-blue glass lantern no longer burned outside the large, two-story house. And John Allen's brothel on Water Street, where the girls had displayed their charms in low-cut, short red dresses, and red-topped boots with bells around their ankles—that, too, was gone.

He turned again, going west this time, walking without any destination. Maybe when he came back from Cuba, he would ask Maria to marry him. He smiled wryly, wondering if she had been aware of how much she had stirred him, kissing him that way. He walked faster, hardly aware of the drizzle that was changing now to a steady rain. At Canal Street he saw the row of tall, narrow houses, each with its red tinted gas lamp, and its sign: "Flora," "Lizzie,"

"The Forget-Me-Not," "The Black Crook."

He stopped in front of one bearing the sign, "The Gem," mounted the short flight of steps, and went inside.

It was early morning when Miguel took Drucilla from the cave. He lifted her in his arms and started for the opening, and she protested weakly: "What if we're seen?"

"There's little danger now, señora," he told her. "Most of the slaves have fled into the Sierra de Escambray."

"And the rest?"

"Up at the house—the shell of the house—sleeping off the effects of the cane brandy."

She blinked as he carried her outside. The pale pink light of early morning was fluttering through the branches of the cedar trees. She could not repress a cry of pain as Miguel lifted her into a rickety little wagon, to which a bony old mule had been hitched.

"This is the best I could do," he said. "They burned the stables, too, you see. The volante's gone, and the calèche."

"And the horses?" Julio had always been so proud of his horses.

"They got out. They're roaming around loose. And the cattle, as well. Those that weren't butchered and eaten."

"The house was completely destroyed?"

"Yes, señora. Now, please don't talk any more. Save your strength."

Inez was waiting in the wagon, with Andrew beside her; the child wasn't crying, but he looked frightened and confused, and no wonder. Later, when Drucilla could find the strength, she would try to comfort him. Now she closed her eyes, feeling an overpowering weakness.

Inez touched her gently on the shoulder. "Where are we to go, señora?" she asked.

Drucilla realized that even now, with Julio dead and Villanueva a smoking ruin, Inez's training still made her turn to her mistress for orders.

"Havana," Drucilla managed to say. "West to Havana."

She let herself sink back on the heap of straw and old cane sacks that covered the bottom of the wagon. She heard Inez and Miguel talking.

"Cienfuegos is nearer," Inez said.

"There may be slaves on the road between here and Cienfuegos—it's on the way to the mountains. Havana is best. It's such a big place, we'll be able to lose ourselves there."

Both Inez and Miguel had been to Havana a few times, but always in attendance on their master and mistress; they had been confined in the quarters provided in Havanese hotels for the body slaves of guests, and would have been too timid to venture out onto the streets, even if they had had permission to do so. Still, Miguel tried to sound confident.

The next few days were agonizing for Drucilla, for each time the wagon hit a rock or jounced into a rut along the road, pain jarred her body. She felt weak and nauseated, unable to eat the food Miguel had been able to find: some coarse bread, a small cask of salted cod, and a sack of corn meal. She could only swallow a little water, mixed with cane brandy. She knew that the slaves had lived on salted cod and corn meal, and had worked in the fields and the mills on such fare, but her stomach rejected these foods.

Andrew fussed and whined until Inez said roughly, "You'll eat what's here, or go hungry." Drucilla, knowing how badly disturbed the child was, wanted to reprove Inez for her harshness, but she knew that the slave girl had every reason to resent Andrew. If Andrew had not betrayed Inez and Ernesto to Julio, the girl's lover would not have been flogged to death before her eyes. Drucilla knew, too, that Inez and Miguel had only spared her son out of consideration for her.

Drucilla reached out and drew Andrew's head down against her breast. "It's all right, darling," she said. "Soon, we'll be back in New York and you'll have all sorts of good things to eat."

"I'd rather go on to Charleston," he said. "To Aunt Gwen and Aunt Hazel. Can't we see them, too?"

"Of course we can," Drucilla said, relieved to hear the eagerness in the child's voice. She had been terrified that the sights of the past few days might have damaged his mind in some way.

He sighed and moved closer to her. "Aunt Hazel's nice," he said. "She used to give me pecan pies and peppermints, and she told me stories. I wish I could have a big piece of pecan pie right now."

Drucilla stroked his dark curls. "Try to eat a little of the corn meal," she urged.

Miguel, taking pity on the boy, turned in the seat and said: "You know, sometimes it's possible to find honey right here in the forest. There are certain trees where the bees live. Maybe we'll find one."

"I'd like that," Andrew said. Then, turning back to Drucilla, he asked, "Will we go home on a big boat, Mother? Like the boat I came on to Cuba?"

"We'll take the first boat we can find." Drucilla said. She did not ask herself how they would pay their passage. If she could get word to Charlotte Tremayne, or to her sisters-in-law, they would provide her with money. Or maybe . . . But pain and exhaustion blurred her thoughts, and she drifted off to sleep.

Miguel did not dare to follow the well-traveled roads, but kept to the by-paths. It made the trip slower, and more difficult, but he was terrified of being seen and taken prisoner. By now, the destruction of Villanueva must have been discovered. Government troops would try to round up every escaped slave they could find and inflict brutal punishment. And he had done more than burn and loot. He had been instrumental in the killing of his master. He had struck one of the blows that had left Julio Vargas a bleeding carcass in the yard in front of the stables.

The señora might speak for him, if he should be taken, and for Inez, too. But the ways of the law were strange and she might not be listened to. Or perhaps, he thought gloomily, she would not survive the trip at all. She looked like a dead woman, lying there on the cane sacks. Her face was chalky white, and there were dark circles under her eyes. Her once bright hair was tangled and dark with sweat. She had lost much blood during the miscarriage. She might still be bleeding. She needed rest, not a long ride in a wagon without springs along a rutted road.

The following day Miguel found a honey tree and filled a small, cracked basin. Andrew was pleased. He clambered up on the seat beside Miguel, and when he had finished his treat, he licked his sticky fingers and smiled.

"Are you coming to Charleston with us, Miguel?"

"I don't know," Miguel said.

"It will be strange for you, if you do. You won't be a slave anymore, you know." He thought for a moment. "Maybe my aunt will give you a job on Seaton Barony."

He chattered on, and Miguel thought: "And how are we to get to Charleston, wherever that may be. The señora has no money, not a penny." After her ordeal, she looked almost like a slave herself, except for her red hair concealed under her shawl, and those blue eyes of hers. Her face was smudged and dirty, and her dress was stained.

Miguel glanced up at the sky. The air had turned very hot, and gray clouds were moving across the sky. "You'd better cover Señora Vargas with those sacks," he said to Inez. "We're going to have rain any minute."

Inez had hardly finished, when the first drops started falling, and then the path ahead was blotted out by the fierce tropical downpour. The mule, old and decrepit to begin with, began to falter; his hooves sank into the mud, and he stopped in his tracks, head down. The rain continued all that day and into the night. And the next morning, Drucilla awoke with a pounding head and a sore throat; a little later, she began to cough, in hard, racking spasms.

When Miguel hit the mule with his whip, the animal lurched forward, then stopped again.

"This mule's in a bad way," Miguel said. "I don't know how much more I can get out of him."

"No matter," Inez said. "Stay here for awhile." She clambered down from the wagon.

"Where are you going?" Miguel asked.

"I'll try to find some cuajaní berries," she said. "Mixed with honey, they're the best thing for a cough. My grandmother told me so."

"Don't go too far," he warned.

She found the berries, and Miguel built a small fire, using a *yesca*, a black ash he kept in a tinderbox. He rubbed a stone on the tinderbox until he struck a spark, but it wasn't easy to get the fire going because the wood chips were damp. Still, he persisted and when the flame was glowing, Inez made the brew of honey and crushed berries.

"You are as wise as your grandmother," he said. "And very pretty, too."

She gave him a cold look, and he guessed that she was still remembering Ernesto. All the same, he had often eyed her trim figure as she had moved about the halls of the great house. Perhaps, now, he might have a chance with her. Not right away, of course. But a woman like that needed a man, and he knew women thought he was good-looking, in spite of the scar left on his cheek by Julio's riding crop.

Inez got Drucilla to drink some of the cuajaní and honey, and for a few hours, her cough was less severe; but then she told Inez that her arms and legs ached, and she began to shake with a chill.

"She should not spend another night out of doors," Miguel said. "Perhaps, if we could find a small, out-of-the-way tavern—"

"And how would we pay?" Inez said. "Besides, we'll be getting to Havana soon. Won't we?"

"And what of that? They use money in Havana, too, I suppose."

"Mind your tongue, Miguel. The señora told us to take her to Havana. No doubt she knows how to get assistance there. She and Senor Vargas visited friends there—"

"And what about us? What will happen to us?"

"She will provide for us," Inez said calmly.

But by the time they entered Havana, Drucilla was unconscious, breathing with difficulty. Both slaves were frightened by the bustle of the city, the crowds of people— and no one to tell them where to go. The city was a noisy, brightly lighted maze of narrow streets. Miguel tried to remember the name of the hotel where they had stayed before; then realized that even if he found it, he would not be admitted. Questions would be asked, the police would be called, or the soldiers. Miguel was too afraid to think about it. Later, when the señora recovered her health, when she could give them instructions, then everything would be all right.

In the meantime, they would have to find some sort of lodgings. He guided the wagon through the narrow, dirty streets and tried to remember his last visit to the city; surely it had not been so noisy then. Perhaps this was some fiesta, unknown in the back country.

Inez covered Drucilla's hair and part of her face with her shawl, and ordered Andrew to lie down beside his mother and say nothing. When they reached a street lined with open-air food stalls, Miguel got down and approached a fat woman, who stood behind a pile of melons.

"Señora, *por favor*—where can I find a place to sleep tonight?"

She looked him up and down. "You have no money?"

"None," he said. "But my—my wife's sister is ill. She needs to rest."

"Go down to the harbor, over that way. It's not far. You might find some kind of shelter on Murella Street." Seeing his blank look, she added: "That's where the old city wall used to stand—before you were born. Parts of it are still standing, and there are a bunch of lean-tos built against the ruins. If you find an empty one, it's yours."

She gave him a broad smile, showing her blackened teeth. "Too bad you've a wife with you. Plenty of whores live down there. They'd give you a place to sleep for nothing, a handsome young man like you. They'd even share their earnings with you."

"I don't understand—"

"You are a country boy, aren't you? No matter. You will learn fast, here in Havana."

She glanced at the wagon. "What's wrong with your wife's sister? Cholera? Yellow fever?"

Later, Miguel was to learn that both diseases were common in Havana. "No—nothing like that. She—lost her baby, and she is ill and tired. She needs rest, that's all. And food."

The fat woman hesitated, then handed Miguel a melon. "It's too soft to be sold tomorrow, and I'm getting ready to close up the stand for the night."

He began to thank her but she shook her head. "*De*

nada," she said. "Now, you're sure you'll find your way to Murella Street?"

"I'll find it, señora."

He returned to the wagon, climbed onto the seat, and cracked the whip. The exhausted mule lurched forward.

Twenty-eight

KEVIN set the bird cage down on the cafe table. "Think Maria will like it?" he asked Tim Cleary, who had arrived a little while earlier.

Tim looked at the green and yellow parrot and shrugged "I know something she'd like a lot more," he said. "A ring."

"Drop it, Tim."

"She's a fine girl, Maria. Pretty as they come, and from a good family."

"Too good for me," Kevin said. "In the long run, she'll be better off with one of those transplanted *criollos* in New York. She's had proposals from a few of them."

"But she hasn't said yes, has she?" Tim drained his glass and set it down on the table. "I tell you, she hasn't been able to think of any other man since the day she met you."

"Because you filled her head with a lot of foolishness about me on the trip to Key West."

"I only told her the truth—"

Kevin laughed. "The Irishman hasn't been born who doesn't like to embroider a story—and you're one of the worst I've ever known in that respect."

Kevin signaled the waiter, who came pushing through the crowd. The Cafe La Dominica, like all the other cafes in Havana, was crowded tonight. Only that afternoon, the news of emancipation had been released here in the city, although rumors had been flying all the past week. The city was in chaos. Whether a Havanese was for or against the freeing of the slaves, he was eager to get out to one of the cafes and discuss the matter with his friends.

"Look at them all," Tim said. "Sound like a flock of parrots themselves, and what's all the excitement about? The blacks won't be much better off when they're free. Most of them don't even know how to take care of themselves."

"It's always better to be free," Kevin said quietly. "Besides," he added, "the provisions of the law are most sensible. There will be an eight-year period of apprenticeship on the plantations for those who want it. The *patronato*, they call it. The younger slaves will be taught useful trades. And kept up until the age of eighteen by their masters."

"That'll go down hard with the masters," Tim said. "Spain's not going to pay any compensation, like France and England did when they freed their slaves here in the islands."

Kevin swallowed his rum. "To hell with the masters," he said. "I'm glad we're sailing in a few days. Everything went well this time."

"You think the rebels stand a chance?" Tim asked.

"One day—but not yet. Still, I've completed my end of the bargain. And once I'm out of Havana harbor, I won't ever come back here again."

"Unless it's to bring Maria back for a honeymoon." Tim grinned.

"I told you, there are a dozen reasons why it would be wrong for me to marry Maria."

"A dozen? I'm thinkin' there's only one. If you ask me—"

"I haven't," Kevin said, and there was something in his gray eyes, in the set of his mouth, that silenced even Tim Cleary.

La Murella was less a street than a cluster of shanties that clung to the ruins of the old city wall. In the shanties lived the drifting population that made up the lowest level of Havanese society: *emancipados* who had been able, in one way or another, to buy their freedom, but who had not been able to find steady work; prostitutes whose customers were the sailors on the docks; deserters from the Spanish army and from the merchant ships in the harbor.

"At least we'll have a roof to keep out the rain," Inez had said on their first night in one of the empty shanties.

Miguel looked up at the patched canvas that covered the spaces between the broken planks and shrugged. Then he helped Inez get Drucilla and Andrew bedded down for the night, and went out again, to dispose of the mule and wagon. Because he was unfamiliar with the ways of the city, and because he was afraid to attract attention by vigorous bargaining, he let both go for a few pesos.

It did not take long for Inez to make the acquaintance of her new neighbors. At a public fountain, at the end of the row of shanties, she struck up a cautious conversation with a tall, large-breasted girl with a mane of coarse black hair, who was called Rita. Following the plan she had worked out with Miguel, Inez told Rita, in answer to her questions, that she and her husband had arrived from Puerto Principe, that there was no work there for dock laborers, and that her sister, whom they had brought along, was very ill.

"The boy is hers?" Rita asked.

"That's right. There was another one on the way, but she miscarried."

Rita did not bother to ask about the sister's husband; in La Murella, few women had husbands.

"Your man won't find it any easier getting work here in Havana. Besides the slaves, there are the Chinese. And a dozen *emancipados* for every odd job. You'd better come down to the docks with me. A good-looking girl like you won't have any trouble finding plenty of customers."

But Inez was repelled by the thought. True, at Villanueva, the master and the *mayoral* were free to take any slave woman they wanted. But for several years, Señor Vargas had not exercised that particular right, and Inez, in the safety of the great house, was not troubled by Ruiz or Cespedes, the *contramayoral*. She had never given herself to any man but Ernesto. She had given herself to him freely, drawn by the hard strength of his body, and his passion for freedom.

To sell herself for money—that was disgusting. Besides, Inez knew little about money, since she had never handled any of her own, getting what she needed from the master.

She had heard that on some plantations, slaves were permitted to do odd jobs in near-by towns, and to save their earnings toward their freedom; but Señor Vargas had never allowed anything like that.

"Well, what do you say?" Rita demanded, lifting her water bucket and preparing to return to her shack.

"I can't—my husband would kill me."

"When his belly shrinks with hunger, he'll change his mind," Rita said. She turned and walked away, her round rump swaying under her thin cotton skirt.

Miguel did not find work, and in a few days, the money from the sale of the mule and wagon were gone. Miguel and Inez, as household slaves, had slept in beds and eaten with cutlery, not with their hands, like the field workers. But even the few cheap household utensils Inez bought, along with food, soon used up their small store of coins.

On the fourth day in Havana, Miguel went scavenging among the garbage heaps behind the large cafes. On the fifth day, Inez sold Drucilla's wedding ring.

Drucilla was conscious but completely apathetic. The shocks, physical and emotional, that she had sustained since the uprising had left her unable to think coherently or to plan. Although the bleeding that followed the miscarriage had stopped, she was pitifully weak. She made no protest when Inez slipped the diamond wedding band from her finger. She did not even appear to be aware of what was happening.

"A pretty trinket," Rita said, when Inez showed it to her. "See how those stones sparkle. As if they were real."

Cold terror shot through Inez, as she realized her danger; suppose Rita should guess the truth about her "sister" and report her suspicions to the authorities. Visions of jail and flogging arose in Inez's mind. "What would my sister be doing with real jewels?" Inez said forcing a smile. "It was a gift from one of the dock workers back home."

"I'll give you two pesos for it," Rita said. "I had a good night's work last night. One sailor after the next. A rough bunch, but free with their money when they get a little rum inside them."

Inez did not want to hear the details of Rita's business. She hurried to the nearest market to buy goat's milk, vegetables, and a bit of beef for broth.

It was at the market that she heard the talk of emancipation. "It's true," the woman who sold her the beef said. "All the slaves are to be free. Not right away, but soon. All children of slave mothers will have their freedom as soon as they come into the world, and—"

Inez stood still, while the crowd jostled around her. She thought of Ernesto. Freedom had come too late for him.

She went back to the shack, and she managed to get Drucilla to swallow a little of the goat's milk. Drucilla was coughing again, and her face felt hot to the touch.

Inez sighed and went to prepare the broth. She was stirring the mixture of meat and vegetables in an iron pot when Miguel came in, his eyes shining with excitement. "You've heard?" he asked her.

She nodded and went on stirring the broth.

"But this changes everything," he said.

"Not for Ernesto. And not for us, either. We led the uprising at Villanueva, didn't we? And you helped to kill the master. If we're caught, we'll be hanged."

Miguel said: "We won't get caught. I've been careful."

"Have you found work yet?"

He shook his head. "But I will, soon." He sniffed at the steaming pot. "Where did you get that food?"

"I sold the señora's wedding ring to Rita, down the street."

"Did the señora give you permission?"

"How can I ask her, when she looks at me as if she

398

does not know me? She needed the food to get her strength back, didn't she?"

"You're right," he said. "And the child must eat, too. Where is he?"

"Running with a pack of other brats out in the streets. He'll be here when he smells the food."

But Inez was wrong. Andrew was hanging around outside the shack, and he heard her speaking. He wasn't hungry at the moment, because he and his new friends had stolen some bananas from a stall in the market, and had devoured them in a nearby alley. In the little while since he had come to Havana, Andrew had learned to lie and steal and fight with his fists; it was his ability as a fighter that had made the other boys accept him.

Inez had taught him to lie, warning him that if he gave his right name or said anything about Villanueva, she would cut his tongue out; he was sure she meant it. She had made him put away his shirt, his shoes and stockings; he wore only a pair of torn, filthy pants, the ones Miguel had put on him the night of the uprising.

Now, with his hunger satisfied for the moment, he lingered outside the shack, listening to Miguel and Inez. And he was confused and afraid.

"The señora doesn't look any better to me," Miguel was saying.

"She's weak and her mind is confused. She speaks now of people and places I don't know."

"We must get her back to her own country. She has a family there, rich people who will care for her."

"Perhaps you would like to go down and get passage for her—for all of us—on a fine boat," Inez snapped.

Andrew heard the ladle scraping against the side of the iron pot. "She's eaten hardly anything for the last two days," Inez said. "I hope I can get this broth into her."

"She's got to eat or—Inez, she's not going to die, is she?"

"How can I tell?" Inez sounded angry and afraid.

Andrew did not wait to hear any more. He wanted to run away and find a dark place where no one would see him crying. But he couldn't let himself do that. He had to do something to help his mother. Inez had talked about a boat, to take them back to the United States. His mother had talked about that, too, when they were together in the wagon, coming to Havana. Now, she didn't talk at all. She didn't even know when he was there beside her.

He rubbed the back of his hand across his eyes, and ran off to find his new friends. They knew all about this big, noisy, confusing city. Maybe they could help him.

Kevin stood on the dock, looking out over the harbor. He was tired of Havana, and it would be good to leave tomorrow. With the *Medea*'s powerful new engines, he would make the run to New York in five days, and the tropical fruits he had loaded on board would bring a good price there. Pineapples and melons were still considered luxuries up in New York.

A breeze blew in across the water, and the sky turned from blue to red and gold; the setting sun laid a pathway of blazing light across the water, and then the swift tropical twilight fell and the first stars came out.

"We're about finished," Tim said, coming up to Kevin.

"A profitable voyage."

"Our last night in Havana. Let's go get a few drinks."

"I've had enough of the city," Kevin said. "I don't want to go to the center of town again."

"We don't have to. These last few nights, I've been going to a place not far from here. Nothing fancy, but the rum's good, and the girls are better."

"Haven't you had enough girls since we came here?"

Tim grinned at him. "No such thing as enough girls. Or enough good rum."

"I've got plenty of rum in my cabin," Kevin began.

"You don't have any girls there, though, do you?"

"Afraid not. All right, Tim. Let's see this cafe of yours."

It was a short walk from the docks to the Bougainvillea, a small, noisy open-air cafe which was like a thousand others Kevin had known here in the islands; it was filled with sailors and ships' officers, talking a dozen languages, musicians playing guitars, drums, maracas. Couples dancing, and then drifting upstairs together.

Some of the girls who strolled by on the street, or threaded their way between the tables, looked no older than eleven or twelve, but their faces were white with powdered egg shell, and their lips and cheeks were rouged. Gangs of ragged small boys whose skins were every shade from ebony to yellow lingered outside, or came in to beg from the customers or to sell lottery tickets.

"There's your abolition," Tim said, pointed to one group of boys. "You'll see twice as many soon—begging, stealing. As soon as the owners turn them all loose, Havana will be full of them."

"You're probably right," Kevin said. "But every seaport I've ever seen has had its share of homeless children who had to fend for themselves or starve. The years I spent in Liverpool, before I went to sea, I had a taste of it myself. What about you?"

"I guess I was one of the lucky ones. My parents scraped up enough to get passage to Quebec. We had relatives there. We managed. Not that it was—"

He broke off. There was some sort of disturbance at a nearby table. Kevin, looking in the direction of the uproar, heard a drunken ship's officer say, "Get the hell out of here, before I belt you one."

A moment later, Kevin heard a child's shrill voice. "I'm not a beggar like these others—I can pay you."

There was the sound of a blow and a cry of pain.

A waiter hurried over, but Kevin reached the child first. It was a boy, small, skinny, half-naked. He was getting up from the floor slowly, but with determination.

A sailor at the next table laughed. "You've got it all wrong, *muchacho*," he said. "The sailors are supposed to pay your mother. Not the other way around."

For a moment, the child looked bewildered. Then he understood, and his face went scarlet under the dirt. His lips drew back from his teeth. He picked up an empty bottle and ran at the sailor who was still laughing.

Kevin reached out with one quick movement and grabbed the boy's arm, then hauled him away, kicking and struggling. Tim, who had seen the whole thing, looked from Kevin to the boy, then back at Kevin again.

"Are you hurt?" Kevin asked the boy.

"No, sir."

"You're not big enough to start a brawl in a cafe—not yet," Kevin said. The boy was trying to look defiant, but Kevin saw the fear in his eyes. Light gray eyes under black brows. He didn't look like a mulatto, or even an octoroon, but Kevin knew that the mixture of the two races produced unusual coloring sometimes.

"You'd better go home—if you have a home," Kevin said.

"He's been here these last two nights," Tim said. "I think his brains are a bit addled. Keeps telling everyone who'll listen that he wants passage on a ship for himself and his mother. And their servants. They keep kicking him out, but he keeps turning up again."

Kevin reached into his pocket. "Here," he said. "Go buy yourself something to eat, and stay away from the cafe."

"I'm not a beggar. I tried to tell that pig over there. I want to book passage for myself and my mother and our servants. My mother's a very rich lady."

Kevin looked at the child with pity. He was addled, all right. But there was something about him.

"Where do you and your mother live, with these servants of yours?"

"On Murella Street, sir—"

Kevin knew the place. He'd never been there, but some of his men had gone down there to find themselves a whore. A couple of nights before, one of them had been beaten and had had his money stolen there.

"You're lying," Kevin said. "Your mother has no money."

"Not now—but she did. We only had to go to live in that place after we—after they—"

"All right, anything you say." Kevin pushed the coins into the boy's hand. "Go on, now. Get along."

The boy looked down at the coins in his hand. He shook his head. "It's not enough," he said.

"Well, I'll be damned," Tim exploded. "You save the brat from a beating, you give him money, and he tells you it's not enough. Cheeky little bastard."

He shoved the boy away. "Let's find ourselves a couple of girls and go upstairs, Captain."

The boy turned around and stood planted on the spot.

"You're a captain, sir? You have a ship? You could take us home."

"I don't carry passengers," Kevin said. "Certainly not those without money."

"Please, sir, we could all stay in one cabin—or on the deck—I can work and so can Miguel."

Tim half-rose, but Kevin motioned him back to his chair. Havana was full of child beggars but this one was different. "Who is Miguel?"

"He is—he used to be a valet—he's a very good worker, sir."

"And I suppose your mother travels with a lady's maid."

"Yes, sir. Inez. She—"

The boy searched Kevin's face and his lips started to tremble. "We've got to go home—we've got to—"

The boy might be addled, but he spoke perfect English, and he held himself with dignity, even now.

"Where is home?" Kevin asked him.

"Charleston, sir. My aunts live there. Grandmother Seaton used to live there, too, in a big house but she died and then—"

Kevin gripped the boy's shoulder. He put a hand under the boy's chin and looked into the face. The gray eyes were wide with bewilderment, under their straight black brows. The boy began to squirm, but Kevin did not release him. He was studying the face, the wide thin-lipped mouth, the short, straight nose, the line of the jaw.

He heard Tim saying softly: "For the love of Christ, the lad—he's—"

"What happened to Vargas?" Kevin asked.

The boy hesitated.

"Answer me," Kevin said, not letting him look away.

"Señor Vargas is dead. The slaves killed him. They burned Villanueva, and we had to run away."

A look of terror came into the boy's face. "I wasn't supposed to tell. Inez said she'd cut my tongue out if I told."

"I won't let anyone hurt you. Come on, now. Let's go see your mother."

The boy looked up at Kevin, as if he hardly dared to believe what was happening. "Are you going to take us home?"

Kevin put his arm around the boy's skinny shoulders. "That's right," he said. He lifted the boy into his arms and shoved his way through the crowd, with Tim following.

Drucilla ate the hot broth with the meat and vegetables in it. Later, she swallowed a brew of herbs.

"You wouldn't believe what they cost here," Inez said, encouraged by the slight tinge of color in Drucilla's face; and by the flicker of awareness in her eyes. She was coming around now; she was beginning to take notice of her surroundings.

"Where are we?" she asked Inez.

"In Havana, señora." Inez held the cup of steaming herbs to Drucilla's lips. "Drink it all," she said. "You would not believe what simple herbs cost here in this city. And they're dried, not fresh and green as they were in the fields at Villanueva. All the same, they will make you well again, you'll see."

Villanueva. Drucilla shut her eyes. She did not want to remember the plantation. The red flames licking at the walls of the house, the sound of shattering glass and falling timbers. The yells of the slaves as they had surrounded Julio, their machetes rising and falling. She would not let herself remember. Better to go on drifting in this curious hazy state, where there was no past at all . . . where time did not exist. . . .

The herb brew had made her sleepy, and she lay back on the bed of straw and cane sacks. From somewhere outside, she heard people shouting, singing. She heard drums and guitars and maracas. She wanted to ask Inez what was happening. Her tongue felt thick and her eyelids were heavy. "Is it the harvest celebration . . . ?"

No, that had been a long time ago, at Villanueva. The day she and Andrew had tried to make their escape.

"Sleep now, señora," Inez said gently. "The herbs must have time to do their work. Tomorrow, I will make you a charm of black and white river pebbles and cock feathers. . . ."

When Drucilla awoke again, she felt a little stronger. Inez brought a basin of water and washed her face with a bit of sacking. Then she tidied Drucilla's hair with a comb Miguel had found during one of his scavenging expeditions. "In a little while I will give you more broth.'"

Drucilla heard a burst of shouting from the street. "Don't be afraid," Inez said soothingly. "The people are celebrating."

"Is it some holiday?" Drucilla asked.

"A great holiday," Inez told her. "The news came from Spain only a little while ago. The emancipation, señora. All the slaves in Cuba are to be free."

Drucilla smiled, but the smile froze on her lips. She was wracked with guilt. "If only I had waited, Ernesto need not have died. And Julio—"

It was coming back now, all of it. She remembered the night when they had entertained the Santovenias and the Talaveras at dinner. And Julio had said, "I hope I don't live long enough to see the end of slavery in Cuba."

"It wasn't your fault," Inez said. "How could you know about the emancipation?"

Drucilla did not answer. She was seeing Julio, mounted on Conquistador, as if leading his troops into battle. She was hearing the cries of the slaves, and Julio's last scream.

Inez stood quickly, and looked toward the half-open door. Drucilla, too, heard the sound of carriage wheels in the street outside the shack, heard Miguel saying: "What do you want here, señores? You must not come in. There is sickness here—"

"Out of my way," a man's voice said.

Drucilla gave one sharp cry and sat up. Her head was swimming, but she clung to Inez and tried to get to her feet.

"No, you mustn't, señora—please—"

But Drucilla did not hear her.

"Kevin." His arms were around her now, holding her, supporting her. She looked up into his face. She raised a hand and touched his cheek as if to reassure herself that he was real. "I thought you were dead—all those years—and then, when Julio admitted he had lied—"

Her voice faltered and she rested against Kevin's arm.

He kissed her and held her face against his shoulder and said her name. When he drew away she tried to cling to him. "There now, love," he said soothingly, tenderly. "I won't leave you."

Then, turning to Inez, he said: "Get her dressed and wrap her in a blanket."

"I have no blanket, señor. And I won't let you take her out of here—"

But Andrew was saying, "It's all right, Inez. Captain Farrell has a boat. He's taking us back to the United States. All of us."

"You know this man, señora?" Inez asked, still cautious.

"I know him," Drucilla said.

After that, everything happened with bewildering speed.

Kevin took off his jacket, wrapped it around Drucilla's shoulders, and lifted her in his arms.

"You want these two to come along?" he asked her, indicating Inez and Miguel.

"Oh, yes," she said. "They saved my life and Andrew's. We'd both have been killed, along with Julio, if they hadn't—"

"All right, then," he said. "Come on, both of you."

"You'll take us out of Cuba?" Miguel asked. He looked at Inez as if not daring to believe the possibility of such a miracle.

"That's right," Kevin said. "Make up your minds, fast. We sail in a few hours."

Miguel did not wait for a second invitation. He was throwing Andrew's clothes together in a bundle, his hands trembling.

Then they were all in the carriage, with Kevin holding Drucilla across his knees, her head resting in the curve of his arm. She felt him brace himself each time the carriage wheels hit a rut, to spare her the jolting of the ride. She heard the music around her, on every street, as the colored population of Havana went on with their celebration. The wide avenues and the narrow alleys were packed with men and women, dancing, drinking, embracing. Several times the carriage was forced to jerk to a stop, to make way for a reveler, drunk on cane brandy and freedom.

Down at the waterfront, Kevin said: "Get us a small boat, Tim. Pay whatever you have to, but hurry."

Drucilla raised her head. "Tim?" she said. "You're here, too?"

"You bet I am," he said. She felt the scratchy stubble on his face as he kissed her cheek. Then he was gone, his heavy footsteps pounding along the dock.

"Captain Farrell's going to take us home, Mother," she heard Andrew say.

"I know, darling—I know." Drucilla looked up at Kevin, and saw the warmth, the tenderness in his eyes. He had never looked at her that way before. "How did you find me?" she asked.

He smiled but his voice shook a little as he said, "Andrew brought me to you. He—" Kevin held her more tightly, as if afraid he would lose her. "When I think that I might have sailed out of Havana tonight, without knowing you were there in that hellhole."

She reached up and drew his face down to hers, and their lips met in a long kiss. At that moment, she felt that she was home already, safe and loved. The past no longer had any power to hurt her now. There was only the future, rich and golden with the promise of happiness.

Twenty-nine

———

DURING her first night on the *Medea*, Drucilla, wearing one of Kevin's shirts for a nightgown, slept in his cabin. Kevin did not move from her side; even when she drifted off to sleep, he held her hand in his.

During the voyage, as they made their way around the tip of Florida and up the eastern coast of the United States to New York, her strength began to return. They spent hours in the cabin talking, and she told him what had happened to her since they had been together that last time in the garrison at San Rafael.

"I didn't know," Kevin said. "When Diego Barbosa and his men got me out of the garrison, I didn't know you had been behind it all. That you'd provided money for the guns and explosives." Kevin's face darkened. "Diego never had a chance to tell me—he was killed, getting me back to the ship."

"He wouldn't have known about me in any case. I never met Barbosa," Drucilla explained. "An English newspaperman acted as go-between. I'm sorry about Barbosa—he must have been a remarkable man."

"He was," Kevin told her. "Diego Barbosa was the

heir to a sugar fortune, the same as Julio Vargas. But he turned his back on the plantation, the money—all of it—to fight beside the other rebels—his own slaves, some of them were—to try to free Cuba."

Then he added: "Tim was able to get Barbosa's sister, Maria, out of Cuba the same time he was getting me out. She's living in New York City now."

"That's where we're going, isn't it?" Drucilla asked.

"Yes, to unload the cargo." Did she hear uneasiness in his voice, or was she imagining it?

Later that day, when Kevin took her up on deck for air and exercise for the first time, she spoke of her marriage to Julio. "I had to become his mistress, or he'd have had me sent away from Cuba. I couldn't have helped you then. He led his troops into Oriente the same time Barbosa's people were attacking San Rafael, and when he returned and told me you had died in the escape, I believed him. After that, nothing mattered. I thought I would never be able to feel anything again."

"Was he good to you, Drucilla?"

"He tried to be. He loved me in his way. But I couldn't love him. And then there was the business of the slaves. I couldn't stand the way he treated them. And he was teaching Andrew to accept such cruelty as a fact of life."

She went on to tell Kevin about the events that had led to the uprising. And about the loss of her baby.

"I can't remember much after that. I think maybe I didn't want to remember. I blamed myself for Julio's death—"

"You weren't to blame. He deserved what he got." He put an arm around her and drew her close. "Try to forget the past."

When the *Medea* docked in New York harbor, Kevin left Drucilla on the boat while he went ashore to dispose of the cargo. She had expected him to be back by evening, but Tim came to her instead, explaining that Kevin would be late.

"He brought a few presents for Maria Barbosa," Tim explained. "He always brings her things when we go ashore here. And takes her around town to fancy restaurants and theaters."

"And that's all?" Drucilla asked uneasily.

"I don't know what you mean."

"Of course you do, Tim. Don't pretend with me. Kevin said that Maria helped nurse him back to health after he got out of San Rafael. What's she like?"

"She's a fine girl," Tim admitted. "And, of course, Kevin's grateful to her for takin' care of him that time. And I guess he feels some kind of obligation, too, because her brother died getting him out of the garrison."

"Is she pretty?"

"I don't know— Listen here, Drucilla, there's nothin' like that between her and Kevin. He's only tryin' to take her brother's place. Kind of lookin' out for her, that's all. Gave her money to start the dress shop, but she's paid most of it back. Besides, there's lots of young Cuban bucks after her."

"She is pretty, then."

Drucilla had no right to be jealous. Kevin had thought that she had married Julio because she had loved him. Now he knew the truth, but maybe it was too late.

Drucilla had looked at herself in the shaving mirror in Kevin's cabin. Her face was thin, the cheekbones prominent, and there were blue smudges under her eyes. She was terribly thin: her breasts were smaller and her hips as flat as a boy's. She remembered the lush beauty of the Cuban girls, their gleaming blue-black hair, their huge, brown eyes, their fine figures. And they were born coquettes, skilled in all the arts of seduction: the provocative sidelong glance, the enticing sway of the hips.

When Kevin returned after midnight, Drucilla pretended to be asleep; they had not occupied the same bed since her first night aboard, and even now, when she had regained her strength, he continued to share a cabin with Tim and Andrew.

Even the next morning, she said nothing about Maria. Kevin, however, had news of his own. "I found out Charlotte Tremayne has opened the house in Newport for the summer, and I wired her, telling her I was bringing you there. That's all right, isn't it? She'll see you're well taken care of at Peregrine Court, and Andrew, too. He's a fine boy, Drucilla. Everything a man could want in a son."

"You'll stay with us in Newport, won't you?"

"If you want me to," he said, but his gray eyes were distant, and once more Drucilla was uneasy.

Although Newport had changed, particularly Bellevue Avenue, where more and more imposing stone and brick "cottages" had been built, some of them modeled after Renaissance palaces, others after French châteaux, Peregrine Court had remained exactly as Drucilla had remembered it. On a morning in August, nearly two months after she and Kevin had arrived here with Andrew and the servants, Drucilla was seated on a wide, cushioned bench in the summerhouse at the end of the topiary garden. She wore a summer dress of striped lilac and pale yellow muslin, with a form-fitting, low-necked bodice trimmed with lace and lilac ribbons; a wide straw hat rested on the seat beside her.

These last weeks spent amid the luxury and comfort of Peregrine Court, had restored her completely. There was color in her cheeks again, and her lips were a deep pink. Her figure had filled out a little, too. Charlotte Tremayne had ordered Inez to ply Drucilla with rich concoctions of milk, eggs and brandy, and although, at first, Inez had insisted that her own herb brews were better, she had gradually learned that one did not contradict La Abuela, the stately white-haired Señora Tremayne. Andrew had been given into the care of a Miss Winterbury, an English governess who kept him in stiffly-starched sailor suits, stuffed him with oatmeal and lamb chops, and took him for brisk walks around the estate.

Miguel had a fine position as a valet in the Norman château of a newly rich railroad tycoon, who bragged about his new attendant and drew the line only when Miguel tried to give him a bath. "That's too damn much," the tycoon had roared, adding a stream of Anglo-Saxon obscenities that fascinated the young man. "Nobody's bathed me since I was in diapers, and nobody's going to start now."

Miguel had dismissed the outburst as an eccentricity of these peculiar *americanos*. He could afford to be tolerant, for he got good wages, which he had turned over to Inez each week to add to her own. One day soon, when they had saved enough money, they would marry and set themselves up in a small shop.

Kevin remained at Peregrine Court through the summer, and had several long private talks with Charlotte Tremayne; Drucilla knew the old lady liked him, in spite of his lack of family background.

But the summer would soon be over, and Kevin had said nothing to Drucilla about the future. Now, as she waited for him in the summerhouse, she was uneasy. At last, she saw him striding through the topiary garden, past the hedges clipped into the shapes of birds and animals. Did he remember, as she did, the night she had run out to meet him here? The night he had made love to her, here on this very bench.

Now he came into the summerhouse and her heart lifted at the sight of him. He did not sit down beside her, but stood near the doorway, his eyes distant and unreadable. He was looking out at the topiary garden.

"I've always hated those hedges," he said. "A hedge should look like what it is, not like a chicken. And those new mansions, all crowded together. Stables with monogrammed sheets for the horses. So help me, it's true. Miguel told me that railroad baron he works for provides his horses with monogrammed linen sheets."

He began to pace restlessly across the little summerhouse. He looked like an animal in a cage.

"You don't like Newport, do you?" she asked.

"I like parts of it. The wharves and the ships. Those old houses on Thames Street that look like homes for people to live in, not museums. But Bellevue Avenue—" He made a wide gesture. "You fit in here, love. And I guess Andrew will have to learn to."

"But you don't, is that it, Kevin?"

He didn't answer, and she went cold inside. "You're

leaving Newport, aren't you? That's what you're trying to tell me."

"That's right."

"Where will you go?"

"To New York City, first," he said.

"It's Maria, then, isn't it?"

"Maria? Good Lord, what gave you that idea?" He came and stood looking down at her. "Maria and I said good-bye that day the *Medea* was anchored in New York harbor. I went to see her and I made her understand how I felt. I never loved her, and I know that one day soon, she'll realize that she never loved me either."

She rose and faced him. "But then—why are you going to New York now?"

"To get rid of the *Medea*. I'm selling her to Tim. He plans to set up a cargo run between New York and the Caribbean."

"And you—"

"I'm going to head west, I think. Maybe California. Or even up to Alaska. They've made a gold strike in Alaska, you know."

"Somewhere else," she said softly. "It always has to be somewhere else."

He looked at her in bewilderment.

"You said that to me, that day at San Rafael. You told me that when you got out, you'd never settle down. You told me some men were made that way."

"It's true, love," he said.

She gripped his arms with all her strength. "But you said something else, too. You told me you loved me. And I—I know you love Andrew. I've seen you with him and I know—"

"Of course I do. That night in the cafe in Havana, when I realized he was mine. My son. I was so damn proud of him."

"Then take us with you. Andrew needs a father. And I—Kevin, my darling, I don't want to let you go —I won't let you go—not this time."

"Don't you think I want you both with me? But to ask you to turn your back on all this. I'm not a poor man,

413

Drucilla. I can take care of you and the boy. But I can't promise you all you have here."

"But I have—"

"I won't take your money." He searched her face, and his dark brows drew together. "What the devil are you smiling at?"

"You. Once you'd have taken a share of the Tremayne fortune. You said that for people like us, honor and decency were impossible without money."

"To hell with what I said. I'm telling you now—and you'd better believe it—I won't live off my wife."

She gave a wordless cry of joy and flung herself into his arms. "Say it again."

He understood. As he had always understood her. He held her close, his gray eyes warm and passionate. "My wife. My wife and my love."

His mouth claimed hers, and in his arms she knew that wherever he might lead her, there would be her home, her sanctuary—her fulfillment.